MW01493478

MEN OF THE NORTH
#9 NORTH

THE FIGHTER

Books in this series

The Men of the North series can be read as standalone books – but for the best reading experience and to avoid spoilers this is the recommended order to read them in.

The Protector – Men of the North #1
The Ruler – Men of the North #2
The Mentor – Men of the North #3
The Seducer – Men of the North #4
The Warrior – Men of the North #5
The Genius – Men of the North #6
The Dancer – Men of the North #7
The Athlete – Men of the North # 8
The Fighter – Men of the North # 9
The Pacifist – Men of the North #10

To be alerted for new book releases, sign up to my list and receive a free e-book as a welcome gift.
elinpeer.com

PLEASE NOTE

This book is intended for mature readers only, as it contains a few graphic scenes and some inappropriate language.

All characters are fictional and any likeness to a living person or organization is coincidental.

DEDICATION

To the ones who go first

Pioneers are often considered crazy until they prove
that the so called impossible was in fact, possible.

Never let yourself be limited by what others failed to do.
Maybe they would have succeeded if they were you.

Elin

PROLOGUE
The Academy

Raven

My legs were shaking from exhaustion and my jaw was shivering from the ice-cold water. All around me, bigger and stronger recruits were struggling, too.

Half an hour ago, we had been asleep. Our bodies were burned out from days of endless torturous stress, tests, and severe sleep deprivation. The desperation in the eyes of the men around me reflected how I felt myself. It had been quarter to midnight when we were allowed to go to bed. Fifty-three minutes later, the nightmare had begun again when they woke us up with loud sirens. Ninety-seven of us were left from the original two hundred and fifty recruits that had been given the chance to try out for a spot at the academy. Now we were facing the last test, which was simple in nature. We had to get out of the lake and press through the chain of faceless men standing in front of us. If we didn't secure one of the fifty red sticks in the box that the masked men were guarding, we would be packing our bags and leaving the academy. Only the fifty strongest recruits got to stay.

I am getting one of those sticks!

As the only woman, I wasn't just fighting for myself but for any woman who dreamed of becoming a police officer. This was my chance to prove that we had what it took. Three times I'd made it onto the shore already. Each time, the chain of masked men had pushed and thrown me back in the water.

It was October, past midnight, and at least forty of the red sticks had been taken by now. The desperation in me and the other recruits still in the water was tangible. Screams, growls, and roars filled the air as the men getting pushed off the shore landed on other recruits that sunk deeper into the muddy, cold water.

Come on, Raven, get out of the water, now!

"What are you weaklings waiting for? No one is forcing you to do this. Just give up and we'll take you inside to get a warm shower and some sleep. Doesn't that sound nice? The police force doesn't need you. We only need the strongest, and that's clearly not you," one of the men on the shore shouted in one of his constant attacks on our psyche. "Is this really worth dying for? You know you'll either drown or die of hypothermia if you don't make it out of that water fast."

The sound of the faceless men laughing triggered me. I was dying after only ten days at the police academy, and they thought it was funny. I wanted to punch them in their faces and make them suffer as much as I was suffering.

More frozen recruits clawed their way onto the shore only to get into desperate fights with the masked men on the shore.

When one of the recruits tore off a mask from the man he'd been fighting, I saw the rage on the now un-masked man. He shouted, "You fucking asshole" at the recruit, who triumphantly held up the red stick he had secured.

"Get him a blanket," someone else shouted and pointed the victorious recruit to a large tent.

"Only nine more sticks left and fifty-two of you are still in the water. Why don't you join the four who gave up? They're in the warm tent sipping hot cocoa now. There's no shame in quitting when you're simply not good enough. You always knew that only twenty percent make it through the initial two hell weeks, and you didn't really think you would be one of them, did you? Why go through all that trouble and pain when you might as well quit now?"

I blocked him out. I hadn't suffered through the other thirteen days of physical and mental torture to give up now. *Think, Raven, think!*

"We have to work together," I called out to the three large recruits closest to me. Like me they were smeared in mud from failed attempts at getting through the chain of men on the shore, and their jaws were shivering. "We have to pick the weakest link and go at him together. It's the only way."

"Stay away from me," one of them hissed, while another pushed past me muttering, "You shouldn't be here anyway."

"You two, follow me," the largest of them ordered and the three of them moved to the side, forming an alliance and targeting the smallest guy on the flank of the shore.

I couldn't feel my toes, my teeth were chattering, and seeing them go ahead with my plan without me made me furious.

Don't get mad, get even. How many times had my dad told me that? *Assess, plan, attack.*

My teeth were chattering even worse as I looked around, searching for an alternate route to the box with sticks, but the instructor had specifically told us the only way was through the defenders. "We have fenced in the area around you. Don't make the mistake of trying to dig your way under the fence. Trust me, each year we find dead students who ran out of oxygen or got tangled up in the fence and died that way."

But what if he had been lying? What if I could find a hole in the fence?

With the three recruits attracting attention on the shore, I moved backward and out of the light from the

3

projectors that were shining down on us recruits in the water. It was counterintuitive to lower my body further into the ice-cold water when all I wanted was to get out, but after taking three deep inhalations, I dived and swam to get away from the masked men standing guard on the shore.

My lungs were hurting and every muscle in my body screamed for oxygen. I kept my eyes closed to protect them from the muddy water and counted on my sense of direction to pull this off.

Every second I was expecting to touch a net of some kind. *Where is it? Am I going in the right direction? Come on, just a little longer.*

Feeling like I was about to pass out, I had no choice but to break the surface in a greedy gasp for air. It was hard not to laugh with relief when I saw that the shore was only a few feet away. There was no net to keep us in. It had all been a bunch of bullshit. It felt like a mile to the shore when I forced my tired legs and arms to do a few more swimming strokes to get there.

Come on, Raven! Hurry or there will be no more red sticks left. Get your ass out of the water. Do it, do it, do it!

I was pumping myself up while listening to the men shouting and fighting further down the shore.

As I crawled out of the water, my white t-shirt and pajama pants weighed a ton. Even with the large spots of mud on the fabric, the white color still worked against me and so did the squeaky sound my wet shoes were making. Without hesitating, I stripped down to my black sports bra and panties before running barefoot to where the masked men were protecting the red sticks. My brown skin worked to camouflage me in the darkness.

I ducked down behind a bush to assess the situation. The wide human chain of what I assumed were all second and third-year cadets were doing to us newcomers what had probably once been done to them. They all had their backs to me, focused on keeping the other recruits in the water and protecting the box with red sticks that stood between them and me.

Getting to the box would be a short sprint from where I was hiding, but I would have to get past the large man standing close to it. To fight off a man his size would be hard on a good day, and I was wet, cold, and weak. I shifted position as my feet were sinking deeper into the cold mud.

"What are you fuckers waiting for? There's only one stick left," the instructor shouted again. "I knew you didn't have it in you the moment I saw you losers. I can smell a bunch of failures when I see them."

Don't listen to him. My only failure would be to give up. I'm not giving up! I was just about to make a run for it, but then a fight broke out between some of the masked men closest to me.

"I fucking told you to keep an eye on her. Where is she?" The man talking pulled his mask off and pushed at two other men with a low growl of aggression. I recognized him as another of our instructors.

"I swear, she was there a few minutes ago." Another man my age pulled his mask off, pointing to the water.

"Just fucking *find* her!"

When the two younger men followed the instructor out into the lake, others on the shore began shouting questions.

"What's happening?"

"The woman. She fucking drowned or something…"

"What?" The rusty voice of the headmaster of the academy had been calm when he welcomed us new recruits two weeks ago; now his tone was furious. "You fools better fucking find her or I'll drown every one of you myself."

5

More of the men walked into the water and it created holes in the long human barrier, giving wet recruits the chance to push their way through. They were all running for the box with the last red stick in it.

That stick is mine!

That thought made me sprint ahead to beat the four other recruits running for the box. But my sprint was no sprint at all. My frozen feet and weak legs made my movements uncoordinated and slow.

Nooo! My mind was screaming for me to get there first, but two of the male recruits were moving much faster than me and there was no way I would get to that box before they did. Trying to go faster made me slip on the muddy ground and I fell flat on my back.

It's over! I knew it and my eyes closed, waiting to hear the howl of victory from the last recruit to pick up a stick.

But the howl I heard was one of pain and it made me lift my head and look up. The large masked protector of the box was fighting with everything he had.

As if a puppet master controlled my body, I got up and zoomed in on the box. The ten running steps felt like a trip around the world, but I reached the box at the same time as one of the male recruits and both of us threw ourselves onto it to get the stick. My hands were on it first, but he ripped it from me.

"Yeees..." he screamed and raised the red stick in the air. And then he sunk to his knees, his face scrunched up in agonizing pain as his hands went to his crotch and the stick fell to the ground.

"It's mine!" I picked it up and took a step back, not feeling the least bit bad about kicking him so hard. Raising the stick high above me and giving an ear-splitting whistle, I called out to the headmaster in the water. "Are you looking for me?"

Everyone turned in my direction

"Raven." The headmaster's immediate expression of relief was quickly gone when he saw the stick in my hand. The way his eyes widened in complete disbelief was almost comical, and then his mouth opened and his fist slammed down in the water as he spewed a long string of profanities.

No one offered me a blanket or hot cocoa. All I received were hateful glances from the forty-seven recruits who hadn't made it and would be going home. As the men around me pulled off their masks, their curses matched the headmaster's as he came out of the water to stand in front of me.

"Who let you through?"

"No one did."

"Then how did you get that?" He pointed to the stick in my hand.

Raising an eyebrow, I spoke in a flat tone. "I dug my way under your fence."

He was shaking like me, but I couldn't tell if it was from the cold or from anger. Stepping closer with his jaws tensed up, the headmaster hissed low. "Go home, woman! There's no fucking way I'm letting you make a joke of this fine academy. You won't get through the training so you might as well give that stick to someone who is worthy."

"You mean someone who is male?"

His upper lip lifted in an expression of disgust. "Yes, and get some goddamn clothes on. You're practically naked."

My fingers squeezed around the stick like I was expecting him to tear it from my hands. "I earned this stick and I am staying!"

We stared into each other's eyes and I saw the moment he concluded we were done for tonight.

"Pack up and get the recruits warmed up." His order made all the men around us move into action. "You and I

7

aren't done. I'm going to make it my personal mission to make sure you don't succeed in making a mockery out of my police force. I guarantee that you won't have a mere two weeks in hell like others. You'll have four years, unless you're smart enough to give up before then. That is my promise to you." As he moved past me, he shoved me with his shoulder and because my legs were already so weak it knocked me off balance and made me fall down.

No one helped me up.

Sitting in the cold mud, I clung to the stick in my hand and muttered low under my breath, "And my promise is that I will *never* let you break me. I will *never* give up! When I leave here, it will be as the first woman police officer in the Northlands." Planting my hands in the mud, I pushed myself up from the ground again but there was nothing left in me to give, and I'd only stumbled ten steps toward the school when I collapsed.

I felt hands on my shoulders, and a voice calling my name, but I couldn't open my eyes or respond. I was slipping away; the last thing I heard was "Bring her to the medic, she's going into shock."

CHAPTER 1
Station 7, District 3
One year later
Raven

What if the first person to try something new had waited for someone else to do it first?

What if no one had dared cross a mountain or sail a sea to see what was on the other side?

The world needed pioneers and I was proud to be one of them.

When I was eleven, my favorite teacher, Kya, brought me with her from the Motherlands to the mysterious Northlands, where I became one of twenty students at the first experimental school to mix children from each side of the border.

For a pioneer like me, living in the Northlands was exciting and from the day I arrived, I wanted to do everything that the Nboys could do. That's why when they ridiculed me and said that girls couldn't fight, I would train harder. And when they made jokes about women being weak, I'd push myself to do more push-ups and run faster than any of them.

What they didn't understand was that I came from the Motherlands, where only women could rule. I knew what great things women were capable of and if I ever needed proof, Laura Aurelius was there to show me. Unlike me, Laura was born and raised in the Northlands, where women were protected and cared for by their fierce and strong men. But Laura wasn't content watching the action as a bystander, so she ran away to the Motherlands and learned how to fight.

For years I trained with her, with my father, and anyone who would teach me. And by the time I turned twenty-one, I was ready to pursue my dream of becoming the first female police officer in the Northlands.

At first it had seemed like a miracle that the ruler, Khan Aurelius, allowed me a chance to prove that I could do it. But after a year at the academy, I knew that he had only agreed because he felt certain that I wouldn't succeed.

My first twelve months as a recruit had been hellish, and every week felt like running an obstacle course trying to deal with whatever absurd obstacle the headmaster, teachers, or classmates came up with to make me quit.

They cheated and never played fair and so I adapted and became good at being sneaky myself. Like the time they created a test that required height and would be impossible for someone below six feet to finish. I couldn't let that stop me, and luckily, I succeeded in convincing Hanson to let me sit on his shoulders. It wasn't hard when I pointed out he could say he'd had his face between a woman's thighs.

I counted the days until the twelve months were over and I finally moved from the academy to Station Seven in the third district where I would get six months of practical experience.

None of the policemen wanted me there, but my mentor Leonardo da Vinci was a high-ranking inspector and everyone knew that he had been appointed to look out for me and that he took his role seriously. It was obvious that Leo resented the role as my mentor, but the request had come from Commander Magni Aurelius, and no one refused a direct order from the brother of the ruler.

Leo came up with a strategy to keep me from getting close to danger by assigning me the task of sorting unsolved cases in a dusty archive room in the basement. For five weeks I'd been down there six to seven hours a day, and the isolation and boredom were driving me insane. My only escape was fight training four times a week with the others at Station Seven.

Today was Friday, the only day without fight training, and feeling extra frustrated, I went upstairs to complain to Leo about the mind-numbing work he was having me do.

"I'm not learning anything, Leo. How am I supposed to pass my tests if I haven't done any real police work?"

As always, Leo felt no need to explain himself, and when an important call came, he pushed his chair back, got up, and gestured to some of the others that they needed to move.

"What's going on?" My eyes were darting around the police station, my heart rate picking up as I sensed the suppressed excitement from Leo.

"The Huntsmen found Hannigan and they are waiting for us."

"Can I come?"

"No. This is a serious police matter. You stay here and focus on the task I gave you."

"But, Leo, sorting irrelevant files in the basement has nothing to do with real police work. I would much rather come along and see you in action."

He was already walking away, signaling who could come and who couldn't. Two of the men close to us looked as disappointed as I felt.

Hannigan, the man the Huntsmen had found, was believed to have killed three men in one night two weeks ago. He'd been on the run ever since and his capture was exciting to all of us.

11

"It's not too late to change your mind," I called after Leo, but he didn't look back and just threw an answer over his shoulder.

"Stay here, Raven. It's a fucking order!"

I made a mocking facial expression but was smart enough not to mouth back.

Station Seven fell quiet the minute Leo and the other lucky officers left.

Monroe, another young officer in training, looked over at me and the small smirk on his face annoyed me. "What are you looking at?"

Monroe stood by a large screen where documents from the case he was working on were open. "Shouldn't you be down in the archives?"

"Shouldn't you shut your mouth?" It bothered me that he got to be involved in real police work while all I got to do was categorize boring and inconsequential cases of first-time theft and fraud.

Walking with clattering steps like I could stamp out the unfairness of it all, I left the large room and took the back stairs down to the basement.

Cursing in a low mumble, I returned to the four large piles I had already made. The cabinet in front of me was just one out of twenty-two cabinets and it was still half full.

According to Leo's instructions, I had divided the cases according to the level of crime and number of years the case had been unsolved.

He was just trying to find a way to keep me busy and make his life as my mentor easier, but it was pointless work. Leo had no intention of opening up any of these cases, and the worst part was that they were all digitized anyway. Why anyone insisted on keeping paper copies was a mystery to me, and the best explanation I could come up with was that it worked as a punishment to crush a person's soul.

Picking up a handful of the files that I hadn't yet looked through, I scanned the first page in one of them. "Theft of drone." I placed it in the pile with the lowest priority.

The next one was a case from 2407 of assault, but the accuser had been drunk and didn't remember any details about the man who allegedly attacked him and broke his nose. A forty-one-year-old case like that with no clues to work on was destined to stay archived.

With a sigh, I placed it on top of the last file and scanned the next one.

The category of the case had me frowning and reading aloud: "Death by suicide – huh!"

This case had been filed in the wrong place, but one detail caught my eye and made me stare: the name of the young woman who had died. "Dina Aurelius."

With my head still in the file, I walked over to sit by a desk, my index finger trailing over every detail of the file to confirm my suspicion that this woman was related to our ruler.

Name: Dina Aurelius
Closest family: Daughter of Marcus Aurelius and Erika Aurelius. Sister of Khan and Magni Aurelius.
Date of birth: February 3rd, 2400
Date of death: March 18th, 2415
Status: Married
Cause of death: Suicide by fall from window.

I sat back in my chair, a small triangle forming between my eyebrows as I wondered why I had never heard about a sister to Khan and Magni.

Mila, my best friend since childhood, was the adopted daughter of Magni and because of that, I'd been a regular

13

visitor at the Gray Manor, which housed the ruling family. I couldn't recall seeing a picture at the Gray Manor of a sister.

According to this file, she had been dead for thirty-three years. Another glance at her status had me swallowing hard. Fifteen years old and married. Intellectually, I knew it had been the norm back then, but it was disturbing to think that a young woman seven years my junior had been married.

There weren't many details in this file, but my fingers began tingling and my head was popping with questions. *What if Dina didn't jump from that window?*

What if she was pushed?

Maybe it was my bored brain looking for an escape, but I was convinced that I might be looking at a murder mystery. If Leo wouldn't allow me to get close to any action, then maybe I could solve this old case on my own. Who better to find out what happened to Dina than me? After all, no other police officers had the connections to her family that I had.

I didn't need more arguments than that to decide that this was going to be my private investigation into the possible murder of Dina Aurelius. It was a golden opportunity to show all the people hoping for me to fail, that I was born to fight crimes and solve murders.

CHAPTER 2
Best Friends

Raven

"Mila, honestly, this room is as good as the last one. Jonah won't care one bit." I was following Mila around at the Gray Manor as she was trying to decide which room to pick for her friend Jonah. "He's only staying a few days, so why does it matter?"

Mila gave me a patient smile. "It might not matter to you or him, but it matters to me. I want every guest to feel welcome."

We were now in the hallway on the third floor and I pointed from one door to the other. "They're all the same. It's what, eighteen guest rooms and the only difference is the color of the walls?"

"That's not true at all. Some of them have a better view. Some of them are slightly bigger, and one had the carpet replaced last year because of water damage. I want Jonah to feel comfortable here."

"Why is he coming again? I feel like he was just here."

"That was two weeks ago, and he's here to discuss some political matter with Lord Khan and Pearl."

"What political matter?"

Mila shrugged. "It's something about the new public transportation system that Pearl is working on, I think." She opened a fifth door, turned on the lights, and looked around. "I'll give this room to Jonah. It faces the garden and he liked that the last time he visited."

15

I sighed. "Fine. Now, can we focus on me for a moment? I told you something important happened at work today."

"Yes. But you didn't say what it was."

"Because it's top secret."

Mila gave me a troubled look. "Then maybe you shouldn't tell me."

"I have to because it involves your family." Grabbing her left hand, I pulled her to the edge of the bed and sat down. "Mila, do you know that your father had a sister who died?"

Mila blinked her eyes before nodding slowly. "Yes, I've heard of Aunt Dina. My sister is named after her."

With eagerness in my voice, I squeezed her hands. "Tell me everything you know."

"Okay." Mila's eyes went to the ceiling as if she was remembering details from the past. "My dad told me about her years ago. He was only seven when she died and it sounded like it was a traumatic experience for him."

"What happened?"

"Dina and Magni were close. She would sing to him, play with him, and teach him things. He has few memories because he was so young, but he told me that the last time he saw her was at her tournament. Dina picked a large warrior whom she married, and less than a week later she was dead."

"Did Magni tell you how she died?"

Mila brushed her hand over the bed cover and looked down. "Erika told him it was an accident and that Dina fell from an attic window, but Magni doesn't believe it."

My eyes widened. "He doesn't?"

"No, he said that Dina was far too sensible and careful to fall out a window."

"I found her file at work today."

Mila was quiet, waiting for me to continue.

"Cause of death said suicide, but what if it wasn't? What if her husband killed her?"

Mila jerked back her head. "Why would he kill her? He fought for her. She was his bride."

"I don't know. Maybe she refused to have sex with him and he got furious."

"Yeah, but Raven, if he was mad that she wouldn't have sex with him it wouldn't make sense to kill her. You would think that he'd force her instead."

I wiggled my finger in front of my face. "Maybe he did force her. Maybe that's why she ran up to the attic and when he came for her, she had nowhere to go but out the window."

"So, you think she really did kill herself?"

"Maybe she didn't intend to. Maybe she thought she could crawl to safety and get away from her abusive husband."

"You don't know that he was abusive."

"True, but don't you find it suspicious that she died only a week after marrying him?"

Mila pushed up from the bed. "Yes. And, so does Magni. He told me that he would like to know what happened to his sister, but it's been decades and the husband died right after she did."

"What do you mean?"

"According to Magni, his father Marcus went to investigate and he ruled it suicide, but still the husband was found dead a few days after her."

"Aha!" I joined Mila by the door. "That has to be proof of foul play. Two young people don't just die."

Making sure to turn off the lights in the room before we exited, Mila agreed, "No, they don't. So, what do you think happened?"

I straightened up. "I'm so glad you asked that question. Since the husband is dead it has to be one of three

17

scenarios. Either it was murder-suicide, murder-murder, or suicide-murder."

Mila raised her eyebrows. "What does that mean?"

"It would be murder-suicide if the husband killed Dina and then committed suicide out of guilt. But if the husband murdered Dina and Marcus then murdered him, it would be murder-murder, right?" I paused only long enough to suck in air. "But there's also the possibility that Dina committed suicide and that her father blamed her husband and killed him for it. That would make it suicide-murder."

Mila was walking at a slow pace when she tilted her head to one side. "Hmm, yeah, but I guess we'll never know."

"That's where you're wrong. I'm going to investigate, Mila. Don't you think Dina deserves for the world to know the truth about her death?"

"To be honest, I don't think most people remember that she lived."

With a hand on Mila's arm, I stopped her. "We know she lived and now I want to know how she died."

For a moment she watched me as if waiting for me to break into one of my signature laughs, but I was serious.

"Okay. And how are you going to investigate her death more than thirty years later?"

"I don't know. I've never done anything like it, but my logic tells me to follow any clue I can find."

"All right, and were there any clues in the file?"

"No."

Mila walked on. "It sounds like it'll be a short investigation then."

"We can't give up this easily. There are people in your family who knew Dina. One of them must have information about her death."

"I told you everything that my father told me. I don't know anymore."

"Okay, but Khan, Magni, and Erika would know more."

"That's right, but who says they're willing to talk about Dina now?"

Mila had a point, and either way, I couldn't just waltz in and ask the ruling family to answer my questions. "It would be so much easier if I had the same kind of access to them as you do."

"You mean because I live here at the Gray Manor?"

"Yes, you see them all the time, and they're your family."

"I don't know, Raven. They treat you as family too." Mila looked thoughtful. "Remember when I suggested that you should stay here while you work at Station Seven?"

"Yes."

"Well, didn't you say that you felt a bit old to be living with your parents? I mean, you know there are plenty of empty rooms here and that you're always welcome."

A smile grew on my lips as a thought formed in my head. "Living here would give me a better chance of asking questions and finding clues."

Mila returned my smile. "You know I'd love to have you closer, and I'll find you a nice room close to mine."

As we walked down the hallway, I linked my arm with hers. "Will you make sure I get a nicer room than Jonah? You know, because I'm your bestie."

"I didn't think something as mundane as a room mattered to you. Didn't you just tell me they were all the same?"

"It doesn't, but I know it matters to you. If you give him a nicer room than me, I'll know that he has taken my spot as your closest friend."

"Raven." Only Mila could say my name like it was a protest against my craziness.

"No, Mila, I'm warning you, woman. If you like Jonah, you'd better give me the nicest room because otherwise I'll challenge him to fight for the spot as your best friend, and we both know I'll whip his ass."

"I doubt Jonah has ever fought in his life."

"Then I'll battle him the Motlander way."

"With words?"

I raised my thumbs. "I'll declare a thumb war and defend my rightful spot as your best friend."

Mila's sweet laugh had always had a calming effect on me and I smiled back at her.

"You know I love you, Raven."

"But do you love me more than Jonah?"

"Where is this coming from? I've known you for a decade while Jonah and I met less than a year ago. Besides, he lives in the Motherlands."

"I know, but anyone can see the two of you are like magnets and he makes you laugh."

"Jonah is easy to be around and I enjoy his company, that's all. You make me laugh too."

"Hmm… admit it, he's your new girlfriend."

Mila stopped and took my hand. "Raven, just because I love you doesn't mean I can't love others too. I have infinite love in my heart and I don't rank my friends from best to worst."

Tilting my head, I squinted my eyes. "Fair enough, but if you did, I would be on the top, right?"

Mila's melodic laughter filled the hallway as she walked on with one word hanging in the air. "Obviously."

CHAPTER 3
Keeping in Shape

Leo

I had never spent as much time in the gym as I did after Raven became my mentee. The woman was relentless and kept a rigorous training program. Technically, no one asked me to supervise her while she worked out, but her preferred method was fight training, and I figured that my presence would deter any of her opponents from getting too rough with her.

In the beginning, none of us eighty-five men at Station Seven would spar with her. Not only was it ingrained in us from early childhood never to touch a woman, we also had strict laws that could put our lives in jeopardy if we overstepped our boundaries and touched a woman without her permission. Those laws had been lifted when it came to Raven's fight training, but the thought of hitting a woman was so alien to us that no one wanted to do it. Raven didn't give up, though. Being resourceful and sneaky, she played mind games with young Monroe until she riled him up enough to fight her.

As an opinionated rookie who felt entitled to respect, Monroe wasn't popular among us experienced policemen. After Raven lost to him in her first fight, she was able to persuade some of my colleagues to train with her under the pretense that she needed their help to beat him in a future fight.

Three weeks later, she had beat Monroe twice and the whole damn station was lining up to spar with her. Some of the men were taking pride in her explosive

21

improvement rate and loved teaching her, while others enjoyed beating her to put her in her place.

For most of these men, Raven was the first female they got to touch. I worried that the raised testosterone and excitement level that occur during fighting might make some of the men unable to control their urges. That's why I stayed around to make sure she was safe.

Today, I worked out in one end of the gym while Sergeant White was sparring with Raven. He was in his late forties and from what I'd seen, she was giving him a run for his money. The eight colleagues watching the fight were blocking my view, but I could hear them call out and make comments – some encouraging Sergeant White, and others helping Raven improve her technique.

"Come on, White, you can't let her get away with that."

"Raven, be ready, he's coming on your left."

"Get that fucking elbow up, woman."

"That's it, White, show her who's the boss."

That last comment made me walk over to the ring area to get a better view just as Cameron shouted:

"Turn, Raven, fucking roll like I showed you. Yes. that's it!"

I stopped next to Cameron, a large man a few years older than me. "How is she doing?"

"She doesn't have his strength, but she's compensating with speed and technique."

Just then Raven got a kick in and Sergeant White, who was sweating profusely and panting hard, doubled over with a deep groan.

"Don't just stand there, take him down," Cameron ordered, and Raven was quick to sweep at her opponent's feet, making him fall flat on his back.

"Arrghh!" Sergeant White roared with irritation and banged his hand down the floor.

Raven's face was red and sweaty too, but she was dancing on her feet with a large grin on her face. "Did you see that, Cam?"

Cameron, who was normally always so stoic and brusque, grinned back at her. "I saw, Raven, but you still have to move faster and be more precise. There was no reason for you to let him get that blow in. Had Sergeant White fought you when he was five years younger, he would've nailed your ass to the floor."

The man in question was already back on his feet and he scowled at Cameron as Raven tried to ease his embarrassment.

"I just got lucky. We all know that even experienced fighters have bad days. Next time, it'll be me on that floor for sure."

White was leaving the ring, but he turned and answered her, "Fucking count on it."

That led to a satisfied smile on Raven's face and then she looked at me. "What about you, old man? Do you want to go a few rounds with me?"

I hated when she called me old, and I suspected that was exactly why she did it. Raven had a special gift for riling people up. She was an expert at finding things that would give her a strong reaction.

"How many times do I have to tell you, I'm not interested in fighting with you?"

She gave me a cocky grin. "What if I go easy on you?"

Cameron's deep chuckle next to me made me narrow my eyes. "You wouldn't stand a chance against me, Raven."

"That's what Sergeant White, Monroe, and the others said before I beat them." Looking straight at me, Raven still danced on her feet, jumping from side to side with a lot of energy. "Come play with me, Leo. It will be fun."

23

The other men looked to me, and one of them muttered. "What the hell, Inspector, did she just call you Leo?"

"Raven, for the last time, you'll refer to me as Sir or Inspector."

"Cameron lets me call him Cam."

Cameron avoided my hard look. It was clear he had a soft spot for Raven. "I don't care what Cameron does. You'll call me Sir or Inspector."

Raven tilted her head with a playful smile. "How about you come in here and make me?"

Some of the other men couldn't hide their amusement with her putting me on the spot like this.

"Um, are you gonna spank her ass for being a brat, or can I do it?" Cameron's question was for me, but he was looking at Raven.

"Okay, I'll teach you a few lessons, Raven. But I don't want a fucking audience when I take you down."

The men protested when I pointed to the door. As they walked out a few of them shared their opinion, "Fucking highlight of the year and then we don't get to see it. Way to be a dick, Inspector."

"He's just afraid she'll take him down and he'll be humiliated."

"Nah, I think it's more like he's hoping to have her go down but in a more pleasant way, you know." Gruff male laughter was heard until the door slammed behind the last one.

"Is that true?" Raven asked with an amused smile. "Are you hoping for me to go down?" Her eyes fell to my crotch, but I knew her mind games and didn't take the bait.

"Stop trying to fuck with my brain. It won't work on me."

She tilted her head to the other side and gave an innocent smile. "I'm not very experienced with sex but I'm having a hard time seeing the anatomy of it. How do you fuck with someone's brain exactly?"

"You don't! All you have to worry about for now is understanding and using the right titles when you speak to me and other employees at this station." While talking I was putting on thin safety gloves made of Protego. "First there's you, a recruit, then there's Monroe, who's a cadet. After that comes officer, sergeant, and then comes inspector, which is what I am. Are you following so far?"

"Yes. I'm just wondering why you're not putting on a helmet..."

"Because we won't have any blows from the neck up. Maybe a black eye would teach you some humility, but I'm sure as hell not sending you home to your dad with one."

Raven removed her helmet and tossed it to the side while shaking her large mane of dark curls.

"As I was saying, I'm an inspector and the next time I get promoted I'll be a chief inspector. After that comes lieutenant, and captain. Captains are typically mature men and they don't see much action as they mostly work at the station."

"Got it."

"After captain comes Commander, and we only have one in our country."

"Magni Aurelius."

"Yes."

"So, are we going to get physical today or should I sit down and take notes, Professor?"

I clapped my hands together and with a hard expression, I took up fight position. "You're being disrespectful again."

"I'm sorry about that. It's just that it takes *so* little." Raven had a smug smile on her face when she got into position as well.

25

"Cameron was right, you know, you shouldn't have allowed White to get so close to you. Let's see if you do better with me."

Raven's eyes were shining with excitement and her nostrils were flaring in anticipation of my first attack.

My first high kick she blocked and with incredible speed, she placed her foot where my face would have been if I hadn't ducked.

I puffed out air. "I told you, neck and down only."

"My bad, I mistook your head for your ass."

"Very funny." I moved in a circle, my body expecting her to attack.

"Yeah? If you think I'm so funny, then why aren't you laughing?"

My next attack came swiftly and the sheer force of my blows to her body forced her back. Raven took three punches while trying to protect her core. When I pulled back to launch my fourth punch, she sidestepped and placed her fist in my ribs.

"Umph."

Encouraged by my groan of pain she jumped back and screamed when she launched a roundhouse kick to my chest. For all her small size her impact was hard and it hurt. Like always, I let my pain fuel me to fight harder and this time, I used my body to force her to the ground. Maybe Raven remembered Cameron's words because she rolled like a fucking anaconda and used her legs to wrap around my body. Like two wrestlers, we were grappling for control but my problem was that I was too fucking conscious about not wanting to place my hands between her legs or on her chest area.

Raven was panting and her hair was in disarray from our rolling around on the floor, but tight as a damn parasite, she clung to me, trapping my right arm. "What kind of fighting is this?" I growled, but her only response was to twist my nipple hard.

"Stop that shit." I got up, but instead of letting go of me Raven clung to my back. Fuck, this woman was a fucking acrobat with unbelievable core muscles and persistence. Falling on top of her to make her lose her grip didn't work, so I rolled to get her to let go. That move backfired as it gave Raven a chance to reposition herself, this time wrapping her legs around my neck and strangling me.

There was only so much humiliation I would take and by now it was clear that she was a lethal fighter. Using my strength, I tried to tear her off me. All I managed, however, was to get her in front of me, her thighs still locked around my neck, and her arms hooked around my waist. No matter how much I tried to push and hit her, she only squeezed her thighs harder. I was fucking struggling to breathe and at that point I was done playing nice. I let my dead weight fall to the ground with her underneath me. It was satisfying to hear all the air whoosh out from Raven's lungs and I didn't care that my crotch was in her face. If I couldn't breathe, I had no fucking sympathy for her gasping for air like me.

By now my face had to be blue and I reckoned her thighs to be on fire. I could feel her pounding on the backs of my thighs, signaling that she couldn't breathe, but I wasn't letting go until she released her hold on my neck. Using the muscles in my legs, I kept her from rolling, while I wriggled and pushed my hand up between her legs to force her thighs apart. It worked. First, I got my whole arm through, then my shoulder, and I could finally break her hold and breathe again. Sucking in a large gulp of air, I rolled off of her and heard Raven cough and suck in air too.

My eyes were wide as I stared at her while panting. "What the hell was that?... Do you call that fighting?"

Raven's chest rose up as she heaved in oxygen and spoke on the exhalation. "What would you call it?"

"Porn!"

"Porn? What are you talking about?"

"It was like doing a sixty-nine with clothes on."

"What's a sixty-nine?"

"You had your head in my crotch, I had mine in yours. That's a fucking sixty-nine." I was angry at myself for having allowed this situation to begin with.

"Oh, now I get it." Her eyes fell to my crotch. "When I couldn't breathe, I thought about biting. Good thing I didn't."

I frowned and got up. "Only a coward would bite in a fight!"

"My dad taught me to use every trick possible and if this hadn't been a training situation, I would have used my teeth."

Offering her a hand, I pulled Raven up and when she stood in front of me, she kept her hand linked with mine. "So, I guess this wasn't what the others meant when they joked about me going down on you?"

I raised an eyebrow. "Are you trying to be funny again?"

Raven used her free hand to brush her hair back and then she gave me a smile. "I *am* funny! I might not be able to take you in a fight, yet, but I'll consider it a personal victory when I make you smile." Her eyes were full of amusement and it felt intimate to stand this close with her eyes shining up at me. Taking a step back, I pulled my hand from her grip, cleared my throat, and changed the subject.

"I heard you moved into the Gray Manor."

"Who told you that?"

"Magni did." I moved to the fridge to get a few balls of water. "Do you see Mila a lot?"

"Of course. She's my best friend and it was her suggestion that I should move in there."

After popping two balls of water in my mouth, I held one up, asking, "Do you want water?"

Raven nodded and caught the one I threw to her.

"Any chance you could put in a good word for me with Mila? I'm fighting in her tournament and I have a good chance of becoming one of the five champions."

Raven looked down at her torn tank top. "You ripped my shirt."

"So? You strangled me. And why are you changing the subject? I asked you if you could put in a good word with Mila for me."

Raven lifted her gaze and stood for a second. "Sorry, but she's my best friend and I would never recommend that she marries a guy who has no sense of humor."

"I have a sense of humor."

"Do you?" Like it was the most natural thing in the world, Raven pulled her shirt over her head.

"What are you doing?" My eyes were like magnets drawn to the drops of sweat traveling down her belly. I'd never seen a real woman in only shorts and a sports bra. The amount of naked skin had my heart hammering faster, and other parts of my body reacted as if she was wearing lingerie.

"I'm throwing my shirt out. Told you, it's ruined."

I watched as she tossed it in the trash and picked another shirt from her bag. "Thanks for sparring with me today. You're a fabulous fighter. If only you weren't so damn serious all the time, I might like you enough to put in a word with Mila."

"I don't need you to like me. I just need you to respect me. You can start by addressing me as Sir or Inspector."

Raven gave a low chuckle and left with her hips swaying. "See you tomorrow… Sir Inspector."

As soon as the door closed behind her, my eyes fell to the trash can. Like a magnet had been dropped in it, my feet moved closer and I couldn't resist picking up her tossed-out shirt. My mind was reeling from what had just happened between us and my hands shook when I lifted the fabric to my nose, closed my eyes, and inhaled the arousing scent of Raven.

CHAPTER 4
Clues

Raven

Mila was in the garden with Jonah and her three dogs. I was no expert on dog breeds but one of them was small like a cat, another was a mix with a happy personality, and then there was Holger, who was a great Dane and the newest of Mila's dogs. He was my favorite because being big and strong like a small pony, he never had a need to bark. Mila's small dog would drive me crazy with all its barking, but not Holger. He was above that and just walked around with Mila, all nice and calm, letting her pretend that she could control him if he chose to run.

"Hey, Raven, it's so nice to meet you again. May peace surround you." Jonah came and took my hands while the smallest of the dogs was nipping at our feet.

I greeted him back, and when Holger came to sniff me, I rubbed the huge dog behind his ear.

"Raven, I'm so glad you're here. I was just telling Jonah about the mysterious death of my aunt Dina and how I spoke to my dad about her last night."

"You spoke to Magni?"

Jonah picked up the little dog, whose name I could never remember, and by stroking it, he made it quiet down.

"Yes. He even gave me some articles about her."

Jonah was holding his chin up to avoid being licked on the mouth by the little dog. "It's like a real mystery. I've already told Mila that I would love to be her partner in crime and help solve it."

31

"Excuse me?" Planting my hands on my hips I gave Mila a hard stare. "I'm the policewoman here. How did this become *your* mystery to solve? And why is *he* suddenly your partner?"

Mila had always hated confrontations and she hurried to take my hand. "Raven. I'm so sorry. We're just trying to help. Of course, it's your investigation! Why don't we go inside and I can show you what I found." Putting her arm around my shoulders, we walked back to the house together.

"How many have you told about my investigation? When you spoke to your dad, did you tell him that I'm investigating Dina's murder?"

"No, I just told him that I was curious about the young woman my little sister is named after."

"Good."

"I figured if you didn't succeed, he would be disappointed. So, for now, there's no need for him to grow hopeful."

Once in her room, Mila handed me a large envelope. "Magni said that after Dina died, their father purged the house of all evidence that she ever lived. Pictures of her were taken away, and her room was made into a bathroom for one of the guestrooms. Allegedly, it was because Erika was grieving. But even if she wasn't around, Dina's name was never spoken and when Magni asked about her, he was either ignored or told to never mention her again."

"How old was Magni again when his sister died?"

"Seven. But later, when he was around eleven or twelve, he searched for evidence that she had existed, and he found a photo of her under his mom's bed. He doesn't have it anymore, but after his father died, he checked the archives to find more information about Dina's life, and that's where he found that." Mila's eyes fell to the envelope in my hand.

I opened it and pulled out an old article with two pictures in it. In one of them Dina was smiling with her new husband. In the other they were surrounded by seven people.

"Wow, it's so weird to see pictures of Magni and Khan this young." The two boys stood on the outskirts of the picture, Magni looking away and Khan looking up. Marcus stood between the bride and groom with his arm around their shoulders while Erika stood next to Dina holding her hand.

"Who are those three men?"

"I asked my dad about it and he said that this man was called Mr. Zobel. From what I understand he was Marcus's best friend and instrumental in the revolution that helped Marcus take power in the Northlands." Mila paused and rubbed her collarbone. "That's why it's a paradox that Mr. Zobel was later executed for treason."

"How long ago?"

"At least ten years. It was about that time when my dad disappeared into Alaska, remember?" A ghost of pain flashed over Mila's face and I reached out to touch her hand.

"Of course, I remember."

"What happened?" Jonah asked and Mila looked down with a sad shake of her head.

"Oh, it's a long story, but my dad was frustrated with the world and for weeks he disappeared into Alaska where no one could find him. I grieved and cried a lot during that time."

"And I tried my best to cheer her up. Remember when I directed that song competition in your honor?"

Mila angled her head. "That's right. You sang horribly to make me sound like an angel and I won. Huh, you know what I just realized?"

I waited for her to tell me.

"You became the class clown during that time. Always coming up with a funny face or a joke to make me smile. Maybe Magni's absence is part of why you became so funny."

Jonah sat down on the corner of Mila's desk. "Do you remember any of her jokes? I love humor."

Tapping her lip, Mila thought about it. "There were so many but one that had us all crack up was when Kya asked the class, 'What is math?' and Raven raised her hand with a serious face and said, "Mental abuse to humans."

Jonah raised his chin. "Ah, I see, a clever acronym."

I groaned. "I hated math then and I still do today."

"Yes, and then there was the time William fell asleep during class and Archer shouted, 'William, are you sleeping in my class?' Raven answered loud and clear, 'Well, now he's not, but if you could just be a little quieter maybe he could get a good nap.'"

Jonah smiled at me. "I'll bet you weren't too popular with your teachers if you were cracking jokes like that."

Waving a dismissive hand, I shrugged. "It was harmless. But back to the picture. If that's Mr. Zobel, then who are those two other men?"

Mila bit her lower lip. "Magni didn't know."

Jonah leaned in to see them. "They could've been friends of the groom. They are standing right next to him."

I studied Dina's husband for a moment. "Do we know his name?"

"Yes, the article mentions it halfway down." Mila used her finger to search while reading out in a mumble, "After three impressive victories, Henry Hudson fought and won the final match, making him one of the five champions to stand in front of Dina Aurelius, daughter of our strong ruler, Marcus Aurelius."

I studied the picture again. "Hmm, it's weird…"

"What is?" Mila went to sit on a couch and right away her three dogs followed. The small one jumped into her lap, while the two bigger ones lay down by her feet.

"I don't know, it's just weird to me that the husband is actually handsome. I imagined him as some kind of ogre. I mean why else would Dina refuse to have sex with him?"

"How do you know that she refused to have sex with her husband?" Jonah sat down on the floor next to Holger, who decided to use Jonah's leg as a pillow.

"I'm speculating here. A young girl gets married and five days later she falls from an attic window. The logical conclusion would be that she was trying to escape someone, and it's not a far stretch of a theory to assume that she was trying to escape her husband, who probably wanted to have sex with her."

Mila looked thoughtful. "I don't know, Raven. I'm getting married and I would expect my husband to want to have sex with me. It can't have been a surprise to Dina."

I was pacing the rug in front of them. "Maybe the sex was painful to her or maybe he wanted to have it ten times a day and she just needed a break."

"No man wants to have sex ten times a day," Jonah pointed out.

"Jonah, we are talking about an Nman here. Compared to you Motlander men they are…" I hesitated.

"Freaks of nature?"

Mila pushed at his shoulder. "Heeeyyy, you make them sound like mutants."

He shrugged. "I didn't mean to offend them, but they are insanely large men and if they love sex as much as sports and fighting, then I can see why a young teenage girl like Dina would be overwhelmed."

35

"That reminds me... about your tournament, Mila." I paused. "Leo wants me to put in a good word for him, but I told him I wouldn't."

"Why not? I like Leo."

Jonah got up. "Sorry, ladies, as much as I would love to stick around and help solve the mystery, I have a meeting with Pearl and Khan soon."

"Okay, then Raven and I will just see you at dinner."

"Uh-huh."

I picked up a funky energy from Jonah that made me study him for a second. It didn't seem like a coincidence that he left just as we were discussing Mila's upcoming tournament. *Is there something going on between Jonah and Mila?* I quickly dismissed the idea since I'd never picked up on anything but friendship between them, and it was normal for Motlanders to dislike tournaments. "I don't want you to marry Leo. He wouldn't be a good match for you."

"How can you say that? I've heard you say that he's a strong warrior, and my parents praise him a lot. You know how rare it is for my father to approve of anyone fighting in my tournament?"

"Honestly, Mila, you should have never made that stupid bet to begin with.

She sighed. "I know, sometimes I wonder..." Her eyes wandered to the door.

"If you could just run away from it all?"

Mila pulled her legs up underneath her. "You know how I feel about violence. The idea that some men might die because of me makes me sick. When I made that bet with my father I never in a million years thought he would do it."

"Wearing a bead in his beard for a full year is a small price for him to pay. You know how badly he wants you to marry the strongest man in the country."

36

"Well, at the time, no Nman with respect for himself would put beads in his beard. That was a fashion only seen among the men in the Motherland. You know how Magni resents the femininity of the Motlander men. I was so sure he wouldn't do it."

"Well, he did. And now every other man in this country is wearing a black bead in his beard to look as fierce as your father."

Mila threw up her hands. "He's trying to protect me by making sure that I marry someone who is strong enough to secure my safety."

"I know. I would just never have a tournament myself and I would've sworn you were the last woman to have one."

"Why? My parents married in a tournament and they are very happy together."

Taking three steps I walked to the sofa and sat down next to Mila. "If you marry someone like Leo, things are going to be a lot different in your life. There's no way he would be okay with you having male friends like Jonah. Leo is just as overprotective and annoying as every other Nman. If you ask me, they are all one colossal pain in the butt."

"So, what do you suggest I do?"

"For now, I suggest you take me to talk to Erika. I'll bet she can tell us who the two men in the photo are."

"All right. But you have to be gentle with my grandmother. She lost a daughter and I won't have you interrogating her with hard questions."

My smile was innocent. "I promise to be mild as a lamb."

"Good. Then let's do it."

CHAPTER 5
Erika's Puzzle

Raven

Mila and I found Erika doing a jigsaw puzzle.

"Hey, darling, are you here to help me?"

"Sure. Do you mind if Raven helps too?"

"Of course not."

Erika smiled and waved for us to take a seat at the table, where only the frame and a quarter of the puzzle had been assembled. "I might have been a bit ambitious with this one – it's four thousand pieces and I've been working on it for more than a week."

Picking up the box, I looked at the cover picture. "I've seen these people before?"

"Yes, they are some of our founding fathers."

Studying the picture, I saw antique motorcycles and a group of twelve sinister-looking men in leather jackets.

"Why did you choose this motif? Why not one of a beautiful forest or flowers or something."

"Because I'm a patriot at heart." Erika pointed to one of the bikers. "And I've always thought he was very handsome."

I scrunched my nose up. "Really? He doesn't look like he's any fun."

Erika gave me a small wink. "I think I could have had a lot of fun with him. Except, we were born in different centuries."

Mila snatched the box from me. "What does fun have to do with handsome anyway? It's like your comment about Leo not having any humor. I'm sure Leo would laugh if he felt relaxed but even if he doesn't, he's still an impressive man."

Erika tilted her head. "Are you talking about Leo, the policeman?"

"Yes." I picked up one of the pieces of the puzzle, letting my eyes search for its place.

Mila's finger tapped on the box with the image of the bikers. "I would say that he's even more handsome than these men."

"I'll agree that Leo is strapping, but I'm sorry, girls; no one compares to John Hanson." Erika gave a last look at the box and sighed. "If only we had time machines."

I smiled at her. "It's funny because we actually came to talk to you about something from the past."

"You are interested in the history of the Northlands? That's so nice to hear." Erika lit up as she said it.

"Yes; more precisely we are interested in knowing what happened to your daughter, Dina." I looked down at the puzzle as I asked the question, but even so, I felt Erika stiffen.

"Raven, we don't speak about her."

Mila reached out her hand and placed it gently on top of Erika's. "Grandma, why don't you ever talk about Dina and why did Marcus erase all signs of her?"

It took Erika so long to answer that I thought she might not want to answer at all, and when she finally spoke it was in a low voice. "Marcus was always protective of me. We people of the North are not as accustomed to discussing our emotions as you people from the Motherlands. He did what he thought was right."

"But if you didn't talk about your emotions, then how did you deal with your grief?"

There was a trembling in Erika's voice. "We moved on. What choice did we have?"

"But why did you move on like Dina never existed? Didn't you feel the need to honor her memory?"

"It was Marcus's decision to remove everything that would remind us of her. He said he did it for my sake, but to be honest I think it was as much for his." Erika paused and her fingers played with the puzzle piece in her hand. "People think Marcus was a cold and ruthless man but they never understood him the way I did. He wasn't always like that."

Mila leaned in and squeezed Erika's hand. "Who was the Marcus that only you knew?"

Even though Erika was looking down, I could still tell that she was tearing up. "Marcus was a graceful warrior and so tall and handsome. It was the happiest day of my life when he fought for me. I didn't think twice before choosing him as my champion." In a sudden movement, Erika pushed back her chair, got up, and moved over to open a closet. "Every Christmas he would make me an ornament for the tree." She pulled out a wooden box and brought it back to the table and opened it. "This one was my first." The year 2399 was written on an ornament in the shape of an angel.

"Wow, did Grandpa make this himself?"

"Yes. He was an artist and one of his preferred materials to work with was glass."

"Wait, did he decorate it or did he make the glass angel from scratch?"

Erika lifted her chin. "Marcus made it from scratch."

Mila was picking up more beautiful ornaments from the box. "How many did he make you?"

"He made me one every year for Christmas." Erika sighed and looked down. "Until the year Dina died."

For a moment none of us spoke. We just admired the artistry of Marcus Aurelius.

With a church-bell-shaped ornament in my hands, I leaned back in my chair. "Never would I have thought that an artist could go on to become the ruler. Aren't artists supposed to be gentle souls?"

Mila looked from her grandmother to me and back. "Was Marcus a gentle soul, Grandma?

"I wouldn't say that, but I do know that Marcus was a much better ruler than his predecessor. That man was a monster."

"Who was the previous ruler again?" I looked at Mila hoping she had paid better attention in school than I had.

"Wasn't it Nikolai something?"

"His name was Nikolai Wolf and he was an example of how power corrupts." Erika was quiet before she added, "Not that Marcus was an angel, because he certainly did some questionable things that were awful in the later part of his life, but Nikolai Wolf was a pig in comparison."

"What happened back when Marcus came to power?"

My question made Erika raise an eyebrow at me. "Raven, if you think Marcus just came to power, you are wrong. Marcus *took* the power in a well-orchestrated coup and millions were happy, including me. We all celebrated the day Marcus killed Nikolai.... Well, except for his wife of course."

"What happened to her?"

"Lord Wolf had four sons and a young daughter. It's rare for any member of a ruler's family to survive a coup, and many disagreed with Marcus's decision to let the wife and her two youngest children live."

I frowned. "Why is that? The family shouldn't pay for what their father did."

"Don't be naïve, Raven. Little boys eventually grow into men who want to avenge their fathers." Erika said it like it was a given.

41

"Did you see Lord Wolf's execution?" Part of me felt bad for making her relive a traumatic past, but this felt like real police work and I was a little giddy on the inside.

"I wasn't there in person, but I saw a recording of Nikolai Wolf's execution." Erika's eyes glazed over as she muttered, "Marcus made him apologize to me."

Mila and I exchanged a look. "Why would the dictator apologize to you, Grandma?"

"What?" Erika was blinking as if coming back from the past. "What did you ask?"

"You said that Marcus made the dictator apologize to you. Did you know him?"

"No. I don't know why I said that. It's all a bit blurry at this point." By the way she was picking up new pieces from her puzzle and focusing on finding the right place for them, I could tell she wasn't interested in discussing it further.

"We found this old article, and we wanted to ask you if you know who these two men are..." I gestured for Mila to show Erika the photo.

Erika's hands were shaking when she reached for the article with the photo. "Where did you find this?"

"My dad had it."

I pointed to the two men standing in the background. "Do you know their names?"

Tears were welling up in Erika's eyes, and she gave a dismissive shake of the head and returned the paper to Mila. "No. They were friends of the groom. One of them was a roommate, I think."

"Do you remember which city they lived in?"

"Raven, it's been so long. Please." She was fiddling with the sleeve on her dress.

"I know, but anything might help us. Do you know if there's anywhere we could find some of Dina's belongings?"

When Erika didn't answer, Mila followed up on my question. "Grandma, do you know what happened to Dina's things?"

With a voice thick from suppressed crying, Erika brushed back her hair. "Well, as far as I know, everything was taken to the storage room down in the basement."

"What storage room?"

"You'll find it if you continue all the way down in the long hallway. It's directly under the library, but I never go there."

"Because of all the painful memories?" Mila's face was full of sympathy.

"Yes. That's right. It's better to leave the past in the past."

"But what if we could find out what happened to Dina, wouldn't you like to know?"

This time it was Erika who patted Mila's hand. "It's been more than thirty years, darling. You're asking for the impossible, and going around asking questions will only cause pain. My mother always told me that the dead are best left in peace."

When Mila and I left Erika that afternoon, I was more determined than ever to find answers. "Did you see how your grandma had goosebumps on her arms when she spoke about Nikolai Wolf and how Marcus killed him?"

"Yes, but it's because he was an evil dictator. She lived through his tyranny, so it probably gives her the chills to think about him."

"I get that, but the way she said that Marcus had made him give an apology to her...hmm." I narrowed my eyes. "I'm telling you, Mila, your grandmother only told us half the story. We are definitely on to something, you just wait and see."

CHAPTER 6
Action

Leo

"She did what?"

I'd been a police officer since I was twenty-four, and in those seven years, I had seen many strange things, but nothing like the policeman reporting a domestic violence case was telling me about.

I listened, and as the computer produced a transcript of his words on a screen in front of me, I was underlining things he said such as wife, attack, vicious, and humiliation.

"I have no fucking clue how to deal with this shit," the man ended. "Do you?"

There's no way I would tell him that I was unsure how to deal with it, too. "We'll figure it out. I'm coming to meet you."

Ending the call, I gave a loud outburst of frustration. "Fucking hell!!"

"What's up?" Cameron and Raven were standing by his desk, both looking over at me.

"A wife just tried to chop off her husband's dick."

"What?" Cameron looked as pained as I had felt when I first heard it.

"Apparently he cheated on her."

More colleagues came over. "Did you say a husband cheated on his wife?"

"Yup, and she didn't take it well."

Cameron lifted his hand with a coffee cup in it. "How is that even possible? Did he go to the Motherlands? Where would he find a woman to cheat with?"

"Her name is Gennie and the wife found her husband in bed with her."

"Wait a minute, that has to be Storm's wife."

"Storm who?" Cameron asked.

"Storm. I went to school with him and he married some wacko woman from the Motherlands."

"Maybe your friend should have kept a better eye on his woman."

Raven was waving her hands. "No, no, they aren't married anymore. She divorced him last year."

"Then why is she still here?" I asked.

Raven lifted her shoulders in a shrug signaling that she had no idea. "It's lucky for her that most women here don't have fight training. If she had been with *my* husband, the bitch would've been dead."

To call a woman a bitch was not done, and I gave Raven a reproachful glance while Cameron focused on another detail of what Raven had said.

"You plan to have a tournament, Raven?"

Raven wrinkled up her nose. "Not a chance."

"Then why did you mention that if she'd been with your husband, she would have been dead?"

"I'm not saying that I'll never marry. Just that I'm not having a tournament. And why would I? I don't need a strong warrior when I can take care of myself."

With a snort, I crossed my arms. "Are you saying you want a weak husband?"

"No."

"Then what?"

Raven mirrored me and crossed her own arms. "The right man for me will be someone I can laugh with and

45

who will support me and my dreams the same way I'll support him."

"Hmm." I frowned because I understood her comment about laughter was aimed at me. Raven had called me stiff and boring plenty of times. "Well, good luck finding that while I go find a solution to this mess."

I was walking out of the room when I heard Cameron talking to Raven behind me. "I've been supportive, haven't I?"

The man was twenty years her senior and a strong warrior in his own right. We could all see how he had fallen for Raven, but I didn't think any of us stood a chance with her. Still, I slowed my step, wanting to hear her answer.

"Yes, Cam, you've been supportive with my fight training, but I'm still stuck in the basement sorting files that no one really cares about. That's not exactly my dream of police work."

The door closed behind me before I could hear any more. My head was spinning as I kept thinking about something one of Raven's friends had once told me. *She grows on you.*

After my initial strong attraction to Raven when I first met her, I hadn't wanted the job as her mentor. It was one thing to admire an unattainable woman from afar, but working with her was a nightmare. I had little experience with women in general, and having responsibility for her safety had me worrying all the time. My life had been much easier and more uncomplicated before she got the crazy idea of joining the police, but at least I'd been able to use my irritation to suppress my attraction to her. The fact that she was annoying and disrespectful had pushed me to act cold and hostile to her.

So why was Raven the first thing I thought about in the morning? Why did I wonder if she would come to work wearing her hair up or down? Why did I stand close enough to see if I could smell her perfume? And why did the days when she didn't poke fun at me feel longer than the rest?

I didn't have time to ponder about it when I had a historic case waiting for me. Under normal circumstances, I would call in the Doom Squad in cases of domestic violence, but with a female aggressor that seemed like overkill. We men of the North believed in "an eye for an eye" but it wasn't like we could beat up a woman or cut off her nonexistent penis. I would have to come up with something else, but what?

When an idea struck me, I pivoted around and walked back into the station.

"Raven, come here."

Popping her head around the corner, she looked at me. "I didn't do anything."

"You said you wanted action, right?"

"Yeah."

"Then you're coming with me."

Raven beamed as if I had just told her Christmas would now be celebrated four times a year. "For real?"

"Hurry." I spun around again and had made it a few steps outside when I heard her running footsteps behind me. "What about a jacket?"

"You told me to hurry, so I just ran."

"It's raining."

"I don't care."

"That's because you have no clue what police work is. We might be standing outside in the rain for hours interviewing people." I pointed to the door behind us. "Get your jacket, right now."

"Yes sir, Inspector." Raven sprinted inside and returned a minute later with a jacket in her hand.

I was already by the drone. "Get in and let's go."

Climbing in with eagerness on her face, Raven buckled up. "You know, it's kind of sweet when you think about it."

"What is?"

"You telling me to get my jacket. It's like you care about me or something."

"I don't."

"Not even a little?"

"I'm your mentor. It's my job to teach you stuff, that's all."

"I'm still going to choose to think that you care about me."

I sighed. "Do you want me to leave you here?"

"No, of course not. I want to come."

"Then stop talking about me caring about you. It's a fantasy."

"What about Mila? Do you care about her?"

"Raven." There was a warning in my tone.

"All right, all right, I'll be quiet now."

"Good."

It took us twenty-five minutes to get to the crime scene, where a young uniformed officer who couldn't have been out of the academy for more than a few years came to shake my hand. "Nice to meet you, Inspector, we spoke on the phone."

"You're Officer Flannigan."

"Yes, sir." His eyes kept going to Raven but for some reason, I didn't want to introduce him to her. I should have known it wouldn't matter, because she spoke up anyway.

"I'm Raven. The first female police officer."

Flannigan smiled. "I've heard of you."

"You're not an officer, yet," I reminded her in a dry voice and walked into the house. "Where's the husband and wife?"

Flannigan was right on my heels, eager to answer my questions. "They went to the hospital."

48

"Both of them?" I turned.

"Yes." Officer Flannigan pointed down to his crotch. "The husband was bleeding severely after she tried to... You know."

"Yes, I know." I had phantom pains in my crotch just from thinking about it. There was no need to repeat what she had done.

"How bad was the wife hurt?"

"She wasn't hurt at all, sir."

Lowering my brow, I moved through the living room and into the bedroom. The torn bedsheet told a story of a fight and the bloodstains revealed how severe it had been.

"Why did the wife go to the hospital if she wasn't hurt?"

"She was in remorse over hurting her husband and he wanted her to come."

"Why didn't you arrest her?"

"Because he didn't want to press charges, sir." Flannigan had a big question mark on his face. "I didn't know what to do."

"Hmm. Is this the couple's house?"

"No. It's the residency of Gennie Manning, the woman he slept with. Not sure how his wife knew he was here, but she must have suspected what was going on since she walked right in."

"And where is Gennie now?"

"She's in the kitchen, sir." He pointed out the bedroom door. "It's right through the living room."

At first glance, Gennie Manning was an attractive woman, with symmetrical features and high cheekbones. She sat on a chair with her knees pulled up in front of her and a blanket wrapped around her body. Her hair was wild, making me conclude that her lover's wife had yanked at it, and there was a long scratch on her jaw.

"Oh, great, more police."

"My name is Leo da Vinci. I'm an inspector and I deal with domestic violence cases."

Gennie gave him a bored glance. "I didn't do anything. You should go and talk to that crazy woman who attacked me."

"I will, but first you need to tell me exactly what happened."

"Just talk to him, I already explained everything." When she lifted a hand to point at Flannigan the blanket fell over her shoulder and revealed that she wasn't wearing a shirt underneath.

I averted my gaze, pulled a chair over in front of her, and sat down. "Take me through it anyway."

"All right. If you insist. Nigel and I have been seeing each other for a while and then today we were in my bedroom when suddenly his wife barged in and started screaming at us."

"Were you having sex?"

"Yes."

"Did she attack you physically?"

"Yes and no."

I waited for her to elaborate.

"She had this crazy look in her eyes and a knife in her hand. Nigel was on top of me and he got up from the bed to calm her down, but she just grabbed for his penis with one hand and the next thing I saw was her hand with the knife coming down."

"And then what?"

"He was shocked, and he just stood there looking down at his bleeding penis with disbelief. I think she would've attacked him again if I hadn't intervened."

"How did you intervene?"

"I threw things at her and shouted at her to get out. I think she was in shock too from the sight of all the blood on her husband because she threw the knife down."

"Did she leave then?"

"No. She was crying and yelling about trust and loyalty. Calling her a psycho probably wasn't a good idea, because she came for me and we ended up fighting on the bed." Gennie touched her head. "She tore out my hair."

"Did you fight back?"

"Of course I did. I was scared. That's why I asked my home-bot to call the police."

"I understand that you got divorced from your husband last year. Who is your protector now?"

There was a shift in energy from Gennie, who let the blanket fall a little further down her arm and leaned forward. "Whomever I choose for the day of the week."

I pulled back, narrowing my eyes. "And they let you?"

"It's not like I give them a choice. I'm an adult woman, and I don't need anyone's permission to live my life the way I choose to."

My eyes found Raven's and I could see the eagerness radiating from her. With a small nod I signaled that she was allowed to ask questions too.

"How do you afford to live in a house like this?"

"I have an entrepreneurial mind. Why would I settle for one man when I can have many who want to impress me and buy me things?" While she spoke, Gennie's fingers toyed with a gold necklace.

Raven stood with her feet spread. "But if you're not going to marry any of them, then you're just using them."

"Nonsense, I'm being very generous with myself. As I see it, I have lots of love to give, and I'm spreading it out. Because of me, more than twenty Nmen can say they've been with a real woman. I look at it as a modern form of philanthropy." Gennie gave us an overbearing smile. "I'm simply feeding the hungry."

51

Raven lowered herself to the edge of a small dining table, still facing Gennie. "Interesting, and what are you getting in return?"

Gennie rose up in her seat and pushed her jaw out, making her look defensive. "I'm getting variety and fun. I've been married, and I'm not interested in living with one of them." As she said the last word, she made a nod with her head to me.

"I know your husband. Storm and I went to school together and he's a good man."

"He's a pig who couldn't clean up after himself and who would fart and burp with me in the room."

Raven didn't look disgusted. Instead she answered in a dry tone. "Sounds human to me."

"Yeah, maybe, but he was over-possessive and we fought a lot."

"From what I heard, you two fought because you kept flirting with other men."

"Why wouldn't I? Storm annoyed me while all these other men loved me. I'm telling you, woman to woman, don't ever marry one of them. You're much better off letting them love you with no strings attached."

"Really?"

Gennie gave Raven a sly smile. "You wouldn't want to eat in the same restaurant for the rest of your life, would you?"

I didn't like where this conversation was going and moved in my seat.

"Men aren't restaurants." Raven's tone was defensive.

"To me they are. Each one tastes different and I sate my hunger when I'm with them."

I almost jerked a little when Gennie returned her attention to me. It was like a transformation happening right in front of my eyes when her eyes became hooded, her face tilted to one side, and her smile became soft.

52

"You look appetizing. Maybe I should sample you?"

I shifted in my seat. "Um, what did you say?"

Gennie was looking straight into my eyes, now, and speaking with a sultry voice. "Have you ever been kissed by a woman?"

"No."

She leaned a little closer. "Would you like to?"

My eyes were staring at her lips as I tried to make my brain work.

"That's enough, Gennie, back the fuck off." Raven rose to her full height and came to stand next to me.

"There's no need to be vulgar."

"If you want to sleep with a thousand Nmen, go for it. I really don't give a shit but pick someone else."

Gennie broke into a small chuckle that sounded fake. "I see the Northlands rubbed off on you. Look at you swearing and being possessive."

"That's right, and you know what else I learned here?" Raven had a challenging glint in her eyes as she looked down on Gennie. "I learned to kick ass and since I'm not a man I won't be held to the same laws. I could literally beat you up and not go to jail for it."

"Are you threatening me?"

"I'm educating you! Stay away from married men and get yourself under control."

Gennie's eyes darted between me and Raven, and even though she appeared to look calm, it was a telling sign that her fingers were fiddling with that necklace of hers again. "My mistake. I didn't realize he was your husband."

Raven placed her hands on her hips. "What Leo is or isn't is none of your concern. Touch him and I'll break your arms."

I rose up from my chair. "Raven, calm down."

"I *am* calm."

"Is this interrogation over now?" Gennie pulled the blanket back over her shoulder and looked away.

"Yes. You didn't commit any crime, but I'm warning you: you're playing with fire. Gennie, our culture isn't like the one you know back in the Motherlands. You are lucky that none of your lovers have killed each other yet."

Gennie didn't respond to my warning.

"Let's go, Raven." Placing my hand on the small of her back, I pushed her forward. It was unheard of for an unmarried man to touch a woman, but that rule was suspended with Raven during fight training, and as her mentor, I felt closer to her than most.

We had only just taken off in the drone when I turned to her. "What the hell was that about? You'll break her arms if she touches me?"

Raven was looking straight ahead. "We were supposed to do our job, but you lost focus."

"No, I didn't."

"You were literally drooling."

"I was surprised, that's all. She said I looked appetizing."

Raven rolled her eyes.

"What? You can't blame me for wondering if she might have..."

"Might have what?"

"Tell me honestly, do you think she would've slept with me?"

"Of course. Didn't you hear her? She's on a mission to spread her love by feeding the hungry Nmen, and you definitely qualify. Anyone can see that you're love deprived."

"What's that supposed to mean?"

"It would explain why you're always so serious." Raven's voice rose a little, as she crossed her arms and turned to face the other way. "You know what, on second thought, why don't you take Gennie up on her generous offer and bang her brains out? Maybe then I won't have to deal with you being grumpy all the time."

For some reason her little outburst made my day. "Sorry, Raven, but I'm pretty sure your threats ruined my chances with Gennie."

"And now you want me to apologize?"

"Nah, it's fine, she wasn't my type anyway."

In a slow movement Raven turned to look at me. "She wasn't?"

"No." I was waiting for her to ask me what my type was, but Raven chose to swallow her endless curiosity and change the subject to the husband and wife. "What's going to happen to her?"

"I'm not sure. I'll have to discuss this with Magni after we have talked with the couple. If the husband refuses to press charges, there's not much I can do. We've never had a situation like this before."

"Another 'first' in the Northlands."

"Yup, they seem to be standing in line these days.

CHAPTER 7
Treasure Hunting

Raven

Mila enlisted both her dad, Magni, and her uncle, Khan, to go searching with us for Dina's belongings in the basement.

So much for my secret investigation!

I had wanted it to be just Mila and me, but she made a good point that Magni and Khan might be able to recognize Dina's possessions, and that the more sets of eyes, the better our chance of success.

To be honest I was surprised that the two most powerful men in the country took time out of their day to do this with us. It strengthened my feeling that Dina might be gone, but not forgotten. Finding answers to how their sister died was important.

Jonah came with us as well, and when I asked why, Mila gave me no other reason than his being a good friend who enjoyed the sense of adventure.

It was like my murder mystery had been overtaken by the four people walking down the long corridor in front of me. With his long steps, Magni led the way and spoke in his deep voice "Don't be disappointed when we don't find anything. I remember searching this room when I was a kid and there was nothing."

Jonah gave me and Mila a wide smile. "I'm excited. This feels like going treasure hunting."

"Hmm, more like trash hunting." Magni walked another ten steps before he stopped in front of an old wooden door that screeched on its hinges when he pushed it open. "Prepare for half a century of unwanted things."

Once the light flickered on, my eyes took in a room much larger than I had expected. This wasn't some small storage room, this was the size of the upstairs library and then some.

Khan stepped into the room and groaned. "Holy crap, I had no idea we had this much shit down here."

"It's not all rubbish, look at this." Mila stood next to a painting of wild horses on a beach.

Khan didn't look impressed but let his gaze wander over the stacks of boxes, piles of books, picture frames, rolled-up rugs, and furniture of different kinds.

Jonah craned his head to get an overview. "Do you remember anything specific from Dina's room that we can look for? If we can find one thing, we might be lucky in that the rest of her stuff is next to it."

"Good thinking." Magni turned to Khan. "You were thirteen, so maybe you remember her room better than me."

Khan drew his eyebrows close together and ran a hand through his hair. "Yeah, she had an… ehm… bed that was purple, I think. Or maybe it was blue."

We were all looking at him waiting for more details, but he threw up his hands. "I don't know, I can't even remember how my own room looked back then."

Magni was looking around the storage room. "It was a wooden bed, and it had a heart engraved in the headboard. I remember because I would let my fingers run across it when Dina let me sleep in her bed."

"All right." Mila walked into the room. "We'll look for a purple or blue bed with a heart engraved."

Khan pointed to his right. "I'm searching over here. The rest of you spread out."

I went to the back where the clutter was worst. A large shelf stood against the wall full of boxes. Some of them had writing on them indicating that it was Christmas decorations or cutlery.

We searched around for ten minutes and I repeatedly heard Mila make comments like, "Oh, look at this," and "Why would anyone not want to keep this?"

Magni laughed. "What are you doing, Mila honey?"

"I'm making a pile of things that I want to bring to my room."

"Nobody tell Pearl about this room, I don't want my suite filled up with old crap."

"You've got a point, brother." Magni chuckled and called out to me. "Hey, Raven, can you imagine your mom in this place? Christina would be like a kid in a candy store. She loves everything old, doesn't she?"

"She's an archeologist. I'm sure she would love to go through this room to see if there might be something ancient down here."

"Like this one?" Jonah held up a book that was coming apart.

I nodded. "Yes. Old books are precious. None of them should be hidden away in a storage room."

"That's right. Did you hear that, Jonah?" Khan stood with a metal device in his hands but was looking over at Jonah. "Remember what Pearl and I told you about the forbidden books in the Motherlands? You people need to stop treating your people like children. If someone wants to read a scary book or a bunch of steamy novels it should be their choice. You call me a tyrant when you council members are the ones suppressing your people's freedom."

"I know you see it that way, but the council members think of themselves as responsible protectors of their people. That's why it's so hard for them to agree with me on higher speed limits, and why Jenna McFulham called me a danger to society when I suggested making it legal to consume alcohol."

Magni opened a box and roamed through it. "They are a bunch of worried mother hens is what they are. You know, Jonah, it's a wonder how you turned out so sensible despite growing up surrounded by Momsies. But at least when you come and visit us, you can drink some beer and fly as fast as you want to."

"I appreciate that."

Turning back to my searching, I picked out a box that said, Costume Party 2418. It was a bunch of garments and I put it back. A few other boxes had glasses and cups in them and when I took out the fourth box, I spotted a picture frame in the back of the shelf.

I couldn't help laughing when I saw the two boys in the picture. "Mila, come see this. You're going to want to add this to your pile."

"What is it?"

When she got close enough, I handed the picture frame to her. "Recognize these two gangsters?"

Mila's eyes widened, and her hand flew to her mouth. "Oh, Raven, this is precious. Thank you."

"What's precious?" Jonah came over to see while I leaned back and called out to Khan and Magni.

"We found a picture of you men from when you were children."

"Huh. Let me see." Khan came over with Magni following him. "Jonah, give me that picture."

Amusement was written on Jonah's face when he handed the frame over. "I think you look very nice, both of you."

They both groaned. "Why the fuck are we naked?"

Magni shook his head. "How would I know? I can't be more than two in that picture."

59

"Looks like it was taken in the park. Maybe you were going swimming in the lake." Mila reached for the picture. "Can I have it?"

"No!" Magni took it from Khan. "I know you'll just put it in a prominent place in your room and display our dicks to the world."

"It's hardly the whole world if I keep it in my room, is it?" Mila tried taking it. "It's such a sweet picture. I want to show it to Mom."

"No. Why would Laura want to see Khan naked?"

"Come on, Dad, you were just children."

"Where did you find this anyway?" Magni asked me and I told him how it had been hidden behind a box.

"That sounds like the right spot for it." Leaning forward Magni reached in and placed the picture frame as far back as he could, but it only made the picture fall down behind the shelf.

"Look what you did." Mila gave a displeased sound and got down to the floor.

"No, honey, leave it there."

Magni's words were pointless because we all knew how persistent Mila could be, she already had one arm and half her head under the shelf trying to reach for it.

"Jonah, I can't see. Would you shine some light, please?"

I hated that she asked for his help instead of mine, so I got down on my knees and used my wristband. "I've got it."

"Good, I see it." While Mila reached for the frame, my eyes focused in on something much more interesting.

"I think there's a door."

"What do you mean?"

"I see a doorstep and the outline of a door."

Jonah offered Mila a hand to get up and Magni reached out for me, but I was back on my feet in no time, reaching for the first box. "Let's clear the shelf and you'll see for yourself.

Everyone helped and sure enough, there was a hidden door.

"That's weird. Why the fuck would anyone block a door?" Khan muttered.

Mila moved behind Jonah. "I'm scared now. What if there's something awful in there, like a body or something? Some of the people who lived here in the past were not very nice."

"It could be that they were trying to trap something immortal in there," I teased Mila. "Maybe we're about to release some kind of monster into the world."

Jonah played along. "Like a vampire or a werewolf. If that's the case you'd better stay behind me, Mila, because it's gonna be hungry if it was trapped in there for so long."

Magni snorted. "Ha, and what were you going to do about it? It's not like you're a fierce warrior with fight training."

Jonah shrugged. "That's true, but I figure that if it eats me first, Mila has time to run away."

Khan and Magni exchanged a look and shook their heads. "That's some weird-ass altruistic Momsi shit to say."

"Be nice, Dad. I think it was a sweet thing to say."

"How about you all just move back and let me and Khan handle this?" Magni gestured for us to move back, and the two brothers huffed and puffed to move the massive metal shelf that was more than five doors wide and went all the way to the ceiling.

"Let us help." I stepped forward and Jonah and Mila followed. With the combined strength of the five of us, we moved the shelf enough that we could open the door enough to get in.

"I'll go first." Magni drew in a deep breath before he opened the door and used his wristband to shine a light inside the room. We were all silent until he spoke again, "What the…"

"What do you see?" I asked with eagerness, my blood pumping faster and my sense of adventure making me stand on my tiptoes trying to get a peek.

"A coffin with scratch marks."

Mila gasped but then Magni's deep rumble of laughter made us all relax again.

"Hang on, let me find some light."

A few seconds later light came on and I was able to see a bit around Magni's large body. It looked like more of the same. Furniture, boxes, and books.

Magni backed out and turned to Khan. "You take a look and tell me if you see what I see."

The two men changed position in the narrow space and Khan moved just inside the door. "So, the bed wasn't purple. It was crimson."

"You found Dina's bed?" My voice was much too loud, but I was already pumped and the excitement that we'd found some of Dina's things made me want to cheer.

Turned out that the small room was full of Dina's stuff and slowly, as we began pulling them out, Khan and Magni unpacked boxes and picked up small items with their eyes glassy. No doubt they were taken back to memories of their lost sister.

In the end, it was only larger items like her bed, a small desk, a tall dresser, and some rolled-up rugs that were left in the room.

"I love this one." Mila was letting her hands slide over a keepsake box. "Look at how pretty it is. I think little Dina would love to have this in her room."

"Does your sister know that she's named after a relative?"

"We told her, but she's four. I doubt she understands what it means."

Mila opened the box and Jonah, and I both leaned in to see what was in it. A bracelet made of braided leather straps, hairbands, and a few drawings from Magni were among the things Mila picked up.

"Dad, look at this drone you painted when you were five."

Magni lifted his head from the box he was going through. "Hmmm."

"It's cute how you turned the G in Magni the wrong way."

Magni gave a small smile and returned to his box. "I think I might have found something." Lifting a stack of five leather-covered books, he showed them to us. "These are diaries."

"Can I see?"

Magni handed me one and I opened it fast. "This one starts in March 2411 when Dina was eleven."

"What does it say?" Mila came to stand next to me as I read aloud.

"Dear diary, I don't like red roses as much as white roses. Today, we had some vile stew for dinner and if they ever serve it again, I'd rather go hungry and not eat at all."

Khan had picked up a diary as well. "This one is from 2414, so she was fourteen then." Khan was skimming through the pages. "Looks like it's mostly about clothes, Magni, and complaints about our father being a strict disciplinarian."

"Is that the last one?" I nodded at the book in Khan's hands.

He flipped to the last page. "This one ends a few months before the tournament."

"Let's see if she continued in a different book after that."

We searched through the seven books, but the one Khan had was the latest.

I wanted so badly to ask if I could read through them, because going through the diaries of a possibly murdered woman would feel like true police work.

Mila looked over and saw me biting my lip and like the best friend she was, she was quick to say. "Can I add the diaries to my pile? I would love to learn about life at the manor when you were children."

At first Khan hesitated but when Magni shrugged and handed over the stack of books he was holding, Khan flicked through a few more pages and handed his over as well. "I don't have time to read through them right now, so you can have a go at it. Just let us know if you find anything interesting, okay?"

"I will."

"Even if you don't, I'd like a chance to read them when you're done."

"Of course, I'll make sure you and my dad get them as soon as I'm done."

Looking at his wristband Khan frowned. "It's late. We should get back. Mila, pack your pile in a few boxes and we can help you carry it to your room."

"It's okay, I'm sure Jonah and Raven won't mind helping."

"All right." Khan scratched his shoulder. "Magni, one of these days we should have this room cleaned out. It's like a hoarder lived here or something."

"Yeah, one of these days." Magni picked up a few pictures he had found in one of the boxes. It was of him, Khan, and Dina "You think Mom would like this?"

"I don't think so. Mom doesn't like to be reminded."

"Then I'll keep it for me."

Khan patted his younger brother on the shoulder. "You do that."

"And you, Khan? Anything you want to keep?" Magni looked around. "Maybe something that reminds you of Dina."

"I haven't forgotten her in the thirty-three years that she's been dead. I don't need some object to remember her by now."

"I know, but these are her things."

With a sigh, Khan bent down and picked a small statue of a bear. "I'll take this one. It's glued together from the time she threw it at me and it hit the wall."

We heard the two men continue talking as they walked through the large storage room to the exit. "Remember what a temper Dina had? But how could she not, I mean being in our family and all."

"What did you do to make her so mad that she threw things at you?"

"I can't remember. I just know our dad glued the bear back together." Their voices became low as they left the room.

"Hey, Raven." Mila was packing a box and smiling at me. "Let's carry this stuff upstairs. I assume that you want to read through the diaries?"

"Yes, of course. I'm all giddy inside with the prospect of doing some real detective work."

"This was so exciting. We should do it again." Jonah looked around. "I'll bet there's a lot of interesting things down here."

"Yes, and now that we know you're willing to sacrifice yourself if something jumps at us, we'll need to bring you every time."

I picked up the box with Dina's diaries and some of the other questionable things that Mila had stuffed in there and I began walking. "Nothing is going to jump out at us down here, unless you count a rat or a ghost."

"There's no rats."

"But there's ghosts. You told me so yourself, Mila." I laughed. "And ghosts don't eat people, so Jonah isn't going to be very helpful, is he?"

"Ghosts are just residual energy, they're not going to hurt us." Mila sounded like she was trying to convince herself.

Jonah frowned and balanced another box. "Who told you that?"

"Laura did."

"Do people here believe in ghosts?"

"Of course. There's more to the world than we can see."

"I know, but surely ghosts aren't real."

Mila stuck her tongue out a little in concentration when she balanced the box she was holding on her thigh while trying to turn off the light. "Then how do you explain that we found one little picture among the thousands of things in here? Do you think it was a coincidence or could it be Dina's spirit who was leading us to that hidden room?"

"I don't know, Mila, I'm not a superstitious person."

The two of them chatted about it while I put down my box and closed the door. I didn't know if ghosts were real, but I sure hoped that the girl who had once lived in this manor had written some clue in her diary that would lead me to her possible murderer.

CHAPTER 8
Dina's Diaries

Raven

There were seven of Dina's diaries in total. The first began on the evening of her tenth birthday, and the last one ended when she was fourteen, only three months before her death. As I was looking for any sort of clues to who might have killed Dina, it was a no-brainer to begin with the last diary. For the most part, it was small talk about her life at the manor, but on page fifty-three a detail caught my interest.

December 13, 2414
The manor looks so pretty with all the decorations, and I begged Mom to let me add another Christmas tree to the house. She said we already had four, but I argued that the library would look so pretty with a tree. Mostly because I was bored, and decorating trees is so much fun. The best part was that she said that I could ask one of the guards to help me chop it down and bring it inside. I asked old Kevin and he assigned the job to a new guard whom I hadn't seen before.
The guard was young and much better-looking than any of the old guards. We walked side by side to find the right tree and it might have taken me a little longer than necessary, but I swear it wasn't because I was trying to be mean. It was just that I was hoping that maybe he would speak to me. I hate the rule about guards not being allowed to speak unless spoken to because with me being too shy to say anything, it was awkward. If I had been

*braver, I would have asked him his name but the only thing
I said was. "I like that tree." He must think that I don't care
about anyone but myself and that's not true at all.
Maybe I should bake cookies and spread some joy in the
manor tomorrow. If I give him a homemade cookie, maybe
he won't find me so self-absorbed, but I suppose that I
would have to give cookies to all the guards and not just
him. Otherwise it would be weird – like I just made cookies
for him. I wonder how I'll find him since I don't know his
name and I've never seen him before. I can't exactly go up
to old Kevin and ask for the handsome guard with the red
beard and the kind blue eyes, can I?*

I scribbled down notes on my pad and then I
continued reading the next page, where Dina made
cookies and was disappointed that she didn't find the
guard anywhere. It wasn't until five days later that he
appeared in her notes again.

*December 18, 2414
Today was the best day ever.
I found out the name of the new guard. It's Scott.
He and Kevin escorted me and Magni to Mr. and Mrs.
Carlson's house, where we were allowed to use the indoor
pool. Magni kept chatting with the guards and I learned
that Scott has worked at the manor for three weeks now,
but mostly outside. At one point I think he smiled at me,
but I'm not one hundred percent sure because Magni was
standing behind me so he might have been smiling at him
instead. Scott is so handsome and for some reason, I get
really shy around him.
I almost didn't want to go swimming because I didn't want
Scott to see how small my breasts are in my bikini, but
Magni threatened to throw me in the water with my*

clothes on if I didn't go in. I know he's only seven, but he's strong and I know he could do it. That would have been so embarrassing. Now I wonder, though, what would Scott have done if Magni had thrown me in the water? Would he have interfered if I screamed for help? Or would he have laughed and found it amusing?

I wish I could ask if he's planning to fight in my tournament, or just say something to him instead of behaving like a tongue-tied fool when he's near.

I was hoping for more entries about Scott in Dina's diary, but only two days after going to the pool with him Dina ended with a comment saying, "Dear Diary, there are no more pages for me to write on. Time to begin my next diary. Thank you for listening to my thoughts."

Only, I didn't have any more of her diaries.

Putting down the book, I speculated: could Dina's death somehow be a crime of jealousy? What if Scott and she had fallen in love over the next months before her tournament?

I had no other choice than to pick up the diary from before the one I had just read. Unfortunately, it was nothing but thoughts and worries of a thirteen-year-old girl without any clues to my important murder case.

The third book was a disappointment too. With a sigh, I picked up the fourth diary and saw the first entry was made on January 2nd, 2412. Dina had been eleven years old back then, and the chance of her revealing anything about her murderer a little over three years before she died was pretty much nonexistent. Still, after reading through three of her diaries, I was beginning to really like Dina and I was curious to know more about her as a person.

She had humor, a big heart, and dreams that sadly never came true. All her thoughts about hosting large theme parties with her future husband and having guests show up in funny costumes made me smile. Her plan to name her future children Millie, Max, Maddie, and Marvin made me tear up a little bit, because here I was in the future and knew that she never got to experience any of that. If she had still been alive today, Dina would have been forty-eight years old. But because of her early death, she would always remain that young woman who had written about longing for friends her own age. The diaries spoke about her thoughts on being home schooled and lonely, with few girlfriends and very little contact with males that weren't related. It made me reflect on how much better my own life was, and how lucky I was to have close friendships with Mila, Willow, Hunter, and others.

Lying on my bed, I read for hours and it was well past midnight when I got to March 18th, 2412. What I read gave me goosebumps and made me sit up to read it one more time.

I was so excited about my birthday this year, but this day turned out to be a birthday from hell. Dad was in a worse mood than ever. He snapped at Khan and Mom at dinner and said some awful things that made Mom tear up. I could tell Khan was hurt so I tried taking his hand under the table, but he pushed it away and just sat there all stiff and looking down.

Later when I wanted to check up on Mom in her room, I heard them fighting again and even though I know I shouldn't have, I listened through the door.

Dad said something about being tired of people asking why Magni and Khan looked so different. "I'm fucking tired of the question."

Mom answered, "I don't believe anyone would ask you that question, Marcus."

"Maybe not to my face, but people aren't blind, Erika. Khan looks nothing like me and I see the question in people's eyes."

"He's your son. You know he's your son."

"No, I don't know that. Not after what happened."

I couldn't see Mom's face, but I could hear her voice break when she spoke. "Marcus, please! You said that we would never speak of it. You said that no matter what Khan would be your son."

When Dad didn't answer Mom cried hysterically, and I wanted so badly to go in and comfort her and tell Dad that he was wrong. Khan might be darker than me and Magni, but that's just because Mom's side of the family have brown hair and brown eyes. She has told us so many times.

But then my dad hissed, "I know what I said. It doesn't change that he's not my blood, and we both know it. Every time I see the boy's face, I'm reminded of that fucker."

After that I ran back to my own room, and now I'm shaking and I don't know what to do. Should I tell Khan what I heard or not? Nothing will ever be the same now.

I lowered the diary and I realized that I'd been holding my breath while reading. Sucking in air, I stared at the pages of the old book where some of the letters were smeared from what I assumed had been Dina's tears.

Who would have known that in between the pages of trivial thoughts from a twelve-year-old girl lay a bombshell of a secret? Khan wasn't Marcus' biological son.

Of course, I had noticed how different Magni and Khan were in appearance, but like Dina, I had believed that Magni was blond after his father, and that Khan took after his family on his mother's side. Growing up in the Motherlands I was used to siblings looking different because we all had different fathers due to the anonymous sperm donors that were used at the fertility clinics. Maybe

71

that's why I never thought much about the two brothers being opposites. But now that I thought about it, Khan was a few shades darker than his mother and with a white father, that was unusual.

With my pulse hammering away, I couldn't sit still any longer. My mind was like an antique popcorn machine popping questions at a high speed, and it made me get up to remove two paintings from the wall to make room for an overview of my investigation. With a picture of Dina in the middle, I plastered the wall with my suspects and the most pressing questions.

Husband – Henry Hudson.
Did he kill Dina in a fit of rage?

Guard Scott (last name unknown).
Did a relationship evolve between the guard and Dina?
And if so, could jealousy be the motive for her death?

Who is Khan's biological father?

Did Erica cheat on Marcus or was she already
pregnant with Khan when she married Marcus?

Who knows that Khan isn't Marcus' biological son?

Did Dina tell Khan about it? And what about Magni,
does he know?

Did Dina find out who Khan's real father is and is he
still alive today?

Could this secret somehow be related to Dina's early
death?

CHAPTER 9
Leo's Type

Leo

All day Raven was acting weird.

She didn't give me any of her endless shit about working in the basement and she didn't poke me or tease me like she usually did.

For my part, I hadn't been able to stop thinking about her strange reaction to Gennie the other day, and it was distracting me from my work.

First of all, why would she threaten to break Gennie's arms if she touched me? It wasn't like Gennie would be a physical threat to me in any way, and I was none of Raven's concern. She didn't even like me much or was that just what she wanted me to believe?

My head kept going back to the first time I met Raven, which had been about a year ago when I was in charge of the security for an ensemble of artists from the Motherlands who were touring the Northlands.

We had arrived at the Gray Manor after a hectic day of fighting and were met by Mila and Raven in person. The two of them had been like two goddesses but opposites in looks. Mila resembled an angel as she stood smiling at us with her large blue eyes and cute dimples. She was the essence of femininity with her blue summer dress and flowers in her blond braided hair. I imagined it would have taken her a long time to arrange her hair like that, while Raven's black curls were pointing in all directions like she couldn't care less. She was gorgeous, though, and I had to pretend to rub my forehead clear of sweat just so

I could close my eyes and get my heartbeat under control. Raven was wearing clothes, but my imagination had no problem removing the shorts and tank top because she was already showing off plenty of her caramel colored skin.

Get yourself under control.

I had spent the last days with beautiful female artists from the Motherlands, but none of them had made my hands shake like this. If she could read my mind, she would think me a creep because all I could think about was that I wanted to lick her toned legs to see if she tasted as delicious as she looked.

Fucking get a grip! I scolded myself and focused on what was happening in front of me. Solo was talking to Mila's younger brother, Mason, who was ten and bragging about how good a warrior he was.

"My dad says that you're the best warrior he has ever trained and that when I can beat you, I can call myself the greatest warrior of my generation."

"Magni said that?" Solo looked surprised. "How good are you now?"

Mason threw a nod in Raven's direction. "I can take her."

Raven objected, "You took me by surprise, Mason. That was all."

"Have you ever fought a real fighter, though?" My question to Mason made Raven spin in my direction.

"Hey, wait a minute. Are you saying that I'm not a *real* fighter? Who are you anyway?"

Solomon was quick to answer her, "Sorry, Raven, let me introduce my friend, Leo. He's a police officer."

"Police Inspector," I corrected him and squared my shoulders. I wanted all the leverage I could get with this beautiful woman.

"Right. Sorry, I always forget about your promotion."

Raven's face glowed with excitement. "I plan to join the police force too."

She had to be joking, so I gave her a smile. "Women can't be in the police force here. It's too dangerous. Maybe if you go back to the Motherlands…"

Raven's left hand landed on her hip, which she pushed out to the side. "The Motherlands don't have a police force. They have mediators and it's not the same thing. For the record, I'm not going anywhere. This is my home and has been for ten years. Just because there are no women in the police force yet doesn't mean there never will be. Times are changing, or haven't you noticed?"

I didn't believe she was serious for one second. Even her tank top had a joke on the front saying: Support bacteria – they're the only culture some people have. It was unexpected and refreshing to see a woman with a sense of humor so I grinned. "You're a funny one, aren't you?" Shaking my head, I placed my hands in my pockets. "Female police officers, now that would be a sight."

Mason, Mila's younger brother, looked from me to Raven. "She's a good fighter." He bit his lip. "But not as good as me."

A few minutes later, I watched her walk away with a group of people and it gave me a chance to question Solo about her. "Tell me about Raven."

"Ahh, Raven." He grinned. "I know she's stunning, but trust me, that woman is a handful."

"Is she with anyone?"

He chuckled. "My friend, I've watched some of the finest boys and men of this country be burned by her rejections. One of my classmates, Nero, had the biggest crush on her for a long time and she ripped his soul apart with cruel jokes. If Raven has a special talent, it's to make men look stupid."

"Maybe she hasn't met the right man yet."

"Maybe. But personally, I wouldn't waste my time. I'm pretty sure Raven isn't into men at all."

"Is she a lesbian?"

"Or asexual." Solo shrugged. "Either way, if I were you, I'd go for Mila. She's the kindest and most amazing human being you'll ever meet, and she's going to have a tournament."

"But isn't she a Motlander? Why would she have a tournament?"

"She is, but Magni and Laura adopted her. I guess they influenced her to want to marry the traditional Northlander way."

"Is Raven going to have a tournament, you think?"

Solo patted my shoulder. "I can see you're taken with her, but no, Raven isn't that kind of woman. I can't imagine she'll ever want to marry. At best, you might be her toy for a while, but I wouldn't wish that on my worst enemy. I know what loving and losing feels like. It will destroy a man."

Refocusing my thoughts on the present, I tapped my fingers on my desk. Solo had known Raven for ten years and he had been right about her. The times I'd tried talking to her during our stay at the Gray Manor, she'd teased and provoked me. There had been no signs that my attraction to her was mutual. Eventually, I had redirected my hopes upon Mila, who would make any man a fine wife.

Still, the dream popped up when I was alone at night. Raven was always there when I fantasized about making love to a woman. What if I hadn't been reading Raven right?

Looking around to make sure no one was close, I cleared my screen from the case I should be working on and brought up a blank slate to write on.

Clues that Raven doesn't like me.

- *She won't put in a good word with Mila for me.*

- *She says I have no sense of humor.*
- *She's being disrespectful on purpose*
- *She's mad that I don't allow her to come on dangerous missions and she tells me so all the time.*
- *She never flutters her eyes or lifts her shoulders to her cheek as an invitation like the women in the books I've read.*
- *She tried to strangle me with her legs when we fought.*

Clues that Raven likes me.
- *She won't put in a good word with Mila... maybe she wants me for herself?*
- *She acted jealous when Gennie came on to me.*
- *I've never seen her fight anyone the way she fought with me. I don't care what she says, that was fucking porn.*
- *She has joked that she flirts with me, but what if she wasn't joking and she really is flirting with me in her own strange way?*

"Inspector, can I have a minute?"

I had been so engrossed in my own thoughts that I hadn't seen Cameron approach. With a quick swipe of my hand, I brought back the case I'd been working on before I got stuck on whether or not Raven liked me. What the hell had I been thinking anyway?

"What's up?"

"It's Raven, sir."

I lifted my gaze to meet his eyes and leaned back in my chair. "What about her?"

"Something is wrong with her, but I don't know what it is. She didn't come up for lunch, so I went down there to see if she was alright. She tried to tell me she forgot about lunch because she was distracted by her work, but we

77

both know that's a bloody lie. She's always dying to get out of that room."

"Hmm…" I narrowed my eyes. "Did you see her do anything suspicious?"

"No, she was looking over some papers. I assume they were files that she was sorting. But here's the next thing that worries me; I offered to spar with her and she said she wasn't in the mood."

That part got me out of my chair. "Yeah, something is wrong here. Raven would never pass up the chance to have some fight training."

"That's what I thought. I worry about her. What if some ass hurt her or something?" Cameron scratched his beard.

I was already making my way around my table. "Then that ass would die a slow and very painful death."

Cameron groaned in agreement. "Don't tell her I sent you. I don't want Raven to think that I fuss over her or anything."

"Don't worry, I won't. I'll just go down to check up on her."

Three minutes later I walked into the archive and saw Raven sorting files at a desk.

"You changed your system."

She didn't look up. "What do you mean?"

"You used to stand over by the file cabinets, now you're sitting by the desk."

The normal Raven would have given me some kind of sharp reply about me being a fine inspector and very attentive to details, but not today. Raven showed no interest in talking to me and simply shrugged her shoulders.

"Raven, what's going on?"

"Not much." She kept her eyes on the papers, but I wasn't that easy to shake off.

"It's Friday."

"Uh-huh."

"That means no fight training. Is that why you're a little down today?"

"I'm not down."

I moved over and pulled a chair out, turning it around and sitting astride it. "Wanna take another round with me in the gym today?"

Raven shook her head. "I can't."

"Why not?"

"Just can't."

"Ahh, I see…" I gave her a slow nod. "I've read about this sort of thing in books. You have your monthly bloodbath, don't you?"

That got Raven's attention and she crossed her arms. "I have work to do."

It was almost painful to see her be such a pseudo version of herself. There was no playful energy and no provocations. She just wanted me to leave her alone, and it drove me a bit desperate to fix whatever it was I had broken.

"Is it because of what happened between me and Gennie? Is that why you're so down?"

Raven tilted her head. "Did something happen between you and Gennie that I don't know about?"

"No, I was referring to Gennie coming on to me."

"Oh."

"You got upset about it and I've been thinking, Raven."

She kept looking at me, tapping her pen on the table with impatience while waiting for me to go on.

"Are you in love with me?"

Her eyes were blinking a few times. "Yes, Leo, I'm madly in love with you. How did you know?"

"Wait, you are?"

She rolled her eyes. "No, you idiot. Why would you think that?"

"Because you didn't want Gennie to have me. And don't call me an idiot. I'm your boss."

Raven sighed. "I didn't want you to be with Gennie because a man almost lost his genitals because of her. She's just bad news."

"True, but I'm not married. I don't have a jealous wife."

Raven leaned forward. "And what about the other men she fucks? Do you want to be in her bed when one of them shows up thinking she belongs to him?"

"I can take care of myself."

Raven looked at the door and back to me. "Leo, honestly, go be with her if you want to. I don't care."

"I don't want to. Told you that she isn't my type."

"Right." A small smile grew on Raven's lips. "So, what is your type exactly?"

"I would tell you, but you just said you don't care." I got up and moved the chair back.

Raven picked up a stack of files on the table and pushed her chair back. As she walked past me, she brushed my arm and it made an electric current run up and down my spine. Raven was the only woman whom I'd ever been alone with and I was reluctant to leave.

"What are you doing this weekend?"

Placing files on top of different piles, Raven spoke without looking at me. "Mila and I have plans tonight and Saturday I'm taking a shift for Laura at the school."

"What school?"

"The one where I grew up. Laura teaches fight training there and since she and Magni are going to the east coast to visit Laura's sister, I promised that I'd do it for her."

"The kids have school on Saturdays?"

"No. It's an advanced class that's voluntary, but there's always more than ten who show up."

We were standing only a few steps apart when she turned and went for another pile of files.

"If you want, I could help you train the children and we could spar after."

Raven wrinkled her nose. "What is it with you and Cameron? Did you know he asked me to spar with him less than an hour ago?"

"I'm just trying to be helpful."

Raven moved closer and leaned her head back to look up at me. "Is your type of woman someone who can kick your ass? Is that why you're being weird right now? Did it turn you on when I wrapped my legs around your neck and squeezed?"

"Very funny."

"No, it's a serious matter because if you're into that sort of role-playing you probably shouldn't fight for Mila. I doubt she could handle a man who needs to be submissive to get off."

I pushed my chest out and spoke in an offended tone of voice. "You know I'm not submissive."

Tilting her head, Raven gave me a skeptical once-over. "Then why do you keep begging me to spar with you?"

"I'm not begging, I was offering because we both know that you need all the fucking help you can get."

"Is that right?"

We stood head to head, neither of us blinking.

"I wish we were in the gym so I could take you down right now. I'm not submissive, Raven."

"Then what are you?"

Taking a step forward, I spoke in a low gruff voice: "You wanna know what I am? I'm more man than a young girl like you can handle." I knew my mistake the moment I said it.

81

"Hmm, in that case I should warn my friend. I doubt Mila can handle you if I can't. She's a year younger than me, you know."

"That's different."

"Why?"

"Because Mila is sweet and she doesn't rile me up all the time."

Raven had a sly smile on her pretty face when she rose up on her toes and whispered in my ear. "Admit it, Leo, you love it when I rile you up."

I folded my hands into fists, refusing to admit the obvious. I was down here because I had become a fucking addict of her riling me up. There was no one like Raven. The attention she gave me could be negative for all I cared, as long as she wasn't indifferent to me.

"No? Are you too proud to admit it?"

"Be happy that we're not in the gym or I would put you in your place." The rules that allowed us men at the station to touch Raven only covered fight training, where it was necessary.

She didn't back down. Her pupils were dilated and her stare challenging. "What would you do? Huh, Leo? How would you put me in my place?" Knowing that I couldn't touch her, Raven began circling me slowly, while looking up at me. "Would you throw me to the ground and pin my hands, huh? Would you get on top of me and use your larger body to keep me in my so-called place?"

My breathing was picking up as my pulse was racing. "You sure you want to provoke me like that? You know I could do all those things to you."

Raven gave a small shrug. "Oh, I'm sure you will the next time I allow it."

"Allow it?"

"Yes. I have to allow you to touch me."

"I don't want to touch you, I want to fight with you."

82

Reaching her hand up, Raven placed it on my cheek. "You're just like the others. The only reason you want to fight me is so you can touch me."

My fingers closed around her wrist in an iron grip. "Don't touch me."

"Why not?"

"Because I fucking said so."

It was hard enough to control my need to be physical with her when she didn't touch me. The last thing I needed was for her to break that barrier between us.

"You don't like it when I touch you?" Raven didn't try to move her hand away and I didn't let it go.

"If I can't touch you, then you can't touch me either."

"But you *are* touching me." Her eyes lowered to her wrist caught in the air by my hand. "Does that mean I can touch you too?"

I didn't move a muscle when she bored a finger into my shoulder. "Good thing I don't have long nails or this might hurt."

"I'm not afraid of pain, Raven."

She laughed. "It's sweet how you Nmen are always trying to be tough to impress me."

My face hardened. "Who? Who has been trying to impress you?"

"Who hasn't? I'm the only woman here. Did you think no one would make a move?"

The anger I felt in my stomach almost knocked my breath away. "And have any of them made you laugh yet?" I hadn't forgotten how she had told me that she would choose a man who supported her dreams and made her laugh.

Twisting her wrist, she gestured for me to let go. "Leo, people are going to wonder what's taking you so long. They might think we're having an affair."

I let go and stuffed my hands into my pockets to keep me from doing something stupid like pulling her against me. "I'm pretty sure no one will think that. It's kind of obvious that you don't like me like that."

"True." She turned and walked back to the table. "And that you don't like me like that either. I mean, why else would you be fighting for Mila?"

"Why do I get the sense that it bothers you?"

Raven avoided looking at me. "Why would it bother me?"

"Maybe you're jealous?" My heart was speeding from the thought, but Raven crushed my hope with a dismissive snort. Tilting my head, I watched her move some papers around and cover a book and even though I knew I should just go, my instincts flared up. Raven was trying to hide something. When she took some more file cases and carried them to a pile, I moved over and picked up the book. "What's this? I didn't take you for someone to whine about me in a diary."

Her small gasp when she turned to see me with the book in my hand made me raise a brow and look down to see papers and pictures stuffed into it. Opening the book, I saw old pictures and lots of little notes with questions on them. I read the first one aloud, "Did Dina tell Khan about it? And what about Magni, does he know?" I looked over at Raven. "Know what?"

"Nothing. It's nothing. Just give it to me." She tried to take the book and the notes from me, but I moved around and kept it out of her reach while reading the next questions, "Did Dina find out who Khan's real father is and is he still alive today?"

Like a ship crashing against an iceberg, I stopped and gaped at her. "Raven, what the fuck?"

"You can't tell anyone." She tore the book from my hands and it made some of the other notes with questions fall to the floor. In silence, I read, *Did Erica cheat on Marcus and could this secret somehow be related to Dina's early death?*

My heart was hammering as I bent and picked up the notes. "Start talking, right now, Raven."

"Okay, but before I do, you have to promise me that you won't stop me from investigating."

"Investigating what?"

"Dina's death. She was Khan's and Magni's sister who died when she was fifteen, just one week after being married. I found her case last week and I don't believe it was suicide like it stated. Last night I was reading through her old diaries and I came across her telling that she overheard her parents fighting. It turns out that Khan isn't the son of Marcus Aurelius."

My hands flew to my hair. "Who in their right mind leaves explosive information like that in a fucking diary?"

"A twelve-year-old girl."

"Give it to me." I reached out my hand. "How did you even get your hands on it to begin with?"

"No." She pulled her hands away. "It's my research. Mila gave me permission to read her aunt's diary and I had all the notes on the wall in my room, but I was afraid someone might walk in and see it. You can't have it."

My tone grew deeper. "You don't understand what you've stumbled upon. If people find out that Khan isn't the rightful heir to rule the country and that Erika was unfaithful to Marcus it will be the biggest scandal this country has ever seen."

"Why? What does it matter? Khan is already the ruler. It's not going to change anything."

"Fuck yes it will change things. You don't understand the ramifications if this comes out. Khan won't be able to stay the ruler and if he doesn't surrender power freely, there will be a rebellion."

"You can't know that."

I lowered my voice. "No ruler has ever surrendered power freely, Raven. That diary could set off a new civil war."

She narrowed her eyes. "I doubt it. Really? War?"

"Just because there's been peace for decades now doesn't mean it couldn't happen again. We could face a bloodbath and just to be clear: if Khan loses there's a big chance his entire family will be killed. That includes Mila."

She gasped. "You're not serious?"

"As your boss, I'm demanding that you hand over everything you have and forget you ever saw it."

"No."

"Raven, it's not up for debate. I'm confiscating this." I took the research from her and stayed firm when she got mad. There was no way she could comprehend the magnitude of what she had discovered, but I did. The danger was not only that this information might get out to the public, but also that Khan and Magni would discover that Raven knew about it. Would they trust her to keep quiet, or take precautions to silence her? No one could know about this and I would take it to my grave to protect her!

CHAPTER 10
Confronting Erika

Raven

When I came home Friday night after Leo had confiscated my research, I was hell-bent on not letting him stop me.

He might have all my notes, the diary, and the article, but I had access to a key witness, and all day I had been thinking about how to approach Erika.

Mila had gone with the rest of her family to visit Laura's twin sister, but I couldn't wait for her return on Sunday before talking with Erika about what I had learned in Dina's diary.

That's why I joined the older woman after dinner in the library, where she was playing a game of cards by herself while watching a show on the entertainment center.

"Erika, do you mind if I join you?"

She smiled. "Not at all. Would you like a game of cards?" Erika was always very stylish, but today she wore a large knitted sweater that looked more cozy than fashionable.

"Not really. What are you watching?"

She waved a hand through the air. "It's a dating show."

I sat down next to her and looked at the large screen. "What's a dating show?"

"One Motlander bride deciding between five Nmen. They each get a date with her to impress her but so far they're not doing too well. That one with the braided beard was so nervous that he hardly spoke to her at all.

87

He's from Alaska and had never seen a woman in real life. The third one from the left told her a crude joke that made her wrinkle her nose up in disgust a few minutes ago."

I watched as another man was presented to us viewers as the next contender for the Motlander bride, who was a smiling woman in her late twenties called Saphira.

"Zander is a man who loves nature," a narrator spoke while we saw footage of the large Nman running in a forest, climbing trees, and driving a snowmobile. "But he's also excited to learn more about other cultures and having a best friend to laugh with." More footage showed Zander standing outside a restaurant like he was waiting for someone. With a wide grin and clear blue eyes, he looked straight into the camera.

Erika sighed. "Why didn't they mention anything about how well he fights? Who wants a man who cares about other cultures?"

"Motlander women."

Erika narrowed her eyes in suspicion. "Don't tell me you would pick a man who couldn't fight."

"Not a chance."

"Good. I knew we had raised you better than that." Her eyes returned to the screen, where Zander was trying to impress the Motlander bride, Saphira, with his cooking skills.

"What is your favorite piece of art?" she asked him as they sat down for dinner.

"Does porn count?" Zander quickly swallowed his laugh when Saphira didn't even smile.

"What is porn? Is it a painting?"

I was amused when Zander's ears grew red and he offered her some more food with nervous movement. "It's a very graphic art form. You probably wouldn't like it."

"Maybe you could show me."

"Uh-huh, but not tonight. What kind of art do you like?"

"I enjoy music very much and sculptures. Do you like sculptures?"

A loud snort came from Erika. "These women... it's like they turn everything upside down. They want men who can make them laugh and who know about art, and conversation. Why would they come to the Northlands for that? If they want weak men, then they should have stayed home."

"It's not that they want weak men. They just define strength in a different way than people do here."

Erika lowered her brow. "They are trying to tame our men and make them soft. I don't like it. A real man has to be a bit dangerous."

I thought about the times I'd seen Leo fight at the police station and how it had always excited me to see how lethal he was. "I know what you mean." I nodded at the screen. "Still, maybe it's not such a bad thing that the women get a chance to get to know the men and interact with them before choosing a mate. I've read some of my parents' old romance novels and there's something to be said about a man who makes an effort to seduce a woman."

"Hmmm."

"It's like Marcus when he made you the ornaments; that was a romantic gesture too."

"I suppose you have a point there."

Feeling nervous about asking the rude question that was on my mind, I pulled down the sleeves on my blue shirt. "Actually, I have some more questions for you."

Erika's smile stiffened. "If it's about Dina, I can't offer you more than I've already told you." Picking up her pile of cards from the table, she began shuffling them with abrupt movements.

89

Her dismissive signals were as clear as day, but I needed answers to solve my case or I would never prove to the world that I had what it took to be an officer. An unwilling witness shouldn't be enough to stop me. Taking a deep breath, I blurted out, "We found Dina's diaries and I'm not sure you know this, but she overheard you and Marcus fight one night when she turned twelve."

Erika slowed her shuffling.

"Marcus said that he wasn't the biological father of Khan."

All the color faded from Erika's face, and she put down the cards and placed her shaky hands on the table. "Dina must have misunderstood what she heard. Marcus was the father of all our children."

Even though we were alone in the library, I still leaned closer and lowered my voice. "Erika, I know he wasn't. I'm sorry for the question but did you cheat on Marcus?"

"Cheat?" Her hands were now clinging to the side of her chair like she was afraid she might fall down. "How dare you?"

"I'm sorry, Erika. I don't mean to judge you."

"I would never cheat!"

"But then what happened? Were you already pregnant when you married Marcus?"

Erika's hands flew to her chest. "I can't believe they let you into the police school. You can't even do simple math."

I blinked my eyes. "What do you mean?"

"Dina was a year older than Khan, so if I'd been pregnant when I married Marcus it would have been Dina who had a different dad, wouldn't it?"

Feeling stupid, I moved in my seat. "Did she?"

"Nooo!" The way Erika's voice rose spoke of her indignation. "I never cheated on my husband."

"Then what happened?"

"It's not what you think and it's not something I wish to talk about." Her brown eyes were guarded and her lips were forming a thin line.

"Ah, I see."

"I don't know what you think you see, but this conversation is making me very uncomfortable." Erika's tone was blameful.

"It would be logical to conclude that if you didn't cheat, you slept with another man with Marcus's blessing. That's unusual for Nmen, isn't it? Was Marcus unable to satisfy you? Is that why he allowed another man to sleep with you?"

Erika looked like she'd sucked on a lemon. "You're out of your mind. This is the Northlands, Raven, not some twisted sex club in the Motherlands. We don't jump from one bed partner to the other." She was speaking fast and with anger. "To think that Marcus would have ever allowed that man to touch me is to taint his memory, and I won't allow it." Moving forward in her soft chair, Erika spoke with her lips quivering. "Raven."

"Yes."

She stared deep into my eyes. "What I'm about to tell you can never leave this room, do you understand?"

I said nothing, not wanting to explain to her how police work couldn't be limited like that, but Erika took my silence as acceptance and began telling anyway.

"I was fifteen when I married Marcus, and five weeks before I turned sixteen we had Dina. The country celebrated the birth of a baby girl and when she was two months old Lord Wolf came to see her for himself."

"Nikolai Wolf – you mean the ruler who Marcus killed?"

"Yes, but this was years before that and Marcus was still an artist. Lord Wolf was the one who had performed our wedding ceremony the previous year and he

91

congratulated Marcus on his amazing fighting skills. We were honored to have such a fine guest and invited him and the two generals he had brought with him to stay for dinner." Erika wet her lips and fiddled with the large collar of her sweater, her eyes became unfocused as if memories were playing in her mind. "I cooked for them while seeing to Dina, and the men stayed and drank wine and whiskey after dinner. Before they left Lord Wolf asked to see Dina one more time so I brought her in and held her in my arms for him to admire her." She trailed off, her shoulders sagging and her face sad.

"And then what happened?" I asked to get her to continue.

Imitating a man's voice, Erika spoke in a deep tone. "'This baby girl will make a fine bride in fifteen years,' When Wolf said that we smiled with pride. We even laughed when he told Marcus, 'Make sure to get Erika pregnant again right away. We need more girls.'" In a soft movement, Erika shook her head and even though she was looking down, I saw her eyes filling with tears. "I can still remember the smirk on his face before he took another gulp of whiskey and said, 'Maybe I can be of help.' At first, I gasped and jerked back when his hand slid up my back leg to my behind. Nothing like that had ever happened to me and I wasn't sure how to react. Marcus read the fear on my face and got up right away."

My heart sank as I closed my eyes with a bad feeling where this story might go.

"The two generals held Marcus while Wolf pushed me down over the table."

"But what about baby Dina?" I protested.

With her eyes still glazed over from haunting memories, Erika lifted her arms showing how she had held Dina. "I kept her safe in my arms, but I couldn't protect myself from... from... *him*." The moment she said it, the tears flooded, and her breathing became shallow as Erika's face twisted in mental pain. "There was nothing either of us could do. Marcus screamed 'No!' over and over, but Wolf just laughed and raised up my skirts while telling us that he was doing us an honor and that we should be thanking him. I tried to hold in my tears for Dina's sake because my baby wouldn't stop crying. But it hurt so bad, like he was ripping me in two."

I felt awful for having brought back these dark memories to Erika and wanted to tell her that she didn't have to say anymore, but it was like she didn't see me in the room anymore, so consumed was she with reliving her nightmare all those decades ago.

"I'll never forget his deep panting behind me and the sound of his flesh meeting mine. It felt like endless hours of being sawed in two, and the smell of whiskey hanging in the air... I still can't stand the smell of it. I couldn't look at Marcus, couldn't see his pride as a man being torn from him as Wolf kept grunting that Marcus needed to shut up and be grateful." Again she imitated the dictator in a deep distorted voice: "'Can't you see that she's enjoying it?'" Erika's eyes lifted to mine and blinked a few times. "I wasn't."

"No, of course not. I'm so sorry, Erika. I thought Nmen were respectful of other men's wives. How could he do this to you and walk away from it?"

Erika dried her eyes with the backs of her hands. "When Wolf was done, he stayed inside me telling me that he didn't go through all that work to have me press out his semen. He just stood there, holding on to me, drinking more of his beer and talking about how no one tells the ruler no. It was sickening and there was no one to complain to. No justice for what had been done to me. That's why that night as Marcus held me in his arms, he promised me that he would find a way to kill Wolf and make him regret touching me."

"Did he ever come back?"

"Yes." Erika used the sleeves of her sweater to dry her eyes. "He came back five months later while Marcus was at work, telling me that he came to see if his seed had taken root. When he saw my bulging belly he was satisfied and left again."

"But it could have been Marcus's child."

"That was what we were hoping for, but when Khan came out with olive skin and black hair we both knew whose son he was."

"And Magni is definitely Marcus's, right?"

"Yes. But it took many years for us to get back to having sex. That's why there's almost six years between the boys."

"You and Marcus didn't have sex?"

"No, Raven, I was traumatized, and Marcus had lost his self-respect. There's no greater shame for a husband than not being able to protect his woman. I think that's what drove him to obsessively strategize and plan the attack for years, and when it finally happened..." Erika sighed and closed her eyes. "That wonderful night in 2406 when Marcus finally killed Wolf, everything changed and nine months later Magni was born."

For a minute we sat in silence, digesting the horror and triumph of her story.

"Do you think Dina ever told anyone about what she knew?"

Erika shook her head. "No one knows, and it has to stay that way. If the word came out, the peace in this country would break down and there would be chaos. Khan and Magni can't know either."

"But they must suspect it."

Her tone became firm and close to a hiss. "No, they don't suspect anything, so you'll keep your mouth shut, Raven, do you hear me?"

"Yes. I hear you."

"Good." Erika rolled her shoulders back and lifted her chin. "This world isn't as nice a place as some people would have you believe. Maybe my story will make you reconsider the path you've chosen. We women are fragile, after all."

I understood her pain and trauma, but I wouldn't let it stop me from achieving my dreams. "I don't feel fragile and I guarantee you that if anything like that ever happens to me, I don't need to wait six years for a man to avenge me. I would have killed Wolf on the spot or at least castrated him."

"Well, I never learned how to fight and even if I had, it would have been hard with a baby in my arms."

"I'm not blaming you, Erika. It wasn't your fault. I'm just saying that I won't allow it to happen to me or anyone else. That's why it's important that I join the police force. What better way to fight injustice?"

Erika didn't look convinced. "Just promise me that you'll stay safe, Raven. It's a dangerous world out there. And now you'll have to excuse me. I think I need to go and lie down a little."

"Of course." I walked Erika to the door and hugged her, once again telling her how sorry I was for the pain she had suffered.

"You've always been too curious for your own good, Raven." Erika caressed my hair. "But now that you know, I hope you can let it rest in the past where it belongs."

When she was gone, I sat down and made more notes. This investigation was confusing and I felt like I was finding more questions than answers. If only I had all my other research that Leo had confiscated. I wondered if there was a way to convince him to give it back to me.

Would he have hidden the research at work? My gut told me no. There were too many people at the station. It would be more logical for him to bring it home with him, not least because he was probably curious to look it over himself.

The thought made me frustrated. What if Leo decided to solve the murder case and take all my glory?

This was *my* case!

My friend Willow called me up half an hour later when I was in my room coming up with arguments on how to convince Leo to let me have my research back.

"Hey, my bird, what are you doing tonight?"

"Not much. Some work, what about you?"

"I'm alone with the puppies and I finally got Nora to sleep."

"Ah, okay, is Solo on a mission tonight?"

"No, he went out with the guys."

I smiled. "Really? I thought you two were glued together. Have you even been apart after your wedding?"

Willow laughed. "It was an emergency. Zasquash, Leo, and Solo went out for beers. Apparently one of them had a really shitty day."

"Who did?"

"I think it was Leo, but it might have been Zas."

"Wait a minute, did you say that the three of them went out to a bar?"

"Yes. Solo is so sweet. He's been checking in on me every half hour and he just sent me a video of the three of them singing. They are pretty drunk."

"Huh..." Maybe I didn't need strong arguments to convince Leo. Maybe I just needed to know his address and go get what belonged to me while he was distracted.

CHAPTER 11
The Break-In

Raven

Leo lived in an old house about ten minutes outside the city. What surprised me the most when I saw his house was the state of his garden. It was September and from the length of his grass he hadn't cut it since early August. Leo worked a lot, but for someone so focused on details at work, it surprised me to see that he didn't take much pride in the outside of his house.

The good thing about the location of his house was how isolated it was. There wouldn't be any neighbors asking me questions about why I was out on my own without protection. The guards at the manor had offered to escort me when I left tonight, but I'd told them I was flying home to my parents' house and that there was no need.

There was no light coming from Leo's house and his drone wasn't here either. With what Willow had told me less than thirty minutes ago, I felt confident that Leo was still at a bar with Solo and Zasquash. Just to be sure, I knocked on the door and as expected, no one answered.

Taking a step back, I looked around, searching for cameras or signs of alarm systems, but I saw nothing.

Pressing down on the handle of the door, I groaned low when I found it was locked. At least it was a one-story house and not a tall apartment building, and it didn't sound like he had a large dog guarding his house either.

To go around the house, I had to climb a tall fence and as I swung my leg over, my pants got stuck and I lost my balance, sending me to the ground ass first, with the sound of my pants tearing open from the knee to my pocket. Getting up fast, I brushed myself off and looked around to make sure no one saw me looking like a complete amateur.

"All right, get yourself together," I muttered low and tiptoed to the nearest window to look inside. There was no movement, so I tested to see if the window was unlocked. It wasn't.

Still searching for an opening, I continued to every window on the back side of the house and when I got to the fourth window, it slid up as I lifted it. "Yes!"

Leo had taken something precious from me, and from all the great crime movies I'd seen, I knew that sometimes great police officers had to work around the law to find the murderer. I needed that research and he wouldn't even know that I'd been in his house because I would leave everything where I found it and continue my work with only the photos of my research that I would take tonight.

After crawling through the window of his house, I turned on a lamp and looked around in his living room. It wasn't fancy but cozier than I would have expected. I walked over to study a picture on his wall, tilting my head from one side to the other. It was abstract in nature and I couldn't figure out what it was supposed to be.

Who would have thought that Leo was into art?

Reminding myself that I didn't have time to study Leo's décor, I began searching for my research. It wasn't hidden in his couch or in any of the cabinets in his living room, so I continued into his kitchen. The moment I turned the corner I gave a small shriek at the sight of the figure standing still against the wall.

Because of the darkness, I had mistaken the home-bot for a person. I gave a low chuckle in relief that it wasn't Leo waiting to whack me on my head.

"Geez, you scared me for a second," I muttered to the robot, but it was in recharge mode and didn't respond.

My research wasn't in the kitchen either. I crawled up on the counter to get high enough to check every cabinet, but it wasn't there. I checked the fridge too but found only food and beer in there.

The only two rooms left were his bathroom and his bedroom. I hesitated before walking into Leo's bedroom because even in my eagerness to solve this murder mystery it felt like a major violation to snoop around in his bedroom.

Taking a deep breath, I steeled myself and justified what I was about to do by telling myself that Leo had brought this on himself when he took my research.

The door squeaked as I pushed it open. When I turned on the lights, I saw that his bed took up most of the room in here.

Leo hadn't made his bed which shouldn't have surprised me after seeing the length of the grass in his garden. There was nothing special about this room except that my research might be here. Walking around the bed, I lifted the mattress and looked underneath it, but there was nothing. His nightstand on the right side of the bed had books, paper towels, and some cough medicine in it. When I opened the nightstand on the left side of the bed, I pulled out a shirt. It was *my* torn tank top.

I held it up and stared at it. This was the one I'd thrown in the trash can after our fight. Why did Leo take it and bring it home with him? Even before I had finished that thought, I knew why.

He had fantasized about me. It had to be the only explanation, and for some reason it made my whole body tingle with satisfaction. I lifted the tank top to my nose and inhaled the scent of my perfume mixed with my sweat, and then I smiled. From the first time I met Leo, he had annoyed me with all his talk about women not being fit for the work of a police officer. But sometimes when I read steamy books, I would imagine the male characters with a man bun and serious dark eyes.

My hands spread over his bedsheets and I lifted his pillow to inhale the pleasant scent of Leo. A dirty thought entered my mind, but it made me feel like a deranged person, and I wasn't here to get sexual pleasure. So what if we had sexual fantasies about each other? Even if the thought was hot, I wouldn't let the troublemaker inside me act on an embarrassing impulse to pleasure myself in my boss's bed. Quickly, I put the tank top back where I'd found it and continued on to search his built-in closet. On the top shelf behind a pile of his clothes, I found my research.

"I'm so badass," I muttered feeling proud of myself for not letting anyone stop me. After spreading it out on his bed, I photographed everything. It would have been much quicker if I could have just taken it with me.

When I was balancing on my toes to put the research back in place, a flash of light lit up the bedroom from the outside. A drone. Shit, that meant Leo was coming home. Would he notice my drone? I hadn't parked it right outside but on the back side of the house. If I was lucky, he would be too drunk to notice.

Closing the closet doors, I moved to my only escape route – the window – but the damn thing wouldn't open. I had entered through the window in the living room and needed to get back there, but when I got to the bedroom door, I heard a voice shouting, "Hellooo."

Shit, shit, shit.

It was Leo. I couldn't let him find me in his bedroom. In a state of panic, I searched for a place to hide and fell to my knees thinking I could squeeze under his bed.

"Raven, are you here?

100

I froze. How did Leo know I was here? I hadn't told anyone. Had he found my drone?

"Raven, I know you're here." Heavy footsteps were coming this way and at the first sound of the bedroom door creaking, I moved up to sit on the bed, pushed my shirt over my shoulder, and faced the door with a fake smile plastered on my face.

Leo stopped in the doorway and frowned, his balance a little off as he swayed.

"Hey, Leo."

"Raven. My security system sent me an alert and I saw a picture of you walking around in my living room. Thought that was a bit strange." I could tell from his speech that he was drunk but it wasn't too slurred.

"I didn't know you had a security system."

Tapping his temple, he nodded. "We policemen can never be too careful. We deal with some pretty bad scum on occasion." Taking another step into the bedroom, Leo sunk down on the bed on the opposite side. "Why did you come here?"

"Because I wanted to see you."

His eyes darted around the room as if checking whether something was missing. "I saw your drone outside."

"It's not my drone, it's one of my father's. He just lets me use it."

Leo's eyes fell to my bare shoulder before he rubbed his face. "I thought you were mad at me after today, but you don't look mad."

"Why would I be mad?" My smile was meant to cover up how nervous I was.

"Because I confiscated your research."

"I get why you did it and I kind of like that you're so strong and protective."

I expected Leo to call me out on my bluff, but he was intoxicated and broke into a boyish smile that almost sucked the air out of me.

"You do?" At that moment he was beautiful and radiant as he sat close enough for me to reach out and touch. The thought made me pull my hands back in my lap.

"Uh-huh." I couldn't help smiling back at him. "You should smile more often, Leo."

"I used to, but then Commander Magni gave me the toughest position in the country and I've been fucking tense ever since."

I tilted my head. "If you don't like being an inspector, then why do it?"

He pulled off his jacket and threw it on the floor. "I don't mind being an inspector. But being the protector of a gorgeous young woman who insists on coming to work and putting herself in danger every day is bloody exhausting."

My palm flew to my chest. "Are you talking about me?"

"Yes!"

"You think I'm gorgeous?"

Leo lowered his brow. "That's not the point. The point is that you shouldn't…" He trailed off and just watched me.

"I shouldn't what?"

"Why do you show up to fight training wearing tight clothes that show off your beautiful curves? Or those shorts you wear to show us all your long golden-brown legs." He used his hand to signal how short my shorts had been.

"They weren't that short."

"Fuck yeah they were. You can't wear hot pants or tight outfits like that. You have no idea how it affects all us men." He hiccupped. "I mean the other men."

"But not you?"

"Na-huh. Not me."

Tilting my head to the other side, I smiled at him. "Liar."

"Okay. Maybe it affects me a little bit." Squinting his eyes, Leo underlined his admission by showing a bit of distance between his thumb and index finger while smiling again.

The same feeling of satisfaction that I'd felt when I found my shirt in his nightstand now warmed me from the inside out. Curiosity about how it would feel to let him touch me convinced me that it was time to get out of his bedroom. Getting up, I walked to the door. "You're probably tired. I should go."

"Hey, what happened to your pants?"

Looking down at my torn pants, I felt my face turn hot. "Ehm, they tore."

"When?"

I rubbed my nose and thought about some clever answer, but Leo's closeness and the curiosity that always got me in trouble whispered about this moment's being a great opportunity to try out some of the things I had only fantasized about.

"What happened, Raven?" Leo leaned closer. "Are you bleeding?"

"It's nothing. I just tore my pants when I climbed your fence. I got a scratch, but I'll survive."

Leo's mouth opened as if he wanted to say something, but then he shook his head and reached out his hand toward the tear in my pants. "Do you want me to clean your wound?"

From the back of my mind, the not-to-be-trusted Raven pushed forward and spoke on my behalf. "Would you?"

But internally my head was a war zone between the sensible part of me and my troublemaker.

No, you should be leaving now. You got what you came for, and Leo touching you isn't part of the plan. Just get out!

But the troublemaker inside me tempted, *Come on, wouldn't it be fun to play a little? Leo would never hurt a woman and you always found him attractive. Don't pretend you haven't been curious about men for years, and how often does a chance like this come along? Have a little fun?*

No, don't do it!

Ah, come on, you know how you can't resist the chance to try new things for the first time.

Raven, be sensible. You are going to get yourself into trouble – you always do.

"You sure that you want me to clean your wound?"

Leo's question brought me back from the war zone in my head.

"No," I said while at the same time taking a step closer and almost standing between his legs. "I mean, yes."

Leo who was still sitting on the bed leaned his head back and met my eyes. His hands hovering on the side of my thighs without touching. "Which is it? Yes or no?"

"Yes, I would like you to clean my wound."

This time his Adam's apple bobbed as he swallowed hard again. "Alright, but if I touch you..."

Already knowing what he was going to say, I cut him off. "Don't worry, Leo. I won't tell Magni or my dad."

"I'm only going to clean your wound."

"Yes."

In a slow movement, he nodded his head before taking a deep breath and touching my leg. I stood completely still, suppressing the warnings in my head and enjoying the thrill of seeing Leo separate the torn edges of the textile and assess the scratch on my inner thigh. "You're still bleeding a little."

"Am I?"

"Yes." He pushed me back a little to create space for him to get up from the bed and move to his bathroom. "Why were you climbing my fence anyway?"

"Because you didn't answer the door and I thought you might have gone to bed."

A moment later, Leo stood in the doorway with a first-aid kit in his hand. "And what was so urgent that you couldn't tell me tomorrow?"

"Oh, like I just said, you know…" I bit my lip. "Just that I wasn't mad at you…" I avoided his eyes and flushed red, hoping he would buy my obvious lie.

Walking back to the bed, Leo kept his eyes on me. "Try again. You don't break into a man's house without a good reason. Did you snoop through my drawers?" His eyes fell briefly on the nightstand where my tank top was hidden.

"No, of course not."

"Hmm, admit it, Raven, you were looking for your research?"

"Why would I come here for that? You have it at the station, don't you?" I gave him a sincere look.

Leo pointed to the bed. "Sit down and let me look at your leg."

I watched him kneel down in front of me and use both his hands to tear my pants open even more.

"Ehm, Raven, I hate to ask you this, but would you mind spreading your legs a little for me?" Leo gave me another charming smile and again my insides did a somersault. A strong urge to reach out and touch him spread like wildfire inside me.

Don't do it, my sensible voice warned and made me lean back on my elbows to create distance and keep myself from touching him.

"Like this?" I spread my legs and held my breath a little when he nodded.

105

"I'm just going to lift your leg so I can see it better with the light." With a hand under my knee, Leo raised my thigh up and began cleaning the wound with his other hand.

"I can hold my leg up so you can use both hands."

"Thank you, it's a bit difficult with the fabric getting in the way."

"Do you want me to take off my pants?"

His eyes widened, but then he regained his composure and cleared his throat. "Ehm, sure... maybe that would make it easier to see the wound."

It spoke to my sense of adventure that I'd never been in a situation like this, and from the way Leo touched me with gentle hands, I felt in control. With a small smile, I looked into his brown eyes and raised my hips up from the bed. "Pull."

He hesitated only for a second before he hooked his fingers into the waistline of my soft pants and peeled them off me.

"How did that feel?" I giggled a little. "It's the first time you've undressed a woman, isn't it?"

Leo's ears and neck were red, and he dried his forehead like he was sweating.

"You look hot, Leo. Why don't you lose that thick sweater? This might take a while."

"Yeah, it feels like a fucking sauna in here."

I laughed, feeling giddy because of the strong reaction I was getting from him. "You're just flustered because you've never had a woman in your bed before, aren't you?"

He laughed back. "I'm gonna wake up soon and discover it was just a dream."

"Oh, so you think you're dreaming this?"

"I must be." His hands returned to my thigh and he pushed my leg to the side a little. "It makes complete sense that I would create a scenario like this in my head, with you being vulnerable and needing my help. Soon, I'll wake up in a bar realizing that I passed out from drinking or some shit."

"Yeah, I think you're right. But if this is all just a creation of your imagination, then I have to wonder why I'm the only one in your bed. Why not two women – or four for that matter?"

"Jeezis, Raven."

I giggled again. "Oh, come on. I know you are kind of boring, but I took you for a man with confidence. You don't think you could handle more than one woman?"

"Not if they are your kind. You count for four women at least, what with your ability to break my neck if I don't satisfy you."

A deep roar of laughter erupted from me.

Leo was laughing too. "It's not funny. We both know that you would taunt me for a lifetime if I disappointed you in bed, and you'd probably tell everyone at the station too."

My white panties stood in contrast to my caramel-colored skin, and I looked down to see my hand on my belly, which was bumping up and down with laughter. "You can't blame me for what happens in your dream, though. If you don't satisfy me it would be because you doubt yourself, and some psychologist would get a trip out of that for sure."

Cleaning the wound took much longer than necessary but when Leo pulled back and told me he was done, I wasn't ready for this playful interaction to end.

"I think you did okay, Leo, but honestly, your care-giving needs that little extra touch."

"What touch? I cleaned it and covered the wound. There's nothing more I can do."

"Kya always had a secret weapon when I was young." I let my finger trail from my belly button over my panties and down my thigh to the wound. "She would kiss it to make it feel better."

Leo's breathing got heavier and his tone deeper. "Hmm, and would you like me to kiss you?"

I nodded and tapped my finger on my thigh. "Right here."

Leo's hands slid up my shins to my knees as he leaned forward and kissed my right thigh. It felt so intimate and the way he squeezed my knees made my body buzz with excitement. Pulling back, he watched me with hunger. "Anywhere else you need me to kiss you?"

"When I climbed your fence, I might have stretched a muscle."

"Oh yeah? Where?"

I bit my lower lip and used my index finger to point to a place higher up on my inner thigh.

His Adam's apple bobbed in his throat again as he moved forward again and kissed my inner thigh. I heard him inhale deeply close to my core, like he was taking in the scent of woman, and then his tongue touched my sensitive skin near the edge of my panties. It tickled and made me tense up and gasp out loud.

Leo stiffened like he had done something wrong, so I weaved my hands into his hair to signal I was okay.

Emboldened by my touching him, Leo's hands moved up my thighs again and he pressed his face against my panties with a low growl that vibrated against my clit. "You have no idea how much I want to rip these off."

"Then why don't you? This is your dream, Leo."

Lifting his head, he locked eyes with me. "Don't fuck with me, Raven."

My voice was bubbly from amusement. "You sure about that?"

Leo was studying me like he was trying to read me. "You know what I mean."

"Yes, you just said it loud and clear." I sat up and reached for the pants that he'd tossed on the bed. "You don't want me to fuck with you, so I guess I'd better go now."

Leo's fingers bored into my hips. "No one in this world drives me as insane as you do."

"We all have a gift, I guess, but since this is your dream, I find it bizarre that you would refuse to have sex with me. Makes me wonder if you're not into women after all."

Leo, who had been kneeling on the floor, moved fast and with two hands under my armpits he moved me further back on the bed and crawled on top of me. "If this is my dream then I'm taking you tonight."

"Taking me where?" My eyes were sparkling with humor, but I didn't get a chance to say anything more before he silenced me with a long kiss.

It was like being knocked out in a fight. Suddenly, the conflicting voices in my head went quiet. My mind was always popping with ideas and questions but not while Leo kissed me. It was like the touch of his lips against my lips sucked out every thought process from my brain and left a vacuum of blissful quiet inside me.

I'd never kissed anyone like this, and for someone who had longed to be accepted ever since my mom neglected me as a child, I couldn't get enough. Leo wanted me. His strong hands on my body, his heavy breathing, and his demanding kisses made me feel almost desperate for more. "Say that you want me."

"Oh, you have no fucking idea how bad I want you."

My hands were in his hair, and I wrapped my legs around him, holding him close. "I want you too."

"You sure?"

"Yes." It was the most urgent thirst that I'd ever felt and nothing about this was funny to me any longer. My playful messing around out of curiosity had been replaced with an all-consuming need to have Leo. I was tearing at his clothes and biting his shoulder and neck to satisfy this new and strange hunger that burned inside me.

"Fuck, I knew you'd be a wildcat. Slow down, babe."

But I couldn't slow down and with a sense of desperation I pushed his pants down and moaned in his ear. "Show me how much you want me."

Leo broke out of the hold I had on him and pushed my legs off him as he pulled back on his haunches to rip my panties apart. "You think you can handle it if I show you?"

"Yes."

With a firm grip on my hips, he lowered his head between my legs and used his elbows to keep my thighs apart. "Careful what you wish for. I've got more than fifteen years' pent-up sexual appetite to take out on you." His words were followed by a playful smile.

"You talk too much; how about you show me instead?"

Leo's charming grin made my insides melt and I felt a tingling sensation in my stomach when he nibbled on my inner thigh and licked all the way up to the most sensitive part of my body. In fascination, I watched as Leo devoured me with a ferocious appetite. "Oh... that's... wow..." It was impossible to keep my body still with the amazing sensations of his tongue licking me. There were no male sex-bots in the Northlands and because I'd lived here since I was eleven, my contact with sex toys had been limited.

The sounds of Leo sucking on my clit and the sight of how wet his face was when he looked up at me made me cover my eyes. This was my boss, and I would never be able to look at him again without knowing what extreme pleasure he could give me.

"Look at me, Raven."

I moved my hand and smiled back at him and didn't protest when he lowered his head and suckled on my clit again. "It's so good, Leo... so amazing."

110

He kept at it and when I almost couldn't take anymore and began arching my back, he kept me in place and pushed me all the way to a screaming orgasm with his fingers and tongue.

"Yes... Yes... Yes... Leo..." I moaned and panted, unable to control my breathing or my need to scream out my joy at this amazing gift he was giving me.

While blissful happiness had me on a cloud, Leo moved his kisses up across my belly button, to my breasts, where he let his tongue play with my nipples. "You have the most gorgeous tits," he muttered low and positioned himself with his knees on either side of my waist. I opened my eyes to see him push my breasts together and slide his erection between them.

"You like that?" I asked him and lifted my hand to his ripped six-pack. "You like playing with my body?"

Leo's pupils were dilated, making his eyes appear almost black. He licked his lips and gave me a hoarse "Fuck yes."

My hands were roaming over his strong chest, shoulders, and biceps while he kept pressing my breasts together and playing with my nipples. "What do you want, Raven?"

I wasn't sure what to answer. This was all new and exciting to me and being twenty-two, I had fantasized about sex since I first got my hands on a romance novel at the age of thirteen.

"What do you want?" he repeated but when I still didn't answer, he took over.

"Open your mouth." He moved higher on my body, his knees now on each side of my shoulders as he lowered himself against my lips. With the way he had licked me, I had no reservations in giving back.

"That's right. Open up wide. Ahh, yes, your mouth is so warm." Leo began pushing his hips back and forth but

111

with his size he reached my throat and pushed against my uvula, making me gag a few times.

He stopped and caressed my face. "Relax and breathe through your nose."

Giving a small nod, I used my nostrils to inhale and exhale and ignored that my eyes were watering. Leo had his eyes fixed on my mouth, making sounds of deep pleasure. The raw desire in his eyes filled a void inside me.

"Relax, beautiful. Just take me in your mouth and use that delicious tongue of yours for what it was meant."

I stiffened.

"I fucking fantasized about shutting you up like this from the day I met you."

"What did you just say? With some force, I pushed him off me and sputtered. "I can't believe I let you touch me when you're nothing but a douchebag misogynist."

"What are you talking about?" Leo was on his knees on the bed with his hands spread out in a gesture of "what-the-fuck?"

"You think all we women are good for is shoving your dick down our throats, is that it?"

He scrunched up his face. "What? No! Of course not. Why would you think that?"

"You just said that my tongue was meant to be used for sucking you off and that you've wanted to shut me up from the first time you met me."

"Devils and demons, will you calm down, woman? It should be bloody obvious by now that you turn me on. Of course, I've had erotic fantasies about you, and yeah, I might have had a few when you were riling me up at the station."

"I'm not some puppet you can shut up. I'm opinionated and stubborn and if you can't deal with that, go find yourself a brainless sex-bot."

Reaching for my clothes, I stormed out the door and ran to my drone. I didn't care that I was naked with only a bundle of shoes and clothes in my arms. Leo called after me, telling me to wait a minute, but being angry and hurt I needed to get away and collect myself. Just the idea of having to go back to the station on Monday and see Leo made it hard to breathe. What we had shared for those precious moments had been like finding Nirvana, until he opened his mouth and ruined it all.

CHAPTER 12
Fishing

Leo

After Raven ran from my house, I was left wondering what the hell happened. Not only did I have a nasty hangover on Saturday from all the beers and shots that I gulped down on Friday night with Zasquash and Solo; I was also worried that Raven might be so upset that she would tell on me.

Everything that had happened between us had been consensual but who would believe me if she said otherwise?

I shut myself inside my house all Saturday thinking the incident through. It was so surreal that I almost wanted to believe it truly had been a dream. But the sock that Raven had forgotten was a reminder that despite how insane it sounded in my own head, Raven had truly been here, and we had made out.

Why had it made her so mad when I told her I'd fantasized about having oral sex with her? I knew she had enjoyed receiving oral sex from me, so what was her problem? Her rant about me being a misogynist had made me confused because I didn't know the word. But I looked it up and read the definition as dislike, contempt, or prejudice against women, which had me snorting out loud. What a pile of elk-shit. I fucking loved women and maybe we Nmen got a bit overprotective, but that had nothing to do with contempt or prejudice. Did it?

On Sunday, Solo asked me to come and hang at his and Willow's place. It was a welcome change from staying home and torturing my brain, so of course I went.

What I didn't think through was that being at their place was a different kind of torture. My eyeballs were hurting from seeing all the loving gazes between Solo and his woman, and now that I'd had a taste of what it meant to kiss and touch a real woman, my longing for a connection had exploded.

I was happy when Solo asked if I wanted to go fishing by the river, as it would just be the two of us.

"Why are you so quiet today? Is something wrong?"

I kept my gaze on the water. "Nah, I'm just working on a case that has me questioning everything."

"What case?"

"Last week we got called out to a domestic violence case that blew my mind."

"Why didn't we hear about it?" Solo turned to me.

"We don't always call in you Doomsmen. Some cases we handle ourselves."

"Tell me about this case."

"A married man had an affair and his wife got so mad that she tried to cut off his cock."

"Uhh... fuck." Solo looked pained and pressed his thighs together.

"You might know the woman he cheated with; her name is Gennie and she was married to your friend, Storm."

"Yes, I've heard of her."

I allowed Solo to digest the disturbing scenario before I continued. "Anyway, what has my mind reeling is the reaction from Gennie. When Raven and I confronted her about it, she showed no sign of guilt or regret. To her it was just sex."

"Hmm. From what I've heard, Gennie is crazy."

"I don't think so. I think she just lives by different rules than us. She is a Motlander and sex is purely a physical need for her. She's not looking to bond with anyone but wants to taste as many men as possible. Her words, not mine."

"But that makes no sense."

"Doesn't it?" I raised a brow. "Think about it, Solo. If the situation was reversed and there were ten million women and a few hundred men, would we be less inclined to settle down with just one or would we want to taste as many as possible? Gennie sees it as spreading her love."

"That's because she doesn't know what true love feels like. Once she finds the man she loves, there's no way she would share him with other women. Urghh..." Solo shook his body. "Just thinking about sharing Willow gives me the creeps."

"Yeah, but you're an Nman. We're wired to want a wife. But now we're dealing with Motlanders, who come with completely different conditioning. They think marriage is archaic and limiting in nature."

"Maybe it is. But plenty of them have married anyway."

I leaned forward, thinking hard. "Fine. But what if Gennie's affair with a married man is just the first sign of a new day? There are divorces now, and what then? Before the integration a woman's destiny was to marry. First in a tournament; and later if he died, she would pick a partner in a widow win or move in with one of her children. The only case of divorce with a Northlander woman that I can remember was that idiot husband who had a drinking problem and threw a bottle at his woman; remember her?"

"Yeah, she married Kilroy after that."

"Exactly. We have no procedures in play when it comes to someone like Gennie. Do we let her play all these

116

Nmen and wait for them to kill each other? Or do we Nmen adapt and take what's offered to us from women like her without expecting marriage?"

Solo shifted his fishing rod from one hand to the other. "You think there will be more of her kind?"

"Undoubtedly. So, let me give you a thought experiment and you'll tell me what you would do, okay?"

"Sure."

"Women are now beginning to work. For instance, I have a buddy who works as a mentor and he's got female colleagues from the Motherlands. One of them is single."

"She's single? As in divorced?"

"Ehm, no, she grew up here."

"Ahh, I see, so her mother married and brought her along."

"Sort of, but the point is that one night he came home to find her in his apartment. He knows that he probably shouldn't have touched her, but she was inviting him, and they ended up in his bed."

"Your friend had sex with a single woman?" Solo's eyes were wide open. "Who is that guy?"

"I'm not giving you his name, and in principle, he didn't do anything wrong. The woman gave him permission to touch her."

"Okay…" Solo shook his head. "That's just a pretty insane thing to happen to a man. Willow kinda did the same thing to me in a bathroom once, and I was convinced you guys would break down the door and kill me for touching her."

"Well, my friend is pretty scared too. Especially because the woman left in anger."

"Shit. That's bad, Leo."

"I know."

"What happened?"

"Well, I don't know all the details but from what he said she was giving him oral sex when he made a comment that upset her."

"What comment?"

"Something about her using her tongue for what it was meant for and him having fantasized about shutting her up like that ever since he first met her."

"And she got mad about it?"

"Furious!"

Solomon lowered his brow. "Women can be sensitive, and maybe this one had no sense of humor."

"Maybe."

Solo looked like he was thinking hard. "Did she say why she got upset?"

"Yes. She took it as if he didn't respect her. You know, as if sex was the only thing women are good for."

Solomon snorted. "Didn't respect her – ha. See, that's where Motlanders get it all wrong. We Nmen respect women a ton, but why shouldn't a man be allowed to play out a few dirty fantasies in bed? If he had said it outside the bedroom it would have been a different story, but in bed, he should be allowed to play around a little."

I made a sound of agreement as Solomon kept talking.

"It's like when Willow and I have sex. She likes it when I place a hand on her throat and squeeze a little, but if I tried anything like it outside the bedroom, she would kick my nuts."

I raised an eyebrow. "She likes it when you strangle her?"

"Just a little. It's a sign of trust, and I fucking love that it turns her on that I'm in control."

"I never took Willow for a submissive woman."

Solo smiled. "That's because outside of the bedroom she's not. My woman controls most things in our lives, and then I bring balance by dominating her in bed. It works!"

118

"Huh." I gave a slow nod. "So maybe it's not what my friend said but rather that the woman didn't feel respected outside of bed."

"Could be, but don't worry; I have a trick that works like magic on women. Give her a foot rub or scalp massage; it makes even hysterical women calm and easy to get along with."

"I doubt he'll be allowed to touch her again."

"Good point. So, what is your friend going to do?"

I shrugged. "Try to talk to her, I assume, but the whole thing has me reflecting on our role in the future. We both know that we're the ones who'll face the angry Nmen who got screwed over. Do we kill a guy who lost his temper when he found out his woman is seeing several men? Do we restrict the women from having multiple men at the same time? Just because monogamy makes sense to us doesn't mean everyone shares our opinion. Historically, other cultures didn't believe in it and it was normal to have lovers outside the marriage."

Solo groaned. "That's just sick."

"For us, yes. But if one of those people were here maybe they would think we're the ones who have it all wrong." I plucked at the grass. "Think about it, Solo."

"Think about what? To me it's black and white. It's the Motlanders who are making it complicated when it's really not."

"What if you and Willow decided that you love each other so much that you will only work out together. From now on you can never work out with me and Zas or your other pals. You can only work out with Willow."

"No way. She keeps herself in shape by dancing and doing yoga shit. I need my hard-core sweaty workouts."

"Then it would be a compromise for each of you. Maybe you could do yoga or dancing from time to time and maybe she'll be sweaty with you in return, but mostly

119

you'll probably have to find something in between that is tolerable to both of you."

"What kind of shitty deal is that?" Solo wrinkled up his nose. "Willow and I could never be partners. I work out every day, she used to do it three or four times a week, but now with the baby, it's even less."

"There's that." I nodded. "But that's how others see monogamy."

"It's not the same thing. Working out is a physical need whereas being married is a deep connection that you share with someone."

"You do realize that working out was a reference to sex, right? Sex is a physical need too."

"Oh..." Solo frowned. "Now I get it."

"Monogamy isn't the only way to live, and from a rational standpoint it makes little sense. Gennie compared it to eating at the same restaurant every night even when sometimes there's nothing on the menu. Motlanders think we're crazy when the street is full of other restaurants with new and delicious food you haven't tasted before."

Solomon shifted in his seat and looked back at his house. "Willow'd better not go searching for other restaurants."

"Then you'd better make sure your menu is always full of the classics and spice it up with a few new things as well."

"What the hell, Leo, how did this conversation get this deep? Did you read some article or something? I feel like I'm talking to Jonah."

I chuckled. "You mean the councilman?"

"Yeah, he was giving me and Hunter shit about us Nmen not being emotionally aware." Solo laughed. "I wish he could see us now, talking about workouts and monogamy when we should be fishing in silence."

Picking up my beer from the grass, I raised it to Solo, who picked up his own beer. "Cheers, my friend."

"Cheers. And be fucking happy that you're not your friend who has to go apologize."

"Huh?"

"You know, the one who had a woman leave in anger. Sounds like he might have to apologize, and I've been there. Apologies are so unnatural and forcing them out is like cutting your tongue with a dull razor blade. Sometimes, all you get in return is more shit. You should warn your friend that just because he apologizes doesn't mean that she'll forgive him. Willow was so fucking brainwashed that she thought she hated me."

I looked back at the house. "Clearly, she got over that."

"Yes. I'm happy I didn't give up." Solo took another sip of his beer. "There will never be another woman for me but Willow. I've loved her from the first time I saw her, and you know what..."

"What?"

"I'll do yoga with her if that's what it takes to stay her gym partner forever."

I raised my beer again. "Cheers to that."

Solo nodded. "Yeah, and cheers to your friend. Good thing that we're not in his shoes."

My smile was a bit stiff as I returned to fishing while looking down at the shoes that would have to carry me to work on Monday, hoping that Raven would talk to me about what happened between us.

CHAPTER 13
Scam

Raven

I called in sick on Monday. It wasn't like anyone would miss me since I was only moving unimportant files around. The thought of seeing Leo again made me miserable. He had been my first kiss, and what happened between us had been like opening a door and peeking through to paradise only to learn that it was a mirage.

At least I had left his house with pictures of all my research. To distract myself I focused on laying out the details I had gathered from Dina's diaries, the article with pictures, Dina's husband's name and address, and the notes from Erika's revealing story about how she had been raped by Lord Wolf.

I kept going back to the picture from Dina's wedding with the two unknown men that Erika had mentioned were friends of the groom. My instinct told me I needed to find them and using face recognition, I was able to track down one of them and call him up.

Michael told me he had been Henry's roommate and that he still lived in the same building where Dina had died. The very idea of seeing the place had me excited. What if I could find a clue that everyone else had missed?

My dilemma was that meeting up with a stranger alone was reckless, and I couldn't ask Leo to come since he had ordered me to stop investigating. I thought about asking my father to go with me, but my need to prove that I was capable made me resent asking a man for help. I was a great fighter and could protect myself. If only I knew if Michael would be unarmed and alone.

Still considering my options, I went down to the kitchen to make myself a sandwich, and that's when Laura walked by the glass door and the solution presented itself.

Opening the door, I called out to her. "Laura, wait up, where are you going?"

"Running. You wanna come?" Laura was married to Magni and she had been a huge inspiration for me growing up.

"I need your help."

"With what?"

Holding the door open for her, I gestured for her to come into the kitchen.

"Can I trust you to keep a secret?"

"Of course."

"I'm investigating the murder of Khan's and Magni's sister, Dina."

"Yes, they told me about your trip to the storage room. Mila tried to tell Magni that she was the one interested in knowing more about Dina, but we're not stupid. With you joining the police it's not hard to figure out that you want to solve the case. I'm just not sure giving Magni hope is a good thing."

"I would like to give him more than hope. I would like to give him answers and closure. I can't even imagine the pain of losing a sister."

Laura frowned. "Yeah, neither can I. Although my sister and I aren't very close anymore, losing her would be awful."

"How can you not be close? Aren't twins supposed to be mentally linked or something."

"We're not identical. I don't see why we would be any more mentally linked than other siblings. To be honest, we don't get along well. Michelle is very traditional, and she

123

never understood my need to learn how to fight or the way I stand up to Magni. She feels women should serve their husbands."

"How can you two have been raised the same?"

"My theory is that we've been influenced by our friends. I have Christina, Kya, Athena, and Pearl, who opened my eyes to other ways of living, while Michelle mostly spends time with her best friend Annelise, who is just as traditional as my sister." Laura's face scrunched up when she mentioned Annelise.

"You don't like her, do you?"

"Annelise?"

"Yes."

"No, but I feel sorry for her. Her grandfather was the richest man in the country until Magni and Khan took him down for treason more than ten years ago. Her whole family lost their social status and influence overnight because of what Mr. Zobel did."

"I remember that name. He was in Dina's wedding picture."

"Sounds about right. Mr. Zobel and Lord Marcus were best friends, and you might not know this, but Erika was planning to marry him before he was arrested for conspiring to kill Khan."

"Wow, that is messed up."

"I know. But back to your investigation. What do you need help with?"

"Right. Okay, so, I tracked down a man called Michael who was a friend of Dina's husband. He's willing to talk to me face to face, but I don't feel comfortable going by myself."

"No, of course not, that would be stupid."

"Right. But, Laura, I really want to show the men that I can do this without a male babysitter. Would you come with me?"

She placed a hand on my shoulder and smiled. "You want me to be your female babysitter?"

"No, I want you to be my sidekick for the day. This is my investigation, but I would feel safer if you were with me."

Her face softened. "I'm honored. Let me just load up with weapons and then we can go."

"I don't expect any trouble so don't bring a large arsenal."

Laura was already walking away from me. "I'll bring my numb-gun; I haven't had a chance to use that thing in ten years, and last time was so much fun."

Ten minutes later, Laura and I were on board my drone and flying full speed to see Michael, a construction worker who lived in the same building that Dina and her husband had resided in.

Michael turned out to be a man in his mid-fifties with a story to tell. "I've wanted to share what happened for years, but no one would believe me, and back when it happened, I kept quiet because I was scared for my life. That's why, when you called today, I knew it was the right time to share it." He gestured for us to take a seat in his small living room.

Laura and I sat down and while her head turned in all directions, no doubt taking in the tired-looking wallpaper and the outdated entertainment center positioned like an altar in the middle of the room, I kept my focus on Michael, who had a weathered face and rough hands. "Who were you scared of?"

"The Ruler."

"Who, Khan?"

"No, he was just a kid back then. It was Lord Marcus who had Henry killed, I'm sure of it."

"How did you know Henry?"

125

"We knew each other from school. He was a construction worker like me and Daniel. Strong as an ox and a great warrior."

"Who is Daniel?"

"He was a good friend of ours who was at the wedding too."

"Is this Daniel?" I showed Michael the wedding photo. "Yes."

"Are you still in contact?"

"Daniel died a few months after Henry and Dina."

"What happened?"

Michael crossed his arms. "He talked too much is what happened."

I frowned. "What are you implying?"

"Daniel and I both speculated about Dina's and Henry's deaths, but the difference was that I was smart enough to keep my mouth shut in public."

"How did Daniel die?"

"Shot in the head. They said it was random, that he got mugged that night, but I always knew it wasn't." Michael fiddled with the fabric of his pants. "I still miss them. Mostly Henry. We had fun together, but we were poor as fuck and that's why we lived together in an apartment. Not that I'm rich now or anything."

I jotted down a few notes as he added, "Lots of men do that; it doesn't mean that we were more than just friends."

"I know."

"Anyway, the deal was that we would put our money together and save up for a tournament. Henry was the better fighter, so he would go first and with a prize of a million dollars, he could pay me back double what I'd lent him. I always knew he could win but that he would marry the Ruler's daughter was unbelievable. It was like a fairytale and we celebrated thinking he would get both the princess and half the kingdom." Michael's head fell forward. "But it was a scam."

That got Laura's attention. "What do you mean it was a scam?"

"The day after the tournament, Henry received one hundred thousand dollars, but the other nine hundred thousand, he never got."

"Why not?"

Michael threw up his hands. "He was told that winning the Ruler's daughter was a reward worth more than money, but the problem was that he planned to buy her a nice house. I mean, we lived in an apartment on the third floor and to give him and Dina space, I had moved down here with a neighbor who was kind enough to allow it. There was no way he could offer her living in a small cramped apartment with two men. One hundred thousand dollars is a fair amount of money, but it's nothing compared to the million he was promised."

"How did Henry react to that?" I asked.

"He felt cheated and he complained about it. Dina was embarrassed too, and I know she called her parents many times begging for the money."

"Do you think Henry took it out on her?"

Michael bit his lower lip. "He was stressed and disappointed, so sure, he might have."

Laura's knee was bobbing up and down. "Do you think he killed Dina that day?"

Michael looked down. "Right when it happened, I would have said a hundred percent that he didn't, but to be honest, Henry had a temper and could be volatile in nature. I just never thought he would harm a woman."

"Can you show us the apartment they lived in and the attic she fell from?"

Michael nodded and took us outside to show us where Dina had landed. "It was the end of March and the ground was still frozen. Not that I think she would have survived if the ground had been softer. The window was too high up for that." He leaned his head back and pointed up to the roof of the building. "She fell from that middle window."

"Who found her?"

"I did."

"How? What were you doing in the back of the house on a cold winter day?" Laura's question sounded a bit accusatory and it made Michael frown.

"You have to understand that there was nowhere for Dina to go without protection. When Henry was working, she stayed inside the apartment. Henry and I were her only friends here, so I made sure to always swing by after work and talk to her. I liked Dina."

"Okay."

Michael licked his chapped lips. "But that day she didn't come to the door when I knocked. That's why I figured that maybe she had gone outside to get some fresh air."

I looked around the closed-off back yard. "And you figured she would have come here?"

"There weren't many options for her to choose from, so yes, that was my initial thought. I went down to check and... well..." Michael pointed to the ground. "That's when I found her lying here with blood around her head."

"How long do you think she had been dead for?"

"It's hard to say, but she was stiff and pale with her lips all blue. I once read that stiffness in a body starts after around three hours, but I could be wrong. It was cold that day so maybe she was just frozen."

"How did you know she had fallen from the attic?"

"I didn't. At first, I thought someone had hurt her because of all the blood, but then I saw a few pieces from the roof had fallen down too and it made me look up to see that the attic window was open. That's when I knew."

Next, Michael took us up to the third floor to see what used to be Henry's and his apartment thirty-three years ago. When no one answered his knock on the door, he typed in a code on the wall and walked in anyway. "I know the guy who lives here and I'm sure he won't mind us taking a quick look around."

The apartment was just as small as the other one that Michael lived in now.

"Is this the only bedroom?" Laura stood in the doorway of a room so small it could only fit one bed and a side table.

"Yes. But we managed."

"Yeah, but how did you manage? Did one of you sleep on the couch then?"

Michael was quick to change the subject. "Did you want to see the attic?"

"Yes."

Both Laura and I followed him up the two flights of stairs to a door that looked scratched and had dents in it. When Michael pushed it open, we walked into a dusty storage room with a beam of light coming from the window. "Not much to see, but it's where Dina spent her last minutes."

There was a heaviness in my chest from the sadness of a fifteen-year-old girl losing her life way too soon.

I walked to the window. "I wonder if she jumped or she was pushed."

Michael nodded. "I think she was pushed. I know she was stressed about the money, but she was still a happy girl. I could never imagine she would take her own life."

Opening the window, I stuck my head out. It would be possible to climb onto the rooftop, but even with dry conditions and a good balance, it would be very unsafe. "How did Henry react when he found out that she was dead?"

129

Michael scratched his neck. "Not well. He was on his way home from work when I called him, and he came running down like a crazy man, roaring out his grief. That's why I would have sworn he didn't do it. His reaction seemed very real, and there was such sorrow when he took her from me and caressed her hair while calling for Dina to come back to him."

"Do you think Henry loved Dina?"

"They only knew each other for five days but he was insanely proud of being her husband."

Laura moved to the door. "Let's get out of this attic. It gives me goosebumps."

Michael and I followed her, and we were coming down the narrow staircase when suddenly Laura gave a shout.

In the door opening onto the apartment we had just been inside stood a middle-aged man with spiky hair and crazy eyes. "Someone broke into my place." He was pointing a gun at us, and in reflex Laura pulled out her numb-gun.

"It's okay, don't shoot," I urged him. "Michael, tell him you showed us the apartment."

Michael, who was behind me, was trying to push his way past me on the narrow staircase. "Jenson, you insane old fart, drop that gun right now."

When the man didn't lower his gun, Laura warned him too, "Put your weapon down, right now."

The horrible thought of Laura getting shot had me pulling my own weapon and pointing at the man. How would I explain it to Magni if his wife lost her life in the same place as his sister?

"I'm not fucking around. Put down the gun or I'll roast your thieving asses," the man threatened.

"No one stole from you. It was just me showing these women the apartment I used to live in."

Jenson was holding his gun with both hands stretched out as he was staring at Laura. "You put down your gun first."

A "pop" sound made me suck in a breath in fear. Had the man fired his gun? My finger was on the trigger, my heart racing with fear, but it only took a split second before Jenson's body froze and he fell to the floor.

"You didn't have to shoot him, Laura."

"It's so typical of men to expect women to back down. I'm done with that."

Rushing to the man's side, I made sure he was breathing and that he hadn't cracked his head open in the fall.

Michael kneeled on Jenson's other side. "Maybe it's better if you two leave now. I'll take care of Jenson – he's a bit of a hermit and as you can see his social skills are lacking."

I looked into the eyes of the older man. "We didn't mean to hurt you. I'm very sorry for the pain you're experiencing but the good news is that it was just a numb-gun. Soon you'll be able to move again."

He couldn't respond so I left him with Michael and nodded for Laura to come with me.

"If I'd know how trigger-happy you are, I wouldn't have brought you."

Laura grinned. "Told you I've wanted an opportunity to try my numb-gun again. What better time than when a stranger is pointing his gun at me?"

"We could have de-escalated the situation."

Laura smiled. "Yeah, probably, but where would the fun be in that?"

Now that the adrenalin and fear were leaving my body, relief that we were both unharmed made me laugh a little. "God, you're such a Northlander sometimes, Laura."

"What? You mean badass and amazing?"

"Yeah, and a little mean too."

Laura climbed into the drone. "There has to be balance in the world and with all you nice Motlanders around, I figured I have some wiggle room."

I buckled up and gave her a mischievous smile. "You must be confusing me with Mila."

"My bad. I shouldn't have insulted you by calling you nice, Raven." Laura's tone was vibrating with irony.

Closing the doors to the drone and taking off, I looked over at her. "So, are you thinking what I'm thinking?"

"About Michael and Henry being lovers?"

I scrunched up my face. "No... why do you think that?"

"Oh, come on, didn't you see how he avoided the question about where they slept? They were living together and saving for a tournament together. I bet they were lovers."

"That's a big assumption."

"But it would give a motive to why Michael got jealous and killed Dina. I mean that story about Henry only getting one-hundred-thousand dollars. I don't buy it."

"Huh!" I thought about it.

"And you, Raven, what were you thinking?"

"That it was strange that Michael was the one to come home from work first. Didn't he say that he and Henry worked together? And why didn't he call Henry the moment Dina didn't answer the door? Was he hoping to have some alone time with Dina and was he maybe in love with her? Could be that she was running from him when she went up to that attic?"

Laura bit the inside of her cheek. "Yeah, could be. We should have asked him about that."

"Yes. We should have." I pulled my foot up on the seat. "Argh, you know what sucks? Now that we're leaving, I have all these questions popping into my mind. Why didn't I think of it when we were with Michael?"

"Maybe because you're a rookie and not a seasoned policewoman yet." Laura leaned over and placed her hand on my shoulder. "At least you got *some* answers."

"Yes, but how do I know if he told us the truth?"

Laura brushed her long red hair back. "You don't know. I'm telling you, that guy was full of shit."

"You really think he and Henry were lovers?"

"For sure. I have a nose for those sorts of things. Michael was so pained when he spoke of his old friend. There were true feelings there."

"I have true feelings for Mila, but you don't think we're lovers, do you?"

Laura, who was Mila's adoptive mom, grinned. "No, of course not."

"Ah, so you don't have a nose for those things after all." I gave her a sly smile that made her stiffen.

"What? Are you saying that you and Mila…"

I shrugged. "Didn't you and Magni ever wonder about our many sleepovers?"

Laura was gaping at me. "But…"

I directed my gaze out the window and sighed. "Don't freak out, Laura, I read somewhere that it's perfectly normal and a phase that young girls go through."

Laura swallowed hard. "And are you and Mila still… ehh… lovers?"

"Why, do you have a problem with it?"

"No. I mean, it's unexpected… but I guess if you love each other…" She was blinking her eyes. "What about Mila's tournament?"

I couldn't keep a straight face any longer and shoving her shoulder, I erupted in a grin. "I'm just messing with you."

"You are?"

"Yes." I nodded and laughed some more. "It's my dark side, Laura. You were the one who said we need to counterbalance all the niceness."

"Oh, geez, Raven." Laura brushed her hair back again. "I was already thinking about how to break the news to Magni that Mila wouldn't have a tournament."

"You think he would mind if she was a lesbian?"

Laura leaned back in her seat. "Our men don't have experience with lesbian women. He wouldn't love her less. He would just be confused and worry about her safety."

"Why? At least if she married me, she would be with a strong warrior."

Laura inhaled noisily. "There's that." Shaking her head, she chuckled. "I can't believe you fooled me like that."

"You know what the worst part is?"

"What?"

"I got my dark side from you."

"Me?"

"Yes. You're my role model and you always give Magni crap."

"That's just because someone needs to keep his ego in check. That man is nothing but pride and confidence."

"Just saying that I learned from the best."

Laura and I exchanged a warm smile. "In that case, Raven, I'm honored!"

"You're not going to tell Magni about today, are you? I really want a chance to solve this mystery on my own."

"I won't tell him unless he asks me, but if you find something, you'll let him know, right?"

"Of course."

"Good." Laura looked out the window. "Maybe that will give him some peace."

"Maybe." I looked straight ahead too. "And then he'll be all soft, relaxed, and sweet."

134

We both burst into loud laughter.

CHAPTER 14
Apology

Leo

When I heard that Raven was sick and wouldn't be coming to work, worst-case scenarios made me sick to my stomach. I was restless and short-tempered with my colleagues all day, and my eyes kept going to the door, worrying that any moment now Boulder and Magni would burst through it and accuse me of touching Raven.

I would be a dead man, and it made me angry with her. Raven had promised it would stay between us and if she claimed it hadn't been consensual, she was lying. She had fucking clung to my hair and pressed my head against her when I gave her oral. She had wanted me. It couldn't have been something I imagined because she had told me so – hadn't she? Ever since she ran out my door on Friday night, I'd analyzed everything that had happened between us and I was going crazy.

Desperate for answers, I decided that I had no choice but to seek her out, even if it meant walking into the lion's den or in other words, the Gray Manor.

I had been at the Ruler's majestic residence before, but only at the park and in Magni's office. Visiting Raven was risky because she might not want to see me, and I didn't want the word of her rejection to get back to my men. That's why I was relieved when I parked and saw Mila come walking toward me with a Great Dane on her right side, and what looked to be a golden retriever mix on her left, while a smaller dog was running toward me, yapping with aggression.

"Loki, come here."

"You named your dog Loki?"

Mila smiled at me. "Yes. Haven't you noticed the theme of people named after Norse Gods in my family? We have Magni, Freya, and Thor, so I figured this little guy should be named Loki. He fits the role as unpredictable and opportunistic."

I kneeled down to let the little dog sniff my hand.

"He talks a big game, but he would be the first to run if there was danger."

"And those two?" I nodded to the two bigger dogs by her side. "Would they protect you?"

Mila nuzzled the Great Dane behind its ear. "It's okay, you two, go say hi." As if they understood her both dogs came over to sniff me too.

"I would like to think that they would protect me, but hopefully we'll never find out." Mila tilted her head. "Do you like dogs, Leo?"

"Yes. And cats too."

"That's good. I could never marry someone who wouldn't accept my animals."

"Ehm... right. No, of course not, that makes sense." Mila's mention of marriage threw me off because after what I'd done with Raven, the thought of marrying her best friend felt wrong. "Mila, have you seen Raven today?"

"No. I thought she was with you."

"She didn't come to work."

"Oh, is she sick?"

"Apparently. I just wanted to check up on her."

"What a concerned boss you are." Mila gave me a genuine smile and it hit me how different she was from Raven. Not only physically, where Mila was blond with blue eyes and long straight hair while Raven had dark skin with large curly hair. I knew they were best friends, but they couldn't be more opposite in nature. Mila was mild

137

and gentle and looked young and innocent with her cute dimples, while Raven was loud, tough, and looked older than she was.

"Come on, Leo, I'll take you to her." Mila led the way and as we entered the Manor, she gestured to a guard that he could stay put and that I was her guest.

"I'm sure Raven will be honored that you came to see if she was all right. I've told her several times that you're not half as old and cranky as she claims."

"Thank you, Mila. Yeah, Raven isn't my biggest fan, that's for sure."

"Oh, it's just because she says you locked her in the dungeon with the dust dragons. She's not happy about that at all. That's why she calls you her warden."

"Like a prison warden?"

"Uh-huh."

It shouldn't have surprised me, but I still felt a need to defend myself. "Just for the record, I did take her on an assignment this week. It was a domestic violence case. Very dangerous."

Mila made a sound of concern. "I heard about that, Leo. It worries me because I can't bear the thought of losing Raven or seeing her hurt. Promise that you won't let her do something too dangerous."

I huffed out. "It's a shitty situation. She's mad if I keep her safe, and if something happens to her, everyone else will have my ass."

"Yes, I see your dilemma; we all want to be supportive of her dreams but keep her from harm at the same time."

We had walked up the wide staircase and were now walking down a long corridor. "It's that door on the right. The one with the purple sign. I made it for her."

I gave Mila my softest smile. "Thank you for taking me to her."

"Of course."

Mila was the one to knock on the door and when Raven opened it, she hugged her. "Are you okay? I heard you were sick."

Raven's eyes darted between Mila and me. "Yeah, I had a headache, but I'm better now." As expected, she didn't look happy to see me and asked, "What are you doing here?"

"I was worried about you. May I come in?"

Raven stiffened. "No, I didn't clean my room."

"That's okay, my place isn't the tidiest either. I wanted to talk to you about some… ehh… stuff." I gave a sideways glance at Mila. "Something related to work."

Mila picked up on my attempt to talk to Raven alone and with a small smile, she leaned in to place a kiss on Raven's cheek. "I'd better leave you two professionals to your boring work talk then. See you later."

As Mila walked away, Raven refused to look at me and kept her eyes locked on Mila and the three dogs.

I spoke in a low, urgent tone: "Raven, we need to talk."

"Fine. But we'll talk out here. I'm not letting you into my room."

The hallway was empty, so I agreed, "Have it your way. You know why I'm here."

When she didn't answer, I continued, "You ran out without giving me a chance to understand what I did wrong."

Planting a hand on her hip, Raven gave me a pointed look. "You're a misogynist; I told you."

I held up both hands. "I'm sorry if you were offended by my sexual fantasies about you. You know that I don't have much experience with women and maybe I fucked up, but your reaction wasn't helpful. If you had stayed, we could have…"

139

Raven narrowed her eyes and cut me off. "Helpful? Oh, you mean I should have stayed and stuck out my tongue for you to cum on like a good girl."

Damn, it was hot in this hallway. I pulled at the neckline of my sweater. "Raven, that's not what I meant." My voice lowered and became more intense. "I've hardly slept or eaten these past days. Have you told anyone?"

"Not yet."

I had been a runner my whole life, but never had my heart beat faster. "Are you planning to tell anyone?"

Raven raised her chin. "That depends."

"On what?"

"On how well you apologize."

"I already said that I'm sorry."

"Yes, but we both know that the only thing you're sorry about is getting yourself trapped in this situation. Your biggest regret is that I now hold the power." Like a goddamn standoff between two alpha wolves, Raven raised her chin and gave me a challenging stare. "The question is, what will you do to make me forgive you?"

I lowered my head, keeping my temper in check. "What do you want?"

Raven looked thoughtful as she began circling me. I turned with her, never allowing her to get behind me. Facing my shoulder, she rose up on her toes and throwing off confidence she whispered in my ear. "Action. I want to see action. No more hiding me away in the basement."

I closed my eyes, knowing that I would be doomed if she told on me and doomed if something happened to her. There was no way I could win this one. "Maybe we can find some assignments for you other than filing. I could have you look into minor violations."

"Now you're onto something."

My voice was low and annoyed. "And in return you promise that you won't tell what happened?"

140

Her finger trailed down my shoulder. "How about weekly sparring, just you and me. You're the best fighter at the station and I want you to teach me."

My answer came without hesitation. "Not if you do that porn shit again."

Raven pulled back and crossed her arms. "Says the man who wanted to shut my mouth with his penis."

"That was different. We were…" I trailed off, not sure how to categorize what we had been doing.

"From now on, all I want from you is better police assignments and fight training."

I crossed my arms as well. "And what about the things that happened between us?"

Raven tilted her head and lowered her brow. "What things? As long as you honor your part, I have no clue what you're referring to."

"And if I don't?"

"Then my memory might come back."

"That's blackmail."

"Is it?" She leaned her head back and let her hands run through her hair, forming it into a ponytail. "Or is it just my way of taking what none of you men want to give me voluntarily? I can see how your life would be so much easier if I just bowed down to your superiority. Wouldn't it, Leo?"

"Do you have to be such a brat right now? I was protecting you."

Raven's smile didn't reach her eyes. "And you'll continue to protect me by teaching me everything you know."

I growled low. "Don't fucking push me, Raven. I'm not your little servant and don't forget I have surveillance at my house. If you accuse me of rape, there will be video evidence to show that you broke into my house. It's not like I kidnapped you and tied you down."

141

"Hmm." Raven shook her head. "Enough with all your sexual fantasies, Leo."

I snorted. "Kidnapping you is not my fantasy, but tying you down might make my top three if you keep blackmailing me."

"I'm simply stating what I want from you."

"Action and fight training."

"Yes." She looked into my eyes. "Action and fight training."

There was something about this woman that spoke to a primeval part of me. "And what about the kind of action we had in my house? Do you want that too?"

Raven turned her face away. "It was nice until you opened your mouth."

My sharp reply came fast. "Funny, 'cause I remember you liking my mouth."

She raised an eyebrow and let her eyes fall to my lips. "As long as you use it for oral, sure."

"Fuck you! How is what you just said any better than what I said that night? You're such a hypocrite."

Raven blinked her eyes. "I didn't say oral is the only thing you're good for. I've told you I want to learn from you as well."

I scoffed. "You're standing here, treating me like I'm some kind of private tool for you to use and blackmail. Fuck that!"

Raven pushed her chest out and tensed her jaw. "Do you want to tell Magni what you did to me? I could get you in serious trouble."

I stepped forward, my chest almost touching hers. "Or you could admit that what we did was consensual and fucking amazing."

Raven's eyes were dilated and her chest was rising and falling. "Maybe for you."

Our eyes were clashing like the two strong fighters that we were. "Admit it. I made you come and you loved it."

"Fine. But I didn't like how it ended."

Taking a huge chance, I lifted my hand and cupped her face. "But you liked how it started, didn't you?"

Her breathing was fast and shallow.

"And you liked everything in between, didn't you?"

She didn't deny it and that was all I needed to kiss her, but Raven was quick to place her hand in front of my lips.

"Don't, Leo."

"Why not? You just admitted that you liked it."

Stepping back, Raven pressed herself against her door, her large mane covering the purple nameplate that Mila had made for her. "I was just curious, but we can't do it again. You Nmen get funny with women and I'm not letting you claim me."

"Funny how?"

"If we have sex, you'll think I belong to you. I'm not like Gennie so I won't lead you on. But I'm not interested in marriage. At least not with someone like you."

"Someone like me? What the fuck is that supposed to mean?"

"For one, you're planning to fight for Mila. The man I marry will want *only* me."

That felt like a slap in my face. "I'm not fighting for Mila!" When I said it, I knew it was the right decision because marrying Mila would mean seeing Raven all the time, and there was no way I could deny how attracted I was to this feisty woman.

Raven hesitated. "Do you love Mila?"

"No. I mean, Mila is lovely, but I don't know her that well."

"And me? You know me pretty well."

I gaped at her. "Are you asking me if I love you?"

143

She shrugged and looked away.

"Why?" I'd never met a person who sent so many mixed signals. "Why would you ask me that question if you don't want someone like me anyway?"

Raven averted my direct stare. "Just curious."

"Yeah? Well, me too." I held my head high and kept my eyes on her. "I'm curious to see what you have in your room and why you're not letting me in."

That made Raven spread her arms a little like she was blocking the door. "It's nothing, Leo."

"I don't believe you. What do you have in your room that you don't want me to see?"

"A bed! I have a bed in my room and last time you and I were alone in a bedroom, it didn't end so well, remember?"

I was trying to read her and figure out if that was all or there was more. "Then tell me this: if I go into your room, I won't find more research on the Dina case, will I?"

Raven met my stare head-on. "You told me to leave that case alone and you're not coming into my room."

I lowered my voice. "I'm getting a funny vibe from you. Please tell me you understand how imperative it is to keep the paternity issue a secret?"

Raven moved closer and it surprised me a little when her voice was low and almost seductive. "The reason I'm not letting you into my room is because there's a bed in there. If you give me the action and fight training that I want, I won't tell about what happened between us, but that doesn't mean that I don't remember what your tongue felt like. It's better if you walk away now before one of us makes a stupid move."

I swallowed hard, my pants tightening and my fingers itching to reach out and touch her. "Would it be so bad?"

"Show me that you aren't a misogynist. Show me that you'll respect my skills and give me an equal chance to prove myself, and then maybe..." Raven's eyes softened.

Like a fucking puppet, I stood there with her dangling the highest prize a man could get in front of me.

"Action and fight training," I muttered like I was in a bloody trance.

"That's right. I'll see you at work tomorrow."

After Raven disappeared back into her room, I walked away with a head full of *what-if* scenarios. *What if she feels the way I feel? What if she's fantasizing about what would have happened if she hadn't left? What if a few more exciting assignments could get her to want me enough to marry me?* My head was exploding with possibilities and when for a split second the thought of missing out on the million dollars in Mila's tournament entered my mind, I turned around and looked back at the door with the purple sign. The strong urge to go back and claim Raven right now made me sure that no amount of money would ever beat that. Raven was the biggest oxymoron personified, with her badass fighter skills and hardcore attitude on one side, and her flirtatious seductive sweet humor on the other side. How could she try to blackmail me for what happened between us one second, only to give me the impression that we weren't done in the next?

I smiled as I walked away, promising myself that Raven and I weren't done by a long shot.

CHAPTER 15
Overview

Raven

My hands were shaking when I retreated to my room after my confrontation with Leo.

The fact that he'd shown up here and been mere feet away from all the research that was spread out in my room had made me jumpy.

I couldn't afford to have any strikes on my record, and if Leo found out that I wasn't following his orders to stay away from Dina's case, he would surely report it as a lack of ability to follow orders.

My only choice to cover my tracks had been to come out more aggressive than he expected. My blackmailing hadn't been planned, especially the part about wanting weekly fight training with Leo. I had plenty of big guys who were more than willing to spar with me down at the station. Sure, Leo was the best, but after what happened between us and his stupid misogynistic comments, did I really want to be physical with him again?

Looking down at my shaking hands, I knew the answer to that question. I had felt drawn to touch him a few minutes ago and it made me mad at myself.

From now on, I will keep my distance.

In an attempt to distract myself, I took another look at my research that I'd organized this morning. The growing numbers of suspects, the open questions, and the blind alleys of dead people who couldn't give me answers made it a huge puzzle with no solid leads. What I wouldn't give to talk to Dina, her husband, or even her father, Marcus

Aurelius. If my hunch was right, I had a case of a double murder on my hands. I just wished that I knew if the murderer who killed Dina was the same who killed her husband Henry.

Around an hour after Leo had left, Mila called to invite me to a late lunch with her and Willow. Since I was hungry and needed a break anyway, I was quick to accept and go with them.

"Let's take that table in the corner." Willow pointed to a wooden booth, but I shook my head.

"No, if something happens, we don't want to be cornered. It's better if we sit closer to the door."

"Nothing is going to happen. There's three of us and the two guards are right outside." Willow scanned the room. "There's hardly any people here anyway."

Walking to the table that I wanted, I pulled out a chair. "That can change, and we all know that I'll be the one to defend you two if something happens, so I say we sit at this table."

"All right." Willow sat down next to me. "You're almost worse than Solo, you know that?"

"He's a smart guy and he understands security. I've learned a thing or two at the police academy and one thing is to always have an escape route."

"Hmm." Willow picked up a thin tablet and went over the menu. "I don't know, Raven, you've changed after you joined the police. You used to be funny but now you're more serious."

That hit me hard in my chest. "I'm still funny."

"Not as funny as you used to be before the academy."

Mila pulled up her sleeves and gave me a small smile. "Careful that you don't turn into a new Leo."

"Why, what's wrong with Leo?" Willow pointed to the menu tablet. "Ooh, that looks delicious."

"Raven thinks Leo is too serious."

147

Willow looked from Mila to me before tilting her head. "Huh... I don't know. I've seen him joke around plenty of times with Solo and Zasquash."

Mila agreed, "Exactly. That's what I said. And he has a beautiful smile."

I gave a small snort. "I wouldn't know, he never smiles around me."

When a bot approached us to ask what we wanted, Mila asked for a few more minutes to decide.

"It's just that Leo is my boss and he's... well, bossing me around. Sometimes he says things that are chauvinistic in nature, and I have a problem with misogyny."

Mila fiddled with her earlobe. "I know, Raven, but we talked about it before. The Nmen haven't relied on women for centuries. They aren't used to expecting great things from us females."

"Of course, they have relied on women. Who do you think gave them their young ones?" I tried reading the menu card while being part of the conversation.

"I know, but the resentment they've been holding on to about being isolated up here has made them negative toward strong women."

Willow objected, "That's not true. I'm a strong woman and Solo never had a problem with that. Who wants to share a salad and some brussels sprouts or maybe the red beets with pears?"

I nodded. "Sure, how about we just order a bit of all their side servings and share it? They have good bread here and a really nice selection of olives."

We called over the bot and got our order going before returning to the subject of the Nmen.

"Leo just drives me crazy with his views on women. I'm tired of men seeing us as fragile and inferior to them."

"He said that?" Willow lowered her brow. "That's so strange because Leo was amazing during the tour with all us performers from the Motherlands. He was furious when we were attacked, and I have no doubt that he would give his life to save any woman."

I leaned back in my chair. "Yes. But he wouldn't let her work in a position equal to him, that's for sure. All the men are misogynistic. I even see it with my dad at times."

"You've got to stop using that word, Raven. It means that he would have to hate women. And Boulder definitely doesn't hate women."

"Okay, so maybe there are levels of it, but misogyny also means to hold a prejudice against women, and you can't say that the men here don't hold strong prejudices against us."

Willow rested both forearms on the table. "They do but it's a matter of conditioning and ignorance. For centuries they have been taught that women can't do what men can, but that just leaves it to us to prove them wrong."

I threw my hands up. "Which is what I'm doing but it's hard when I'm surrounded by bigots and chauvinists."

The bar-bot brought drinks for us and we cheered.

Raising her glass, Willow whispered, "Let's just enjoy that we are here together and ignore the five guys across the room who are staring in our direction."

"They are just curious." Mila turned around and smiled at the group of men.

I spoke without moving my lips. "Don't do that, Mila. You'll only encourage them."

"I'm just being friendly."

"I know, but your friendliness might make them come over here, and then we'll have the guards storming in asking them to back off. I just want to enjoy a quiet meal with my good friends."

Willow backed me up. "Yeah, Mila, less smiling and more updating, please."

"Okay, but what do you want to know?"

149

Willow's index finger was circling the rim of her glass. "How are things with Jonah?"

"You mean in the council?"

"Yes."

"Well, he's working hard to get some of his ideas through, but it's hard with him being the only male on the Motherland council. He did have one victory last week, though."

"What victory?"

"There's a blended family who live up here in the Northlands and the father has never been allowed to go on vacation to the Motherlands with his family."

"Why not?"

"He could never get a visa because he had a criminal past. But the wife has been advocating for it for years and with Jonah's help he finally had his first visa approved."

I lowered my brow. "What kind of criminal was he? I hope they didn't allow some psycho into the Motherlands."

Mila picked up her glass. "According to my mom he got in a bar fight once and killed a man, but that was way back in the late twenties. He served his time and hasn't been violent since, except for the time when he and my dad were in a drunken fight." Mila placed her index finger on her forearm. "My dad still has a scar right here from that fight."

Blowing a lock of my curly black hair out of my eyes, I stared at Mila. "Wait a minute, are we talking about that man your mom helped catch after the earthquake?" My fingers were snapping in the air as I was trying to recall his name. "Laura told me about him. What was his name again, Demon, or Devil or something?"

"Surely not." Willow raised a hand to her chest. "I mean the Nmen have strange names, but I can't imagine it would be legal to name a child *that*."

Mila shrugged. "I don't remember his name either, but my mom told me how he got through the wall during the big earthquake and that his wife, Julia, hid him. Apparently, she had a major thing for Nmen."

"Yes, Laura told me that story too. He was sent back to Northlands and Julia was forbidden to come and be with him."

"Why?"

"With his criminal past, the council deemed him dangerous and they saw her as mentally unstable for wanting to put herself in danger. He was a convicted murderer after all."

Willow moved in her seat. "Then what happened?"

I let Mila tell the story. "Julia arranged protests and had people sign petitions. The council sent her to reflect on it, but every time she came out, she went back to fight for her right to go to the Northlands. I guess that in the end they got tired of dealing with her and gave in."

"Devlin. His name was Devlin," I bellowed out as I finally remembered.

Mila smiled. "Yes, that's right. And anyway, he and Julia have three kids together and live here in the Northlands. I haven't met them, but I was happy that Jonah spoke for them and helped them get a visa so Devlin could finally meet Julia's family and go on vacation with his wife and children."

I placed my crossed arms on the table. "That's kind of sweet and a little crazy too. Don't you think, Willow?"

She looked thoughtful. "The heart wants what the heart wants. Sometimes you just can't fight it no matter how hard you try."

Leo's face popped into my mind when Willow spoke of love, and the annoyance and resistance against him coming to mind made me physically shake my shoulders and arms.

"Are you cold?" Mila asked.

"Me? No, why?"

"You just shivered like you were cold."

"No, no, I just had goosebumps from what Willow said. It sounds awful to fall in love against your will. What if you fall in love with someone who is the complete opposite of what you want? I don't like that idea. I read somewhere that the tingly little feeling you get when you like someone? That's your common sense leaving your body."

"I didn't like it either." Willow still had that serious expression on her face. "I've told you how I was so blinded by my anger that I said some horrible things to Solo." Willow looked down, her nail scraping along the edge of the table. "I still feel awful for telling him that I wished he was dead."

Mila rested her hand on top of Willow's and gave her a look of sympathy while I shrugged.

"You were hurting at the time. Remember how you used to hate him?"

"That doesn't make it better. I'm ashamed of it." Willow was looking into my eyes.

"I get that, but I remember wondering if you had lost your mind when you got back together with Solo. I didn't understand how you could go from hating with such intensity to loving him again."

"I understood." Mila blinked her big blue eyes. "I always figured that your anger with him was just a shield to protect you from the greatest love of your life."

"Then why didn't you tell me that?"

Mila drew in a sigh. "I tried, but you didn't want to hear it. Solo's name was practically taboo around you and Hunter. But either way, Willow, your love story should give hope to all of us. If I'm paired up with someone whom I don't love, I'll remind myself that you went from hating Solo to loving him."

"That's not the same at all. Solo was my first love. Mila, I wish you wouldn't do that tournament. You can't gamble with your future like that."

Mila had a soft smile on her pretty face. "It'll be fine. I get along with most people and a promise is a promise."

"The food is taking a long time, isn't it?" Willow turned in her seat and looked toward the kitchen. "Nora was sleeping when I left, and I told Erika that I would be back by two. She usually takes a three-hour nap this time of day, but I'd hate for her to wake up before I get back."

"Then we'll just have to eat fast." Mila straightened up in her chair. "I'm sure Erika can handle it, though; with all the grandchildren Khan and my dad have given her, she's amazing with babies."

When the service-bot brought us our food a little later, we dug in and tasted from the many plates. Mila asked me, "So how is the investigation going?"

I tightened my lips and bulged my eyes, signaling that it was a secret, but Willow saw it and frowned.

"What investigation."

Before I could come up with a white lie, Mila had already revealed more.

"Raven is investigating a murder mystery."

"Yeah, an old one that was never solved, but I've told Mila that it's a secret so we really shouldn't talk about it."

Willow lit up. "Who's your suspect?"

I pursed my lips and skewed my mouth from side to side, tempted to talk about something that I was passionate about. "I think Marcus Aurelius might have ordered the assassination of a man."

Willow looked from me to Mila and back again. "Is that your *mystery*? Marcus had many people killed. Everybody knows that. The man was a psychopath and a cruel tyrant."

"True, but I'm investigating a specific murder that I think he ordered."

Willow gave me a small smile. "Are you going to tell me who this prominent and important victim was?"

"I'd rather wait until I have solved the case."

"All right." Willow raised her glass to us. "At least let's give cheers to the fact that they're finally letting you do some real police work."

Mila clinked her glass with Willow's and when I hesitated, Willow frowned.

"What's wrong?"

"Actually, they didn't assign this case to me. It's more like a hobby case that I'm doing in my spare time. Would you mind not mentioning it to Solo?"

"Oh, I see." Willow scratched her shoulder. "Sure, I can keep a secret."

I clinked my glass with them and we drank.

"So how is it going with the case?" Mila asked again and reached for the plate with olives.

"Slow. I'm running into a lot of dead ends. That's the problem with old unsolved murder cases, I suppose. Not only is the victim dead, but so are many of the people who knew the person." I sighed and popped an olive into my mouth. "If any of you know a psychic who can speak to the dead, let me know."

Willow grinned while Mila gave it some thought.

"Hmm, I once heard about a woman who claimed she could feel the presence of dead people, but it was Pearl who told me about her, and I think they met when Pearl was in a place of reflection. I'm not sure how stable that woman was."

Giving a small laugh, I kept digging my fork around my salad. "You should know that I wasn't serious, Mila."

She shrugged. "I'm just trying to help, but I guess you'll have to make do with the things the dead ones left behind. Did you go through the box with Marcus's name on it?"

"What box?"

"The one in the basement."

I had been lifting my fork to my mouth, but my hand stopped in mid-air as I stared at Mila. "You never told me about a box with his name on it."

Her head tilted to one side. "Yes, I did."

"No. When?"

"Huh. I'm sorry about that. It was right next to the broken piano and the weird-looking clock." Mila began touching her wristband. "I took a picture because I thought your mom might like it, Raven. You know, with Christina being an archeologist and all."

The three of us leaned in to study the picture Mila showed us.

"How tall is that thing?" Willow asked.

"Taller than any of us and look at those weird lines and dots. It's like a secret code of sorts."

The round shape with the many symmetrical lines had me confused and Willow complained, "Are you sure it's a clock, Mila? Why doesn't it just say what time it is? Is this some kind of math thing? I'm horrible at math."

I leaned closer. "No, I think Mila is right. My mom has something similar in her office but hers has numbers on it. I think twelve is on top and then it goes this way with one, two, three, and so on."

"Okay, but then what? How do you know what time it is," Willow asked.

"I don't know. My mom tried to teach me, but it's super complicated and all I remember is that the fat arrow shows hours and the long slim one shows minutes, or maybe it was the other way around. Either way, I gave up because you would have to be as passionate about artifacts as Christina to appreciate it. It's not like the rest of us will ever need it."

Mila lowered her wrist and it made the picture disappear. "No. Thank god that we modern people have real watches that actually show the time. Sometimes I think that people back in the days were either incredibly stupid for making things so complicated, or insanely smart for understanding how complicated things work."

It was a quick dinner since Willow was eager to get back to her baby daughter, and I was impatient to see what I might find in the box with Marcus' things that Mila had spoken about. As soon as we got back to the Gray Manor, I almost ran down to the basement and because of Mila's instructions that the box was close to the antique clock and the broken piano, it didn't take me long to find it.

It didn't surprise me that the box was sealed. With the storage room being overwhelming and a little creepy with no one else around, I dropped the idea of searching for a pair of scissors or some kind of tool that could help me break the box open. Instead, I half carried, and half dragged the heavy box to my room like a giddy squirrel carrying the biggest pine cone back to its house. Despite my eagerness and excitement, I was careful not to get caught and peeked around each corner to make sure no one would see me.

Unlocking my door, I pushed it open with my butt and lifted one end of the heavy box. The room had carpet down, so hopefully no one downstairs would hear me dragging the box over the floor.

My focus was entirely on the box as I backed into the room and maybe that's why it didn't occur to me that the lights were already on. With a satisfied sigh, I decided that the box could stay next to my bed while I searched for something to open it with. My hands were tingling from the heavy lifting but all of that ceased to matter when I straightened up and felt the strong presence of someone behind me.

CHAPTER 16
Answers

Leo

"What do you have there?"

Raven turned fast and looked like she was ready to fight.

I stayed by the window, still leaning against the frame. "Told you. You're not the only one who is curious."

Raven looked pissed and stepped forward. "You have no right to be here. This is a break-in."

"You're right. But aren't you Motlanders the ones preaching the Golden Rule? How does it go again?" I pretended to be thinking. "Only do to others as you want them to do to you."

Raven stepped in front of the box as if I would forget that it existed.

"Since you broke into my place, I figured that I could break into your place too."

Raven shot a sideways glance at all the pictures, articles, and notes spread out on her bed. "Are you going to report me for insubordination?"

I shrugged. "That's such a fancy word."

"We both know you asked me not to pursue the case."

"Yes. But you did it anyway."

Raven met my eyes. "What choice did I have? You won't let me get close to any real police work."

"Not true." I changed position, folding my arms and taking a wide stance. "I brought you with me to a domestic violence case." Throwing a nod to the research on the bed,

158

I continued. "How about you walk me through what you've found out so far?"

"Why?"

The last thing Raven had told me when we had our little showdown in the hallway two hours ago was "Show me that you aren't a misogynist. Show me that you'll respect my skills and give me an equal chance to prove myself, and then maybe..."

I had come back because I couldn't stay away. What I'd found in her room hadn't come as a surprise. I should have known she was too feisty and stubborn to give up on the case, but I was disappointed. Part of me had hoped that I would only find a bed and that she had spoken the truth when she talked about her attraction to me being the only reason that she wouldn't let me in. Clearly it had been a lie.

The thirty minutes I had waited for her had given me a chance to think it over: this case could be my chance to show Raven that I respected her. My chance to reach whatever "maybe" meant.

"Did you hear me, Leo?" Raven stepped closer. "Why do you want to know what I found out? You're just going to ask me to forget about it anyway."

"I was considering helping you."

She narrowed her eyes in suspicion.

"For practice, Raven. We'll work on this case without telling anyone and I'll help you solve it. It'll give me a chance to educate you on my methods, but whatever we discover will stay between us."

"That's not fair," she protested. "I want everyone to know that I've solved the case, and that's why I want to do it alone."

Leaning forward, I spoke in a non-negotiable tone. "I'm not letting you jeopardize the safety of our country. This is a high-profile case. What makes you think that people desperate enough to kill the daughter and son-in-law of the ruler won't do the same to you or me if we begin asking questions?"

"So, you think they were murdered too?"

Inhaling deeply, I let my chest rise and fall. "The first rule of investigating is to never rule out anything."

For the next few moments, Raven and I stood in her room not speaking any words but still communicating.

"Yes or no, Raven."

"I didn't invite you to be part of this investigation."

"When I leave your room, we will have reached one of two possible decisions. Either we do this together, or I'll report you for not following an order."

"So now you're blackmailing me?"

I shrugged. "At least I'm giving you a choice."

Raven's head fell forward and her hands clamped into fists. "Fine!"

"Good. Then take me over what you've learned so far." I lifted pictures of what looked like logbooks. "What are these?"

"Dina had a crush on a guard. I've been searching through old logs to find him and it turns out he still works at the Manor."

"Interesting."

"Yes." She explained about every suspect and clue and I listened. "So, you see, I'm curious to see what I can find in Marcus' box."

"All right, then let's open it, but I'm warning you. It's not like you'll find a diary with a list of all the people he murdered and the reasons why. Small girls write diaries, but not Nmen."

Picking up a pair of scissors, she began breaking through the sealing of the box. "You don't know that. Maybe there are some who do it. Hmm, I wonder what you would write in your diary."

160

"That you have to be the slowest person to open that box. How about you give me the scissors?"

Raven kept cutting the box open with her right hand while pushing away my hand with her left. "I've got this."

When she finally opened the flaps, we almost banged our heads together to see what was in the box.

Mostly, it was things that I guessed had been in his office once. A framed picture of Marcus, Erika, Khan, Magni, and two dogs. Another with his friend Mr. Zobel.

I picked up a heavy marble bust of Marcus Aurelius. He looked as serious as he had in every picture I'd ever seen of the man.

Some old electronic products came out of the box and I took one of them from Raven, who asked, "What is this?"

"That's a burner."

It was the length of my underarm and the width of my wrist. "This will print out anything you need by burning the letters or symbols on the paper."

"Oh, I have a burner, but it looks different."

I turned the burner around in the air. "This one is at least twenty years old."

"So is this, I think." Raven gave me a wristband and when I checked the model number online it turned out to be from 2414.

"This is thirty-four years old." I chuckled. "The rumors were true then. Old Marcus was a technophobe."

"Why do you say that?"

"Because he died in 2433, Raven."

Raven bit her lip like she still didn't understand.

I held up the wristband. "In 2433 this wristband was nineteen years old? That's crazy."

"Oh, now I understand. I've never been good at math, so I didn't catch that part." She shrugged. "It's unusual, but not everyone wants the newest gadgets."

"No." I was quiet and thoughtful. "But maybe his phobia about new technology can be helpful to us. *If* we can get access to the information on it, that is?"

Raven pointed to the burner. "Maybe there's a log on the last printed papers."

"Wow, you're really serious about being bad at math, aren't you?" I gave her a smile. "Marcus died eighteen years after Dina. I doubt this burner existed in 2415, around the time of her death."

"Ahh, but what if one of his last printed papers was a confession of what he did to her?" Raven tapped her temple with a sly smile. "The first rule of investigation, boss, never rule anything out."

She was so bloody cute at that moment that I had to get my brain to stop thinking about all the things I wanted to do with her.

Raven kept looking through the box while I worked on the burner and the wristband.

"I'm sorry, Raven, but I think we'll need an expert to access this. It's completely dead and I'm not getting anything."

"Give it to me." Raven reached for the wristband and placed it around her wrist. "Maybe it needs heat or movement."

"It's an oldie, so yeah, probably."

Raven sat back against the bed tapping on the wristband, but it remained dead. "Well, this is disappointing."

"I warned you not to expect too much."

She shrugged but kept her eyes on the wristband. "It would have been nice if he had left a confession letter."

My laugh made her look up. "I agree. The criminals really ought to think of us poor detectives and make it a bit easier to solve their crimes."

162

Raven smiled back at me. "At least we agree on something."

"Come on." I got up and reached out my hand to pull her up. "We're going to the station to see what's hidden on that thing."

As we stood by her bed, I couldn't help a small complaint. "You know what bums me out, Raven?"

"What?"

"That all that talk about your bed being the reason you couldn't invite me in was just an excuse, and so was what happened at my house." I picked up a picture of the diary that was in my closet. "A part of me wanted to believe that you really came to see and that you enjoyed making out with me."

Raven's eyes fell from my face to my shoulder and her voice was low when she answered, "I did."

I scoffed low.

"Leo, it's not what you think."

I held up a hand to stop her. "You're an opportunist, Raven, and you worked with what you had. I'm not blaming you. I'm just sad that I got caught up in your net."

"What net? I thought you liked making out with me."

I shrugged. "It doesn't matter what I did or didn't like. You took what you needed and left me with nothing."

Her eyebrows were close together and she bit her lip. "That was never my int…"

Cutting her off, I moved to the door. "At least now that I know it was all just a hoax, I can focus on my job again."

Raven stood with her shoulders low and her arms hanging by her sides. She didn't have her usual feisty energy, and I had to call out from the door. "Are you coming or what?"

We hardly spoke on the way to the station and were disappointed to find that our gadget expert had already left for the day. I called him up and he explained how to

163

unlock the wristband and where to find the extractor that we would need to do the job.

"You're going to love this." I gave Raven a smile. "The extractor that we need is stored down in the archive."

"Oh, you mean in my room?"

"Uh-huh. If you want, I could make a purple sign for the door like the one you have at the Gray Manor." I was trying to make a joke to ease the tension a bit, but Raven stayed serious.

"Mila made me that sign."

"I know. She told me."

We were taking the stairs at a run.

I almost wished that I hadn't confronted Raven about being an opportunist, since things between us had become stiff and awkward.

We worked together to extract the information on the wristband. She was cordial and polite, but her wicked humor that I'd come to appreciate was safely packed away. I hated how fast we'd become impersonal, but I didn't know how to change it.

"There it is." The large screen showed a long list of messages, videos, and sound files.

Raven's eyes were darting around on the screen. "Can you search for activity around Dina's death?"

"When was that again?"

"March 23rd, 2415."

I searched and a list of calls came up. "Looks like these are the unanswered, the outgoing, and the incoming."

"Wow, busy time for old Marcus, huh?" Raven was standing while I was sitting, and she let her finger run down the screen. I don't think she noticed but as she leaned in, she supported herself with a hand on my shoulder. "There's a lot of unanswered calls from Dina."

"Yes."

"Okay, so let's be systematic about this and look from her wedding day, which was March 18th."

The first two days there was nothing from Dina, but then there had been two incoming calls on the third day, followed by thirteen unanswered until the day of her death.

"Did she leave any messages?" Raven asked.

"If she did, they would have been received as transcribed text messages."

We searched but there was nothing.

"Wait a minute. This wristband is ancient. Maybe the technology worked differently back then. Do you remember anything about this type of wristband?"

I gave Raven an are-you-serious look. "How old do you think I am? I told you this wristband is thirty-four-years old. I'm sorry to burst your bubble, but I didn't wear a wristband three years before I was born."

Raven rubbed her face. "Okay, let's just keep searching. What about the videos?"

We looked through videos on fast forward but except for a few videos of the family it was all from hunting trips where Marcus was filmed with his foot on the head of a large bear or elk that he had killed.

"What about the sound files?"

"There's over three hundred." I groaned. "I hope you brought some food."

"Let's focus on the ones from the week where Dina got married and died." Raven pulled a chair over and sat down next to me as I played the first file. The first five were low-quality recordings of meetings where a lot of people spoke at the same time. It was hard to make sense of any of it, except that they were angry and there was a theme of money.

The sixth sound file had us both sit up straight as the sound of a woman crying came through loud and clear.

"It's me again. Why won't you pick up? How can you do this to me? Am I worth so little to you? Call me, Dad."

Raven blinked. "That was her. That was Dina."

"I know."

"Play the next one."

I pressed play and again Dina came through with a brittle voice. "I'm begging you, Dad. Pay Henry the money you owe him. I don't understand why you would steal it from him. He fought for me and he needs the money to get us out of this tiny apartment. It's his money, Dad. Please, I'm begging you. Call me."

Tears welled up in Raven's eyes.

"Are you okay?"

"Yes. It's just that I've been thinking about Dina non-stop since I found her file and to hear her voice..." She brushed her hair back. "I don't know, it's just very powerful."

"Yeah, but you can't get emotionally attached, Raven. We're only working on this case for you to learn."

"I know that."

"Good, because no matter how well you do your job, Dina is still going to be dead."

She nodded and gestured for me to play the next ones. There were nine sound files, with Dina growing more and more desperate – from her initial sad and begging tone to the seventh, where she was speaking in a harsh tone.

"Dad, I know what you did and why you took that money. You are bankrupt! Mom told me, and I would help you, except you already stole my husband's fortune so I can't feel bad for you. You're a thief and a liar. But here's the thing. I also know that Khan isn't your son. That's right, I heard you and Mom talk about it years ago. Since you won't answer my calls or do the right thing, I guess you leave me no choice than to play dirty too. If you don't make sure to pay Henry his money, I'll share that piece of information with anyone who will listen. Just pay what you owe us and I'll never mention it again."

There were two more sound files of Dina making threats and in the last one she made a comment that had Raven and me exchanging a long look.

"Khan has been trying to get in touch with me. Did you know that? Does he know that you're not his father? So far, I haven't picked up, but next time he calls I'm telling him everything unless we have the money."

"How old was Dina again?" I asked.

"Fifteen."

"Wow, she is threatening the biggest psychopath in the country like she's some kind of immortal warrior. What was she thinking?"

Raven frowned. "Don't call him that. Everyone has a back story, and you don't know his."

"And you do?"

Raven gave a sharp inhalation and nodded. "I spoke to Erika, who told me about Marcus and the things that made him a bloodthirsty cynic."

"Care to share?"

Raven told what she had learned from Erika and it made me sit back with my mouth open. "I can't imagine what it must have been like for Marcus to see his woman raped like that. If anyone touched yo…" I stopped before I finished that sentence and tried to cover up my slip. "…touched young women without consent, I would kill them."

Raven studied me. She had to know I had meant her, but she didn't say anything. "But not if they touched an older woman?"

"Yes. Of course. Any man who raped a woman would be dead if I came across him."

"Right." She broke eye contact. "Anyway, all I'm saying is just that Marcus wasn't always evil."

"Fair enough, but apparently he was broke and willing to rob his daughter and son-in-law for a fortune."

"According to Michael, who was Henry's roommate, Marcus only paid one hundred thousand out of the million."

I whistled. "Poor Henry shouldn't have signed up for that tournament. If he had just stayed home, he wouldn't have had to go through hellish fights in a tournament, only to be cheated out of nine hundred thousand dollars, and shortly after, become a widower, before he was killed himself. Shit, that is a lot of bad luck for one man."

"At least, Dina was nice to him. She went against her father on Henry's behalf."

"Yes, she was like a female version of Magni. Fearless."

"Do you think Dina and Henry consummated their marriage?"

Raven's question surprised me. "Why wouldn't they?"

"Because she was so young and he was a stranger to her."

I ran my hands through my hair. "Raven, things were different back then. Men like Henry, they..." I trailed off, not sure how to say it.

"They what?"

"You've mostly been around men who grew up with you at the school, but those men are very different from the rest of us. I mean, I didn't see a woman for the first time until I was an adult. For someone like Henry, a wife symbolized the unique chance to have a family, and he would have wanted to start it the moment he got Dina to himself."

"But she was a child."

"No, not in his eyes, Raven. Not in anyone's eyes back then. She was a young woman able to give birth and that was what mattered."

168

"So, you're admitting that to Nmen, we women are nothing but breeders."

I wanted to swallow my own tongue for being so clumsy with my words. "I don't know if I can explain it right, but you women are the reason we get out of bed in the morning. You are what makes us strive for greatness, you make us push to be the best version of ourselves. You women are the ultimate reward for a warrior and we treasure you as a group and as individuals. A few are privileged to get close to you and those men are admired and envied by all of us."

While I spoke, Raven's features softened. "So, tell me this: if you had won me in a tournament tonight, what would we be doing right now?"

I licked my dry lips, not sure what she was up to. "You know what we would be doing."

Her breathing picked up and her eyes dilated. "How would I know? I've never been married."

My breathing picked up too, my heart racing as fast as my mind, which was frantically screaming not to touch her and warning about what had happened the last time.

"Do you want to get married?"

"Maybe. But it would help me if you could show me what to expect if I do. You are my mentor, after all."

I wanted to strip her naked and take her right here on the table, but I found a bit of self-control and looked deep into her eyes. "Not here. All rooms at the station have cameras and although I really don't care if anyone sees my naked ass, I don't want anyone to see yours."

I transferred everything we needed from the wristband for later use and closed down the system. "We're going to my house."

"Oooh, how exciting." Raven smiled at me. "Just remember your own advice."

"What was that?"

"Don't get emotionally attached. We're only doing this to learn."

CHAPTER 17
One on One

Leo

Raven flew with me and called up the security team at the Gray Manor to make sure they didn't alert her father because of her absence. I didn't say anything when she programmed her drone to fly over.

"Hey, Oscar, I'm just letting you know that I'll be home late tonight. I'm at my parents' house."

"Thank you, Raven. I'll note that down. Just need you to put Boulder on the line first to confirm."

She frowned. "You're not serious – I'm not a child."

Oscar cleared his throat. "I know that. I'm just following protocol."

With an annoyed sigh. Raven reached her wrist out to me. "Dad, would you mind telling the nice and overprotective guard that I'm safe with you?"

I looked at her wristband and back to meet her eyes. Pretending to be Alexander Boulder was not a good idea. Raven's father was powerful and would show no mercy if he found out I'd messed around with his daughter.

Raven lifted her wrist higher and mouthed, "Say something."

Having no choice, I imitated Boulder's voice, "Everything is fine. Raven is with me."

"Thank you, sir. Have a nice evening."

"You too, and oh, one last thing... if it gets too late, we'll just have Raven stay for the night."

"Understood, sir."

171

Finishing the call, Raven gave me a crooked smile. "Thanks, *Dad.* I feel like such a rebel."

I rolled my eyes but smiled. "That's because you are. If your dad finds out about this, he'll kill me."

"For pretending to be him – I doubt it."

"Make yourself comfortable while I get us something to drink. And just for the record, if he doesn't kill me for impersonating him, then he'll surely kill me for the things I plan to do to you tonight."

My last comment was gutsy, and I watched her from the open kitchen to read her reaction to my words.

"Why? Are you going to hurt me tonight?"

"No."

"Then I don't see why my father would kill you. I'm here voluntarily and as long as whatever happens between us is consensual, it's no one else's business."

When she spoke like that, it was easy to forget how much younger Raven was than me. Bringing over both beer and wine, I asked what she preferred.

"Hang on, I'm just telling my drone to come here." After closing down the remote connection on her wristband, she gave me a smile. "I'll take wine, please."

I poured Raven a glass before joining her on my leather couch.

Raven's hands were shaking a little when she swallowed half the glass of wine and gave me a poor imitation of a confident smile. "Are you afraid of me now?"

I was nervous and dried off my sweaty hands on my pants before reaching for a beer. "Of course not."

"Then why are you sitting so far from me?"

Moving closer, I took a big swig of my beer and set it back on the table.

Raven emptied her glass and looked up at me. "So?"

Our eyes played the invitation game of switching between looking deep into each other's eyes and down to each other's mouths, and when she wet her lips, I knew I should just kiss her, but confusing questions in my mind were holding me back. I was nose to nose with her and could almost feel her lips on mine when I pulled back and placed my hands on her shoulders. "Raven, what are we doing exactly?"

Her eyes blinked. "You were about to kiss me, I think."

"Yes, but the thing is that I'm not sure I understand what your motive is. I mean, you've made out with me and flirted with me to distract me from knowing that you were still investigating after I had ordered you not to. But this... what is this?" I swung my hand between us. "I agreed to help you solve the case, so why are you here? What is your motive this time?"

"Do I need a motive?"

I rubbed my forehead. "No, but I like to make sense of things, and your mixed signals are fucking confusing."

"It's confusing to me too."

Sighing, I waited for her to continue.

"I'm an explorer by nature and for years I've wondered about sex. I guess that when you came home that day and found me here, an opportunity to explore presented itself, and so I took it."

I raised an eyebrow. "You make it sound like you would have done it with anyone!"

"No." She trailed a finger down my face and leaned closer. "There's something about you that makes me curious."

I wanted to believe her but had to ask, "Other men don't?"

She shook her head. "There's been a few that made me wonder what sex would be like, but you're the first to make me want to try it."

"I'm honored." I felt myself soften again and gave her one of those smiles that she seemed to like so much. Raven didn't resist when I moved her down on the couch or when I got on top of her. Instead she laughed.

"Don't tell me that I'm the first woman to make you want to try sex."

I laughed with her. "You're not, but then I'm older than you and I've met a lot more people."

"If by people you're talking about women, then I doubt that to be true. I'll bet that I've met far more men than you have met women."

"Fair point, but I'm counting the women I've seen on-screen."

Raven snorted in protest. "Most of those women are from the past so they don't count." She laughed. "You can only include women who are alive and whom you've met in real life." Tilting her head, she asked, "What about Mila? Did you fantasize about having sex with her?"

I hesitated before answering, "Do you want my honest answer?"

Her eyes were saying no, but her mouth said, "Yes."

"I have, Raven, and my guess is that so have all men who come in contact with her. Mila is beautiful and sweet."

Raven's arms stiffened around my shoulders and her mouth fell.

"It's the same with you. I fantasized about you from the first day I met you. You have to know that you have that effect on most men."

"Why? I'm not sweet like Mila."

I brushed a lock of her hair from her face. "No, but you're gorgeous and feisty. You speak to every hunting instinct we Nmen have. Mila is the pretty deer in the forest while you're the sleek cougar with sharp claws."

"How about a panther? I prefer panthers over cougars."

"We don't have panthers in the Northlands."

Raven lifted her brow. "I wasn't born here."

174

"Fine, you're like a panther then. A graceful predator that all hunters admire and respect."

"That's right, and don't you ever forget it. If you try to hurt me, I'll scratch and bite you hard." She let her nails dig into my back.

"I'll take my chances." I changed position, sitting up on the sofa, and pulling Raven astride me. "Will you?"

"What? Take my chances?"

"Yes. What if you fall in love with me?"

Her brown eyes were much darker than mine as they studied me, but she didn't answer.

"That could happen, you know."

Nuzzling my neck with her fingers, Raven kissed me. "Is that what you're hoping for? That I fall in love with you?"

"I would be a poor hunter if I let my panther go."

"But a panther is a wild creature and needs to roam, Leo. She would never be happy in a cage."

"Ahh, but what if the cage was so big that she never felt like she was in one?"

Tilting her head, Raven grinned. "It would have to be huge because a hunter with his prey in a small cage grows lazy and bored. The hunter would have to feel like the panther was free, so he could hunt her down again and again and keep things interesting."

"Good point, especially if she became the only one he was allowed to hunt."

We were smiling at each other.

"Are we still talking about us?" I asked. "It got a little complicated there."

"Did it? You want me to sum it up for you?" She kissed my nose. "You're the hunter and you have to lure me into your bed to get what you want. But you have to make the sex so good that I will want to come back."

"It takes two to have good sex. It's not my fault if you're bad at it..."

"Wow." Raven leaned her head back and laughed again. I loved how relaxed my lame jokes made her, or maybe it was the kissing. "I can guarantee you that I'll be the best lover you've ever had."

My heart was full of mischief and I used a playful tone of voice. "Compared to my other nonexistent lovers, you mean?"

"Yup."

"Then I can guarantee you as well that I'll be the best lover you've ever had."

"Sounds like we have nothing to lose."

I knew that wasn't true. There was a big fucking chance that this hunter might shoot himself in the foot by obsessing about a delicious panther he could never fully catch. I didn't tell her that because I was done talking and began pulling off her clothes one item at a time.

Part of me expected her to say stop, but for every item that came off, my confidence grew. "You really want this, don't you?"

Raven was so goddamn beautiful when she looked into my eyes and nodded. "Yeah, I want this."

I was painfully aware that this wasn't the scenario I had grown up picturing for my first time with a woman. Raven wasn't my wife and there was a big chance she would only allow this to happen once. It was like being served a delicious meal with no guarantee you could ever have it again. Something so tasty that you'd want to eat it with gusto and at the same time lick it slowly to make it last.

"Your beard tickles," Raven chuckled when I sucked on her breast. She was astride me and naked while I still had my briefs on. My hands were on her firm buttocks and with our difference in height, her sitting on me put us almost eye to eye.

"Do you feel that?" Our eyes were locked, and my breathing was getting heavier. "Do you feel how hard I am for you?"

Raven's hands were on my chest and she rotated her hips in a slow deliberate movement, creating a magical kind of friction between us.

"Yes, I feel it." With hooded eyes she leaned down and kissed me like it was an erotic art form – her teeth gently biting my lower lip, her tongue tasting me, and her hands weaving into my hair.

"Fuuuck." I growled low and bored my fingers into her cheeks.

"Sorry about your briefs," Raven mumbled into my mouth. "They are getting wet."

I could feel it and it made me fucking lose my mind that her pussy was dripping wet because of me. *Me!*

"Spread that juice all over me." I moved underneath her, grinding against her while pressing her hips further down. Raven sucked in air and closed her eyes.

"Ahh…"

"I'm never fucking washing these briefs again."

Raven rose up on her knees and gave me a seductive smile. "Wanna take them off?"

I was quick to comply and moaned out loud as she closed her hand around my cock when it sprang free. "Raven… I… I…" My eyes closed and I couldn't form a sentence.

"I'm not the only one who's wet. You are wet too." It sounded like a question, so I opened my eyes and explained.

"It's pre-cum."

"Hmm… does that mean you like it?"

177

The question was redundant, and I could tell she was feeling a little too powerful, so hooking my right arm around her waist I moved her down on her back on my couch and sat on my haunches in front of her. She was compliant when I placed her ankles on my shoulders. Yes, this was better and I was back in control.

Looking down, I let my cock slide between her thighs, touching her slick folds but not penetrating her. Raven was looking at me with expectation, but something was holding me back.

The strong urge to claim her as my woman was scary, even to me, so I held her ankles straight up in the air while pushing my cock back and forth on top of her pussy, telling myself that the feeling of her soft thighs surrounding my cock would be enough and that I didn't have to penetrate her. Instinctually, I knew that if I pushed inside her – if we merged like that – it would be over for me. I would be the hunter who didn't just shoot himself in the foot. I would blow off my whole leg, leaving me a cripple for life. There was no way I could just fuck Raven. Not with how I felt about her already.

"I want to feel you inside me." Raven was looking deep into my eyes. "I want you to be my first."

Another growl escaped me. The first implied there would be others.

Don't be an idiot. You have a goddess asking you to take her; what are you waiting for?

Pulling back, I watched Raven open her legs for me with an inviting smile.

I hesitated only a split second before I positioned my cock against her entrance and looked on in fascination as I pressed myself inside her. The sensation of her snug warm pussy stretching to accommodate me, and the sounds Raven was making, made me want to save this memory for life.

178

"Holy...." I pulled back a little only to push inside again, and slowly I found a steady rhythm.

Raven locked her feet around my waist and pulled me down on top of her. I took off some of my weight by leaning on my elbow and stared into her eyes. "You are so beautiful."

She just smiled back at me.

I poured all my gratitude into a deep kiss wishing I could make her feel how much I treasured her gift. "This is special to me, Raven."

She nodded and moved her hips faster. "How strong are you?"

I raised an eyebrow. "Is that a trick question?"

"Could you take me standing? I've wanted to do that since the time we fought."

Pulling out, I stood up on the living room floor and offered her a hand to pull her up. Raven was agile and got up fast, standing in front of me on the couch.

"Don't drop me."

I gave her a confident smile. "I won't."

"Okay." She linked her hands behind my neck and lifted one leg around my hip.

I grabbed her and pulled her onto me. "You could be an acrobat," I joked with her, hooking her to my body.

Raven wasn't heavy and with her strong core muscles, she held herself up. It wasn't until she slid down on top of me that I understood what a workout I was in for. My biceps flexed as I lifted her up and down. She helped and we found a rhythm.

"I want to try that sixty-nine position you talked about."

"You sure?"

"I'm sure."

Turning her upside down, I hooked my arms around her waist and let her thighs weigh down on my shoulders.

Like the time when we fought, my head was between her thighs, only this time there was no pain involved and there was no fabric between us.

The sensation of receiving and giving oral sex at the same time blew my mind. The sounds, the taste, and the delicious scent of her had me so horny that I was sweating and getting lightheaded from the amazing sex.

Making a quick decision, I carried her to my room and placed her on my bed. "I want you from behind."

Raven crawled up on all fours and looked back at me. "Don't come inside me."

"I won't." She was sleek and wet, and it was fucking fantastic to see my cock slide in and out of her while I held on to her delicious round ass. The smell of our mixed juices and the sound of Raven's moaning had me close my eyes for a second.

"Ohhh, Leo, don't stop."

I wasn't stopping. I would *never* stop. All I could think about was more, more, more, so I kept pumping in and out of her.

"That's it, right there, yes, Leo, yeeess."

I scrunched up my face trying to hold back my own orgasm to make it last, but Raven's panting and the way she arched her back was so sexy that I couldn't think straight.

"Leo, it's so good... faster."

What I needed to do was pull out and get myself under control. If I went faster, I would explode inside her, but Raven was my goddess and I couldn't deny her anything at that moment.

"Yes. That's it..." Raven leaned her head back and screamed out her orgasm.

I should pull out but the way her insides cramped around my cock like a soft hand jerking me off was the ultimate feeling in the world and even if my drone were on fire, I couldn't have moved away from her.

Pull the fuck out!

I was one split second from coming when I pulled out and looked on with large eyes as my semen sprayed over her back and buttocks. Her caramel-colored skin was glistening with our sweat and my sperm.

Raven lowered her head to the mattress but kept her ass in the air. Spreading her cheeks, I used my cock to smear my semen around, spreading it from her front entrance to her back entrance.

"What are you doing?" Her tone sounded a little nervous.

"Fulfilling a fantasy."

"What fantasy?"

"If you could see what I see. It's so fucking hot to watch my semen smeared from your pussy to your asshole."

"Did you come inside me?"

"No, I came on you."

Raven turned her head. "Leo, tell me the truth. Did you come inside me?"

"No. It was close, though."

"Geez, you scared me for a second."

"Let me get you some tissues to dry you off."

I enjoyed every second of cleaning her off and when I was done, she rolled to her side with a sated smile. I curled up behind her and pulled her closer to my body while intertwining our fingers.

"Leo, why are most of your tattoos on the inside of your arms? Most men have them on their shoulders."

"I'm not most men."

"I like the grizzly on your forearm."

"Yeah? It's from a hunt I did seven, no, eight years ago. That bear was the biggest motherfucker you can imagine."

"I don't like hunting."

181

"That's the Motlander side of you." I kissed her hair. "This bear killed two boys from a school up in Alaska. Three friends and I were up there on a fishing trip when it happened, and we immediately volunteered to track down the bear and kill it. Took us days, but eventually I got it."

Raven's fingers continued to slide around my arms. "I don't see any tattoos of deer or cougars."

"There's one of a wild boar on my back. It covers the scar I got when I was nine and the devil chased me and took a bite of me."

"A wild boar chased you?"

Leo chuckled. "Only because we were stupid boys who threw rocks at it to provoke it."

"Ahh, I think I'm on the wild boar's side then."

"Me too." I squeezed her tighter. "We were jerks and I learned my lesson. That's why I got a tattoo as a reminder. What about you? When did you get your tattoo?"

"The summer I turned eighteen. Do you like it?"

"Uh-huh. Who made it?"

"A tattoo artist in the Motherlands. I was going to have it done up here in the Northlands, but the tattoo artist I spoke to got so nervous from the thought of touching me in that place that his hands were shaking."

"Yeah, I can imagine." I let one of my fingers trail down her body to her hipbone where a nice thumb-sized P was tattooed.

"Why a P?"

"It stands for pioneer."

"Oh, I see. I thought it was short for pestilence."

"Ha-ha, very funny." She pinched the skin on my arm.

"Ouch." I retaliated by playfully biting her shoulder. "And why on your hipbone?"

"Because the hip is a place of movement. Pioneers move forward. Do you get it?"

182

"Yes, it makes sense – and talking about firsts, you're definitely the best lover I ever had."

She gave me a blinding smile. "Thank you. Knowing that sex is this amazing makes me feel a bit better about what Dina must have gone through after her marriage."

"Good." I stretched and yawned. "If Henry felt like I do right now, he would have made love to Dina morning, noon, and evening."

"You think?"

"I guarantee it. And you know what else he would be doing?" I averted my eyes when I said it.

"What?"

"He would have been coming inside her."

My heart beat fast waiting for her response. The fact that Raven was taking a chance with me knowing that she could get pregnant blew my mind. Yes, chances were slim, but it was possible, and she had to know that.

"You can't know that."

"Henry would be trying to impregnate Dina."

Raven groaned. "Yeah, well, we can skip that part."

"You sure?" I gave her my most charming grin and bit her earlobe. "Because I wouldn't mind coming inside you if you need to really feel what Dina felt."

"Are you crazy? I could get pregnant."

"So?"

She raised her eyebrows and spoke in a tone of disbelief. "Do you want everyone to find out what we've done?"

"Is that another trick question?"

"No, seriously, Leo. We said this would be our secret."

I spoke the truth, "*You* want it to be a secret. Not me."

Turning her body around, she stared at me. "Promise you won't tell anyone."

This was the part where the panther got up to run away again and there wasn't anything I could do about it. "Okay, on one condition."

"What?"

"You have to promise me that you won't sleep with anyone other than me."

Pushing herself up, Raven got out of bed and walked into the living room to get her clothes.

I followed. "Raven, promise me."

"I can't promise you that. A few years ago I would have sworn I'd never marry, but I might."

With my hands on her upper arms, I pulled her around to face me. "If you marry someone, it will be *me*."

Raven jerked out of my hold. "Don't make things awkward between us. We had a good time. Let's just leave it at that."

My face was drawn tight with suppressed emotions as I squeezed my fist and reminded myself, *you knew it might be a one-time thing only.*

Raven tried to ease the tension. "I would be okay with doing this again with you, but not if you make it weird."

Like her, I dressed, and when she walked to my front door, I didn't try to hold her back. "When, Raven?"

She turned. "When what?"

"When do you want to do this again?" I had my shoulders squared, eyebrows drawn close together, and my eyes on her collarbone. I was holding my breath.

Reaching up on her toes, Raven hugged me, and I responded by closing my arms around her.

"Stay with me tonight." My voice was low, but my tight squeeze screamed how badly I wanted it.

"Maybe I shouldn't. I think you're falling in love with me, Leo."

She was right, but I didn't deny or confirm it. "I want you to stay, Raven."

She sighed. "All right, but just for tonight."

As soon as the words left her lips, I picked her up and carried her back into my bed.

CHAPTER 18
Sparring with the Ruler

Raven

I had told Leo to keep our night together a secret. But the next day at work it felt like he was shouting to the whole station that we'd slept together. Four times he smiled at me across the room and each time colleagues frowned at the unexpected change in his behavior.

"You have to be grumpier," I whispered in a warning when I passed him in the hallway.

"Why?"

"Because they'll know something is different if you aren't your usual grumpy self."

Leo just grinned and walked away with a whistle. Later I saw him in a meeting with the top boss at Station Seven. The old captain looked like he was chronically annoyed, so I'd always stayed as far away from him as I could. Rumor had it that he was friends with the demon headmaster from the police academy who had made my life miserable for an entire year. That alone made me avoid him. I didn't need more powerful enemies in my life when I was already struggling with how to approach the most powerful man in the country.

It was Leo who had suggested that I find a way to interview Khan. Of course, he had said it this morning after we had woken up early to enjoy a fourth round of sex, and so we had both been lightheaded and full of endorphins when I agreed that it was a great idea.

Now it seemed like a dangerous plan. Not only was Khan the ruler of the country but he was an exceptionally sharp individual with a gift of getting people to tell him things that were secret. What if he didn't know that he wasn't Marcus' son and I accidentally told him?

I wanted information from Khan, but I didn't want to give him any information from the case yet.

The whole day, I thought about the best way to approach Khan and get him to squeeze me into his busy schedule. He was a good friend of my father and I'd known him since I was a child, but I needed more than a friendly conversation with him. When I made it back to the Gray Manor, I was determined to at least give it a try; and to pump myself up, I did fifty push-ups before I went to Khan's office that afternoon. My plan was quickly crushed when his assistant stopped me and informed me that the Ruler was in a meeting.

Changing my strategy, I got up extra early the next day and was in the dining room at ten to six when Pearl and Khan came in for breakfast.

"Good morning dear." Pearl kissed me on my forehead and Khan gave me a nod as he steered to the breakfast buffet and asked:

"What has you up so early?"

Already sitting at the dining table with a plate of food and a glass of juice in front of me, I smiled. "I'm waiting for Magni."

"Magni – why?" Khan reached for an apple and threw it from one hand to the other.

"One of the guys at the station told me my high kick needs work. I'm not sure if he was just messing with me, so I thought that I'd ask Magni if he has time to spar with me today. He's such a great fighter."

"Honey, didn't Magni leave already?" Pearl walked to stand next to Khan at the small buffet.

187

Khan nodded. "Yes, he's off to plan Mila's tournament. His first meeting was at six."

I knew that but let my face fall. "That sucks. Who has meetings at six in the morning?"

"People with busy calendars, Raven." Khan squared his chest. "But you know that Magni isn't the only great fighter here, right?"

It was hard not to smile since my whole strategy was based on Khan's vanity. With a shrug, I looked up at him. "Yes, but I haven't seen Solo around lately."

Khan went over to sit at the table with his cup of coffee and some fruit and bacon. "I was talking about me."

"Oh, I'm sorry. It's just that obviously, I would never disturb you about it. Not that I wouldn't love to spar with a fighter as experienced as you."

Pearl laughed and sat down with a plate of bread and fruit from the small buffet. "Flattery will get you far, Raven."

"Please! It's not flattery! Raven is just acknowledging that I'm a great fighter. What's wrong about that?"

"Nothing." Pearl looked amused.

Khan turned his attention back to me. "I was supposed to spar with Magni at seven but since he's not here, you can take his place and I can correct your high kick if needed."

I lit up. "Really?"

Khan nodded. "Meet me in the gym at seven, and you'd better fuel up because I won't go easy on you."

I almost jumped in my seat with glee and it made Khan and Pearl laugh.

The Gray Manor had a gym in the basement with a boxing ring. At seven I was ready and had all my questions lined up in my head. The hard part was knowing when to ask them. We sparred a few rounds with Khan correcting my kicks and teaching me a few new moves.

"Wow!" I burst out. "It's funny because I've seen Magni fight plenty of times, but not you. I'd heard you were good from my dad, but it's still surprising how fast and dangerous you are."

Khan loved the praise. "Ha, you should have seen me when I was your age." He jabbed in front of him.

"Speaking of that, I was wondering about something... that week when Dina got married did your dad act funny in any way?"

Khan lowered his hands. "There was nothing funny about my dad, Raven."

"No, I meant did you notice any strange behavior?"

"How would I remember that? It's so long ago and I was just a teenager."

"Okay." I shrugged like it was no big deal but in reality, I was disappointed and wanted to pressure him with more questions.

We circled each other and he made an attack that I blocked before asking, "What do you think happened to Dina? Do you think she killed herself?"

"Not a chance. Magni and I always knew that there was no way Dina would have fallen out of a window; she wasn't stupid or reckless, and it seemed weird that she was in an attic to begin with."

"Uh-huh."

"Magni thinks it was her husband who killed her, but I disagree."

My eyes widened. "Really?"

Khan narrowed his eyes. "There's something you need to understand about us Nmen, Raven. It's obvious that my father didn't think Henry killed Dina. If he thought so, my father would have executed him in public."

"So, how do you explain Henry dying so close to Dina? How can you know your father wasn't responsible for his death?"

"You misunderstand. I'm sure my dad was responsible for Henry's death, but there's a difference between having someone killed and killing them yourself. Henry died because of what he failed to do, not because of what he did."

I tilted my head. "You mean he failed to protect Dina."

"Yes." Khan raised an eyebrow. "Henry failed to protect my sister and for that alone, my father would have him killed."

"But if Henry didn't kill Dina, then who did?"

Khan stood still and lowered his hands as he told me, "I blame my dad for Dina's death. He might not have killed her with his bare hands, but I know he was being blackmailed, and I believe it was the blackmailers who killed Dina in an attempt to get my dad to comply with their demands."

"How do you know this?"

Khan huffed out air. "Some days before she died, I overheard a heated argument between my father and his best friend Zobel. It was unusual for them to fight. Mr. Zobel was one of the few who knew how to handle my father's violent temper, and they had been best friends since childhood. What was even more unusual was that Zobel was accusing my dad of being weak."

"Do you know why?"

"The details weren't clear to me, but Mr. Zobel wanted my dad to kill someone."

"Kill Dina?"

Khan shook his head and frowned. "No, of course not. It wasn't about her. Someone was trying to blackmail my father and Mr. Zobel wanted him to slam his fist down and kill the bastard right away." Khan scratched his shoulder. "If he hadn't been weak, Dina might still be alive."

"You think she was killed by the blackmailer?"

"Yes, who else? That's why I never go easy on threats. I think Dina became an innocent victim in a game of politics. Someone wanted power over my dad and when he didn't yield, they killed Dina to make him comply."

My eyes were wide open. This opened up a whole new level of potential villains in my case. "And do you think Marcus complied with their demands after that?"

"No way! If my father taught me anything it's that a ruler can never show weakness. I'm sure Dina's death was a harsh reminder to him and that he killed whoever was responsible." Khan shrugged and looked down. "I just wish he had done it sooner."

"Do you happen to know the identity of the blackmailer?"

"No."

"Do you think Mr. Zobel had anything to do with Dina's death?"

"He was very loyal to my father." Khan shifted his weight from one foot to the other. "It was Zobel who helped my dad to power and he was awarded for it many times over. There's no way he would have hurt Dina."

I cleared my throat.

"But isn't Mr. Zobel the man who was executed for treason years ago?"

"Yes."

"Didn't he conspire to have you killed?"

Khan narrowed his eyes. "That's different." He paused. "If Zobel was responsible, my dad would have killed him back then."

Remembering the unanswered calls from Khan that Dina had mentioned in the sound files I'd heard, I had to ask. "Did you talk to Dina after her wedding?"

"No."

"Did you call her?"

"No." Khan pulled off his gloves. "I'm sorry that I can't be of more help in the case, but I've always found a sense of peace in the fact that my father avenged Dina. I'm sure he crushed whoever did it."

"What makes you so sure?"

"There was a major shift in my dad after Dina died. I have no doubt that he regretted his weakness because he became twice as hard and ruthless as he'd been before her death. Sometimes when I think back to how cruel he could be, I try to remember that he was a man battling demons and that it would have haunted any father to know that it was his own weakness that caused his daughter's death."

"Did you ever ask Zobel if he knew who the blackmailer was?"

"Yes, but he didn't know. He said that my father just informed him that the matter was taken care of." Khan exhaled noisily. "But it's all history now, and I never felt the need to dig up that sad part of my life. As a ruler there are always urgent matters that need my attention."

"I get that." I stayed in the ring while Khan moved to the door. "Thank you for teaching me today."

Khan turned and gave me a smile. "You're a great fighter, Raven. Your father taught you well, and I'll make sure to tell Boulder when I see him later today."

It was rare for Khan to praise anyone. I could feel myself grow an inch and I was still smiling when the door closed behind him.

Khan had given me more information than he realized. From the sound clips I had of Dina, I already knew that she'd gone from begging Marcus to pay her husband to threatening him to reveal that Marcus and Khan weren't father and son. It had to be Dina who was the blackmailer that Marcus and Mr. Zobel had fought about. That would explain why Marcus refused to kill the person blackmailing him.

I bit my lower lip. *If only I knew if Mr. Zobel did it for him.*

As I sat down on the edge of the boxing ring, another thought popped into my head. "Why has Khan denied calling Dina that week? It was possible that he simply didn't remember calling her, but what if..." I gave a small gasp from the thought alone, and then I called up Leo and told him what I'd learned.

"What if Khan overheard more than he told me? What if Mr. Zobel and Marcus discussed the threats and Khan learned that he's not Marcus' son? Do you think it's possible that Khan might have killed Dina?"

"Geez, Raven. Khan was fourteen."

"Yes, and destined to take over for his father one day. It would have been a threat to his future. Don't you see? Maybe he tried to call Dina to ask her to keep silent or to figure out how to best get to her if he planned to kill her"

"Or maybe he tried to warn her, Raven. That's more likely isn't it? I mean, if he heard Mr. Zobel encouraging Lord Marcus to have his sister killed, wouldn't he try to warn her?"

I bit my lip. "He said he didn't know the identity of the blackmailer."

"Do you think he was lying to you?"

Closing my eyes, I rubbed the bridge of my nose and tried to remember how Khan had looked while telling me what he knew. "No, I don't know."

"Some people lie because they don't remember. They suppress what happened to them, and those lies are hard to spot because they feel real to the person who tells them."

"You think Khan suppressed something from back then?"

Leo sighed. "If he did it's going to be hard to find out. We can't exactly ask our ruler to do a session with a hypnotist to unlock memories."

"Right. No. I'm sure he wouldn't go for that. It's weird how he seems content and doesn't want to dig around to find out exactly what happened."

"You have to remember that this case is new to you but for Dina's family it's a scar that's more than thirty years old. They had to find peace with what happened somehow."

"Khan thinks Marcus avenged Dina, and that's all that matters to him."

"Maybe Marcus *did* avenge her."

I tapped my fingers on the edge of the boxing ring that I was still sitting on. "Yeah... or maybe Khan doesn't want to dig around because he knows that he was the one who killed her."

"Raven, for fuck's sake, don't say things like that while you're in the Gray Manor. What if someone hears you?"

"Sorry. You're right. We can talk about it at the station. I just need to shower, then I'm coming in."

"I told you, I'm meeting up with Magni and some of the Huntsmen at eight. It's a full-day thing so I won't see you at the station today."

My tone of voice carried my disappointment. "Oh, okay."

"But we could meet at my house tonight..."

"Tonight?" I straightened up.

"Yes, I want to talk more about this."

A smile grew on my lips. "Are you throwing out panther bait now?"

Leo laughed. "If that's what it takes to have another night with you."

I laughed back and gave a small playful purr. "See you tonight then."

194

As soon as I hung up, I called up Laura. "Quick question; didn't you tell me that your sister is friends with the granddaughter of Mr. Zobel?"

"That's right."

"I have a new lead in the investigation and it would be very helpful if we could get access to whatever personal items his family inherited from him. Maybe an old wristband or notebooks… do you think you can ask them about it?"

"Sure, but I doubt Annelise would have anything. Maybe her mother or her aunt. I can ask."

"And Laura, if they agree that I can take a look, would you join me as my wingman again?"

Laura chuckled. "Only if I can bring my numb-gun again!"

I grinned and jumped down from the boxing ring. "Deal. I'll be ready to leave in an hour."

CHAPTER 19
Magni's Concerns

Leo

"Mila's tournament is only a few months away and I have several concerns that we need to address." Magni stood in a strong stance with his arms crossed as he spoke to my captain, me, and four Huntsmen from his elite soldier unit.

"This tournament will be bigger than any in the history of the Northlands."

"Are you sure about that?" my captain asked and looked down at the stats on his wristband. "We have thirteen hundred men signed up so far and that's about the same as for the previous four tournaments."

Magni gave the captain a dirty look. "This is my daughter. Of course, there will be record numbers."

"No one is questioning how desirable Mila is. It's just that with the Couples Matching Program, Nmen have alternatives now. It takes a lot to raise the money to participate and they don't want to risk their lives when the odds of winning are so small."

Magni looked like he was about to explode and spoke through gritted teeth. "Mila is worth dying for."

The four huntsmen and I all nodded with serious faces.

"Any man who isn't willing to risk his life and fortune to be with my daughter should stay the fuck away."

"Agreed." The captain nodded. "I'm just trying to be realistic here. I have no doubt that the entire population of single men in this country dream of marrying Mila, but the fact that she's your daughter might scare away some."

"What's that supposed to mean?"

Every one of us exchanged looks. We knew exactly what the captain meant.

"What are you implying?" Magni stepped closer to the captain.

"That every husband upsets his wife at some point. Having the greatest warrior in the world as a father-in-law complicates things."

Magni leaned back and placed his hands on his hips. "Huh." His eyes shifted to me. "You wouldn't let that stop you, would you, Leo?"

I frowned and averted my eyes. "No, Commander, that wouldn't stop me."

"Good." He turned to the four Huntsmen. "Are all you men signed up for the tournament?"

They confirmed it, and Magni nodded with satisfaction before continuing going over his concerns. We discussed entry points, medic stations, guards for Mila, number of fight arenas, positions of beer tents, distribution of police officers and Huntsmen, as well as the logistics of getting spectators to and from the area.

By the time we had been talking and planning for almost four hours, we were drenched from the heavy rain, which Magni ignored. There was thunder and lightning rolling in, and a collective sigh of relief sounded among us men when Magni finally called a lunch break.

Fifteen minutes later he and I were standing by the bar in a local pub when he leaned in. "I would like to see you win the tournament, Leo."

"Thank you, Commander." It was hard to meet his eyes knowing that I couldn't fight for Mila after what had happened between me and Raven.

"What's wrong?"

"Nothing, it's just that…"

"What?" Magni narrowed his eyes. "Speak up, man."

197

I was struggling with what to tell him. After all, Raven had asked that I keep our relationship a secret, so I chose to focus on something else. "I was just wondering why you don't have Mila's tournament in the summertime. It's unusual to have it in the winter and I wonder if more spectators and participants would show up in summer. That's all."

"Fair question. I guess the answer is that I'm an impatient man." Magni was distracted by an incoming call. "Hang on."

The pub wasn't crowded, and his voice was loud, so it was impossible not to overhear him.

"She did what? No, you did the right thing in calling me. Let me talk to Mila." Magni moved away from the bar, but with the small room it made no difference and I could still hear him clearly.

"Mila, why were you trying to leave without protection? What were you thinking?"

I couldn't hear Mila's explanation but from the way Magni's back stiffened and he growled low, I sensed that he wasn't happy.

"Get the exact address, and you can call Raven and tell her I'll spank her ass when I see her – and the same goes for Laura."

At the sound of Raven's name, I was on alert. "What's going on?"

"Apparently Raven and Laura went to visit Mr. Zobel's daughter together and they didn't bring an escort." He groaned. "Because their drone was making funny sounds, they had to go down in Mortenstown and they called and asked Mila to pick them up."

"Mortenstown. That's a shithole. Why didn't they call one of us?"

"Because they know we would be furious at them for flying out without protection in the first place."

198

I remembered Raven telling me that she and Laura had gone to visit Michael together, but I had always assumed that they had brought guards with them.

"At least they are both good fighters. Of all the women in this country, Raven and Laura know how to take care of themselves."

Magni scowled at me. "They are women, Leo."

"I know, but they aren't helpless."

Magni stabbed a finger against my chest. "They are our responsibility, and no woman should be alone in fucking Mortenstown. I'm going to go get them." Pointing across the room, Magni called out to the captain and the four Huntsmen. "Laura needs me. We'll do this another day."

Grabbing my leather coat, I was right on his heels. "I'm coming with you."

When Magni ignored me, I added, "I'm Raven's mentor, so I'm going."

The rain was still coming down in buckets and thunder was putting a soundtrack to the way Magni and I ran to the drones with serious faces.

"We'll take the Doom's Bird and leave the Angel Maker to the others."

The Doom's Bird was a heavy military drone; I knew my police drone would have been faster. Problem was that I'd left it behind at the open field where we had met this morning and where we were supposed to return to after lunch.

"Laura should know better than this," Magni muttered as we got in, and he quickly got the drone in the air.

It was my first time inside a Doom's Bird. It only had room for four and was an old but powerful and lethal weapon with large guns and the capacity to have rockets attached. I kept looking around taking in all the electronics while Magni muttered: "It's a shame this bird isn't loaded with rockets, 'cause I'm telling you: if anyone touched Laura or Raven, I would gladly fire a rocket up their asses."

"I hear you!"

"I guarantee you that it was Raven that got Laura to go. She's always been fearless and won't stop pushing boundaries." Magni snorted. "Khan should have never allowed her to join the police. Now she thinks she is untouchable. I've told Boulder countless times that he needs to talk some sense into her before she gets in over her head. She might be a great fighter, but she and Laura won't stand a chance if a group of men gang up on them."

My face hardened just from thinking about the cases I'd seen in Mortenstown, which was one of the shittiest places in our district. "Can't this machine go any faster?"

Magni gave me a sideways glance. "You'd better hold on tight."

I was strapped in but felt the force of gravitation push me back in my seat when he took the drone straight up in the air. We needed to go high to get to maximum speed, and I would take whatever Magni could push out of this old war machine.

With a desperate need to hear that Raven was fine, I called her up and with every unanswered ring, I grew more nervous. "Raven isn't picking up. Can you call Laura?"

"I already did, twice. She's not picking up either."

The heavy rain and rumbling of thunder made it impossible for me to hear the string of curse words that followed from Magni.

I looked to the right, seeing flashes of lightning illuminate the dark gray sky in the distance. "How old is this machine?"

"At least twenty years. Military budgets are low in times of peace."

"Maybe you should go around the storm."

Magni's laugh sounded hollow. "Not when my woman is in danger."

I kept calling Raven and was cursing for every time I got no answer.

"Why hasn't Mila sent us the location like I told her to?" Magni called up his daughter and sounded grumpy when he asked, "Where's the location?"

"Don't get angry, Dad, but I spoke to Mom and she said that she preferred if someone else picked them up. Someone calm."

"Calm. Are you fucking kidding me? Is that why she and Raven aren't picking up when we call them?"

"Probably."

Magni growled. "Laura's ass is going to be so red."

"Dad!"

"I'm sorry, honey, but you're a grown woman now. You need to know what a husband does to a wife who pulls idiotic stunts like this."

"And you wonder why Mom doesn't want to be rescued by you. Just give her a hug and tell her you're happy she's unharmed."

"Yeah, well, I'll do that after I spank her. And Mila, call Raven and tell her that if I don't have her exact location within two minutes, she's no longer a police recruit."

"That's not fair."

"Mila, it's not up for discussion. Mortenstown is a fucking dangerous place and we need to get your mom and Raven out of there, right now."

"Okay, I've got the coordinates here." After telling us, Mila promised to call Laura and Raven and tell them to pick up their phones or call us.

"Thirteen minutes to destination," Magni muttered.

When Mila called back three minutes later, we could both hear the fear in her voice. "Dad, I'm scared. Mom isn't

201

picking up and neither is Raven. I've called them both over and over. I have a really bad feeling."

Magni's face paled. "Yeah, me too, baby. Leo and I are flying as fast as we can."

Without consulting Magni, I called up the Mortenstown police force and asked them to send both police and medics to the coordinates we had been given by Mila. I made sure to inform them that two women were in danger, knowing that it would make this case a high priority.

"Seven minutes." Magni hissed through gritted teeth just as lightning lit up all around us and the drone shook.

"Did you feel that?"

"It was a lightning strike. We're fine."

The storm was intensifying, and my fingers squeezed around the armrests as the wind created turbulence inside the drone.

"Six minutes... call Raven again."

I shouted because of the loud crashes of thunder. "That's all I'm doing. She's not picking up."

"Keep calling her. I'm keeping my line open if Mila calls back."

The minutes ticked by slowly and finally, when the display said two minutes to destination, I saw something. "Down there. Do you see the flashing light?"

"Where?"

"Right there." I pointed again. "It must be the police drone and medics."

The drone shook as another lightning stroke hit us, and this time a loud beeping sound filled the drone with an alert.

"Fuuuck!" Magni was pushing buttons like a madman.

"What the hell are you doing?" I screamed over the robotic voice alerting us.

Magni growled. "Something's wrong."

202

"I can hear that, but what is it?"

A robotic voice overpowered what Magni was saying. "System failure. Landing initiated. Prepare for impact. System failure. Landing initiated. Prepare for impact."

As the blinking lights on the ground came closer, I pressed myself back in the seat trying to see through the rain that was crashing against our windshield.

"Fuck, fuck, fuck," Magni hissed. "We're gonna crash."

"Ejection recommended." The robotic voice sounded as calm and matter-of-fact as if it was reminding us to use seatbelts.

I was looking left and right to find the eject button, seeing the ground come closer, and then I found it on my left side.

"Eject, Leo. Now!" Magni was pulling at his handle but nothing happened. "Shiiit!"

With my hand on my own handle, I screamed at him. "Pull it, Magni."

"It's fucking stuck."

I lifted my hand to try and help him but with a quick side glance, Magni locked eyes with me, and then he pulled my handle.

It felt like my body was torn in half from the force of the ejection. Rain hammered on my face and I was screaming my lungs out as I watched the Doom's Bird fall toward the ground with Magni still inside it. "No, Magni, nooo!!!"

CHAPTER 20
Mortenstown

Raven

"It's never made that sound before. I don't get it; this drone isn't even a year old." I looked over at Laura, who was sitting next to me. "If only Tristan were here, I'll bet he could fix it."

Laura was wearing tight black leather pants and when she crossed her long legs the leather rubbing against leather made a squeaky sound. "He's not, and even if he were, Tristan would still need the right equipment. Try to shut the drone down and see if it still makes that clacking sound."

I did as she asked but the moment I pressed power, the clacking began again. "I'm not getting any alerts. Maybe we should just try to fly home."

"No, Raven. Something is not right, and I'm not flying in a defective drone."

"We could call my father."

"Yes, we could, but he would tell Magni, and I already had an argument with him last week about going out without guards. You know how protective Magni is."

"I could call Leo... except he's with Magni, I think."

Laura pulled at her lips with a speculative glance. "How far are we from the Gray Manor?"

"About half an hour."

"We need someone to pick us up that won't tell Magni about it."

"What about Mila?" I looked out at the heavy rain. "She's not the best at keeping secrets, but unless she's asked directly, I don't think she would tell anyone."

"I don't want Mila going out without guards. She's not a warrior like you and me."

"But you could argue that it's not really going out since she won't be in public anywhere."

Laura sighed and after a moment of hesitation, she called up Mila.

"Honey, Raven and I need a favor."

"I'm always happy to help."

"I know you are, dear. Listen, all we need you to do to is program a drone with our location and send it to us. Can you do that?"

"Where are you?"

"We went to interview someone. We'll tell you about it later, so send us a drone, will you?" Laura repeated.

"Of course, but I'm coming to pick you up."

Laura shook her head. "No, darling. There's no need for you to come, I'd rather you stayed back at the Manor. We're in the middle of nowhere and really just need a drone to pick us up."

Mila was being licked on her face by that small dog of hers. "Are you kidding me, Mom? I never get to do anything heroic. This is my first rescue mission and I'm excited."

I laughed at the sight of Mila's wide smile of self-satisfaction. "You want to be our knight in shining armor?"

"I would love to. Mom, it's not like I'm going to leave the drone. I'll just fly to you and open the door for you to get in. What could go wrong?"

Laura lifted her hands. "The same thing that happened to us could happen to you. The drone could break down and leave you stranded somewhere."

"Don't be so negative, Mom. You're being as controlling as Dad, and you know how you hate it when he limits you."

"Okay, honey, I guess there's no harm in it if you stay inside the drone. Just come quickly, okay? We want to get back before your dad gets home."

Mila gave a small shriek of excitement and then she was gone.

"Did you say we're in Mortenstown?" I leaned forward trying to see out of the wet windows.

"That's what the map says." Laura pointed to the display.

"I see a barn and a dirt road. This can't be the city center. It looks more like a farm from the olden days."

Laura didn't seem interested in what was outside the drone. "Maybe we're on the outskirts of Mortenstown, or maybe this whole place is rural countryside. I've never stopped in this town and I don't think we should get out."

"Because of the rain."

"Yes. And because we don't know this area. Let's just stay here and wait for Mila."

We talked about my job at the police station and my dreams of becoming the first woman to join the force as a real cop. After ten minutes Mila called us back.

"Hey, honey, how far are you?"

Mila's tone was sad. "I'm still at the Manor. One of the guards saw me in the drone and he stopped me from going."

Laura and I exchanged a glance and sighed.

"Security called Dad and he's coming to get you."

Leaning her head back, Laura closed her eyes and ran her hands through her hair. "Oh fuck. I can't deal with Magni's temper right now."

"I'm sorry, Mom. He sounded pretty mad that you and Raven went out without an escort."

"Yeah, well, your father is a control freak and he forgets that we can protect ourselves."

"That's a good thing because he told me to warn you that he will be spanking you both."

My eyebrows shot up high and my index finger flew to my chest as I gave Laura a questioning look. "Me too?"

She shook her head. "Of course not."

"But will he spank you? For real?"

She gave me an amused smile. "If I allow it." Looking down at her wristband, which was vibrating a little, she gave a heavy exhalation. "Ah, if it isn't my angry husband."

"You're not going to answer?" I asked as I saw her dismiss the call.

"Trust me. With Magni it's better to give him time to calm down. He'll be yelling at me the minute he gets here and I can't control that, but I'm not stupid enough to accept the call and have him yell at me for twenty minutes while he flies here."

My wristband showed an incoming call from Leo. "He's with Magni."

"Then don't answer."

"But he's my boss."

Laura lowered her brow. "If he's next to Magni then don't answer. I guarantee Magni is in a fit and he's like a small child when he's angry."

I felt awful for not answering. "Maybe I could at least text him that we're okay."

"Do what you want, but it's easier if we tell a white lie and pretend that we didn't know they were trying to call us. If you text, they'll know we ignored them on purpose."

"Come on, Laura. What excuse would we have to not see them calling?"

She threw her hands up. "I don't know. Maybe we went outside to investigate the noise from the drone. With this rain it would make sense to leave our wristbands inside."

I raised my wrist. "Mine is waterproof."

"Yeah, but maybe you forgot that detail." Laura shrugged. "Remember that time when Magni knocked out Solomon and threatened to kill Marco?"

"Yeah. I mean, I was a kid but I remember." I felt awful when I silenced my wristband, which kept buzzing with Leo's calls.

"Well, Magni has gotten a little calmer with age, but the emphasis would be on *little*."

The sound of three loud shots had Laura jumping in her seat and me clinging to my armrest.

"What the fuck was that?" She stared at me with wide eyes.

"I don't know, but we've got to get the hell out of here." I was pushing the button to make the drone start up again and this time I didn't care about the clacking sound it made.

Laura screamed when a man stepped in front of the drone and pointed a large firearm directly at the window. He was drenched and with the heavy rain on the windows, his features looked distorted. "Raven, tell me this drone is bulletproof."

"It's not." I couldn't take off and risk him shooting us.

A sound of someone trying to open the door on my side made me jerk and turn my face to see a bald man stare at me and slowly let the tip of what looked like a large bear gun slide up the window until it was pointing straight at my face. "Open," he mouthed and tapped at the locked door.

"I have a man on my side too." Laura's voice was low and shaky. "I see three men, Raven. Two of them have Bear Guns and the last has a Gut Cleaner. My numb-gun is no match."

208

"I only brought a knife and my smallest gun." My eyes were still on the man staring at me through the window in the door. Again, he tapped his gun on the window and this time he was shouting loud enough for us to hear. "Open the fucking door."

"This one looks out of shape. I think I can take him."

Laura whispered back, "Raven, no. What if they shoot?"

She was right. Laura and I were great fighters, but so were most Nmen and we were outnumbered. I swallowed hard. "Maybe they just want the drone."

"Yeah, there's no way they would dare touch us." Laura's voice didn't have her normal ring of certainty to it. "Our best chance is talking with them."

Laura opened the door slowly and when the man waved his gun signaling for us to come out, I climbed out on her side thinking we were safer if we stuck close together.

"Where are your protectors?" The man who had been in front of the drone had bushy eyebrows and a blond beard.

"They are on their way." I looked the man straight in the eye when I told him.

He narrowed his eyes and spat on the ground. "I can recognize a lie when I hear one."

"There's a problem with the drone so we're being picked up by our husbands." Laura swiped rain from her face while I stuffed my hands in my back pockets to look relaxed and hide that I wasn't wearing a wedding band.

"What kind of husbands let their wives fly around without protection?" Mr. Bushy Eyebrows waved his bear gun, signaling for us to step away from the drone.

I was quick to answer, "I'm sure you've heard of Leo da Vinci, who's a police inspector, and if not, you'll know Laura's husband, Magni Aurelius."

They all stared at her for a second before the bald man smirked. "Nice try, but I've seen the Commander's wife on the news and that's not her."

"I assure you that I'm Laura Aurelius."

"No, you're not," the man scoffed. "Laura is much shorter than you and she..." The bald man looked to the others for help. "It's not her, right?"

"Na-huh. The commander's wife has red hair, hers is brown."

"That's because of the rain, you moron, and I only look short next to Magni because he's so bloody big."

The third man was irritated and spoke with a nasal voice like he had a cold. "They think we're imbeciles. As if the Commander would ever let his wife fly around without an escort." He snorted and pointed to the large barn. "Let's take them back to the farm and then we'll decide what to do with them."

Ignoring the rain dripping from my eyebrows, I raised my chin and squared my shoulders. "We're not going anywhere. Leave us alone."

The three men smirked and moved closer as Mr. Bushy Eyebrows looked me up and down and licked his lips. "If their protectors are reckless enough to leave them alone then they can't want them very much, can they?"

I stepped back when he came too close.

His smirk grew. "Don't be scared. Clearly, you need better protectors who would appreciate you. Sounds like you ladies got unlucky in the Couples Matching Program."

A loud crack of thunder swallowed Laura's first words, but she was stabbing her hand through the rain. "Do I sound like a Motlander to you? I was born and raised here."

Ignoring her, the bald man held his gun over his shoulder and turned to his two friends. "I say we take them home."

Laura and I moved closer.

"I agree. If other men are stupid enough to leave their homes unlocked, we shouldn't be blamed for walking right in. It's like an invitation, really." The one with the nasal voice waved his gun, signaling for us to start walking.

"We're women, not houses!" I hissed in frustration just as the man with the nasal voice hooked his fingers around my arm. The pain from his nails boring into my wrist as he jerked me toward him, and the shock of being touched without my permission, had me reacting by instinct. Spinning around to get out of his grip, I stamped on his toe and planted an elbow against his jaw before I tried to jerk his gun from him. It didn't work and with a sharp push, the man shoved me to the muddy ground.

Looking up I saw Laura was being held back by Mr. Bushy Eyebrows, who had his bear gun in one hand and an arm around Laura's neck. Her eyes were full of rage and she was panting from what I assumed had been an attempt to help me.

Seeing her manhandled like that made me snap. In a fast attack on the man who had pushed me down, I made his leg disappear underneath him and with a roar of surprise, he fell on his back. Laura had spun out of the grip of the blond guy holding her and this time we had both secured the two men's weapons. Years of training had paid off and we were now standing back to back pointing the guns at the men.

With a growl of humiliation, the man on the ground lifted his hand from a puddle of water and shook it before he got up to attack me again. This time I was ready and sent him back to the wet ground with a hard kick to his chest. "Stay the fuck down." I was pointing his own gun at him while Laura faced the other two men. "Don't make the mistake of thinking we're defenseless."

211

"What fuckery is this?" The bald man, who was still armed, fired a shot above our heads and Laura screamed at him to put his weapon down.

"They're just women," the bald man yelled at his friends. "What is wrong with you?"

Mr. Bushy Eyebrows growled and scowled at Laura, who had his gun. "She took me by surprise, that's all."

The bald man was swinging his aim from me to Laura and back again. "Who the fuck taught you women to fight like that? It's unnatural."

"I'm training to be a police officer," I replied and kept the weapon in my hands aimed at the man on the ground. "Maybe I look different in real life too, but don't tell me you haven't heard about a woman police officer in training?"

Holding his gun in front of him, the bald man stepped between me and his friend on the ground and hissed, "Get up, Jake."

The man with the nasal voice looked humiliated and angry when he pushed up from the ground just as the bald man answered my question.

"I've heard they let a woman into the academy, but I thought it was a joke."

"Nope, it's the real thing so please, if you feel the need to attack a woman – go ahead. It'll give me someone to practice on."

"Stop provoking them, Raven."

The bald man growled low. "I'm not fighting with a woman."

"You sure? Because we just learned how to break necks and I'm sure no one will miss any of you."

"That's enough, Raven." Laura gave me a reproachful glance and faced the men. "You know what pisses me off about this situation? This past week I had a fight with Magni about going out without a guard. I told him to have

212

trust in our fellow countrymen and that I believed ninety-eight percent of you would be protective of any woman you met. He said I was being naïve."

The three men just stared at her as another burst of thunder rumbled.

"I'm tired of women having to rely on guards to get around in the Northlands. Every Nman has it in him to be a protector of women, and I don't want my daughters growing up to be wary of men the way I did. So, what kind of men are you? Do you have a sense of honor and integrity or are you really cowards who attack women?"

"I've got honor and integrity," my attacker defended himself.

"Shut up, Jake." The bald man took a step closer to Laura and lowered his voice a little. "Of course we would protect you. That's why we're offering to get you out of this storm and into our home."

Laura's eyes fell to the gun he was still pointing at her before she tilted her head and gave him an are-you-serious look.

The bald man got the message because he muttered, "Fine. I'll put mine away if you and Miss Curly over there lower your guns as well."

I didn't move. "How about you three just go home and leave us alone? I like that idea better."

"Don't let them leave with my Gut Cleanser, Vic. It was your stupid idea to steal their drone," Jake with the nasal voice protested just as a loud blast from a siren made us turn to look toward the village. A police drone was flying toward us.

"Well, fuck me sideways, it's the police, Vic. You better take the blame for this mess. Me and Jake were just following your orders." Mr. Bushy Eyebrows looked nervous.

Vic raised a hand to rub his bald head in frustration and sputtered, "I didn't order you to be idiots and attack two women. I'm not taking the blame for any of this shit. All we did was offer to help the women out of the rain."

"Put down your weapons and place your hands in the air." The large guns on the side of the police drone were pointing straight at us. Vic, Laura, and I were quick to comply and put down the weapons we'd been holding and raise our hands in the air.

Another drone appeared at high speed and from the cross on the bottom, I could tell it was an ambulance.

"How did you call for them?" Mr. Bushy Eyebrows sneered at me.

"I didn't."

"Of course she did." Jake with the nasal voice scoffed. "Only a Motlander with a brain implant could have called them while talking to us."

"Brain implants are illegal," Vic pointed out.

"Not in the Motherlands, you dumbass."

We watched as a police robot was lowered while the drone kept hovering above us shining a strong light on all five of us. The robot walked over and used a firm voice. "Are you two Laura Aurelius and Raven Pierson Boulder?"

"Yes, we are," Laura answered while I raised my chin giving the three men a told-you-so look.

Vic and Jake exchanged a glance with Mr. Bushy Eyebrows, who shook his head with defeat.

"Inspector da Vinci dispatched us to make sure you are safe until he arrives. Does anyone need medical assistance?"

I looked at Jake, whom I had knocked down earlier. "Do you?"

He snorted offended. "Fuck no. I can handle a girl. It didn't even hurt. I was just off balance."

That made me want to kick him again and harder this time.

A huge stroke of lightning flashed across the sky and almost blinded us.

The only one unaffected was the police robot, who continued, "Have these men caused you women any trouble?"

Laura turned her head and whispered to me. "They deserve to eat shit, but if Magni finds out what happened he'll double down on my security."

I gave all three men a sharp glance before I addressed the robot. "No, officer. We had a firm conversation with them and solved the disagreements we had."

"In that case we'll dispatch the ambulance."

I looked up to see the medics' drone and that's when my eyes caught something in the sky.

"What is that… Laura, look." My hand pointed up.

Laura leaned her head back and used her hand to shield her eyes from the rain. "It looks like a falling drone." As soon as she said it her hand grabbed for my arm and she gave a small scream of panic.

Her strong reaction made them all turn to look up and see the drone falling from the sky.

"Fuuuckk…" Jake elbowed Vic. "That guy is going to crash."

"Laura, it's not them." We knew Magni and Leo were on their way, but surely it couldn't be them.

A deep whistle came from Vic, followed by a long "Whooaaw. What's that above the drone? Is that the pilot? Do you see it?"

"I see it, he must have ejected from the drone," Mr. Bushy Eyebrows commented while both Laura and I stood with our faces painted in fear.

"Officer, do you see two pilots?" My question came out as a breathless cry while my eyes searched the sky. The robot would have the ability to zoom in.

"No, just one," the robot answered in a calm voice.

"Laura, it's not Magni and Leo then. They would have both ejected from the drone. This drone only had one pilot. It's someone else."

Laura stood pale, quiet, and with her fear-stricken face turned to the rain. Her eyes were narrowed into slivers as she followed the descent of the drone.

"It's not them, Laura. It's not!" My heart was racing and I stared as another lightning stroke lit up the gray sky displaying the two objects in the air like it was a dramatic art installation. Only this was real life, and right in front of our eyes, a drone was falling out of the sky at high speed while a smaller object was descending with the pilot.

Vic cursed. "It's gonna crash on our barn." He began running as if he could prevent the large drone from destroying his property.

We were too far away to see the face of the pilot and I didn't recognize the drone.

"It's not Magni's drone, and Leo would fly a police drone. It's not them, Laura!" I kept saying it because I needed to believe it myself.

"The drone is a Tyrant model 760851A. It's also referred to as a Doom's Bird and used by the military. I have alerted the medics to stay ready for potential casualties." The calm tone of the police-bot made me want to scream at it.

Magni flew military drones often and when I opened my mouth to tell Laura it wasn't him, my throat was dry and I couldn't speak.

We stood as powerless spectators watching the pending disaster. I didn't breathe. I didn't blink. I just folded my hands into fists and wished that I had super powers so I could slow down the deadly speed of the drone. The collision with the ground was inevitable, and Vic had been right. The drone crashed partly on the barn, which was around eighty yards from us, causing parts to fly in all directions. A large metal piece landed only ten feet from me and Laura.

"Stay back," the police-bot told us, but both Laura and I were already on the run.

The ambulance and police drone made it to the crash site in seconds and when we got there, two human police officers were helping a team of two medics tear at the door to the drone.

"Is someone inside?" I yelled while Laura ran straight in to help as well.

"We don't know yet. You'd better stay back."

From the sight of the drone it was clear to see that if someone was inside, there was no chance they would have survived. Protective airbags had exploded in every part of the cabin of the drone, but the front of the machine had curled up and was so bent out of shape that it was hard to see how it had originally looked.

"I see a man," one of the police officers yelled out, loud. "Help me remove the door."

Jake and Mr. Bushy Eyebrows caught up to the rest of us and all hurried over to help.

Laura was pulling with tears running down her cheeks, and with the combined strength of six men and two women, the broken door came off. The heart-wrenching scream that followed from Laura echoed inside me.

"Magni, I'm here. Magni talk to me!!!"

I ran forward to hold Laura back. "Let the medics help him." Even as I said it, I knew I was asking for too much. Laura was strong, and only when the police-bot helped me did we manage to move her out of the way and give room for the medics to work.

"I've got her," I told the bot and with a nod it returned to assist the medics.

Laura and I clung to each other as we watched them pull out a donor unit to pump blood into Magni. We heard them count, one, two, three, before the two medics and the strong police-bot pulled Magni's body from the drone.

His head was dangling and his large body was limp, and then the shock hit me. He was missing both legs and half of his left arm. I couldn't hold Laura up as she fell to her knees and screamed her pain out. "Noooo…"

The medics got him on a stretcher on the ground and we watched them work on him. One was applying blood blocker gel while the other did CPR.

"Let's get him into the drone," one of them shouted and in less than a minute they were airborne and flying away from us.

"He's not dead, Laura. They wouldn't be working on him if he was dead."

Laura turned her wet and grief-stricken face to me. "Medics don't do CPR on people who are breathing. I've lost him, Raven. I've lost him."

"The other pilot is landing," Jake announced and the three of them ran to help the survivor, who had to be Leo. I wanted to go with them and make sure Leo was alive, but Laura was in a full-blown panic attack, hyperventilating, crying, and clinging to my hand as I whispered for her to breathe through her nose. I was holding her, hugging her tight, while my eyes searched for Leo.

When he came over, he fell to his knees next to us, planting his hand on my shoulder. "Magni?" It was a question and I gasped for air through my own tears to shake my head.

Leo shrunk back on his haunches and covered his face with his hands.

"The medics took Magni with them but he wasn't breathing and he…" I couldn't say it and heaved in air. "He lost…"

Leo's eyes were large as he stared at me.

I couldn't say it in front of Laura, so I leaned against Leo and whispered it in his ears. "Both his legs and one of his arms were detached from his body."

Leo turned his head and frowned at me like he didn't understand what I was saying.

"Inspector da Vinci, a second ambulance just arrived. You need to go to the hospital?"

Leo and I looked up and saw the police robot talking to him.

"No, I'm fine."

"You're not fine. You're injured and need medical assistance."

Only then did I look at Leo and noticed that he had the facial color of a vampire and that he was all bruised, with blood on his pants and shirt.

"We're all going." I pulled Laura up on her feet. "We need to follow Magni, and Leo needs to get checked over."

"I'm fine," Leo repeated and refused when the medics offered to put him on a stretcher. Instead he limped badly toward the ambulance when suddenly he stopped and groaned with pain.

"Are you okay?"

"Yeah, it's just…" Leo's face turned into a grimace of pain.

I had just called out to the medic, who was only one step ahead when Leo's eyes rolled back in his head and he collapsed on the ground.

"What's wrong with him?" I cried as the two men took over.

"We don't know. Could be internal bleeding," one of them answered as they got him strapped on a stretcher.

This time, Laura and I followed inside the ambulance and sat holding each other's hands.

"It's going to be all right," I whispered and squeezed her fingers.

Laura sniffled and looked down. "No, Raven. Without Magni nothing will ever be right again. At least not to me."

CHAPTER 21
In the Hospital

Raven

The hospital quickly filled with Magni's loved ones. Khan and my dad, Boulder, were pacing the waiting area with Solo. My mom, Christina, was trying to comfort Erika, who was sobbing. Mila and her younger siblings sat with their mother, Laura, who refused to eat or drink.

It had been three hours since the accident and Magni's life was hanging on a thin thread. While we knew that Leo was sleeping after undergoing surgery for internal bleeding, it had been more than two hours since any information left the operating room where doctors were working on saving Magni's life. Once again, we were left powerless, just waiting to hear if he would make it.

Willow had her arm around me and our heads leaned against each other.

"It's my fault."

"Why would you say that?" Willow stroked my arm.

"Because it was my idea to go and investigate. Magni and Leo weren't supposed to be in that place at that time. They came to rescue Laura and me. If only we had stayed home the men wouldn't have had to come. If Magni dies, I'll be the one who killed him."

Willow took my hand and wove our fingers together. "That's just survivor's guilt. You can't blame yourself. You didn't even ask them to come, did you?"

"No. But that doesn't matter."

Willow spoke in a low tone. "It's natural to feel that way, Raven. I'll bet your dad is blaming himself that his

221

drone broke down and Laura blames herself for going. But those thoughts will drive you insane. None of you are to blame. Do you hear me?"

My dad looked over. "Finn and Athena will be here any minute."

A doctor's assistant came into the waiting room and everyone looked up as he spoke. "Leo da Vinci is awake now. You can go and see him but only one or two at a time."

I got up from my chair, but Zasquash, who had been waiting in a corner, jumped up to follow the doctor's assistant with Solo. It made sense since the two of them were close friends of Leo, but I was disappointed because I needed to see him and apologize for causing all of this misery.

Twenty minutes later, Zasquash and Solo returned.

"Any news?" Solo asked.

"No." Khan sighed. "How is Leo?"

"He'll survive. He worries about Magni like the rest of us." Solo walked toward Willow and when he reached for her, I gave him my seat.

"I'll go say hi to Leo."

"All right." Solo gave me a nod. "He'll like that."

Leo was in a hospital room by himself. His dark hair wasn't in a bun for once but lay against the white pillow.

"Hey." His eyes followed me as I walked from the door to sit at the side of his bed.

"Hey. How are you feeling?"

"Like shit." Leo moved and groaned from the pain.

"What happened to you? Did you have internal bleeding?"

"No, I don't know." He raised a hand to his head in a slow movement. "The doctor was here, but I'm a bit groggy."

"You passed out."

"When?"

"After you landed."

"Could be. My leg is wrapped up and I think the doctor mentioned something about broken vessels, internal bleeding, and blood loss." Leo lifted a finger and pointed to a screen next to his bed.

I leaned forward and read aloud, "'Patient was ejected from military drone without helmet or safety suit on. He suffered a concussion and fractured his thigh bone, which resulted in internal bleeding. Symptoms were ecchymosis, swelling, tightness, and pain in leg. Operation was successful and estimated recovery with bone accelerator is two to four weeks.'

"Wow, so you broke the bone when you were ejected from the drone?"

"Yes. But the doctor did say that I'll walk again. I remember that much."

"Did they give you something to ease the pain?"

"Yeah." Leo's hand fell down to lie on top of the mattress and he gave me a tired smile.

"I'm sorry for not waiting for you. If Laura and I hadn't gone by ourselves none of this would have happened, and it's not like we found any new clues anyway. We went to see Mr. Zobel's daughter because she said she had a few boxes with his old stuff, but there was nothing of interest. It was all a waste of time and now this happened." I teared up.

Leo reached for my hand as I continued my rant: "I'm sorry that we ignored your calls. Laura was sure Magni would yell at her, but of course now..." I trailed off and lowered my head in shame. "Now his yelling would be the sweetest sound in the world."

"Solo and Zasquash told me the doctors gave him less than thirty percent chance of survival."

"That's what they said." I fiddled with my fingers. "His body was as destroyed as the drone. Three limbs were cut off in the crash, one of his lungs collapsed, he has four broken ribs and his neck, shoulder, and the left side of his face were cut open. They're still operating on him, but the doctor said that it's likely that he has brain swelling so even if they can stabilize him, he'll have to be in a coma until the brain swelling is over."

Leo drew a heavy sigh and closed his eyes.

"I know," I said, "but we have to stay positive. As long as there's a chance of him surviving, there's hope."

Opening his eyes, Leo drew another deep sigh. "To be honest, I'm not sure Magni would choose to survive if it means being crippled for life."

"Don't say that!"

"Magni is a proud man. We all are."

I teared up because in my heart, I knew Leo was right. "Sometimes you Nmen are too proud for your own good. Don't for a minute think that life isn't worth living unless you're the strongest version of yourself."

"Raven, you don't understand."

I fell back on my sense of humor to deflect the gravity of the conversation. Like a strict schoolteacher, I wiggled my index finger. "Shhh, I'll pretend you didn't say it."

"But..."

"No, if I hear you say it again, I might have to crawl up on your bed and beat you up for it."

He raised his eyebrows. "That wouldn't be too hard."

"That's right, so don't tempt me. I've always wanted to win over you. You don't want me to take advantage of your being weak, do you?" In an attempt to change the subject, I took the bowl of water bubbles on his side table and offered him one.

"No thanks." He watched me as I popped a few in my mouth. "Raven."

224

"Yes."

"Not that I want you to beat me up, but I wouldn't mind if you came closer." He patted the mattress.

Tilting my head, I gave him a questioning look. "Are you sure? I don't want to hurt you or anything." I looked down at his legs.

Scrunching up his face in pain, Leo moved over to create room for me. "I know you told me not to expect anything, but I was looking forward to being close to you tonight. Not that I'll be able to do any of the stuff I planned to do with you, but it's just that I'm realizing that if I'd died in that crash…" His eyes dropped to his hands. "I'll bet there's a whole room of people out there waiting to hear news about Magni. His sons and daughters, wife, mother, brother, you know." Leo's Adam's apple bobbed in his throat. "Magni has a family who cares about him while I…"

My heart was crying for him and knowing what he was going to say, I took his hand and squeezed it.

"Raven, I hear you when you say you don't want to hurt me, but it's too late for that. We made love last night and this morning. I already care about you too much to be untouched if you decide to end what we have. I don't think someone like you will ever truly understand how it feels to have no one." He looked into my eyes with deep sadness.

"That's not what I meant, Leo. I was talking about hurting you physically. You've just been operated on."

"Oh."

"And don't say that you're alone. You're not. Even without me you have friends. Zasquash came rushing to the hospital when he heard what happened to you."

Leo used his free hand to scratch his shoulder. "I'm grateful for that, but…" The longing from him was so strong that I got up and sat next to him in his bed.

"I'm here!"

It hurt him to turn onto his right side, but he managed and we lay nose to nose with me caressing his face and neck.

"Magni saved my life."

"How?"

"His ejection handle was stuck and I was going to try and help him, but he pulled my handle to make sure I survived."

I gave a sad smile. "I'll make sure to thank Magni for that when I see him again." If the doctors were right, there was a seventy percent chance that I'd never see Magni again, and the thought made me look down.

We were quiet for a while as I let my fingers caress and play with Leo's dark beard.

"Raven, you know what?"

"What?"

"I've never had a female friend before."

With my eyebrows raised up, I reminded him, "I offered to be your friend. It was you who kept insisting that you couldn't be anything but my boss."

Leo groaned. "I know that, but I was in a tough situation with everyone expecting me to keep you safe and with you messing with my mind. This thing about men and women being friends..."

"What about it?"

"I wouldn't know how to do it. I'm not gonna lie. I want so much more than friendship from you."

"Leo..."

"Yes, I know. You're not ready for marriage and I'm your boss..." He played with my hand before looking into my eyes. "I wish I wasn't, though. I wish I..."

I waited for him to continue but he just sighed.

"You wish I was *your* boss?"

My attempt to cheer him up worked and Leo gave a small laugh followed by a grimace of pain. "Ehhm, no, absolutely not."

"Well, I'm just trying to guess here since you're giving me half sentences. Now you have me wondering what it is that you wish for."

Without words, Leo buried his head against the crook of my neck and entwined our fingers. It was something I had done as a child when I longed for safety, and because I'd lived in the Northlands since I was eleven years old, I knew how rare it was to see such vulnerability from an Nman. With my free hand, I nuzzled his earlobe and neck, appreciating how hard it must be for him to show weakness. Leo was a strong alpha with men looking up to him as a leader and a role model. I was smaller and much younger than him, but in that moment, I felt respected as his equal, a partner, and a friend. It made my heart overflow with gratitude and respect for him.

"You know what it is that I wish for." He spoke the words against my neck, which made them sound muffled.

"You wish we could be more than friends."

"Uh-huh." His lips placed gentle kisses on my collarbone.

"We *are* more than friends, Leo."

"I know that, but being your lover will never be enough for me, Raven." Leo let his finger twirl around a strand of my hair before inhaling deeply and speaking on his exhalation, "I want all of you!"

"Say it again." I had been a neglected child once, with an absent mom who couldn't cope with me. Not until I was adopted by Christina and Boulder had I felt wanted. Fear of abandonment should have no room inside me anymore, but like a ghost from the past, I felt it reach out for the deeply healing and satisfying words that Leo wanted all of me.

"I mean it. I want all of you. Not just the hot sex but the whole package." His finger trailed from my hair down my shoulder and arm.

"I'm not giving up my dream of being the first policewoman."

"I wouldn't ask you to." Leo lifted our entwined fingers and kissed the back of my hand. "I'm not stupid. Being your man will be challenging and scary. If you become a police officer, I'll worry about you night and day."

"You already do that."

"True, but that's because I…"

Again, he trailed off and it made me poke at his shoulder. "Can you please finish your sentences?"

"Okay but don't freak out."

"I won't."

His Adam's apple bobbed. "The reason I'll worry about you is because I like you so much."

"I like you too, Leo."

"Yeah, but I more than like you."

A triangle formed between my eyebrows. "What are you saying?"

We were lying close together and he was looking deep into my eyes. "Promise that you'll stay right here and talk to me instead of storming out of the room."

My heart was racing. "Why would I storm out?"

"I love you, Raven."

Leo looked so serious at that moment; all my words about wanting a man with a sense of humor came back to me. I didn't mind that he was serious, not when it came to how much he cared about me. My feelings for Leo had been strong before I even realized it myself. My irrational aggression toward Gennie for coming on to him should have been a clue, and today's drone crash had wiped away all remaining doubt in my mind. I had met hundreds if not thousands of men and none of them had ever made me feel like Leo did. Watching that drone crash and not knowing if Leo was inside or not had been the worst moments of my life.

"I think I love you too."

Leo used his left hand to cup my face. "You think or you know?"

My face softened. "I know that I love you."

"You sure?"

The hope on his face made me smile. "Yes, I'm sure."

He was searching my eyes. "Don't say it if you don't mean it."

"I love you." My smile widened. "I'm not sure when it happened exactly but I was physically attracted to you from the first day you pissed me off at the Gray Manor. Then at Solo's and Willow's wedding, I tried to get you to dance with me, remember?"

"Yeah, I remember, and when I wouldn't, you danced with that mutant huntsman."

"He's not a mutant."

"I know, I just call them that because they're so fucking large."

"While dancing with him, I kept looking over at you to see if you noticed."

"Oh, I noticed all right."

"Did you also notice that I never teased or provoked anyone as much as I did you?"

"No, but I'll take your word for it."

"Leo, if I'm completely honest, I've probably had a crush on you for over a year."

He leaned in and kissed me. "I could have died today and if it taught me anything, it's to not waste time. You need to know that I'm in over my head. I think about what's ahead and I've never been so scared and excited at the same time. You're going to drive me mad, Raven. I know you will, but I also know that I'll love every day I get to spend with you." Leo kissed my forehead.

I knew he was hinting at marriage, but with Magni fighting for his life and the guilt I felt over the crash, I couldn't think about that right now. "Please don't ask me to marry you. I need time, Leo."

He was quiet but I sensed his disappointment.

"It doesn't change that I love you and that I'm with you."

"You promise?"

"Yes." I kissed him again. "My turn to ask you something. Why did you take my torn shirt from the day we fought?"

He stiffened. "So you found it?"

"Yes, in your bedside table."

"Then you know why I took it, don't you?"

"To jerk off with?"

"Nooo!" Leo wrinkled his nose up. "Well, maybe once or twice, but mostly, I liked to smell the scent of your perfume before sleeping. It helped me visualize that one day I would have a woman in my bed."

"*Any* woman?"

"No, a specific delicious caramel-colored, badass woman."

We were quiet for a moment, listening to the voices coming from outside the hospital room and looking out the window as drones came and left in the distance.

"Raven, can I ask you something?"

"Uh-huh."

"If nothing physical had happened between us yet, would you have let me compete for Mila or would you have told me about your attraction?"

"Who knows? It might have come out the closer we got to Mila's tournament. It was pretty evident that I had a strong reaction every time your name was mentioned."

Leo placed his forehead against mine. "I wish you hadn't hidden your crush so well. There were times when I thought you despised me."

A knock on the door was followed by Mila, who came in and stopped abruptly when she saw me and Leo cuddled up together. "Mother Nature, Leo. You're lucky that you're in a hospital bed already. When Boulder hears about this, he'll be furious."

I sat up in the bed. "I'll tell him when I want him to know, so you'll keep it a secret. You know I would do it for you."

"I don't want to be your secret." Leo reached for me as I got out of the bed. "Even Magni admitted that I'm a good man, so why can't you just tell your family?"

"Because right now they have other things to worry about than you and me."

Leo's eyebrows drew close. "Of course. I wasn't thinking. Mila, is there any news about your father?"

Mila nodded. "That's why I came to fetch Raven. They said the doctor is coming out to talk to us any minute now."

I promised Leo that I'd be right back to update him and hurried after Mila. When we got to the waiting room that the hospital had provided for Magni's friends and family, everyone had their full attention on a middle-aged doctor who was talking.

"So, basically, we'll need another hour or so to finish the operation. My part was successful and right now, Doctor Neiman, our plastic surgeon is working on the large tear on the Commander's face, neck, and shoulder."

"And after the surgery?" Khan asked. "How long before he wakes up?"

The doctor looked down and rocked back on his heels. "Days, possibly weeks. I really can't say. It's a good thing that the Commander was physically strong before the accident and that he has a warrior's mindset because this will no doubt be the greatest battle he's ever had to fight."

Mila stood next to me and was holding on to my arm. "But can you say for certain that he'll make it?"

"No. We can't give you any guarantees. And you should be prepared that even if he does, he won't be the same. There's the physical damage that's obvious, but it's too soon to say if his brain has been damaged as well. We need to wait for the swelling to go down before we'll attempt to wake him up and only then can we run tests."

"Mom, what does that mean?" Aubrey, Magni's young daughter, asked while pressing herself against Laura.

The doctor answered. "It means that there's a significant risk that your father has suffered permanent damage to his vision, hearing, or his cognitive functions."

Pearl translated to the younger children. "It means we don't know if your dad will be able to see, hear, or talk as he used to. We don't know how much he'll remember either."

"He'll remember me, won't he?" Aubrey's eyes were full of tears.

The doctor gave her a look of pity. He looked tired as he nodded to all of us before turning to Finn, who had arrived with his wife, Athena. "Walk with me, will you?"

Finn had worked in this hospital before he moved to the Motherlands; he followed his former colleague down the hallway.

Laura held little Aubrey in her arms, as she wouldn't stop crying. The rest of us were as miserable as her and sat with long faces and teary eyes.

"But if Dad is alive, isn't that good news?" Magni's son, Mason, asked. The twin brother of Aubrey was ten and already the size of a grown man, but at that moment, he looked like a confused young boy.

Solo pulled the large boy into a sideways hug. "Yeah, it's good news, Mason. Magni is alive and right now that's all that matters."

I remembered what Leo had said about Magni preferring to die rather than waking up as a crippled man. If only Magni could see this room full of us, his family and closest friends praying to speak to him again, to share a smile, a hug, handshake, or a laugh. We didn't care if he would never be able to walk or fight again, but something told me that Leo was right. Magni would care.

CHAPTER 22
Recovery

Leo

Despite my friends visiting me in the hospital, the days I spent there were long. Not being allowed to put pressure on my left leg made it difficult to move around and even though I insisted I would do just fine at home alone, the doctors kept saying that they preferred for me to stay another day.

On my sixth day stuck in a bed, I was losing my patience. Raven had visited every night and it was always the highlight of my day when she crawled into bed with me and talked about work at the station, life at the Manor, and everyday things outside of the hospital.

"You missed out on major drama today at the Manor." Raven had brought a bag of candy and was eating some as she was talking. "When I got home, Mila was almost crying because Khan was shouting at her."

"Why?"

Unwrapping a caramel, Raven chuckled. "Because Holger had left a turd on the antique rug in the entryway."

"Which one of Mila's dogs is Holger?"

Raven's chuckle grew to a full-on laugh. "The Great Dane. We're talking this big a pile, and Khan wasn't having it." She illustrated with her hands. "But in Khan's defense it was disgusting and it smelled like death. Not sure what the dog ate to get that kind of food poisoning, but Khan threatened to ban Mila's dogs from the Manor and she responded that he would have to ban her as well before she gave up her dogs."

"Yeah, that does sound dramatic. I feel bad for Mila, though. She has enough on her plate with her dad being here and all."

Raven grew serious and nodded. "You're right, and I think that's why Khan took back his words later. Everyone at the Manor is thin-skinned and on edge these days. We all want Magni to wake up.

"Yeah, me too."

Raven sighed and popped the caramel into her mouth. "Anyway, people are missing you at work."

"Cameron came yesterday."

"Oh yeah?"

"He told me he was sparring with you on Monday."

Chewing, Raven nodded.

"Why didn't you tell me?"

"I did tell you. We talked about how I jammed my finger, remember?"

"Ah, was that with Cameron? I thought that was when you fought Monroe."

Raven rolled her eyes in a playful manner. "Honestly, you're too doped to remember anything. I wonder why I bother talking to you at all."

Tickling her until she begged for mercy had me out of breath, but it was fun. Raven was so unbelievably gorgeous with her soft skin, large expressive eyes, and those full lips that I wanted to kiss all the time.

"Stop it, stop it." She squealed and pushed at me, but I was so much stronger and longing to be physical with her.

"Leo, don't tickle me." In an attempt to roll into a protective ball, Raven raised her knees up, and one of them hit my bad thigh right where I'd been operated on.

The pain that shot through me had me want to scream out loud, but I swallowed my cry and closed my eyes and placed a hand on my thigh.

"Sorry, Leo. I'm so sorry. Are you okay?"

235

When I couldn't respond, Raven scrambled out of my hospital bed and called for help. A doctor's assistant came rushing in while Raven explained what had happened.

"I didn't mean to. It just happened when Leo tickled me."

The man was a no-nonsense type and pulled the cover off me with an abrupt movement. "Spread your legs so I can see."

"I'm fine." I was pushing his hands away and hating that Raven saw me like this.

"I don't see any blood. Does this hurt?" He pushed at where I'd been operated.

"Yes, it fucking hurts," I hissed and shot him a killer look.

"I'll tell the doctor. If it swells it could be a sign that your blood vessels have burst again."

"I'm so sorry, Leo." Raven was standing to one side, her arms crossed with each hand on the opposite shoulder and her face dipped low in shame.

I pushed out a few words through my pain, "It was my fault."

On his way out, the doctor's assistant gave a firm instruction to me before he closed the door. "Stop tickling your wife. I'll find a doctor."

The fact that he assumed Raven and I were married lifted my spirit with pride. I hadn't done anything to clear up the misunderstanding, and with her daily visits, it was a natural assumption for the staff to make.

"I'm okay. Won't you come back here?" I patted the mattress.

"Maybe it's better if I keep a distance."

"My thigh is just sensitive from the operation. It's nothing."

Moving slowly, she stepped a little closer and sat down on the edge of the chair next to the bed. "I can't stay long anyway."

"Why not?"

Raven still looked shaken from what had happened and bit down on her lower lip without answering me.

"Are you still working on the case? Is that why you can't stay?"

"No, of course not. After what happened to you and Magni, I'm done with Dina's case. Erika warned me that nothing good comes out of disturbing the dead, and she was right. If Laura and I hadn't gone, none of this would have happened."

I narrowed my eyes in suspicion. "Just promise me that if you do work on it, you'll include me."

"I won't work on it, Leo. I mean it."

"Good."

She got up and stood behind the chair when a doctor came in.

"I heard there was a small accident in here?"

I stared with my mouth open. "You're a woman."

The doctor was in her thirties. With a kind smile she walked over to me. "My name is Doctor Kim. Let's take a look at it, shall we?" Like it was the most natural thing in the world, she lifted my covers.

I jerked back a little, still surprised to see a female doctor. "But you're a..."

"A woman. Yes, I'm aware, but so are most of the world's population. It's really not that special." The doctor looked over at Raven. "You won't mind if I examine your husband, will you?"

"Ehh..." Raven looked at me as if she expected me to correct the doctor but I was too busy pushing back in my bed when the woman reached for my inner thigh.

"Don't worry, I've practiced medicine for nine years and you're not my first shocked patient. Some of us brides have professions that we enjoy."

"Yes. I'm aware."

Her touch was gentle. "Are you in pain?"

"Not as much as before."

"What if I press here?" Her fingers touched different areas and when she got close to my crotch, my sudden gasp made her furrow her brow. "Did that hurt?"

"Nope. I'm good."

"You sure?"

"Uh-huh!" I sat stiffly and didn't breathe. Only one woman had ever been this close to me and she was watching us right now.

With a satisfied nod, Dr. Kim pulled the cover back over me. "Everything looks fine. How are you feeling?"

"Impatient to go home."

"I understand, and I don't see a problem with it."

"Really?" I lit up. "I was told I had to stay here for at least two weeks."

Doctor Kim frowned. "Yes, I saw that in the file, but that recommendation was based on your living alone. We've had too many cases of Nmen going back to work too soon – despite warnings from us. It prolongs the healing time and sometimes makes things worse. That's why we like to keep our patients in here as long as possible." The doctor tilted her head. "I'm not sure why it wasn't noted down that you have a wife, but if she makes sure you don't do anything foolish, I don't see why you can't leave today." Dr. Kim gave me and Raven another quick glance. "As long as you make sure to follow instructions, keep the leg rested, and you come back for a check-up in a few days."

"I'd *love* to go home today." My eyes were begging Raven to play along.

"It's fine. If you get dressed, I'll go and update your file and have someone bring a hover chair in. Do you need transportation to get home?"

Knowing that Raven's drone had been fixed, I shook my head. "No, we should be fine."

When Dr. Kim left, Raven turned to me, speaking in a loud whisper, "What are you doing? They think we live together."

"I know."

"Why didn't you correct them when they said we were married?"

"Because I'm going crazy here. I need to get out of this hospital. Can't you at least give me a ride home?"

"Of course, but then what? I can't just leave you without any help, and I'm going to my parents' house for dinner tonight."

I pointed behind her. "Zasquash brought me some clean clothes. They're in that drawer. Can you give them to me?"

She found the clothes and handed me the pile. "Do you need help?"

"No, I'm good." I pulled off the hospital clothing and already felt better as I put on some of my own clothing. "When you go to your parents' house tonight, will you tell them about us?"

Raven pulled at her earlobe but didn't answer me.

"What about last week when we said that we loved each other? I thought we agreed to be a couple, Raven."

"I know that, but I want for us to figure out how we want to handle our relationship before we share it with others."

I tensed my jaw because I was bloody clear on what I wanted with Raven, and it included getting married and moving in together. With her it was like two steps forward and one step back. "Look, I get that everything is a bit

239

chaotic now and that you need time. But I love waking up with you in the morning and I want you around as much as possible."

My words carried an invitation for her to move in with me, but Raven chose her usual strategy of making light of the situation. "You just want me as your alibi so you can go home, but if you're counting on me to stay and cook for you, don't. I'm not good at it."

Now wasn't the time to push my luck. "All I'm asking is for you to get me out of here. Once I'm at my house, I'll jump around on one foot. And don't worry about cooking. My house-bot does that." I gave her my most charming grin and twenty minutes later, I was dressed and in a hover chair on my way out. The machine was easy to maneuver and when a long and completely empty hallway presented itself, I had to test the machine to its limit.

Raven's laughter as she ran to catch up with me made me grin out loud. "They should have given me one of these racers days ago. Maybe then I wouldn't have been so bored."

Down in the large foyer of the hospital, there were more people and I had to slow down, but the closer we got to the exit, the lighter I felt inside. "I can't wait to sleep in my own bed." I had only just said it when Mila came running in to the hospital and toward us.

"Mila, what's wrong?" Raven called out to her.

Mila came to a halt and spoke with a sense of urgency. "It's my dad. They're going to try and wake him up. My mom called for me to come as fast as I could. She and Erika are already here and Khan is on his way." Her eyes were full of tears and she grabbed for Raven's hands. "I'm so scared. What if he can't remember us or if he doesn't wake up at all?"

"Do you want me to go with you?"

240

"You can't. They asked for immediate family only, but would you wait outside, please?"

"Yes, of course." Raven's face mirrored Mila's sadness and they hugged.

"It's going to be fine, Mila," Raven's words were meant to cheer Mila up, but it was a guarantee no one could offer at this point.

Mila dried away some of her tears and then she looked at me in the hover chair. "Oh, Leo, I'm sorry. Were you going outside for fresh air?"

"Something like that, but don't worry about it."

Mila began walking and we moved along with her. "You don't mind then?" she asked me.

"Mila, no. I would be honored to wait with Raven. Your father is the bravest man I know. He saved my life."

She gave me a sad smile and held Raven's hand as we made our way up to the intensive care unit. Raven and I went with Mila all the way to the door of Magni's room until we couldn't go any further.

"It's going to be all right," Raven repeated with her eyes full of unshed tears. "We'll be waiting right here for you."

Swallowing a few times, Mila heaved in air before squaring her shoulders and placing a hand on the door. "I'll let you know when he wakes up."

CHAPTER 23
Unexpected

Raven

Leo and I waited in the hallway outside Magni's room, where a few chairs were placed along the wall. After five minutes Khan rushed past us with a short hello. Two of his personal guards walked over to talk to their colleagues, who were here protecting Magni.

We watched two assistants come and go before a doctor entered the room. He didn't close the door all the way and my eyes zoomed in through the narrow opening to see what was going on.

If only Khan weren't blocking my view.

"Have you seen any signs of movement yet?" the doctor asked and I recognized Finn's voice when he answered, "There was movement under his eyelids just a moment ago." It made sense that Finn was with them because even though he wasn't family, he and Magni were childhood friends, and Finn had been Khan's and Magni's personal doctor before he married Athena and moved to the Motherlands.

"Good. We'll just give him a few moments to come around."

"Dad, can you hear me? Dad, if you can hear me squeeze my hand or open your eyes." Mila was the only one of Magni's children in the room.

"I felt something." Laura's voice was brittle. "He squeezed my hand. I'm sure of it."

"Do it again, Dad. Come on. You can do it."

Small outbursts of excitement were followed by Laura, who was now crying with joy, saying, "That's it! Yes, honey, open your eyes."

I had a hand in front of my mouth and didn't breathe. Magni was waking up but I couldn't see anything what with Khan's back in the way. And then by some small miracle, Khan moved out of my way giving me a narrow view of Finn standing at the head of Magni's bed.

"Welcome back, brother. Quite a nap you took there, huh?" Khan's shaky voice revealed how emotional he was.

The sound that came from Magni was hoarse and followed by a cough.

"Let's have him sit up." Finn raised the bed up and it gave me my first glimpse of Magni's face. His beard was gone and his right side was covered with a protective layer of some kind.

"Here, do you want some water?" Magni's right eye was covered but his left was looking down at Mila, who was placing a small ball of water by his lips. Slowly he opened his mouth and she pushed the ball inside.

"Oh, that's okay, babe." Laura got up and dried away the water that ran down his chin.

Another hoarse sound came from Magni and it made me grab Leo's hand and whisper to him. "He's trying to speak."

Leo squeezed my hand and leaned in so he could see a bit through the door opening as well.

"Magni, do you know who we are?" Khan asked.

Magni didn't answer but turned his head and then a long, pained sound cut into my heart.

"Yes, you lost some of your arm. You were in an accident. A drone crash. Do you remember?" Finn's voice was soft and sympathetic.

Magni made a low and throaty sound. It was clear he was trying to speak but I didn't understand.

243

Finn continued, "I'm sorry, friend. There was no way to save your left arm and for a while the doctors here doubted you would survive, but we told them how strong you are and you proved us right."

Magni's left eye was darting around the room. "Do you remember us?" Khan repeated.

"What's my name?" I could see Mila's sleeve as she leaned in and caressed Magni's face.

Another low guttural sound came from Magni, but it was close enough to, "Mila" that I sighed with relief.

"And me, do you remember me?" Laura's voice was breaking.

"Laura."

Mila and Laura were sobbing with joy.

"We were so scared you wouldn't be able to recognize us." Erika kissed his forehead.

"My eye." His right hand lifted to the part of his face that was wrapped up. "I can't see...?"

The doctor leaned in and pulled Magni's hand down. "It's better if you don't touch it. The left side of your face was injured during the crash and it needs to heal. The operation went well, and we're hopeful that we saved enough of your nerves that you'll regain at least some vision in your right eye. For now, it needs to remain covered though."

Magni groaned.

"It was a bad crash, brother. As Finn said, it's a miracle that you're waking up at all. It's going to be a long road to recovery, but you'll get there and we'll help you."

Magni's good eye darted around. "Leo," he muttered.

"That's right. Leo was with you in the drone. Do you remember now?" Finn asked.

"Is he okay?"

Leo squeezed my hand when we heard Magni asking about him.

"Yes, Dad. Leo was injured too, but he's right outside the door. He told me you saved his life."

Magni gave a hoarse cough and sunk back in his bed with a sigh.

Finn placed a hand on his left shoulder. "We know you're tired and we'll let you sleep in a minute. Just know that it's a good sign that you remember the crash and that you recognize us."

"That's right," the doctor agreed. "When you feel better, we would like to do some tests, and later we can talk about robotic limbs for your arm and legs."

"My legs?" Magni looked up at the doctor.

"Yes, there's no good way to tell you this, but I'm afraid both your legs were amputated in the crash. Normally, we can reattach limbs, but unfortunately, yours were too crushed to work.

"Nooo!"

Everyone was quiet in the room, listening to Magni's sounds of despair. Out in the hallway, Leo, the guards, and I all had our heads down as we suffered with Magni at that moment.

"It's a shock, we know." Erika's voice was soft. "You've been in a coma for six days. We've been praying night and day that you'd make it through."

"We love you, Dad. You don't know how happy we are that you're still here. You just need to rest and focus on getting healthy again." Mila's words were swallowed in her crying.

Magni turned his head and closed his eye.

"It's okay, brother, you can go back to sleep. One of us will stay by your side and be here when you wake up. From now on things will get better."

A few minutes later, Khan exited the room with the doctor. "How long do you think he'll sleep?"

"I can't say, Lord. He'll drift in and out of sleep over the next days but he didn't seem in pain, so the medication is working."

"That's good. Thank you."

The two men exchanged a firm handshake before the doctor walked away and Khan faced us. "Leo, Magni was asking about you. I think he remembered that you were in the drone."

"That's good right? That means he still has his memories."

"It's too early to say if he has all of them, but he remembered the crash." Signaling to his guards that it was time to go, Khan gave us a nod. "I'll see you later."

Mila came out and talked to us about her father's few minutes awake. "I'm going to stay here in case he wakes up again. My mom and grandma need a break. They've been here more or less non-stop for the past six days.

"Whatever you need, Mila. Just give me a call and I'll bring it to you. Company, a book, music, food… anything."

"Thank you, Raven. You're the best friend anyone can ask for. I love you so much."

"I love you too, sweetie." After hugging me and saying goodbye to Leo, she went back in and closed the door.

For a moment, Leo and I sat in silence before I sucked in a deep inhalation. "At least he's awake now."

"I know."

"Do you wanna leave?"

"Yeah."

This time we didn't run or laugh as we left the hospital. We were quiet as we flew back to Leo's place, and when we got there, he held on to my shoulder and jumped on one foot to get from the drone, inside his house, and onto his couch.

"Are you comfortable?"

Leo was sitting with his back against the armrest and his feet stretched out in front of him. "Do you have to go?"

We had just witnessed something both miraculous and incredibly sad at the hospital. Normally, I would have been eager to see my parents and talk to them about it, but my feet felt like they were glued to the floor. I wanted to stay here with Leo.

"I can stay a while." Sitting down on the other end of the couch, I curled my legs up and called my mom. "I know I promised, Mom, but I can't make it tonight. Magni woke up."

"I know. Your dad has been speaking to Khan for twenty minutes now, I'm dying for him to finish and update me."

"Leo and I were outside the room but we heard most of what happened. The sounds Magni made when he found out about his legs were soul-wrenching, Mom. I've never heard anything like it."

"Oh, honey, I'm so sorry." My mom's voice was like a warm embrace of empathy. "He'll be in shock for a while but at least his expressing sorrow means that he understands. Remember how afraid we were that he would be brain damaged?"

"Yes, I get that, but it's Magni; his whole identity is to be the strongest warrior and now he's literally been cut down."

Leo reached his hands out, signaling for me to stretch my legs out. I was careful not to touch his injured thigh. He rubbed my ankle, his strong fingers massaging the arch of my foot.

"Magni will get through it. He has so much to live for and a family who needs him. All we can do is give our support. Why don't you come over and get some big hugs? Sounds like you could use it."

"Thanks, Mom, I'd love to, but I made a promise to Mila. I'll come by soon, okay?"

"All right, darling. We miss you."

"I know, and I miss you too. Say hi to Dad and give the little ones a kiss from me."

"Will do, honey."

When I ended the call, I gave a long sigh. "They're complaining that they don't see me enough."

Leo frowned. "I shouldn't keep you from your family."

I gave him a small smile and winked. "Are you kidding? They don't give me foot rubs like this."

CHAPTER 24
A Pair of Mittens
Three weeks later

Leo

End of October, I was at the Gray Manor helping Raven pack her things to move them to my place. I was tired of keeping our relationship a secret while waiting for Raven to make it public, but this morning she had finally agreed that since she slept at my house every night anyway, she might as well move in with me. I had played it cool when she told me, but when she went to take a shower, I'd done a victory dance and raised my hands above my head.

The plan was that we would move her things to my place and tell her family about us being a couple this weekend.

Mila had offered to help pack. She was sitting on the windowsill sorting through some books with a sadness that forced me to ask, "How is Magni doing?"

"Not so good." Mila lowered her hands and let the books rest in her lap.

"Isn't he happy to be back home? Raven told me he was transferred from the hospital yesterday."

"Yes, a month in the hospital would be hard on anyone. My mom and Khan wanted him to come home." Mila's shoulders hung low and she sat with her back hunched over. It appeared to me that her hair looked unwashed and that her skin was grayish.

Raven walked over and gave her friend a sideways hug. "At least he's awake and getting stronger with every

249

day now. Remember how we were all scared he'd never wake up?"

Mila didn't smile. "He's awake but just about unrecognizable. Either he stares at the ceiling for hours and refuses to talk, or he talks but all that comes from him is aggressive verbal abuse of whoever is in the room."

"It's probably the medication and because he's in so much pain."

"Maybe, but this is Magni Aurelius that we're talking about. He has withstood more physical pain than most people, and not even my mom or Khan know this bitter side of him. He won't allow any visitors." Mila sighed. "Maybe he's afraid they'll stare at all his scars."

Raven frowned. "You mean the ones on his face? But why? Magni isn't a vain man, is he?"

"He's proud! It's a lot to take in. I mean, he was already partially deaf on one ear and now he has lost some of his sight on his right eye along with both his legs and left arm." Mila teared up. "All he talks about is wanting to kill himself."

I rubbed my forehead. "Fuck, that's bad, Mila. I feared that might happen."

Mila's voice broke a little. "He's been under suicide watch since he woke up."

Raven sat down on the edge of her bed and wrapped her arms around her waist. "I feel awful that I did this to him."

"Stop saying that. It wasn't your fault." Mila pushed a lock of hair behind her ear and sniffled. "Things will get better. They have to."

I was quick to agree, "Yes. Once he's no longer in pain, he'll feel better."

Mila nodded. "Jonah is coming in a few days. He offered to talk to my dad."

I frowned. "Do you think that will help?"

Mila gave another small shrug. "I hope so. I always feel better after talking to Jonah. We'll see."

"And your tournament? Will it be postponed?"

"I don't know. Obviously, I want my dad to be there but when I asked him about it this morning, he…" Mila's eyes teared up again. "He began shouting and he threw whatever he could get his hands on against the wall. The doctor's assistant had to give him an injection to calm him down."

"Damn, I'm sorry to hear that." I gave her a sympathetic glance.

Mila dried away a tear. "Jonah says to look at it positively. At least my dad can still see, hear and talk. He also seems to have all his memories and his right hand works well enough to throw things."

"Right…" I nodded. "Yeah, I guess, that's a good way to look at it, but I think any warrior waking up to realize he's missing an arm and two legs would be angry with the world. I don't blame him for being grumpy."

Mila pushed off from the windowsill and stood for a second. "My dad's behavior isn't grumpy, Leo. It's hostile like we're his prison guards and he resents us for not letting him kill himself."

Without words, Raven got up and gave Mila a long warm hug. "Give it time."

Mila nodded and walked to the door before turning to us. "I'm happy for you two. I truly am, but I'm going to miss having you around, Raven."

"I'll come by often, I promise."

Mila gave a small smile that dripped with sadness. "I'd like that."

When the door closed behind her, Raven walked into my arms. "I feel so bad for her."

"Me too."

251

"If I had a magic wand, I would turn back time and then I would have never gone out that day."

"Don't beat yourself up about it, Raven. It wasn't your fault." I kissed her forehead and hugged her tight. "Come on, let's just get the last things packed."

We worked in silence for a few minutes until a call came in on Raven's wristband.

"It's Michael."

"Michael who?"

Raven didn't answer me because she had already accepted the call and moved to the window. "Hi, Michael, how are you?"

"I'm fine. Listen, I'm sorry to disturb you but I just wanted to ask if you got closer to any answers about Dina and Henry?"

Raven looked back at me over her shoulder and mouthed, "Dina's neighbor."

I gave a nod of understanding as she answered him, "I wish, but with Magni being injured it's no longer a priority of mine. You heard of the crash, didn't you?"

"Yes, of course. It's all they talk about on the news."

"The thing is, Michael, it was my investigation that caused Magni and Leo to crash, so I'm done."

"I didn't know that."

Raven scratched her shoulder. "I'm sorry that I don't have any answers for you."

"Yes, I was hoping you would, but I guess now we'll never know." The disappointment in his voice was thick, and then he sighed. "Oh well, it was worth a try anyway."

"Yeah, I guess."

"Bye then."

"Bye."

Raven ended the call and we went back to packing but a minute later, Michael called her again.

"I know this is going to sound silly, and it's probably nothing of significance but I kept something that belonged to Dina and I feel a little bad about it."

"What did you keep?"

"A pair of her mittens. We used to have a warming rack outside our apartments for shoes and gloves. After she died, I took her mittens."

"Why?"

"Because I'd never met a woman and Dina was always so kind to me. I kept them to always remember her... And I kept a feather too."

"Did you say a feather?"

"Yes. It's just a small blue feather that I found on the staircase that same night after Dina had died."

"How do you know it was Dina's?"

"You'd know if you saw it too. It's something only rich people would wear on their clothes. Dina had fancy jackets and hats. I knew right away that it was hers. Maybe I shouldn't have kept any of it. It's just that at the time it seemed like such small things, but now I wonder if maybe her family want the mittens and the feather back."

"Send me a picture so I can ask them."

"Of course. I'll send it right away."

After Michael sent her the picture, Raven took one glance at the mittens and the blue feather. "I'll ask Erika if she wants them back as memories of Dina."

While Raven called up Erika, I closed the boxes we had already packed, listening to Erika's and Raven's short conversation.

"Michael wants to know if you want the mittens and the feather back."

"No. How many times must I ask you to leave my Dina in peace? Nothing good will come out of stirring up the past."

253

Erika's response made me look over at her hologram. Her face was stiff and her jaws set in stone.

"I'm sorry." Raven didn't finish her sentence before Erika had disconnected.

"Don't take it personally, babe. They are all grieving and that's why they're lashing out."

Raven gave a sad nod. "I know that." She enlarged the picture of the blue feather with the red dot in the middle. "If Dina had been my daughter, I would have wanted everything with a connection to her, even a small feather like that one."

"Grief is different for everybody. Erika is choosing not to remember."

"Yeah, it's beginning to make sense to me why Marcus removed all traces of Dina after her death. Erika really doesn't like to think about her daughter." Raven closed down the picture. "I'll ask Mila instead. She kept some of Dina's things from the storage room. Maybe she wants these too."

"Yeah, maybe."

"Leo, stop. Put that box down."

"I'm fine."

"Just because you're not limping anymore doesn't mean you should be carrying heavy boxes."

"Not you too, Raven. The guys were giving me crap at work but it's been a month and I'm fine." I had a box in my arms and was by the door when a sudden thought hit me hard. At first, I disregarded it but when I returned for the next box, I asked, "Raven, that article you were looking at when I confiscated your research, can I see it?" I knew she had it since I'd returned all the confiscated research to her.

Raven found it and showed it to me. "What about it?"

I stared at the photo and pointed. When Raven saw what I saw, she gasped out loud. "Holy shit, Leo..."

Looking deep into her eyes, I spoke in a low ominous tone. "We can never tell anyone about this. *Never!*"

"But Leo, what if…"

"No, this is so much bigger than us. Khan being the false heir is a major political bomb that could throw our country into a civil war. With Magni being injured, Khan is already weakened and if any of this gets out, there's no way to know what's going to happen to any of us."

Raven took a moment before she nodded. "You're right. We'll need to keep this quiet and pretend we don't know."

CHAPTER 25
Big Mouth

Leo

Raven wanted to say a few goodbyes before we left the Gray Manor. While waiting for her, I packed the drone and was coming back into the large foyer when Khan came walking through with Solo.

"Leo, what are you doing here?"

"I'm just waiting for Raven."

"How are you feeling? I heard you returned to work – that's good news." Khan patted my shoulder.

"I'm not complaining. I was the lucky one."

"Yeah, Magni has a way to go still." The two men grew somber as Khan spoke. "For some reason, he doesn't want to talk about cybernetics, which is bullshit because with robotic limbs he could walk and run again."

"Mila told me he's not doing well and that you're worried about him being alone."

Khan groaned "He's too damn proud for his own good and he feels sorry for himself. Have you seen him yet?"

"No. I've asked to visit, but Laura says he doesn't want anyone to see him like that."

"Ah, yes, but when he comes around, you'll need to speak loud because my brother lost some of his hearing."

"That's not because of the accident," Solo pointed out. "Magni lost most of his hearing in one ear after a fight with me years ago."

"He never told me that." Khan crossed his arms and then he shrugged. "Anyway, Solo has temporarily taken over for Magni as Commander until we find a solution. It turned out to be a good thing Magni did that paternity test last year. Now I have a nephew to help me out in his father's absence." With a hand to Solo's back, Khan gave him a proud nod.

Solo and I had been friends before he discovered that Magni was his father and it was still weird for me to think of him as part of the ruling family.

"Solo will keep you updated about Mila's tournament."

"I thought you were going to postpone it."

Khan pursed his lips and tapped his foot. "We're not sure. There's still a few months and we're hoping Magni can grow strong enough to attend, but it's tempting to postpone it. I never agreed that it should be a winter event to begin with. Spring and summer are always better for tournaments anyway. It's just that a wedding always brings joy and a lot of men will be disappointed if we don't follow through."

"I'm not one of them."

Tilting his head, Khan lowered his gaze to my thigh. "Ah, because of your injury. Yes, I can see that pushing back the tournament will give you time to heal properly and get back in top shape."

I shook my head. "No, the reason I'm not disappointed is that Raven and I..." I hesitated, but she had promised to make it official this weekend so I didn't feel too bad about telling Khan and Solo.

Khan waited for a second, but then his eyes grew wide "Really? You and Raven? But I thought you found her annoying."

I smiled. "What can I say? She grew on me."

Solo chuckled. "Yes, she has that effect on people, but are you sure she'll commit? Have you asked her to marry you?"

"She's moving in with me today." I squared my shoulders with pride.

257

"What? Without being married?" Khan shook his head. "You're a good man, Leo, but you're not too bright if you let her move in with you without being married."

"Why not?"

"Solo and I have known Raven longer than you. She's not like other women."

"I know that. Raven is fucking strong and amazing."

"Sure, but she carries the pressure of wanting to make a difference in the world. Sometimes, that pressure makes her appear tougher than she really is."

"I understand that."

"Do you?" Khan's expression was serious. "Because Raven is special to all of us and we need to be certain that you can handle someone as complex as her. She's sensitive and soft on the inside but most can't see it because of the way she presents herself as a badass."

I nodded. "I get that."

"Good." Khan patted my shoulder. "Be strategic! Make sure you get her to marry you fast."

"Strategic, Lord?" I shook my head to signal I didn't follow him.

"You don't want her to think it's a possibility to live with you without getting married. If you give her that option, she'll never want to marry. Why would she if she's getting everything that she needs without having to conform to our tradition of marriage?"

Solo crossed his arms. "Lord Khan has a good point. Motlanders think of marriage as archaic. I know Raven used to think of it that way but maybe her many years in the Northlands have made her more susceptible to the idea. Just tell her it can be a small ceremony at our place in the woods or here at the Gray Manor, with only the closest of friends and family if she prefers."

Khan looked thoughtful. "Or it can be a large wedding."

258

"I hear what you're saying, but just because she hasn't agreed to marry me yet doesn't change that she's still mine."

"I hope she agrees." Solo placed his large palm on my shoulder and shook it. "Did you claim her yet?"

"Yes, several times."

Khan gave a satisfied smack of his tongue. "Good, then soon we can finally put this police nonsense behind us."

"Why? Wouldn't you support Pearl if it was her dream?"

Khan groaned. "Leo, if you knew how much Pearl and I discuss all the crazy things she wants to do. Women aren't always realistic about what can and can't be done."

Solo raised an eyebrow. "True, but Pearl has changed a lot of things around here; you can't deny that, Lord."

Khan shifted his balance. "I don't disagree. Much is better because of her ideas, but it's a constant balance between supporting her and protecting her from her own naiveté."

"I get that, Lord." I gave Khan a small smile. "Still, I doubt Pearl could have done any of it without your support. I reckon it'll be the same with Raven. She'll need me in her corner."

Solo shifted his balance. "That woman is the most stubborn daredevil I've met. Willow is a handful, but Raven, oh man, that's a whole different level."

I huffed out air. "I know. So far, I haven't been successful in stopping her from doing anything she wants to. It wasn't until the crash that she stopped inv… ehh…" I had said too much and made a bad attempt at changing the subject. "Anyway, robotic limbs sound cool."

I should have known Khan wouldn't miss a blunder like that. "She stopped what? Are you referring to her investigation?"

It was eerie how he was spot on. I swallowed hard.

"Yeah, I didn't want her to investigate Dina's death and now she finally stopped." Knowing what we had just discovered, I was looking at his elbow.

"I see." Khan frowned. "But tell me: did Raven find any clues to my sister's death?"

"Nothing much." Lying to my ruler could cost me my life; my ears were beginning to get hot.

Khan gave me a sharp glance and I felt like he was doing an x-ray of my mind, seeing every secret I was holding from him. In an attempt to smooth things out, I made it worse by rambling:

"Well, she found the file as you know and I told her to stop. She has stopped. It's not a priority any longer, what with Magni injured and all." My nerves flared up. Dina had died, and so had her husband and his friend. I didn't want Raven and me to be next, and even though Raven didn't seem to understand the significance of Khan's bloodline or lack thereof, I did.

"Huh." Khan rolled his thumbs. "Tell Raven to come and see me. I want to know what she found."

"She really didn't find much."

"Just have her bring her notes. Maybe Pearl and I can help figure out what happened." He tapped his right temple. "I am a genius, after all."

"Are you bragging again?" The sound of Pearl's voice made us turn to see her approach.

Khan opened his arm to hug her. "Not bragging, just stating facts. I just told Leo that we'd like to go over Raven's findings in Dina's case."

Pearl snaked her arm around Khan's waist and leaned against him. "Of course. We're always happy to help."

"It's just that Raven has abandoned the case. After all, it was because of her research that Magni and I crashed that day."

Pearl frowned. "Nonsense. Is that what Raven is telling herself?"

"Yes. She feels very guilty."

"She didn't ask either of you to fly through a thunderstorm, and she certainly didn't cause the breakdown of the drone. You were two grown men rushing to assist two women who never asked for your help in the first place. For her to feel guilty about that is pointless and wrong."

I just stood there, not sure how to respond.

"Anyway, we can't stop the world because of Magni's injuries. He too will need the world to go on and to find his new place in it." Pearl turned to Khan. "We should include him in Raven's findings."

Khan frowned. "But he's not feeling well."

Pearl didn't back down. "Which is why we'll give him something that will distract him for a short while."

Solo cleared his throat. "Magni can't get out of bed yet."

With Solo being more than seven feet tall, Pearl looked up at the giant man. "Then we'll all go to him. I want Magni to be present. It's not like he has anything better to do in his room." With her regal grace, Pearl turned to me. "How long do you think Raven needs before she can go over her findings with us?"

"Ehm, I'm not sure." On the inside I was scrambling to find a way out of it.

Solo looked thoughtful. "You know, Pearl, I think it's a good call to include Magni. You're right, he does need something to take his mind off his own misery. This might do it." Solo walked to the staircase. "Let me go and check in with him and see if he's awake. Leo, will you get a hold of Raven and tell her?"

Before I had a chance to protest louder, Pearl smiled and said, "We should make it a family event. That way we

261

can all surround Magni without focusing on him. It will give him a sense of connection without suffocating him."

It took me a few seconds to find my voice. "When you say family event, what do you mean exactly?"

Solo kept ascending the stairs while Pearl addressed Khan. "I would say everyone should be invited, but maybe not the children. What do you think?"

He nodded. "No children."

"I'll tell Mila and Erika then." Pearl raised her voice when she spoke to Solo, who was already at the top of the stairs. "Solo will you let Laura know?"

"Will do."

Pearl planted a quick kiss on Khan's cheek before she walked off too. "I'll just ask the cook to send up some cake and drinks."

Khan and I were the only ones left in the foyer when he patted my shoulder again. "You'd better get a hold of Raven, she has a case to present."

My heart was racing as I searched for Raven and found her coming down from the third floor.

"I'm sorry you had to wait for me, but the kids wouldn't let me go." She pointed her thumb over her shoulder. "I just passed Solo and he said something about seeing us in a minute. What was that about?"

I took her hands. "Raven, we're in trouble."

"Why, what's wrong? You look like you've eaten something bad."

My tone of voice was low and urgent. "They're all gathering to hear you present what you found out in Dina's murder case. Khan, Pearl, Solo, Erika, Mila, and Laura. It's going to be in Magni's room so he can hear it too"

"But you said we could never tell anyone."

"I know. Trust me, it wasn't my suggestion."

"Then why didn't you say no?"

My voice rose to a high pitch. "How do I say no to Khan and Pearl?"

Raven chewed on her lips. "You could have told them that Erika is upset with me for digging around in her daughter's death and that with Magni being injured it would be better to wait."

I rubbed my forehead. "Yes, I wish I had thought of that, but I didn't. Argh, why the fuck didn't I keep my big mouth shut? I could have just passed Khan with a simple hello."

"But we can't tell them what we know."

"No, we absolutely cannot." My head was spinning rapidly. "Or maybe… I don't know."

Raven waited for me to gather my thoughts.

"Maybe it could work. The more witnesses, the better. If we tell what we know with Pearl and Mila in the room it will improve our chances of leaving unharmed. Don't you think?"

Raven leaned in and muttered. "I can't believe we're discussing this like our lives are in danger."

I scoffed. "Trust me, they are. This is the ruling family, and just like every ruler before them they've had to do what it takes to stay in power."

"Yes, but I'm like family to them."

With a hand at the small of Raven's back, I nudged her forward. "Let's hope that makes a difference. Now let's go get the box with all your research. You're going to need it when you do your presentation. Your accusations are strong, so your proof better be strong too."

CHAPTER 26
Dina's Death

Raven

Leo carried my box of evidence as we walked to Laura's and Magni's suite. Our footsteps were heavy and our breathing shallow. My mouth was dry and when Leo stopped before entering, we exchanged a long look.

"Every instinct I have as a protector tells me to take you away from here. To shield you from whatever is going to happen in that room if we enter."

"The truth shall set you free." My words sounded hoarse because of my dry throat.

"Yeah, but the kind of truth we're bringing often results in an unwanted kind of freedom."

I tilted my head, silently asking him to explain.

"You know, the kind of freedom where your soul leaves your body because you're silenced."

Closing my eyes, I heaved in a deep breath of air. "That won't happen. The Northlands have changed and there are good people in that room."

"Yeah, but just in case." Leo moved closer and shifted the box in his arms to make room for him to lean down and kiss me. "I want you to know that meeting you and loving you has been the highlight of my existence."

"We're going to be fine, Leo. We didn't do anything wrong."

He kissed me again. "Just remember that I love you."

"I love you too." Pressing down the door handle, we entered the suite and found Erika, Laura, Mila, Pearl, Solo, and Khan standing or sitting around Magni's large bed.

"Come in. There's some coffee and tea if you'd like."

Pearl pointed to a table with refreshments. "We're all excited to hear what you have to say."

Leo put down the box and with shaking hands I walked over to stand in front of them all. "Magni, how are you doing?"

Magni sat in his bed, his hair unbraided and wild and long scars showing on his right temple, jaw, and neck. He looked pale and sick. "I've never been better." His tone was sarcastic and there was no smile.

"Can we close the window now?" Mila folded her arms around herself. "I'm cold."

Khan held up a hand to Solo, who'd got up to close the window. "Don't! It's better to be cold than pass out from the heavy air that was in this room when I walked in. A full day of Magni's farts requires at least ten minutes of fresh air."

Magni snorted. "I'm sorry, brother. I would love to be more respectful and go to the bathroom every time I have to pass gas, but I didn't fucking invite you all to invade my space, and it's a little hard to walk on legs that you don't have any longer." The long answer seemed to drain him and his head leaned back on his pillow.

"It's okay, we'll survive – and the women's perfumes have freshened up the air." Khan clapped his hands together. "Now let's hear what Raven has to say. Leo told us she's stuck and dropped the case, so we're here to put the clues together and hopefully help find answers to what really happened to Dina."

They all turned their attention on me except Mila, who crawled up in her dad's bed. "I'm so cold, can I have some of your blanket?"

It pained me to see Magni not open his arms to her. He had always been a hard man but usually Mila had brought out the softness in him. To Mila's credit, she didn't let his cold attitude stop her. Instead, she sat next to him with her feet under his blanket. "All right, Raven, I'm ready."

I took a deep breath and began. "As Lord Khan mentioned, I don't have all the answers, but I can go over what I've found so far." Pulling up the original case file I gave it to Khan, who was closest to me. "This is what I found in the basement of Station Seven. Until then I had never heard of Dina. It doesn't say much except that she was married, the daughter of Marcus and Erika Aurelius, and that she died at only fifteen years old from a fall out of an attic window. The case was closed as it was ruled to be suicide, but I thought it was strange and wanted to investigate. That's why I spoke to Mila, who agreed to help me ask questions of you, Erika." I gave a quick glance to Erika, who sat leaning back on her chair with her legs crossed. It was evident that she didn't appreciate what I was doing.

"Erika explained why there's no trace of Dina at the Gray Manor and how Marcus removed all reminders of her to protect Erika from going into a deep depression again. Maybe he also did it to avoid thinking about it himself, but either way, Erika mentioned that Dina's things were stored away in the basement and..."

"What do you mean by 'again'?" Pearl looked from me to Erika. "Did you suffer from depression before Dina's death?"

Erika hesitated before she nodded and gave a dismissive answer, "Yes, it lasted a few years around my pregnancy with Khan."

When Pearl didn't follow up with more questions, I continued. "So, Mila, Jonah, Magni, Khan, and I went down to the basement storage room and found a closed-off chamber with Dina's things."

"That was when I could still walk," Magni commented from the bed.

"You'll walk again." Khan gestured for me to go on.

"We found some of Dina's diaries and it was while going through those that I stumbled on something interesting." My eyes went to Leo, who looked tense. We were getting closer to evidence that would cause pain, confusion, and potentially anger.

"What did you find?" Laura leaned in.

I wet my dry lips. "Ehm, well, first of all, I found Dina's diary and learned that she had a secret crush on one of the guards at the manor about six months before she got married, and I thought that he might be a potential love interest that got jealous so I noted him down as a suspect."

"I knew it was something like that." Magni gestured from his bed. "There's no way Dina would fall out a window by mistake or jump herself. She wasn't suicidal. Did you get the name of this guard and did you talk to him?"

"I only had his first name but I searched in old logs and interviewed older guards, and the Scott that was around at that time was Scott Livingstone, soo...."

Magni wrinkled his nose. "Oh, I see. Strike him then."

"Why?" Pearl asked.

Khan backed Magni up, "Because Scott Livingstone is a strong and fierce warrior but it seems unlikely that he would have followed Dina to her new home and killed her in a rage of jealousy since he's never been attracted to women. Scott has been open about being gay for as long as I can remember." Khan swung his hand through the air. "All right, moving on, what else did you find?"

I picked up the diary and turned to the marked page. "On March 18th, 2412, which was Dina's twelfth birthday, she overheard a conversation between her parents and..." I looked up at them. "Maybe it's better if I read it to you."

Erika moved in her chair. She knew what was coming but she didn't try to stop me.

267

This day turned out to be a birthday from hell. Dad was in a worse mood than ever. He snapped at Khan and Mom at dinner and said some awful things that made Mom tear up. I could tell Khan was hurt so I tried taking his hand under the table, but he pushed it away and just sat there all stiff and looking down.

Later when I wanted to check up on Mom in her room, I heard them fighting again and even though I know I shouldn't have, I listened through the door.

Dad said something about being tired of people asking why Magni and Khan looked so different. "I'm fucking tired of the question."

And Mom said, "I don't believe anyone would ask you that question, Marcus."

"Maybe not to my face, but people aren't blind, Erika. Khan looks nothing like me and I see the question in people's eyes."

"He's your son. You know he's your son."

"No, I don't know that. Not after what happened."

I couldn't see Mom's face, but I could hear her voice break when she spoke. "Marcus, please! You said that we would never speak of it. You said that no matter what, Khan would be your son."

When Dad didn't answer Mom cried hysterically, and I wanted so badly to go in and comfort her and tell Dad that he was wrong. Khan might be darker than me and Magni, but that's just because Mom's side of the family has brown hair and brown eyes. She has told us so many times.

But then my Dad hissed, "I know what I said. It doesn't change that he's not my blood, and we both know it. Every time I see the boy's face, I'm reminded of it."

After that I ran back to my own room, and now I'm shaking. I don't know what to do. Should I tell Khan what I heard or not? Nothing will ever be the same now.

The room was dead silent as I stopped speaking and raised my gaze from the diary. It was like time had stopped; they all sat with stone faces.

Chewing on my lip, I looked at Leo, who moved a little closer to me.

"Dancing devils." The small outburst from Magni woke them all up. "That's some fucked-up shit right there." He coughed.

Khan stood stoically close to me, his eyes on Erika, who was looking down. "Care to explain, *Mother*?"

My defense of Erika came fast. "Your mother didn't cheat on your father if that's what you think."

Khan held a hand up to silence me and repeated his request for Erika to explain herself. "I'm listening."

Erika didn't meet his eyes; instead she looked at me. "Why don't you tell them what happened?"

I swallowed hard and cleared my dry throat. "When Dina was a few months old, Lord Wolf came to see her." My eyes darted around the room until they settled on the bedspread on Magni's bed. "He and two of his generals drank with Marcus to celebrate a precious girl had been born and then things took a turn." I paused. "The generals held down Marcus while Lord Wolf raped your mother."

Pearl's hand flew to her mouth. Mila gave an outcry and Laura got up from her chair with a row of cusswords, while Magni growled and stabbed a finger at his mother. "Why didn't you ever tell us that? We could have avenged you."

"How? Your father already killed Wolf and we were trying to move on with our lives. No one can know about this outside this room."

My attention turned to Khan, who still hadn't said a word. He seemed way too calm for someone who had just been told this kind of news.

"So that's why Dad started the rebellion – or should I say, Marcus?"

Erika's lower eyelashes were wet with tears. "He loved you and he was your dad."

Khan scoffed. "Loved me. Huh. I don't know if that man was capable of loving anyone, but this explains a lot."

"That's because you didn't know Marcus before it happened. He was an artist and a loving husband."

"Khan, it changes nothing," Magni exclaimed looking paler than ever. "Even if people outside this room found out that I was the rightful heir to the country, it's not like anyone is going to want your crippled brother as a ruler anyway."

"Magni." Laura gave him a pleading look. "Stop talking about yourself as a cripple."

"I *am* a fucking cripple." With his right hand Magni tore the blanket off, showing that from the knees down there was nothing. "Do you see any legs, Laura, huh? Do you?" He held up his left arm, which only went to a little under his elbow. "The sooner you realize that the man you married is gone, the better."

Mila sat next to her dad with her legs pulled up in front of her and her face hiding against her knees. She had wrapped her arms around her legs and from the way her shoulders were bobbing I could tell she was crying.

"Should we take a break?" Leo asked Pearl.

"No. You people don't get to take a fucking break. Welcome to my world where nothing makes sense and everything that comes at you is *shit*." Magni's anger gave color to his face and with the extensive scarring on his left side, he looked scary. "I can't take a break from this joke of a body and you don't get to take a break from the news you don't like either. I demand that we keep going. If someone killed my sister, I want to know who did it."

With the tense atmosphere in the room, it was hard to pull out a picture of Lord Nikolai Wolf and hand it to Khan. "I found this picture and it validates what Erika said. You look a lot like him."

Khan stared at the picture of his biological father but he didn't speak, so I continued.

"I assume you've seen a picture of Lord Wolf before?"

"Of course, but the most famous one is of his corpse after he was killed. I haven't seen this picture before."

"He was forty-two in that picture so four years younger than you are now."

"He was forty-three when he died, wasn't he?" Khan handed the picture to Pearl.

"Yes." I nodded. "Anyway, I felt it was important to talk to witnesses that knew Henry, Dina's husband, so I tracked down his friend and roommate, Michael, and Laura and I went to interview him."

Magni's voice was low, as he looked at Laura. "When was this? Why didn't I know? Did you at least bring guards?"

Laura crossed her arms. "I'm two seconds from being done with your grumpy ass for today. I'm a lethal fighter and so is Raven. Now be quiet and listen to what Raven has to say."

Magni growled low but kept quiet, so I continued.

"Michael still lives in the building where Henry and Dina lived. He showed us the attic and the place behind the apartment building where he found Dina. From the beginning I had Dina's husband, Henry, as the prime suspect, so I asked a lot of questions about him, but from what Michael remembers he was very happy with Dina and they seemed to get along. The thing that stressed them out was the fact that Henry didn't get his prize money."

Khan frowned. "What do you mean?"

271

"He was supposed to receive a million dollars, but he only got one hundred thousand. Apparently, Marcus claimed that marrying his daughter was the highest prize any man could get."

"I thought Michael was a jealous lover of Henry." Laura pitched in.

Nodding my head, I shifted my balance. "Yes, and that made him a suspect as well."

"Why didn't Henry get his money?" Pearl asked.

"Because my father was broke," Khan said matter-of-factly and then he leaned his head back. "Ahh... so the blackmailer I heard Mr. Zobel talk about was Henry."

"What blackmailer?" Pearl waved a hand. "Go back, you lost me."

"As I said, Laura and I were suspicious of anything Michael told us because he was Henry's roommate, and we weren't sure if maybe something more was going on between them."

Laura piped up again. "They shared a small bed."

"Yes, but Michael's story turned out to be true because I found Marcus' wristband with sound clips of Dina begging him to pay Henry the rest of the million dollars."

"Poor girl." Laura rubbed her face.

"Would you like me to play some of the clips for you?"

"Yes." Magni narrowed his eyes. "Anyone who doesn't have the stomach for it can leave but we're hearing it."

I played the nine sound clips, from the first ones begging for Marcus to pay the money to Dina growing harder and colder, to the last ones where she began threatening him.

"Dad, I know what you did and why you took that money. You are bankrupt! Mom told me and I would help you, except you already stole my husband's fortune so I can't feel bad for you. You're a thief and a liar. But here's the thing. I also know that Khan isn't your son. That's right,

272

I heard you and Mom talk about it years ago. Since you won't answer my calls or do the right thing, then I guess you leave me no choice than to play dirty too. If you don't make sure to pay Henry his money, I'll share that piece of information with anyone who will listen. Just pay what you owe us and I'll never mention it again."

I played another sound clip and watched them all sit with stern faces and listen.

"I'm learning about the things you've done, Dad. I always knew you were a tyrant to your family but the fear on people's faces when someone mentions your name, it's disturbing, and now that I know how cold-hearted you are and that you'd steal money from your own daughter, I believe the rumors. I'll never let you see your grandchildren or come close to me again unless you pay the money you owe and make it up to me."

Magni sighed. "I knew Dina had a temper, but for the most part, I remember her as a soft-spoken and good-natured girl. For her to speak like that, it's crazy to think how desperate she must have been."

Dina's voice filled the room again. "Khan has been trying to get in touch with me. Did you know that? I guess that means you told him that you're not his father. So far, I haven't picked up, but next time he calls I'm telling him everything unless we have the money."

I turned to Khan. "Remember I asked you if you'd called Dina after the wedding?"

"Yeah, but I wasn't trying to lie about it, I had just forgotten."

"Nevertheless, it makes you a suspect too. After all, you had the most to lose if Dina spread the news that you weren't the legitimate heir to the Northlands."

"You think I killed Dina?" Khan scoffed. "That's ridiculous."

273

"I'm not saying that you did, but a detective can't rule out anything. With your attempts to call Dina, I figured that you were either trying to warn her about your dad's plans or you wanted to threaten her into silence. That's why I asked you to spar with me."

"I don't recall you asking me. I offered." Khan's brow was low and he looked down at me with an intense stare. "Are you saying you planned it to interview me?"

"Kind of. And the point is that you told me about overhearing Mr. Zobel and your dad arguing."

"We just established that he wasn't my dad."

"Right, but you said that Marcus and Zobel were discussing an issue with someone blackmailing him."

Khan pointed to Marcus' wristband. "And now we know who that someone was. They were obviously discussing Dina."

"Most likely." I nodded. "And that would explain why your father was hesitant over Mr. Zobel's suggestion of killing the blackmailer."

"Fuck, I hate that creep." Magni growled low and looked at Khan. "Did you hear him encourage Dad to kill Dina?"

Khan shook his head. "Not in those words. No names were mentioned. I'm not sure Zobel understood that the blackmailer was Dina or that he knew how Marcus had stolen her bride money." He looked down. "The worst part is that I always thought it was the blackmailer who killed Dina. In fact, I blamed our dad for letting it happen."

"But, honey, I thought you said that you didn't know who killed your sister."

Khan nodded to Pearl. "Because I never knew the identity of the blackmailer until now."

Pearl threw her hands up. "All the evidence I've heard so far leads to Marcus. We know he was ruthless, an awful father, and pressed for money. It must be him."

"Except, Marcus was here when it happened," I pointed out.

Magni growled. "My dad could have sent some of his soldiers to do his dirty job. He did that all the time."

"He could have, but Michael called me today and when I told him I'd stopped investigating, he shared something with me that raised another question." I projected the image of the blue feather for all of us to see.

"What is that?" Khan asked.

From Magni's bed came an annoyed sigh. "It's a bloody feather. Everyone can see that."

"Yes, I can see it's a feather, but what does it have to do with anything?"

"Michael told me he found it on the staircase the same day that Dina had died. He kept it as a memory of her since she was the only woman he ever knew."

They were all looking at me, waiting for me to continue, but I was unsure how to.

"I told you, Raven, he can keep that feather." Erika gave an annoyed sigh. "No need to waste our time on insignificant details like that." She moved to the edge of her seat. "I've heard enough. It's all clues going nowhere. Dina has been gone for more than thirty years and it only brings sadness to keep talking about it."

"I'm sorry that it brings sadness." While talking, I pulled out the picture from Dina's wedding and handed it to Khan.

"I've seen this before. That's the man she married." He tapped his finger on the photo and Pearl leaned in to see.

"His name was Henry Hudson, but since you mentioned that you and Pearl are good with details, let me ask you if anything catches your eye in this picture."

They both stared at it.

"Let me see. I'm good with details too." Magni reached out his hand, indicating that he wanted them to hand him the photo.

"Hang on, I have the picture here. Let me project it so you can all see it." I worked my wristband and enlarged the picture for all to see."

Mila had stopped crying and was leaning forward to see the picture. "Dina looks shy but happy."

"You were so young, Erika." Laura looked over at Erika, who was still stiff and looked like she was ready to leave any second. "And you boys, whoa, talk about change."

"Who are those men?" Khan pointed to Henry's two friends."

"This one is Michael, the roommate, and the other was Daniel, a friend who was murdered shortly after Henry."

"Oh, Mother Nature, are we talking about a potential triple murder case here?" Pearl sighed. "It's hard to wrap your head around."

Leo cleared his throat. "The picture is one of the last photos taken of Dina and the people close to her."

"What detail are we looking for?" Khan looked from the photo in his hand to the enlarged version projected in the air. His eyes were narrowed as he searched from side to side. I observed him and saw the moment when his eyes expanded as he found what Leo and I had seen.

Elbowing Pearl, Khan pointed down to the picture and she was quick to see the detail too. Khan's face was tense as he gestured to me. "Please bring back the picture of the feather."

I added the picture of the feather and put the two pictures next to each other. This time everyone seemed to catch on to the detail I'd been referring to.

"What am I missing?" Laura got up to study the picture closer.

276

Pearl's and Khan's eyes were locked like they were having a secret non-verbal conversation.

"Don't you two even think about it." Magni slammed his right hand down on the bed but the movement was weak and made him pant. "If you see something then you'd better spit it out, 'cause I'm about two seconds from having a fit."

Mila blinked her eyes. "Dad. Calm down."

"Look at Erika's jacket." Pearl nodded at the picture.

"What about it?" Magni narrowed his eyes.

"I see it now." Laura walked over and zoomed in on Erika's jacket. "There." A fine line of feathers decorated the breast pocket and they were all blue with a red dot in the middle.

"That doesn't mean a thing," Erika defended herself.

I couldn't keep quiet. "It means that you were there the day she died, Erika."

"Maybe Dina had one on her. I hugged her on her wedding day. The feather could have fallen off."

"Mom, were you there?" Khan stepped closer to her, his tone hard and insistent.

Erika looked around for help, but all eight of us were pinning her down with our eyes.

"Don't look at me like that. It wasn't my fault." Erika's body was shaking and she stood like a cornered animal.

"Tell us what happened?" Khan demanded.

"You don't understand. None of you lived through those times. The country was poor and people were desperate. Your father had to stay strong and be tough or everything would have fallen."

"What *happened*?" This time, Khan spoke the words through gritted teeth.

Erika took a small step back but her chair was behind her. "I did it for you, Khan."

"What did you do?"

"Dina wouldn't stop making threats and the money was already gone. I had to do something. I couldn't let her destroy our future. *Your future*, Khan. That's why I went to speak to her. I explained that Marcus would pay the money later." Erika's hands were shaking. "I even brought my personal savings of thirty thousand dollars, but Dina she... she..."

We all waited for her to continue, holding our breaths.

"She was so angry with Marcus and being a teenager, she was stubborn and unreasonable."

Magni's next words reverberated through the room. "You killed Dina?"

"Nooo, it wasn't like that." Erika's voice broke and her shoulders bobbed as tears filled her eyes. "She was my daughter, I would never harm her. Dina was young, she didn't understand the devastating level of shame and humiliation she would cost your father and me. We had guarded that secret for so many years and she was threatening to destroy everything we had worked so hard for." Erika raised her voice. "We sacrificed *everything* for this country and she would have destroyed it all. I couldn't let her stay unsupervised in case she talked, so I went to bring her home. Marcus and I were going to talk some sense into her. To make her understand what was at risk."

"But Dina didn't want to come home, did she?" I asked.

Erika's head fell down and she sighed. "No. She said she was done being our puppet and when I called for my guards to bring her to the drone, she ran up the stairs and locked herself in the attic. I tried pleading with her but she wouldn't open the door." The tears were streaming down Erika's cheeks. "The guards had to break down the door and when I entered, Dina had crawled out the window. I ran over and by instinct, I wanted to pull her back in but when I grabbed for her, she tried to break free of my hold on her and it made her lose her balance and then..." Erika's body had shrunk, with her shoulders and head low. She was looking down at the carpet with glassy eyes and I saw tears drip to land on her shoe. "I can still see her falling, my hands reaching out for her and her hands reaching out for me. Her scream mixed with my scream... There... There..." Erika's shoulders bobbed with suppressed sobbing before she forced out the words. "There was nothing I could do."

Complete silence filled the room, and I wasn't the only one with moist eyes.

"I ran down to her but her blond hair was red with blood and my little girl was gone." Erika looked up at us. "At first I thought that maybe... I mean, her blue eyes were open and as pretty as ever... but she wasn't there anymore." Her face twisted in pain and she couldn't hold back the sobbing anymore. It made it hard to understand her words, "Dina was dead and no matter how many times I shook her and called for her to come back, she was gone."

Mila rushed from the bed to hug her grandmother and Pearl rubbed Erika's arm. "Take a deep breath."

Their show of sympathy calmed Erika, who continued talking like getting it all out was a relief. "I can only remember glimpses from back then now, but I remember the guards pulling me from Dina's body and hearing them explain everything to Marcus when we got back to the Manor. After that Marcus left to clean up the mess."

"Mom, do you remember telling me and Magni?"

Erika shook her head. "No, I don't remember that at all. I suppose I was in a state of shock and grief." She dried her nose. "After Dina's death I went back into a depression. Marcus had me on suicide watch because I kept telling him that I didn't want to continue living when our daughter had died because of me."

CHAPTER 27
Reaction

Leo

"Is that why Marcus erased all traces of Dina from the Gray Manor?" Laura asked Erika, who had just confessed to causing Dina to fall from the window.

Mila and Pearl helped Erika to sit down; Mila kneeled down next to her grandmother and held her hand while Pearl returned to stand side by side with Khan.

"I never asked Marcus to remove everything. Even though he said he did it for me, I believe it was as much for him. He wanted life to go on. It had to. We had two sons and a country to think about. We were all grieving, but life had to go on."

Raven crossed her arms. "And Dina's husband, Henry, what happened to him?"

"All I know is that he made accusations after she died," Erika breathed.

Khan had deep frown lines on his forehead and his eyes seemed black at that moment. "So, Marcus had him killed."

Erika met his eyes. "Of course. It was the right thing to do."

Pearl shook her head. "You wanted power that badly?"

"We wanted to live, Pearl. There's no such thing as a retired ruler. We couldn't afford for the public to know the truth. Marcus would have been lynched and we would have been killed by the next men seeking power. It's how things work here."

Pearl was squinting like she was trying to shield herself from all the ugliness coming to light. "But…"

"There's no *but*, Pearl. People would have branded Marcus as a fraud if they knew that he hadn't been able to protect me from being raped. He was playing a role as a mighty ruler exuding confidence and strength but in reality, he felt like a failure of a man. We were broke. The whole country was broke, and if people knew that Marcus stole Dina's bride money from Henry…" Erika waved her hand like she was trying to find the right words. "Every day I feared the people would come for us. Every day I wondered if it would be our last."

Laura's voice was full of sympathy. "I had no idea."

"That's because you're too young to have lived in anything but peace, but I grew up with a steady changing of rulers and kings." Erika dried away more tears. "Living in constant fear is the curse of being the ruling family."

There was a moment of complete silence and then Pearl turned to Khan. "Now do you see why democracy is better *for everyone*?"

Khan groaned and began pacing the room while Laura walked over to sit on the foot end of Magni's bed. "What are we going to do?"

Magni looked exhausted when he muttered, "How many know? We have to eliminate the threat." His face turned to us and his hand shook when he pointed a finger at Raven and me. "You'd better fucking guarantee us that we can trust you!"

"Of course, you can trust us. We haven't told anyone." I pushed Raven behind me, indicating that I wouldn't let anyone hurt her.

"Good, but that Michael – we can't have him talking. Solo, you'll pay him a visit."

Pearl took a big step toward Magni. "No, this stops now!"

281

Magni hissed back in a low strained voice, "This is way over your head, Pearl. We'll deal with this the Northlander way, or do you want people to know the truth and an army of weasels to come and knock down the door, demanding Khan isn't the rightful heir? We have to protect our family. Our children."

Pearl gave Khan a pleading look. "No. There are other ways. You could be proactive."

"How?"

"Put the facts out there and offer to step aside if the people prefer someone else over you. Let your results as a ruler speak for themselves and let the people decide if they want you."

Khan scrunched up his face. "You're talking about an election."

"Yes. Offer to lead as you've done so far. If the people want someone else, we can always go live by that beautiful beach that Magni always talked about."

Magni scoffed and was panting a little when he spoke, "Don't listen to her, Khan. The Northlands is our home country."

Pearl remained calm. "Don't forget that there are ten million people here and it's their home country too. Living in fear that someone finds out and overthrows Khan is no way to live, and I'll have no part in killing any more innocent people because of what happened in the past." Looking around like she was challenging each and every one of us, Pearl asked. "Who in here thinks that Khan could win a democratic election?"

Mila and Raven's hands went up right away, mine followed with Laura's and Erika's. Pearl raised her hand and looked at Magni and Solo. "What do you think?"

Magni groaned. "I can't believe we're even discussing this. Are we talking before or after revealing the truth?"

"After." She looked around at those of us with our hands raised. "Who thinks the people would choose Khan despite everything?"

Solo looked down, Erika lowered her hand, and Laura's raised arm sunk a bit too.

Magni spoke in a gruff voice, "Not me. They'll think you've lost your sanity if you offer to give up your power. Why would you do that?"

"Because it's just a matter of time before the truth about my heritage comes out, and I don't want my fucking head on a spear in the front garden like what happened to King Jeremiah."

"That was two hundred years ago," Magni protested.

"Then you take a pick of how rulers and kings have ended their lives in this country. It's not pretty."

"Listen, we'll do a test. We might still be biological brothers."

Khan picked up the picture of Nikolai Wolf that looked like an older version of him. "I wish, but I don't fucking think so."

"We will always be brothers. We share the same mother." Magni closed his eyes like he was about to pass out of exhaustion.

Pearl pulled at Khan's shirt. "You always knew you were the son of a ruthless tyrant, now it's just a different one."

Khan's voice was cold as he looked down at her. "Yeah, one who raped women." He turned his back on her, but she pulled him around and got close to his face.

"You're almost forty-six years old, Khan, and you haven't raped a woman yet, so it's clearly not been passed down to you."

Khan leaned his head back. "Fuuuck, I just remembered something."

"What?" Pearl was stroking his arm up and down.

283

"When I was around eighteen a man was accused of mistreating his wife. During the trial it came out that he had raped her daily. Dad, I mean Marcus, killed him in a public display of what I assumed was insanity. Do you remember, Magni?"

When no answer came, Laura turned and touched Magni who had drifted off.

He opened his eyes. "What?"

"I was talking about the husband dad killed in public. You remember, right?"

"Uh-huh. To the day I die."

Erika rubbed her face. "Let's not talk about that."

"Now that I know how Dad witnessed Mom being raped, it puts everything into perspective. Back then I just thought he was a sadist getting his kick out of torturing a man."

"I didn't agree with the way that man was executed," Erika squeezed Mila's hand. "No one deserves to be burned from the inside like that."

Pearl gaped. "How do you get burned from the inside? You don't mean literally, do you?"

Khan shook his head. "Let's not go into detail. Just know it was a gruesome way to die."

Magni didn't spare us the details. "The rapist was tied down in public and had a scorching iron stick pushed up his ass. He roared and screamed in pain while people spat on him. It was fucking horrible to watch."

Pearl covered her mouth and turned her face away and it made Khan wrap his arms around her. "I'm sorry, honey. I shouldn't have mentioned it."

Laura moved over to stand next to Magni. "Our people have come a long way since then. There's a higher respect for life today. I would say that what our family has done for this country is nothing short of spectacular. The fact that girls go to school now, that we have more women and therefore more children born into families seemed like an impossible dream back when Khan first came to power. Forty years of peace, better jobs, better infrastructure, more money, and an influx of goods that we didn't have access to before, not to mention the possibility of getting a visa and traveling the world. If the men and women of the Northlands don't vote to keep us in the Gray Manor with Khan as their ruler then they are fucking fools."

Magni looked up at her with his eyes hooded like he was fighting off falling asleep. "Do you get that Pearl is talking about democracy, Laura? She wants us to be like the Momsies. We can't let that happen! Motlanders are repressed and brainwashed. They can't even say the word fuck without getting reported."

"The Northlands will never be like the Motherlands. We'll have a better version of democracy, with the freedom to think what you want and express it with as many curse words as you want to." Laura reached for Magni's hand. "And if the people want someone else to lead them then screw them. We'll find some tropical island to live on in peace – doesn't sound like the worst plan to me."

"Hmm." Khan looked at Solo. "What do you think? You've been so quiet."

Solo held up both palms. "I'm open to thinking outside the box. I'm not sure if we Northlanders are ready for democracy but if you go that route, I'll support it."

Khan huffed out air. "You might be right. The critics already call me too progressive and say I move too fast."

"They say you're Pearl's puppet. That's what they fucking say." Magni grumped.

Mila stood up. "I would like to say something."

We all turned to her.

"I just feel bad for Grandma. She confessed to causing Dina to fall to her death and now she must be afraid of what's going to happen to her. But you're all more focused on how to save yourselves."

Erika sat with her shoulders pulled up and her head down. Mila was still holding her hand when she continued, "I can't imagine carrying a burden like that for that many years."

"I never meant to kill Dina."

"We know that." Pearl sighed and looked up at Khan, who was running his hands through his hair while muttering, "This is such a fucking mess. Why didn't you tell us?"

"You and Magni were children."

"But after we grew up, how could you keep something like this from us?" Khan turned to Magni. "Doesn't it make you wonder what else they kept from us?"

"What good would it have done to tell you? I was trying to protect you."

"That's not your fucking job." Magni was scowling at his mother. "What is wrong with you? How can we protect this family if you're keeping secrets from us?"

Mila gave her father a sharp look. "That's not very helpful and it's the wrong question to ask."

"What is?" Magni's voice was gruff.

"Don't ask what's *wrong* with you. Ask what *happened* to you? Grandma was raped in front of her husband, she lived decades in fear, and all that time she did her best to protect her children from seeing what was really going on. Some would say she was brave and carried a heavy burden of pain on her shoulders to shield the people she loved."

"How is it protecting us by keeping us in the dark? Khan and I stopped being children more than twenty years ago."

Khan had tucked his hands under his armpits and stood with a grave expression on his face. "For years I've

286

resented and hated the man I thought was my dad. If I'd known what demons he was battling, maybe I would have felt differently."

"I did what I thought was best," Erika defended herself. If you want to punish me, do it. I never meant to harm Dina, and that's the truth."

Pearl moved over to stand in front of me. "Leo, you're a policeman. What do you say? Based on Erika's confession to the truth of what happened to Dina, do you see a need to arrest her?"

"Leo doesn't get to do shit without my approval. I may be crippled but he still ranks under me."

Pearl stood strong and looked back over her shoulder at Magni. "No one should be above the law."

"He's not sending my mom to prison. That's for damn sure."

"No, I hope we can all agree that sending Erika to prison won't help anything." Pearl met my eyes. "But what does the law say?"

I opened my mouth to answer, but was overpowered by Erika's outburst, "People will call me a murderer no matter what." Her shoulders bobbed again and she sniffled.

"If what you're saying is true, Erika, and you didn't push Dina out the window, then I'm not seeing any reason to arrest you at this point. This all happened more than thirty years ago but there's no statute of limitation on murder, so I have to ask you, Erika, did you have anything to do with the killing of Henry and his friend?"

"No. Marcus didn't share that sort of thing with me."

"So, you weren't aware of any plans to kill Dina's husband or his friend?"

"No."

"In that case, I'll conclude that the killing of Henry and his friend were orchestrated by Marcus and not you. What about the nine hundred thousand dollars? Did you take part in stealing that from Henry and Dina?"

Erika dried her tears away. "No. I didn't even know how much financial trouble we were in until Dina began calling me. Marcus didn't want me to worry."

I gave Raven a sideways glance. "I'd say that with Marcus being deceased, there's no reason to investigate this case further. What do you think?"

Raven gave a solemn nod. "I agree. Dina's death was an accident and the two murders were the responsibility of Marcus. Let's close this case."

Mila crouched down to hug Erika. "Did you hear that? You're not going to jail."

"It doesn't matter. If Khan tells what happened, everyone will say that I killed my own daughter. People are ruthless and small-minded."

Laura bit her lip. "You're right about that, Erika. But we'll know the truth and if anyone asks, we'll tell them it was an accident, and that you were trying to protect your family. Most Northlanders will understand that."

Erika stared at Laura. "You think so?"

In a fluent movement, Laura sat down on the edge of Magni's bed and pulled one leg under her. "Don't expect Motlanders to understand, though. They judge Magni and Khan for killing people who were plotting to overthrow us. Remember when Mr. Zobel and the others were executed for treason back in the thirties? The council made a big deal about it being barbaric and a violation of basic human rights."

"I remember."

"But we Northlanders never judged them for it because we knew Khan and Magni were doing it to keep us all safe."

"Laura, you're not helping. No one should have to kill anyone." Pearl rubbed her face. "I can't even imagine the burden on your souls."

"My soul is fine."

"Is it, Magni?" Pearl stared at him. "And is this kind of life what you want for your sons?"

Magni looked at Solo, who had kept in his seat the whole time. "It's a man's duty to be a fierce protector of his country and family. I wouldn't hesitate to kill anyone who broke through that door and threatened my kin, and I expect my sons to do the same. We don't kill for joy, we kill for honor and to protect the ones we love."

Solo gave Magni a nod as a silent promise that he could count on him.

Khan nodded. "Yes, I agree. Now, Pearl, Mila, and Laura, would you take our mother to her room? Magni and I have a decision to make."

Solo, Raven, and I began exiting the room too when Khan stopped me with a hand to my shoulder. "Leo, can I have a word?"

"Of course."

He pulled me to the side. "Answer me honestly. Knowing the truth, would you still want me as your ruler?"

I didn't hesitate. "Absolutely."

Khan's tongue ran along the edge of his front teeth. "And if I held a democratic election, would you think less of me?"

I shifted my balance and scratched my neck. "Knowing that you're pressed against a wall, I get that you'll have to make a ballsy move, but democracy... I don't know, Lord. That's a hard pill to swallow."

"Yeah. My critics will have an easy time making me look weak."

"At least you'll have the support of all the women who moved here. They all admire Pearl and love the idea of democracy. You would have their vote."

"The women can't win me an election alone."

"What the hell are you two whispering about?" Magni called from his bed in a low voice. "I thought you wanted to discuss this with me."

We both turned to Magni. "I wanted to know if Leo would vote for me despite what he heard today."

"And?" Magni asked. "Would you?"

"It's hard to imagine anyone can challenge Khan's level of connections and expertise. We may all despise the man who sired him, but Lord Wolf has been gone for more than forty years now and the results you've created as a ruler are impressive."

"Is that a yes?" Magni asked.

"Yes, I would vote for Khan and you to stay in power. I may not agree with everything you do, but I see the progress and the way our country prospers."

Khan picked up the picture of Nikolai Wolf again. "I hate how much I look like him."

"Give me that picture." Magni only lifted his arm a little when he reached for it. "Nah, you don't have the same nose or mouth. I'm still not convinced that he's your dad. We should have a test made."

"I guarantee you that Marcus had a test done already."

"It doesn't matter, Khan. We are brothers. Always!"

Khan sat down on the edge of the bed next to Magni's hip and the two men linked their hands together in a masculine, rough way. "Are you ready to risk it all?"

Magni hesitated and then he gave a weak smile. "You're really serious about having an election?"

"I know it's crazy but Pearl has been talking about this since I met her, and the idea of the Northlands being a democracy doesn't offend me like it once did. Things

290

wouldn't change much if you and I are still in power, but we would have been chosen to lead by the people. Not just our dad, but *the people*, Magni."

Magni shook his head. "I can't believe we're even contemplating it. That's fucking crazy! Yet, a small part of me kind of likes what Laura said."

"About the beach?"

"About saying screw you all."

Khan sat with a thoughtful expression on his face. "Yeah, but you did that once, remember?"

"I went to Alaska. That's different from a warm beach."

"Our country suffered during your absence, and none of us want to surrender power. We are too patriotic for that." With a deep inhalation, Khan leaned his head back and brushed his hand up and down his throat. "I wonder what would happen if we allowed our critics to speak up. All the shitheads who constantly work in the shadows, criticizing what we do. They have no idea about the burden of leadership."

I kept quiet, not sure why the brothers had allowed me to stay.

Magni coughed. "There hasn't been an election in the history of the Northlands, and I can tell you for sure that our father would be rolling in his grave if he heard us talking about democracy."

Khan shrugged. "Our situation is different from every ruling family before us. They never had a place to retreat to in case they lost an election, but with Pearl's connections to the Motherlands, it doesn't have to be a matter of power or death." He pointed out the window. "If the fuckers are dumb enough to pick someone else, we can go live in the sun. And even if that happens, I predict it won't take long before they call and beg us to come back."

Magni groaned. "Or we could just eliminate all threats like we usually do."

291

I took a step back.

"Relax, Leo. I'm not talking about you and Raven. It's that neighbor of Henry that I don't trust."

Khan closed his eyes for a second. "But the thought of winning an election, though. It would be satisfying."

Magni groaned. "Sounds like you're going to follow Pearl's suggestion then?"

The brothers had serious expressions on their faces and their eyes locked. "The question is will *we* follow her suggestion? You know I can't do it alone."

Magni snorted and raised his amputated arm. "I'm not going to be much help to you. Not like this. If anything, I'll make you look weak."

"No, you won't!" It burst out of me.

They turned their heads like they'd forgotten I was there.

"You saved my life in that crash, Magni, and I'll tell that story to any journalist who will listen."

His face was impassive. "It doesn't matter how many lives I've saved. All our people will see is a weakling and a has-been." Again, Magni closed his eyes and it was clear he was drained from the talking.

Khan drew a heavy sigh. "Leo, I'll talk to you later."

I left the room to find Raven and Solo sitting on the staircase further down the hallway, waiting for me.

"What did Khan want to talk to you about?" Raven got up and brushed the back of her pants.

"He had some questions."

Solo rose to his full height too and next to Raven, he looked gigantic. "About what?"

"About this whole election thing."

Solo wrinkled his forehead. "Since when does Khan care what anyone thinks but Magni and Pearl? And why did he want to talk to you about it and not me?"

"Because you're family; he knows he has your vote. I'm an outsider; he wanted to know if I would vote for him."

"Ahh. That makes sense." Solo scratched his head and looked down at his wristband. "I have to get back to Willow. She's called me three times already."

"Is she okay?"

"She's fine, but apparently Nora is whiney and has a fever." Solo raised his arm and we bumped shoulders in a manly hug. "Keep me updated, will ya?"

"Will do."

As he descended the stairs two steps at a time, Raven gave me a hopeful smile. "So, do you think there's going to be an election?"

"They're discussing it right now. Come on." I took her hand and began my way down the stairs. "I need to find a drink. This meeting had me sweating through my shirt."

"I know. Geez, Leo, when Magni said they would have to eliminate all threats and asked if they could trust us, I thought you were going to pull a gun or something."

"Yeah, that was a tense moment for sure." I squeezed her hand tighter. "I'm grateful it ended the way it did."

Raven was quiet and didn't look as relieved as I felt.

"What's wrong? Why are you quiet?"

"Is it wrong that I'm slightly disappointed that it was just an accident? I was so sure that Dina was murdered."

We were at the bottom of the stairs when I stopped and turned to her. "You did good, Raven. You gathered evidence and found answers. That's good work." With Raven on the first step, she was almost my height. Her beautiful smile made me grin back at her. "I shouldn't have said that. You're going to be overconfident from now on, aren't you?"

Wrapping her arms around my neck, she pulled me closer and kissed me. "That's right. I'm so confident that I'm going to make a strong claim."

"Oh yeah?"

She nodded with a smile. "Remember how I told you I would be the best lover you ever had?"

"Uh-huh." I gave her a cheeky grin. "And you lived up to the hype. You're definitely the best lover I've ever had."

Raven tilted her head with a cute smile. "What if I told you that I'll also be the best wife you've ever had?"

My grin morphed into a look of surprise. "Wife? Did you say wife? What the hell, Raven, did you just... did you just agree to marry me?" Her smile was blinding me and it was a good thing she had her hands around my neck, or I might have lifted from the ground with all the butterflies that were swirling around in my stomach.

"It's just that if the Northlands become a democracy more women are going to want to live here, and I saw you first."

My eyebrows furrowed closely together. "What does democracy have to do with us marrying? I don't follow."

With a firm grip on my collar, Raven pulled me in and spoke in a low sexy voice. "You are mine and I'm not sharing. Don't think I've forgotten how Gennie looked at you. Marrying you is just a matter of closing the deal before the competition gets here."

"Hmm..." Narrowing my eyes, I let my hand slide down to the small of her back and pulled her close against me. "You're crazy if you think there's any woman in the Motherlands who can compete with you."

"You haven't seen how many pretty women live there."

"You're right. I haven't. But unlike those women, you are fearless, funny, and not afraid to stand up to me when I get too bossy." I kissed her. "I would pick you any day, Raven."

294

We were almost nose to nose, and she had a teasing smile on her lips when she released her tight grip on my collar. "Okay, well, in that case. Forget about the wedding."

I realized my colossal mistake and hurried to correct it. "No, I mean, I can't imagine wanting another woman, but you're obviously right; I haven't seen them so I can't really know for sure. I completely get why that would make you insecure. We should definitely marry and ease your fears."

We laughed together and Raven gave a sweet sigh when I wrapped her in my arms and whispered in her ear, "The sooner the better. I want all of you, don't you ever forget that."

The sound of running steps burst our bubble, and we looked up to see Khan come down with a determined expression on his face.

"Did you make a decision, Lord?"

"We did. I need to speak to Pearl and start preparations. It's time to be strategic." He hurried past us.

Raven raised her eyebrows. "Is it just me, or did he look excited?"

"No, I got that vibe too. I think it's the part about being strategic and winning over someone else that excites him. I'll bet he and Pearl will stay up half the night and plan the road to victory."

"Let's hope they'll succeed."

"Yeah, but I doubt it. The older generation wouldn't be forgiving when Khan tells them that he's not the rightful heir. That sort of thing matters to them and most of them hated Lord Wolf. Plus, they already think Khan lets Pearl have too much influence."

"But don't they see all the good things that are happening?"

"Sure, but if you're talking about the influx of women, then it's the younger generation who is benefiting.

295

Ultimately none of us want to be included in the Motherlands and lose our sovereignty. We're the last free men."

Raven raised an eyebrow. "Yeah, I know that old motto."

"It's not just a motto, Raven, it's what's in our hearts." My chest lifted as I sucked in air. "Khan might find that he has more critics than he thought. There's always going to be cowards who would normally whisper in the shadows and whose only agenda is to cause trouble. Now those cowards will feel empowered to inflame the Northlands with hateful rhetoric causing riots and fights."

My brave woman squared her shoulders. "Then it's a good thing that we police officers are there to control things."

"Don't get ahead of yourself. We still need to make an officer out of you. You're not even halfway there, and now that you're marrying me, I doubt they'll let me work as your boss."

Raven narrowed her eyes. "Then we won't tell them."

With a firm grip on her hips, I lifted her from the first step down on the floor and gave her an amused smile.

"What's so funny?"

"That you think I can keep being married to you a secret."

"But I don't want another boss."

"It'll just be at work. At home, I'll still be the boss." I winked at her and Raven bumped my shoulder and laughed.

"I'll fight you for the title. If I win you have to refer to me as Boss."

We exited the Manor and walked to my drone, which was full of boxes with her clothes and things. "I'm not going to fight you, Raven. I still remember your porn-inspired fighting moves and now that I'm allowed to act on my attraction to you, I wouldn't stand a chance."

"Oh yeah?"

"Uh-huh, I would be stripping you naked and making love to you as soon as we got physical."

Raven rolled her eyes in a playful manner. "Just for the record, I would take that as an act of surrendering and declare myself the winner."

"I know you would, which is why I'm not stupid enough to take you up on the bet."

"Chicken," Raven teased as we got into the drone and took off.

Putting the drone on auto, I turned my chair to face her. "As I see it, I'm doing us both a favor. You don't really want me to go around at home and say, yes, Boss?"

Raven's laugh grew. "Why not? I would totally get a kick out of that."

"No, you wouldn't. You'd lose respect for me in less than a day." The drone was leaving the craziness of the Gray Manor behind as we flew over green forest. "Come here." I patted my thigh.

Raven unclicked her seatbelt and moved on to my lap. "We're breaking the law, Inspector."

Kissing her and letting my hands weave into her curly black hair, I mumbled into her mouth, "No, we're not. Seatbelts aren't mandatory in the Northlands."

"Yes, they are. It was added a few weeks ago after your crash."

"What? That's bullshit. Magni and I were both buckled in and that didn't help. You're not serious."

"I am. The captain gave a short briefing about it."

"Don't tell me we have speed limits too."

"Only over the cities as usual; otherwise we can go as fast as we want, granted that we stay out of the no-fly zones."

Raven was still on my lap as I bit her earlobe with a low growl. "Let them try and arrest us if they can. I don't think even that can stop me from taking you right here, right now. I've dreamed of having sex with you in my drone too many times."

Raven leaned her head back and gave me room to kiss and lick her neck. "Is there any place you haven't envisioned us having sex? I'm only asking because you said the same thing about your shower, the gym, your kitchen, and my room at the Manor. Or maybe a better question would be: do you think of anything other than sex?"

"Not at the moment, no."

CHAPTER 28
Sex in a Drone

Raven

I don't know why making love to Leo in that drone was so much better than it had been on his sofa. Maybe it was the relief of sharing all the details from Dina's case and still being alive. Maybe it was because I had agreed to marry him before we left the Manor.

We kissed like it was a matter of survival. We touched like we weren't sure we'd ever get the chance again. Leo sucked and suckled and I didn't care that he was no doubt leaving hickeys on my body. I would be walking to work tomorrow with his signs of possession showing on my neck. It *should* bother me but I found a crazy kind of satisfaction in Leo's raw desire for me.

"What if someone flies by and sees us?"

Leo nibbled at my lower lip. "Don't worry about it. There's no one here."

With us both naked and me wet from all our kissing and foreplay, I slid down on top of him with a deep satisfied moan. Leo had his hands planted firmly on my buttocks and used them to control the pace while I let my hands slide across his strong chest, shoulders, and biceps.

"Flying a drone will never be the same after this." He grinned and bit my neck in a playful manner. "Turn around, I want to try something."

I bumped my head against the ceiling as I turned around on his lap.

"Lean your back against my chest – yes, like that –and put your feet up on my knees." Leo sunk lower in his seat and with me on top of him he began a fast pace of pumping in and out of me. We were melting together while I was looking out the windows with hooded eyes and taking in the large woods of the Northlands with the gorgeous fall colors. It occurred to me that it was symbolic of how perfect it was. Leo and I were different in almost every way. We had a different skin color, gender, nationality, and personality but, somehow, we complemented each other as perfectly as the yellow, red, and green colors beneath us. He was strong and the feeling of him inside me made me lean my head back to rest on his shoulder while closing my eyes. "You make me so happy."

Leo pushed all the way in before he stopped moving his hip. As his hands slid around me and squeezed my breasts and waist, he turned his face to kiss me again. "You make me happy too. This, Raven, this is a dream coming true."

I opened my eyes. "The sex?"

"The connection between us. I have friends but this... this is something different. I can't get enough of you."

"It'd better be different, I don't want to think about you doing this with any of your friends."

Leo bit my lower lip and raised an eyebrow. "Very funny."

"But if you do, tell me, would you be on top or below?"

I laughed as Leo pulled me around with a growl. He was cursing when he banged his foot because of the cramped space, but he soon pressed himself against me again and took me from behind in slow delicious movements.

Looking behind me, I watched the man I was going to marry hold on to me with his eyes closed and his mouth slightly open. He was a sight to behold with his chiseled torso and beautiful features. Without thinking I licked my lips and gave in to the feeling of his firm grip on my hips and the magical friction that his large erection created between my thighs.

My breathing got deeper and my moans louder.

"Yeah, babe, take it. Take it all."

The buzzing sensation of an orgasm building made me close my eyes and push back to meet Leo's rhythm. "Yes, yes... yes..."

"Oh fuck, Raven, it feels so good. Can I come inside you?"

I didn't say yes and I didn't say no. My body and mind were on a synchronized chase for that euphoric place that Leo had taken me to before. Placing my hand against the fogged-over window, I let my head fall down and gave a small scream of ecstasy. "Yaaaasssss..."

Leo was pumping in and out of me at high speed now, drawing out my orgasm and making my legs feel like jelly, and then he bored his fingers into my hips and held me firmly against him while leaning his head back and roaring out his own orgasm.

It took me a minute to recover and then I noticed that the drone had landed outside his house. Leo's house was at least twenty minutes from the Gray Manor but the flight had felt short because of our lovemaking.

"We're here." He was panting behind me. "I don't want to pull out of you. It's the first time you've let me come inside you, and you have no idea how amazing it felt."

We were both on a sex high and in no hurry to end what we had started. When I turned around, I playfully bit his earlobe and growled low. "I want more."

"Me too." Leo retaliated and bit my lower lip. "The first time you were here, you ran naked from my house, so how about this time you run naked into my house?"

I smiled. "I can do that. But only if you run naked with me."

"Deal." He kissed my nose. "But you have to run straight to my bed, get in, and prepare to make love all night."

With my right hand I pulled his hair into my fist and gave him a sexy grin. "Deal."

Leo smacked my butt with a playful smile and pointed to the door. "Go!"

The ground was cold as we ran with our clothes in our hands to the house. We were laughing and fighting for the covers once we got into bed, and I planted my cold feet on his legs.

Leo paid me back by stealing the entire cover and as a result, a pretend fight broke out between us. Just like Leo had predicted he didn't stand a chance. As soon as I sat astride him trying to hold his hands down, he forgot about the fighting and went back to loving me. It was sweet and satisfying, and after what felt like hours I was drifting to sleep in his strong arms.

"When are we telling your parents that we're getting married?"

My voice was drowsy. "Sunday, I think."

"No. Tomorrow, Raven. I want to tell them tomorrow."

My eyes were already closed, my breathing slow and deep. "Yes, we'll tell them tomorrow."

The last thing I heard before I surrendered to sleep was Leo whispering into my ear. "I love you, Raven, and I can't wait to make you my wife."

CHAPTER 29
Family Dinner

Leo

I was equally proud and nervous when Raven took me home to her parents' large house on Victoria's Island.

When we arrived, two of her younger siblings, Samara and Jones, were in the kitchen with their mother, Christina.

"Raven, sweetie, what a wonderful surprise. I tried calling you all morning. We're having a party."

"We are?"

"Yes. Didn't you hear the good news?"

"What news?"

Christina had flour on her shirt and her braid was coming undone, but she was glowing with excitement. "The Northland will become a democracy. It's not official yet, but Khan told your father and he has been beside himself all morning."

Raven had gone around hugging her siblings and now she was hugging her mom. "Is he upset about it?"

"Yes, but I don't care. This calls for a celebration. I wanted to invite everybody but Pearl said it's too soon and that they want to announce it to the inner circle themselves in a few weeks. She asked that we make it a small celebration for now so it's just going to be the Aurelius family." Her eyes shifted to me. "And your boss, but Pearl told me you two already know about it."

"Yes. We were there yesterday when Pearl suggested it."

303

Christina tilted her head. "It's the strangest thing. As long as I've known Pearl she has advocated for the Northlands to become a democracy. I can't for my life figure out why Khan and Magni suddenly changed their minds and agreed. Do you know if anything happened yesterday?"

Raven frowned and opened her mouth but I was quicker, and answered before her, "I think it's the situation with Magni. With him no longer being able to do his usual work, Khan must have been more open to thinking of new ways to do things."

Christina tilted her head. "Yes, that makes sense. Huh, imagine that something great could come out of an accident that awful."

"Is Magni coming too?" Raven asked.

"No, he'll need to stay in bed a while longer, but as I said, Pearl, Khan, and their kids are coming, and so is Mila. She's going to be happy that you're here." Christina picked up a large knife to cut some bread. "I'm still bubbling over with joy on the inside whenever I think about the Northlands as a democratic country."

I made a pained noise just from the word.

"Oh, Leo, your face. Don't look like that. I know you think democracy will be the end of your world, but it's going to be the best thing that ever happened to you."

I wanted to tell Christina that her daughter was the best thing that ever happened to me, but the timing seemed off.

Christina pointed to the staircase in the entryway. "If you want, you can join Alexander upstairs. He was brooding all morning, so I exiled him from the kitchen. Maybe you can convince my husband that his world isn't coming to an end."

The energy from Christina was infectious as she returned to supervise her youngest children, who were helping her cook.

Raven smiled. "Anything I can help with, Mom?"

"Yes, you could ask your brother to set the table. Indiana has been hiding in his room refusing to help with anything."

"Why don't I just do it?"

"Because then he gets away with his strategy and that won't teach him to be a useful member of a community, will it? If he wants to eat, he can set the table."

Raven winked at me. "I should have warned you that my mom is a master at putting people to work."

"It's about ingraining values. You never felt too important to help out, so I don't know where he gets that from."

I smiled at the women because it suddenly made sense that Raven had such a strong personality. She had grown up around women like Laura, Pearl, and Christina, and none of them fit my initial expectation that women were delicate and fragile.

"What are you thinking about?" Raven was standing right in front of me. "What's that smile on your face?"

"Oh, nothing, I was just thinking about how my mentors used to describe women to us boys. You two are nothing like that, but then I don't think my mentors had met a woman in real life."

Christina laughed. "Let me guess; they told you that we women cry a lot?"

"Yes."

"And that we have to nap like babies?"

"Yes."

Christina nodded her head. "Alexander heard some of the same stories growing up, but then he also heard horror stories about how we Motlander women emasculated our men."

I shifted my weight. "Yeah, but those are true. I mean look at the Motlander men. Most of them look like women – well, maybe except Jonah."

A knock on the front door made Samara sprint to open it, and a few seconds later Mila came in with Pearl and her two children behind her.

Christina lit up. "Oh, hey. Come in. It's good to see you. I was just explaining to Leo how we Motlander women do not emasculate our men."

Mila walked over and hugged first Raven and then Jones, who was standing on a stool chopping cucumber. "That's a sharp knife for a six-year-old. Careful with that."

Jones held up the knife and flashed a smile that revealed he had lost his front teeth. "This is nothing. Dad taught me how to skin a rabbit with his big hunting knife."

Christina froze. "He did what?"

Khan came into the kitchen, and Raven and I greeted him just as Christina leaned her head back and hollered, "Alexander, Alexander, will you come down here?"

"Uh-oh…" Jones chewed on his lip. "I wasn't supposed to tell you that. Dad is going to be mad at me now."

Heavy steps from upstairs heralded Alexander Boulder running down the stairs. "You're all here." He gave Khan a manly hug and came to shake my hand.

Christina stood with her hands on her hips. "Did you teach Jones to skin a rabbit?"

Alexander's eyes fell on his youngest son, whose lips disappeared as if he wanted to take back his words. "Yeah, I did."

Christina lowered her brow. "He's a vegan."

Boulder shrugged. "Mostly, but not all the time. Come on, honey, you can't blame a man for teaching his sons about survival."

Just then Indiana, who had to be around eleven, came down the stairs and Christina pointed at him. "Darling, do you know how to skin a rabbit?"

Indiana's eyes darted between his parents before he swallowed hard. "Ehm... no, I don't think so."

"Tell me the truth, Indiana. Did your father teach you to skin a rabbit?"

Khan lifted his arm, signaling for the boy to come closer. "You'd better say yes, or I'll be very disappointed in your dad. Every real Nman knows how to hunt and prepare his own food."

"Of course I taught him." Boulder walked over to Christina and wrapped his hands around her from the back. "We talked about this. We teach them our way of living and they get to make up their own minds. I'm not forcing them to eat meat and you can't force them to be vegan."

"Well, speaking about that. If you, Khan, and Leo want some meat, one of you will have to cook it."

Boulder smacked a kiss on his wife's cheek. "See, this is why we need a kitchen bot."

Christina walked over to cut some bread that looked homemade. "Cooking is an opportunity to come together as a family. I wouldn't miss it for the world."

Boulder opened a fridge in the corner of the room and pulled out three large steaks. "Anyone else want some good protein?"

Samara, who was a mini version of Christina with her brown hair and blue eyes, wrinkled her nose up. "Dad, you know I would never eat another living being, that's so cruel."

Freya, who was the daughter of Khan and Pearl and according to rumors highly academically gifted, looked almost bored when she looked at Samara. "They wouldn't be alive if you ate them, would they? Besides, our being vegans isn't very supportive of animals to begin with."

"Excuse me?" Pearl looked at her daughter as if she had grown an extra head.

"The sad truth is this. Before the Motherlands made it illegal to consume animals, there were millions of cows and chickens. The minute the vegans stopped any and all consumption of animal food products they became responsible for the loss of life on a far greater scale than the meat eaters."

Khan grinned. "That's right, honey, you tell them."

Freya nodded and continued, "There was no longer a market for animals bred for food so they would never get a chance to even exist. They would never know the joy of breathing air or running in the fields. What I don't like about being a vegan is that we literally stripped them of their right to live."

I was gaping at the girl, who couldn't be more than ten or eleven, but her parents didn't seem surprised by her eloquent speech. Instead, Khan looked highly amused while Pearl tilted her head and narrowed her eyes a little.

"I assume your father told you this?"

Freya nodded "We've discussed it, but mostly I've read about it in a book by Lee Rinehart – maybe you heard of him?"

"No, but let me guess, it was a book your father gave to you."

Khan confirmed it: "Lee was a fine warrior and a great Nman. His book is a classic in the Northlands."

Freya nodded. "I like when Lee wrote, 'When you think you are truly righteous, morally superior, and better than others, you are blind to other views. All life has a right to live, even if it is only for a short time to feed another life. If you break the circle of life, all will die.'"

Pearl gave Khan a dirty look. "We'll discuss your attempt at indoctrination later."

Christina craned her neck to look back at Boulder behind her, "You men have to stop undermining our teachings about no killing. You knew I wouldn't approve of you showing our boys how to kill."

"Which is why I told them to keep it quiet. Don't say I'm not respectful."

Khan's finger brushed the hair on his young son's head. "Magni and I brought our boys on a survival trip this summer – you liked that, didn't you, Thor?"

The boy nodded his head. "Yeah, I got to make a fire and we built a bridge across a river. It was fun."

Khan grinned. "See, Christina. Pearl wasn't happy about that trip either, but you women will have to respect that men are raised differently up here."

Thor turned to look up at Khan. "Can Jones and I go outside? I want to show him my new play drone."

Khan nodded and the two boys, who were the same age, ran out of the kitchen.

"Stay away from the pond, though," Pearl called after them as she walked over to snatch a piece of cucumber from the cutting board that Jones had abandoned. "Freya, why don't you ask Indiana or Samara if they want to play chess with you?"

Freya still stood leaning against her dad and looked up at Indiana, who was half a head taller than her. "No thanks. Last time I beat Indiana four times and he threw the bishop against the wall."

Indiana scrunched up his face. "Chess is stupid."

"Then find something else to do until lunch is ready." Pearl took another piece of cucumber.

Christina was quick to jump in with a task for them. "Actually, how about you three set the table. Indiana, you'll have to show them how to expand it."

"Argh." He gave a displeased grunt. "Do I have to?"

Boulder and Khan answered at the same time. "Yes!"

When the three children left the kitchen, Boulder threw his hand up. "I don't know what I'm doing wrong but that boy is the most unhelpful child in the world."

Pearl smiled. "It's the age. He'll grow out of it."

Khan shrugged. "Magni was like that too when he was a preteen like Indiana. Always grumpy and contrary."

"Huh." Boulder handed beers to me and Khan. "Leo, can you imagine if we had shown our mentors an attitude like that? My back would have been black and blue."

"Yeah, mine too." I nodded. "Maybe it's what happens when kids grow up in families instead of schools. I mean Magni was in a family and so is Indiana."

Boulder gave a groan. "It would be easier if I could put some fear into the boy, but if you think Christina is weird about skinning a rabbit then you should have seen her the time that I spanked Indiana when he was a toddler. For a pacifist, she just about skinned my ass." Boulder's deep chuckle filled the kitchen. "I had to sit for two full hours listening to parenting tips on how to deal with toddlers in a non-violent way."

Khan took a seat on a high chair by the kitchen island. "Trust me, our dad beat the crap out of Magni and it didn't change a thing. He was still moody and grumpy at Indiana's age."

It was the strangest feeling to stand in the kitchen and watch the interactions between these two families as their children moved in and out carrying cutlery, glasses, and stacks of plates. I'd never experienced anything like it, and soaked up all their conversation and interactions with fascination. Boulder cooked the steaks and told Khan to get us some more beers while waiting for the food to be ready. Christina filled bowls and trays, and it was clear to see that these people spent a lot of time together.

Internally I was wondering why none of them questioned what I was doing here.

"You sure that I can't help with anything?" Mila offered for the third time.

"Wanna learn how to tell when a steak is cooked to perfection?" Boulder winked at her from his place behind the stove. I sniffed in the lovely aroma of garlic, butter, and quality steaks.

"Maybe I could carry something to the table instead," Mila suggested with a smile to Boulder.

"Yes, how about you take this in." Christina handed Mila a basket of bread. "And by the way, Mila, how was your dad doing this morning?"

Mila took the bread. "He was pale and in pain. I don't understand it but he says he feels like his feet are hurting but that's not possible since they are… you know, gone."

"That's called phantom pain. It's a real thing." Boulder placed the steaks on a plate and signaled for us to move into the dining room. "No, Leo, you don't want to sit there, that's the kids' end of the table."

"Oh, okay." I moved to the other end.

Pearl smiled at me. "It's better that way because the kids never sit at the table very long."

I sat between Mila and Raven when bowls and trays of food were passed around and all the time, I wondered why none of them had asked why I was there. To be included without question in a lunch with Raven's family and their close friends who happened to be the ruling family was unexpected. I had braced myself to be roasted about my relationship with Raven, but they talked about everyday things like the co-educational school, Mila's current amount of dogs, and Christina's work on her newest archeological digging site. I was almost done eating my steak when the question finally came up.

"Hey, Leo," Boulder leaned forward to get eye contact. "I forgot to ask you; how is your healing coming along? Raven said you were back to work, but are you going to be ready for Mila's tournament?"

Mila and Raven exchanged a quick glance.

"Actually..." I put my fork and knife down. "I'm not going to be in Mila's tournament."

"Why not? If you need more time to get ready, I mean..." Christina tilted her head and changed her focus to Khan. "Aren't you going to postpone the tournament anyway? I doubt Magni will be ready in only three months. The participants would understand if you give him time to heal so he can enjoy the festivities, wouldn't they?"

Khan was chewing so he didn't answer, which made Christina continue, "It's no secret that I'm the biggest opponent of tournaments, but Magni has been looking forward to Mila's tournament since she was ten, and postponing it would give Leo time to get in shape too."

I was used to seeing Lord Khan at official ceremonies and on TV, so to see him sit around a dining table and eat in a casual manner blew my mind a little.

"Yes, we'll have to postpone it and now with the plans for the election, it's all about timing," Khan agreed.

"Kids, are you done eating?" Pearl smiled at the five children at the end of the table. "How about we call you when it's time for dessert."

Thor, Jones, and Samara were quick to push their chairs back and run off, while Indiana and Freya moved more slowly.

"Today, Freya." Pearl hurried her daughter up.

"I'm not a baby; why can't I stay and listen?"

"Because some things are for adults only and we'll need you two big kids to keep an eye on the younger ones."

"Indiana, will you close the door please? Thank you." Christina smiled as her oldest son complied and closed the two large French doors separating the dining room from the rest of the house.

"As I was saying," Khan continued. "With the election, we'll need to be strategic, and Pearl and I are already working on ideas."

"Of course you are." Boulder had a small tomato on his fork. "But can I just ask again? What the fuck?"

Pearl gave a small groan. "Don't start, Boulder. The decision has been made."

The fork with the tomato on it swung through the air in stabbing movements as Boulder spoke to Khan. "The only explanation I can find for this insanity is that you popped some of Magni's painkillers and that the two of you were fucking high when you made that decision. Democracy is the worst evil and a slippery road to socialism. Next thing you'll have me sharing my wealth and giving up my house and drones. I'm not fucking okay with that."

Khan lowered his brow. "I guarantee you that we'll never have socialism in the Northlands. We'll leave that shit for the Motlanders."

"Hey, if by socialism you mean a safety net to take care of the weaker people in society, then that is a fine thing. Every citizen should have the same opportunities."

"Why, Pearl?" Boulder challenged. "What if they don't work as hard for it? I didn't come to this place in life without busting my ass off."

"And you don't think the men working for you do the same? What about chance and circumstance? Most of your fortune you inherited, Alexander, and that was dumb luck and nothing else. And what about Khan? He was born into the right family. Good for him, but what about the people who aren't that lucky? How is that fair?"

"Fair?" Boulder pulled back in his chair, staring at Pearl. "Life isn't fair! At least I'm providing opportunities for tens of thousands of men to make their fortune. I'm providing workplaces, and you know damn well that Christina and I donate a lot of money to improve education in this country."

Pearl remained calm and nodded. "Yes, it's admirable and generous of you, which makes me wonder why you resent the idea of socialism, as you call it. After all, you already share your wealth."

"That's different. I share what I want and I give it to whom I want to. In your system, people don't have a chance. No matter how much they work they all get the same amount of points."

Pearl was tapping her fingernails on the table. "Not true, Alexander. I've told you this before. The more you work, the more points you get."

"Yeah, but you can only keep the same as everyone else. The rest you need to distribute."

"Exactly. And as you know there is great satisfaction in knowing that you're a large contributor. I would argue the satisfaction of contributing to others is greater than getting more for yourself."

Boulder opened his mouth to speak, but Khan raised his hand. "As entertaining as it is to hear the two of you argue the same thing over and over, I'm going to stop you. Boulder, nothing will change except that I'll be elected by the people."

"But your plan is crazy, Khan. Why would you tell them your darkest secret and give your critics ammunition against you?"

Pearl leaned forward, "Because the truth will set him free."

"That's for damn sure." Boulder snorted. You'll be free but you'll also be out of the Gray Manor on your *ass*."

Christina dipped her head close to Pearl's. "What dark secrets? I thought the reason Khan wanted an election was because of Magni."

My dad sighed, clearly realizing he had said too much, but Pearl didn't look upset. Laying a hand on top of my mom's, she explained, "It's not fair that you're the only one in the room who doesn't know the truth, and soon the whole country will know anyway."

"Know what?"

"Raven discovered that Khan wasn't the rightful heir to rule the Northlands. He's not the biological son of Marcus Aurelius."

"Okaaay… but what is the dark secret Alexander hinted at?"

Khan groaned. "That *is* the dark secret."

My mom gave Pearl a questioning look, as if silently asking her to confirm.

"I know, Christina. It's strange that heritage means so much to Nmen, but apparently, it does." Pearl picked up her glass and glanced at Khan. "I'm confident that honesty is the best way."

Khan didn't answer at first, but cut another piece of steak. "We'll see what happens. Right now, I'm focused on winning the race."

Boulder ran his hands through his hair. "Argh. But what if you don't win and some turd takes your place."

Christina placed her hand on Boulder's wrist. "We've got to trust that Khan and Pearl can pull this off." She turned her face and looked at Pearl. "You'll have to let us know how to best support you."

"Me!" Khan corrected her. "Pearl isn't running for president. I am!"

"Yes, of course, that's what I meant."

"Why president and not ruler?" I asked.

Khan raised his chin. "Because I like the ring to it."

Pearl shook her head. "It's because a new title signals that it's a new type of leadership. Kings, Rulers, and Czars aren't democratically elected. Presidents, prime ministers, and council members are."

Khan sighed and put down his cutlery. "It's a shame about Mila's wedding. I know we have to postpone it, but it would have been perfect because my popularity always spikes whenever I do a wedding ceremony. Not to mention that Mila's tournament is proof that we Northlanders aren't the only ones changing in this integration. For a Motlander-born woman like Mila to let our men fight for her shows that she's accepting our culture."

Mila looked down. "I'm only doing it because I lost a bet to my dad. To be honest, I don't care for the violence."

Khan shrugged. "That's fine, as long as you don't tell anyone outside this room."

"I told Jonah."

Khan waved a dismissive hand. "That doesn't matter. He's not a voter."

Pearl sat straighter on her chair. "Now that you mention Jonah, Mila, I spoke to him this morning. He might have some good input on running a campaign since he did it recently. I've asked him to visit us again soon."

Boulder had stopped eating and sat with his arms crossed. "I like Jonah. I've only met the man a few times, but he was intelligent, pleasant, and different from what I'd imagined a male Motlander would be."

"Yes, Jonah has a good head on his shoulders," Khan agreed. "But back to my numbers spiking around weddings; it would be convenient if we could make a big spectacle out of Raven's wedding now that Mila's wedding will be postponed. What do you think, Boulder?"

Boulder shook his head. "How many times has Raven told you and Magni that she doesn't want a tournament?

It's not going to happen, Khan. Hell, knowing my daughter, she would be more interested in fighting herself than marrying any of the poor champions."

Khan raised an eyebrow and smiled. "I didn't say anything about a tournament."

"What's with the smug smile?" Boulder turned in his chair to look at Raven. "Am I missing something here?"

"Yeah, that's why I came today. We wanted to tell you."

Boulder's eyes widened. "Tell me what?"

I cleared my throat. "The thing is that Raven has agreed to marry me."

Boulder's eyes blinked as he looked from me to Raven and back. "What? When?"

"Yesterday. She agreed yesterday."

"Did you know this?" Boulder turned to Christina, who sat with her mouth open.

"No."

"But what... I mean how..." Boulder's hands tore through his hair. "Is this some kind of prank?"

"No. It's true, Dad."

Boulder held up a hand. "Wait a minute. First you tell me there's going to be democracy in the Northlands and now you're telling me that my daughter is marrying her boss. It's not April first, people, so what the fuck is going on? What kind of elaborate joke is this?"

"It's not a joke, sir." I took Raven's hand on the table. "Raven moved in with me last night."

"She did what?"

"We've been intim... ehm, getting to know each other for some time now and yesterday, Raven, finally agreed to marry me."

Boulder planted both elbows on the table and stared at Raven. "Is this true?"

"Yes."

"Why didn't you tell us?"

317

"I'm telling you now."

Boulder pushed his plate away. "It sounded more like Khan was telling me, so I guess that means he knew before I did."

Khan patted Boulder's back. "Don't worry about it, my friend. I only found out yesterday when I pressed Leo."

Christina raised her glass and sucking in a deep breath, she spoke on the exhalation. "And here I thought you were just bringing home your boss. Leo, forgive us for our reaction, but Raven truly surprised us, that's all. We're excited to get to know you better."

Boulder narrowed his eyes. "How old are you, Leo?"

"Dad." Raven bulged her eyes out, looking embarrassed.

"I'm thirty-one, sir."

"That's ten years older than Raven."

"So what, Dad? You were all excited about him fighting for Mila and she's a year younger than me."

"No, I'm just saying that there's a big age difference. How did this happen?"

Pearl leaned in. "Yes, I'm curious too. When did you fall in love?"

Raven and I smiled at each other. "I don't think any man can look at Raven and not see her beauty, but for me, it's her humor and personality that makes her irresistible."

"Irresistible, huh?" Boulder raised his chin and frowned at me before looking at Raven. "And you're sure about this, honey? Marriage is a life-long commitment."

Her tone was sarcastic. "Am I sure? No, I'm only doing it because I'm forced. Oh, no, wait…" Raven placed a hand in front of her mouth. "That was Mom."

Khan and Boulder groaned. "How many times do we have to hear about that? Things were different then."

"It was the scariest time of my life." Christina still had her glass raised as if waiting for us to join her in a toast.

"You got close to marrying Archer," Mila said with a smile. "Imagine how different everything would have been if you'd married him instead of Alexander."

Christina grinned. "Yeah, there have been days when I've wondered the same thing, but then I speak to Kya and hear her complain about Archer doing some of the same absurd things that drive me crazy in my marriage, and I'm good."

Boulder picked up his glass of beer. "Archer was nothing but a boy compared to me. He wouldn't have been able to handle you."

We all laughed at that comment and Khan elbowed Boulder. "Have you met Kya? If Archer can handle her, I think he would have been man enough to handle Christina too."

Boulder clearly didn't like any talk about Christina with a different man, and scratching his neck he muttered, "Am I to understand that you two are really getting married? You sure it's not just a stupid prank?"

"It's no prank," I assured him. "We're getting married as soon as possible."

Christina planted her elbow on the table and used her free hand to support the one that was still reaching out with her glass. "Are you people going to toast with me or not?"

When we all clinked glasses, Christina smiled widely. "To my daughter and her lucky groom."

After emptying my glass of beer, I set down the glass and saw Pearl reach over the table to place her hand on top of Raven's. "Of all the women I know, I would have thought you'd be the last one to rush into marriage. You've only really known him for a few months, haven't you?"

Raven's eyes were soft when she smiled at me. "Leo and I met when he came to the Gray Manor with all the Motlander artists last August. It's been a little over a year."

Pearl's thumb stroked across Raven's hand. "Don't feel pressured, sweetheart; the Nmen can be persistent when they pursue a woman, but you don't need to marry to be together."

Pearl's words made me nervous. I didn't want her to create doubt in Raven's mind, but my woman answered in a clear and confident manner. "I get that, but marriage means a lot to Leo, and that makes it important to me too." Raven squeezed my hand and gave me a warm smile that made my spine tingle.

"Aww, look at them, they're so in love." Mila tilted her head and placed her hands on her chest. "I want that too."

"Don't get any funny ideas." Khan waved a finger at her. "This business of falling in love is flaky and not a good way to guarantee that you get the strongest protector possible. Raven made a good choice with Leo, but it's better if love grows after you pick the right champion at your tournament."

The talk and the congratulations continued as they wanted more details about when Raven had fallen in love with me.

"You used to think he was boring and stiff, remember?" Mila laughed. "You even said you didn't want me to marry him because he didn't have a sense of humor."

Raven blushed a little. "Sorry about that. I guess I didn't know that side of him until recently."

"Or maybe you just wanted Leo for yourself all along," Mila teased.

"Maybe."

The two friends were smiling at each other when Mila declared, "As consolation for stealing one of my champions away from me, you'll have to let me help plan the wedding."

"We just want a small ceremony." Raven's words were overpowered by Khan, who clapped his hands.

"Excellent. Now that we have confirmed that Leo and Raven want to marry, we'll make it a festive day to bring joy to the entire country. This is exactly what the Northlands need right now. After your wedding, I'll announce the election and then right before the voting day, we'll have Mila's tournament. That way, my popularity will remain high."

Pearl released Raven's hand. "The ceremony will need to be transmitted to the country, though, and it would work better if you had a grand ceremony instead of a small one."

Raven and I exchanged a glance.

"Honey, I know you said you wanted a small ceremony, but if this can help the Northlands to be a democratic country, it's worth considering a large ceremony, isn't it?" Christina asked.

Raven sighed but didn't answer, so her mom turned to me. "Would you mind a big ceremony?"

I hesitated too.

"We'll pay for it of course," Christina added.

"As long as I get to marry Raven, I'm good with whatever. Obviously, Raven has to be comfortable with the scale of it, but I want every man in the whole world to know that she's mine now."

One of the French doors opened and Samara popped her head in. "When is dessert ready?"

"In a few minutes," Christina answered and turned to Raven. "So, what do you say? Will you marry Leo in front of the whole country?"

Raven swallowed hard but then she locked eyes with me. "Yes, let's tell every woman in the world that you're mine as well."

Epilogue
Winter Wedding

Two months later on New Year's Eve 2448
Leo

I looked out my window for the seventh time, feeling anxious for Zasquash and Solo to get here. This time, I lit up as Solo's new drone came in view.

It took a long minute or two for the drone to land and for my friends to cross the frost-covered ground to my front door, where I stood waiting for them.

"You look like a man ready to get married." Zasquash grinned and gave me a masculine hug.

"Did you get any sleep last night?" Solo came in and hugged me too. "Remember how I didn't sleep the night before my wedding. I was fucking terrified that Willow would have regrets and not go through with it."

"I think I slept an hour or two, but it doesn't matter. I'm so pumped with adrenaline."

"Good. And Raven, did you talk to her?"

"Yeah, she's with Mila at the Manor. She called me and complained about having to wear a dress."

Solo laughed. "I've never seen her in a dress."

"No, she told me. Obviously, I don't care what she wears, but it sounds like Mila and Laura have very firm ideas about what a bride should wear. Laura even wanted Raven to wear a pair of her high heels."

Zasquash raised his eyebrows. "Is she doing it? I've been trying to get Darlene to wear some too, it looks fucking hot."

323

"Raven refused. She says they hurt and told them to stop treating her like a doll."

Solo raised his chin up. "Good for Raven. She's never been one to let others boss her around."

I chuckled. "Believe me, I know."

Solo threw his jacket on my couch and took a seat. "I was meaning to ask you about that. Her time at the station is coming to an end soon, right?"

"Yeah, on January 26th. Then she goes back to the academy for three months. I'll only see her on the weekends."

"That sucks."

"Yes. It sucks big time."

Solo moved to the edge of his seat. "Look, I'm only mentioning it because I heard some disturbing things from Willow that worried me."

"What?" Zasquash got three beers from my fridge and returned to the living room, handing us one each.

"Raven told Willow about some of the things that happened to her at the academy and we can't let her go back there if shit like that is going to happen again."

I frowned. "The academy is a tough place."

"Sure. So is the army, but it sounded like the headmaster is a psycho with some kind of vendetta against her. He swore to her face that he would make sure she doesn't pass and he has been sabotaging her every way he knows how."

Opening my beer, I took a sip. "Why would she tell Willow and not me?"

Solo shrugged. "That's Raven for you. Always trying to solve her own problems, but think about it; the headmaster has had six months to cook up new strategies to make her fail."

Zasquash sat on the armrest of my sofa. "Hmm, sounds like someone should pay that guy a visit and remind him that women should be treated with respect."

"But Raven doesn't want special treatment."

Solo and Zasquash stared at me. "Exactly. Raven wants the same fair chance as everyone else at the academy, but it sounds like he already decided to boot her out one way or another. I get that trailblazers have to work twice as hard as everyone else, but she should have a fair chance. Anything less is fucking wrong!"

"I agree, but Raven would be pissed if she found out that I paid her headmaster a visit."

"I get that." Zas took another swig of his beer.

For a moment none of us spoke and then Zasquash groaned. "It's fucking ironic how we're upset about this situation when last year we were all pissed that Khan allowed her to join the academy to begin with."

Solo nodded. "In my defense, it was the idea of something happening to her that made me against it."

"You wanna hear the worst part?" I breathed. "I actually think she'll make a good officer. She is so fucking hungry to prove herself, and these past few weeks that we've let her work on some real cases she has nailed every task we gave her. Raven is bloody sharp."

Solo chuckled. "I could have told you that. Unless we're talking about math because trust me, she's horrible at it."

I smiled. "I've noticed."

"How about Zas and I pay that headmaster a visit? We have a certain effect on people and if you want, we could even bring a handful of our Doomsmen brothers and swing by the school to have a friendly chat with him. What do you say?"

Every soldier on the Doomsmen Squad was more than seven feet tall and bulky with muscles.

"It's nice of you to offer, but the whole academy would be buzzing about it if a group of you mutants showed up. One of you is noticeable but a whole group is fucking terrifying to most people. Raven would hear about it for sure."

"So? Let her hear that her friends have her back."

"No, Zas. She's too much of a fighter. She wants to do this on her own."

"Don't stress about it. We're not police officers who knock on people's doors and ask permission to come in. We're trained soldiers who climb up walls or rappel down from rooftops. We might be large men, but getting in and out without being detected is what we're trained to do."

Taking another sip of my beer, I pondered out loud. "His name is Kaiser Martinez. I've met him a few times and I know he's on the list of invited guests for the wedding ceremony."

Zasquash snorted. "Why? If he's a jerk, he shouldn't be invited."

"More than a thousand people are coming, Zas. The place is going to be bursting with every person of importance and with Raven and me being police, he was included."

"So, what do you want to do?" Solo moved to the edge of the couch.

I thought about it and gave a sly smile. "Let's just be chill about it. We'll show Kaiser a private part of the manor and explain to him that Raven has a husband and some good friends that would get very upset if she isn't treated fairly."

Zasquash grinned. "That's right. Nobody fucks with our Raven. She could get in trouble for beating up her headmaster, but I'll gladly do it for her if needed."

"Let's hope that it doesn't come to that. Problem is that Martinez is good friends with my boss."

Solo crossed his arms. "I wouldn't worry about that. You and Raven are friends with me and while Magni heals, I'm the acting Commander of the police force and the army. Honestly, I went through enough hazing myself when I joined the Huntsmen. I won't tolerate anything less than fair treatment of any recruit at his academy and I'll be happy to tell him that."

Zasquash raised his beer up. "If Martinez is smart, he'll know not to go whining to anyone about this."

We clanked our beers and emptied the bottles before leaving my house.

"When you return here, you'll be a married man," Solo pointed out as we flew away, heading for the Gray Manor.

That thought made me smile.

Raven

It wasn't the thousand people watching me as I walked into the ballroom that made me shy. It was Leo's reaction to seeing me dressed up with the white dress, the make-up, and my hair styled.

At first, he gaped, and then as I came closer, I could tell that he was swallowing hard and blinking back tears.

Taking the last steps to stand with Leo in front of Khan, I smiled and whispered, "You look handsome."

Leo was wearing his formal police uniform that enhanced his wide shoulders and amazing behind. Reaching out to me, he took my hands. "You look like a goddess, Raven."

With a shy smile and soft crinkles around my eyes, I whispered loudly, "Don't get used to it. This will probably be the only time you see me in a dress."

With a big smile, Khan began his speech: "It was a blessed day when Raven and nine other children from the

327

Motherlands first arrived at the Northlands back in 2437. Never had any of us men seen seven girls at once and I would be lying if I didn't admit that I was always hoping that you girls would choose to stay and become Northlanders yourself.

"Raven, you were always one of a kind with your curiosity and desire to learn how to fight like a boy. Those among us who have had the pleasure of teaching you can testify that you're a fast and technically skilled fighter.

"Your father, Boulder, and I often mused about what kind of man it would take to catch your interest. We should have known that you'd pick one of the Northlands' finest. Leo has shown that he has intelligence, ambition, bravery, and superior fighting skills. You couldn't have chosen a better partner, Raven."

Leo and I smiled at each other.

"Traditionally, when a woman marries it's for protection, but with you two, we all know that's not the case. Nor are you marrying for money. The only thing that ties you together is mutual love." Khan paused. "In this day and age, true love is something so precious that it's worth far more than a million dollars."

Murmurs of agreement were heard from the audience as Khan continued, "It's my privilege to ask you, Leo da Vinci, do you take Raven Pierson Boulder to be your wife?"

"I do."

"Do you promise to protect her, respect her, and love her?"

"I do."

"And you, Raven Pierson Boulder, do you take Leo da Vinci to be your husband?"

"Yes, I do."

"Do you promise to honor, respect, and love him?"

"I do."

"In that case, I now declare you husband and wife."

Leo didn't hesitate before stepping forward to cup my face and kiss me.

I lifted my hands and held on to his neck making our first kiss as man and wife deep and long. "I love you so fucking much," he muttered into my mouth.

"And I love you!" When we pulled apart to breathe, we were smiling widely and turned to see the large crowd all cheering for us.

We kept close as people approached to congratulate us. Leo received a lot of pats on his shoulders and I received compliments about how pretty I looked. Some of our colleagues from Station Seven were there and Cameron joked that from now on he would only spar with me if Leo wasn't in the room. "I don't want your jealous husband breathing down my neck."

Leo, who had seen me fight with Cameron, grinned. "I'm sure Raven can and will defend herself if anyone oversteps her boundaries."

Cameron grinned back. "I fucking hope so with all the hours I've spent training her."

The line of people who wanted to congratulate us seemed endless, and at one point I was hugging Willow and Darlene when their husbands Solo and Zasquash led Leo away.

"Where are you going?" I called after him, but he just blew me a kiss and gestured he would be back in a few minutes.

Looking down the long line of hundreds of people, I whispered to Willow and Darlene. "I wish I could sneak off too. Most of these people I don't even know."

Darlene and Willow craned their heads. "It'll take you hours to greet all of them."

I sighed. "Yes, I know."

Mila came over at that moment and Darlene explained the situation to my best friend, who chewed on her lip for

329

a second before she resolutely exclaimed, "I've got this. Go find Jonah. He's over in that corner, I'll join you in a minute."

Willow and Darlene each hooked an arm under my elbow and served as buffers between me and all the strangers in the room.

We were moving through the crowd when I heard Mila's voice in a microphone: "Hello, can you all hear me? On behalf of the bride and groom, I have an announcement. They truly appreciate that so many wish to congratulate them, but let's not waste your evening with all of you standing in a long line to have a few seconds of polite conversation. Instead, you should have a drink, mingle, and make some new friends. That's what parties are for. If you want to congratulate the couple, snap a photo and or a small video and upload it to the wedding site that we created."

A lot of the people in the long line looked as relieved as I felt, and soon they all spread around the room again.

Jonah was standing with a drink in his hand when Willow, Darlene, and I came to join him.

"Can I give you a hug?" he asked me and looked around. "Mila warned me that married Nmen get a bit crazy so I thought I'd asked first in case Leo is around."

"He's not, and even if he was close, he wouldn't mind me hugging you, Jonah."

"You sure?"

"Yes." I hugged him. "The Nmen don't think of you as a threat. They know you're not interested in us women like that."

Jonah squeezed me before releasing me and pulling back to look into my eyes. "That's a pretty big assumption and a generalization."

I tilted my head. "Well, are you?"

At that moment Mila came to join us. "Did you see how it all worked out fine?"

Feeling grateful to her, I planted a kiss on Mila's cheek. "You were amazing. I owe you one, sweetie."

Willow pressed a drink into my hand. "Cheers, beautiful."

I knew I should get around and greet more people, but being in a corner with Mila, Jonah, Darlene, and Willow felt safe and comfortable. We joked and laughed until Khan came over with five giant men.

"Mila, your dad asked me to introduce you to some of the men who will be competing in your tournament. This is Chip, Alan, Morris, Conlan, and Phyton."

Mila gave a polite smile to all the men. "It's nice to meet you."

"If you ask me there's a big chance these are the men you'll be choosing from. I thought that maybe you wanted the chance to ask them some questions. Three of them are Doomsmen."

The five men were different in looks and colors but they all had serious expressions on their faces. Mila, who had been laughing and smiling a minute before, was now fiddling with her hands. "Ehm, okay, well, I didn't really prepare any questions."

"Ooh, I have a good question for you then!" I whispered it into her ear.

Mila nodded. "Right. Okay. Then my first question would be: how do you feel about my friend Raven joining the police corps?"

They exchanged looks and when no one answered, Mila turned to the first man.

"Chip, was it?"

"Yes."

"What's your opinion on women working as Raven does?"

Chip was one of the few Nmen who had trimmed his hair short. He stuffed his hands into his pockets. "I don't have a problem with women working, as long as it's not dangerous work."

"So, if Raven was your wife you wouldn't let her work on the police force?" Mila asked.

Chip's eyes fell on me. "Probably not. It doesn't seem safe."

"All right, thank you, Chip. How about you?" she asked the next guy and one by one they all backed up Chip that women shouldn't work in a place of danger. Only one of the men insisted that women shouldn't work at all. Mila gave him a polite comment, "Interesting," before she moved on with what I assumed was a mental note not to pick him.

"What do you know about me?" Mila asked the men.

"You're the Commander's daughter." Morris stood like a soldier with his legs spread and his hands clasped in front of him.

"Yes, I am. What else do you know?"

"You were born in the Motherlands and you don't like to fight. The Commander wants you to have a strong husband." Morris gave the three facts like he was reading out a report.

"And are you a strong man, Morris?" This time it was Jonah who asked the question, and there was something about the way he stepped closer to Mila that made me straighten up and pay attention.

"Absolutely. I hold a record for the most bench presses in my unit. I can lift two and half times my own weight."

"I wasn't referring to your size of muscles, but your personal strength. Are you loyal and selfless? Do you have integrity and intelligence?"

Morris wrinkled his nose at Jonah. "Who are you?"

332

Jonah stood calmly and faced all five of the giant men. "I'm Jonah, councilman of the Motherlands and one of Mila's closest friends."

The man frowned then smiled a little. "For now."

Jonah tilted his head. "What do you mean when you say for now? Are you implying that if she married you, Mila wouldn't be able to be friends with me?"

Morris raised his chin. "She wouldn't need you. She would have me."

Jonah's jaw tensed up and he linked his hands behind his back. "Right, and I'm sure you and I are so alike that Mila wouldn't feel the difference."

It wasn't the first time I'd heard Jonah use sarcasm and irony but it always threw me off because it was so rare among Motlanders.

Mila gave Jonah a sideways glance and changed the subject. "Please tell me where you live."

The five men informed her and she nodded. "Okay, thank you. And would you tell me what you do for a living?"

As Khan had said, three of them were soldiers in the Doom Squad, one was a ranger in a large forest on the east side, and the last guy, Phyton, owned a workout studio in Kingstown where he taught fighting techniques. Mila asked another question about their view on pets before she gave one of her signature soft smiles.

"Thank you. If my dad and Khan are right, we'll meet again at the tournament."

The five men inclined their heads to her before they walked away.

"Do not pick Alan," Willow muttered. "Solo works with him and I swear that man is either mentally retarded or flat-out gross."

"Why?"

333

"I always hear Solo complain about his lack of hygiene and his sweat that smells like death."

Mila wrinkled her nose up. "Thanks for the warning."

Jonah had been talkative and happy when we first joined him but now he had grown somber and quiet.

"I'm sorry, Jonah, I know you worry about what's going to happen to your friendship with Mila after she marries. Nmen are territorial when it comes to their women. I'm not sure Leo would like it if I had a best friend who was male either."

"But would you let Leo decide who you can be friends with?"

"No, of course not, and I don't think Mila will either. She really cares about you. But it won't be the same as it used to be between you. I mean you two talk more than Mila and me, and that says a lot."

Jonah's gaze was on Mila, who was talking with Willow and Darlene. "She's the best friend I've ever had. I wish she wasn't getting married. These men are..."

"Are what?"

He lowered his gaze to the floor. "Nothing. I'm just frustrated and upset."

"I get that. My fear is that she picks someone who lives at the other end of the country and that I won't see her as much."

Jonah's ears were red. "Please excuse me, Raven, I think I need some fresh air."

He had only just left before I was spun around by my new husband. "Are you looking for me?"

The sight of his warm eyes and bright smile filled me with joy. "Yes. Where did you go?"

"Oh, Solo, Zas, and I just met someone we had to talk to. Did we miss anything?" Leo kissed me.

"No, just some of Mila's nervous suitors whom she interviewed."

"Who is her favorite?"

"I'm not sure. I haven't had a chance to talk to her about it yet."

He took my hand. "I walked past the gift table; did you see it?"

"No, where is it?"

"Right outside. The table is stacked with presents, which reminds me that I spoke to your headmaster and he gave us a special wedding gift."

"He did?" I furrowed my forehead, as I didn't trust the man.

"Yes, he was kind enough to agree that you don't have to live at the academy. You can live with me as long as you're back for class every morning on weekdays."

"No way." I gasped in disbelief. "You're kidding."

"No, I'm serious, Raven."

"Why? He doesn't like me. Why would he do something this nice?"

"It was Solo's suggestion. He mentioned that it was a lot of pressure for Martinez to be responsible for your safety. He agreed and I suggested that you could do like you did at Station Seven when you came in in the morning and went home in the afternoon."

Holding a hand in front of my mouth, I teared up. "I can't tell you how happy that makes me."

"I know, right?" Leo lifted me from the ground when he hugged me tight. "I was dreading sleeping alone without you, but now I won't have to."

"I can't believe how everything is falling into place."

Leo nuzzled his nose against my neck. "I'm happy you feel that way because in a few weeks, Khan is going to announce that he's running for president and encouraging others to run against him. Even though he has been planning his campaign for weeks already, I guarantee you

335

that the next months are going to be unstable and chaotic in the Northlands."

"You keep saying that, but how can you know when it's never been done before?"

Leo tucked a lock of my hair behind my ear. "Try to think of the Northlands like a small room. Right now, everything looks nice enough, but there've been small holes that indicate there might a problem with termites. But every time there was a hole, Magni showed up, sprayed for insects, and patched the hole up."

"Okay."

"Think of the four inner walls as representations of the laws that are currently prohibiting people from talking out against Khan."

"Okay."

"He's preparing to tear down those walls to the studs, and what I'm saying is that we're going to see what's really inside the walls and it might not be pretty."

"Are you expecting major termite issues?" I smiled.

"I am. And termites can cause major structural damage, so one should never take that shit lightly."

Reaching up on my toes, I kissed Leo. "Maybe it's time to remodel the Northlands and get rid of any hidden rodents and termites. Hopefully we can all live in a better room after that."

Leo kissed me slowly before looking deep into my eyes. "Just know one thing. Whatever happens, I've got your back."

"Thank you. I've got your back too. I hope you know that."

He smiled. "There's something I'm dying to show you, babe."

"What is it?"

"I was going to surprise you with it tonight after the celebration, but the wait is killing me."

"Then show me now."

Looking over his shoulder, Leo made sure no one was watching and then he unbuttoned his shirt. Across his heart was a tattoo of a black panther.

"You didn't," I exclaimed in a small gasp.

"Of course I did. Catching you has been my greatest and most satisfying hunt ever."

My initial shock turned to amusement. "Can I touch it?"

"Yes, they sprayed a protective layer on it."

My hand ran over the impressive art piece. "And why does the panther look cute and harmless? If it represents me, at least you could have let it show some claws and some teeth."

Leo pushed another lock of my black hair behind my ear and leaned in to whisper in my ear. "Nah, I prefer my cat purring and happy."

"Huh." I studied the tattoo, feeling honored that he'd chosen that place on his body for a symbol of me.

"Maybe I should have one in the same place as you. Yes, I think I will."

"You want a black panther?"

"No, I think I want a number instead."

"What number?"

I chuckled. "Sixty-nine. You know, as a memory of the first time we were physical."

"Ah, you're talking about your porn fighting moves."

"It was a good fight."

"Except you almost strangled me to death."

I moved closer, pressing myself against him and letting my hands slide from his rib cage down to his firm behind. "I won't apologize for being a fierce fighter. You'll just have to try and keep up."

Leo's face cracked in a large grin. "Shit, if you only knew how sexy you are right now. Damn, I wish we could just get out of here."

"Me too, but it's going to take a while to say goodbye to everyone."

Leo looked back over his shoulder at the ballroom full of people. "Screw that. It's our wedding night and I don't care." When he faced me again, the mischievous smile on his lips should have warned me that he was up to no good, but it still took me by surprise when Leo picked me up and began walking with me bridal style.

"Coming through," he called out to the people who didn't move away fast enough.

"Put me down – I have two feet, you know," I protested at first, but seeing the world from his height and feeling safe in his arms was also making it impossible not to smile.

Laughter and encouraging comments followed us through the crowd.

"Don't go too hard on her, we'll need her back at the station in one piece."

"Everybody move aside. Here comes a man on a mission."

"That's it, Leo, show her who's the boss."

"Hey, what happened to equality? Raven, how come you're not carrying Leo?"

"Enjoy your wedding night."

I had wrapped my arms around Leo's neck and was returning the many smiles that met us as we moved through the crowd and out of the large room.

Leo set me down only when we reached the large suite that Mila had prepared for us at the Gray Manor. I laughed when he threw himself on the bed, spreading his arms out and panting after having carried me all the way here.

"How about a cold beer?" I turned on some nice music and moved to the cooler that Mila had arranged with cold drinks.

"Yes, please."

Leo sat up on the bed and removed his jacket and shirt before reaching for the beer. "Want me to help you remove that dress?"

"Since you did all the work to get us here, how about I do my part and undress myself for you?" Kicking off my shoes, I began swaying my hips to the rhythm of the music, turning my back on him and pulling the dress down over my right shoulder.

"You have no idea how gorgeous you look right now."

I gave him a smile. "Is it the dress?"

"It's your hair, your skin, your smile... it's everything. I can't believe you're my wife. Seriously, Raven, I couldn't have asked for a better partner."

"Give it a few years and you might change your mind."

Leo smiled. "Not if you keep giving me beers while stripping for me."

He was beautiful when he smiled like that. "When did you start smiling so much? I feel like you make jokes and smile a lot more than when I first met you."

He tilted his head to one side. "I wonder why that is? I can't imagine it has anything to do with the fact that I'm no longer a sexually starving man in love with a woman who constantly makes jokes about how boring I am."

"You *were* boring."

"Oh yeah?" In a fast movement, Leo got up and I could tell he was going to tickle me again, so I got out of his way and let him chase me around the room.

When he caught me, we were both panting and he locked my hands behind my back while kissing me. "Here's what's going to happen. I'll sit back down and let you finish that enticing show you started, and when you're

339

out of your dress, I'll show you how imaginative I can be. After tonight, you'll never call me boring again."

"Is that a promise or an order?" My heart was beating fast and my body was buzzing with desire for my husband.

"Both." Holding on to me, Leo moved back to sit on the bed before releasing me. "If this is the only time you'll wear a dress, I'd better take mental pictures of your last seconds in it." He released me and gave me a nod. "Come on, baby, strip for me."

"Yes, sir, Inspector," I teased and began dancing again.

He took a sip of his beer. "I'm the luckiest man alive."

"Yes, you are."

"Will you promise me something, babe?"

I gave him a cute smile with a questioning look.

"When you get to be a police officer and get your official uniform, will you strip for me again?"

"I love it when you say 'when'."

"Will you?"

Walking closer, I let the top of my dress fall down to my waist. I was topless now, but with my back to him. Covering my breasts with my hands I turned to face him, still moving seductively to the music.

"I will... if you do the same for me."

Leo's eyes widened as he pointed to himself. "You want me to strip out of my uniform for you?"

"I do."

"But I've never stripped to music in my life."

I laughed and pushed the dress all the way down. "There's a first for everything, babe. Think of it as an adventure."

Leo was admiring my body and reached for me. "Raven, I swear every day with you feels like an adventure.

I tapped my finger on my hip where the large P was tattooed. "That's because P stands for pioneer."

"After seeing how sexy it looks on your hip, P will forever be my favorite letter in the alphabet." Leo squatted down in front of me and let his finger trail over the P before he licked it. "P for pioneer, and pleasured panther."

"Pleasured?" With a questioning smile, I lifted his chin to look into his eyes.

"Yeah, pleasured. Remember how I told you that I'm the best lover you've ever had?"

"Uh-huh."

"Lucky for you, I'll also be the best husband you've ever had."

"That *is* lucky."

"I'm going to make a bold claim here." He rose up to his full height in front of me.

"Let's hear it."

"I guarantee that tomorrow when you wake up from our wedding night, you'll be a thoroughly pleasured woman."

"And you? What will you be?"

"A fucking proud husband."

"What about your pleasure?"

"I'm not worried about that." He guided me back to the bed with a sexy grin. "After all, you promised that you'd be the best wife and lover that I'd ever have too."

This concludes Men of the North #9 – The Fighter

Thank you so much for reading Raven and Leo's story.
If you liked it, please, please, please take a second to leave a review on Amazon. Your word has power and helps other readers take a chance on this book, which makes it possible for me to write books full time for your entertainment.

Want more?

Can you believe that we're coming to an end in the Men of the North series? Don't miss out on the epic ending to this adventure.

Men of the North #10 – The Pacifist
A promise is a promise but this promise is one I should have never made.

Mila's bridal tournament is coming closer, and pressure on her is growing. Unease is spreading in the Northlands and her family need the event to maintain their political power. But for Mila, the tournament will mean marrying a stranger and giving up on Jonah, the man she secretly loves.

Jonah is everything her dad, Magni, warned her against, and as a Motlander, he would never want anything but a platonic friendship from her anyway. Or would he? As time is ticking down, Mila comes up with the ultimate plan to test how Jonah really feels about her, but it's a plan with a flaw and only too late does she realize the mortal danger she has put Jonah, and her family in.

The Pacifist is the tenth and last book in Elin Peer's wildly successful *Men of the North series*. Don't miss out on this epic ending to a great dystopian adventure that offers both suspense, humor, and romance.

Now available for presale on Amazon. Release date April 23rd, 2019
Sign up for my newsletter on www.elinpeer.com to be alerted when I release a new book or follow me on Amazon and Bookbub.

ELIN PEER

MEN OF THE NORTH

THE PACIFIST

About the Author

Elin describes herself as quirky in a good way.
Being curious by nature, she likes to explore and can tell you about riding elephants through the Asian jungle, watching the sunset in the Sahara Desert from the back of a camel, sailing down the Nile in Egypt, kayaking in Alaska, and flying over Greenland in helicopters.

After traveling the world and living in different countries, Elin is currently residing outside Seattle in the US with her husband, daughters, and her black Labrador, Lucky, who follows her everywhere.

With a back ground in personal coaching, Elin is easy to talk to and one thing is for sure: she is not afraid to provoke, shock, touch, and excite you when she writes about unwanted desire, forbidden passion, and all those damn emotions in between.

Want to connect with Elin? Great – she loves to hear from her readers.

Find her on Facebook: facebook.com/AuthorElinPeer
Or look her up on Goodreads, Amazon, Bookbub or simply go to elinpeer.com

Made in the USA
Las Vegas, NV
17 January 2021